Seeds of Retribution

VOLUME ONE
Germination

Robert B.W. Morton

SEEDS OF RETRIBUTION
VOLUME ONE GERMINATION

Copyright © Robert B.W. Morton, 2021

Published by Robert B.W. Morton, Edmonton, Canada

Paperback ISBN - 978-1-77354-307-9
eBook ISBN - 978-1-77354-313-0

PAGEMASTER
PUBLISHING
PageMaster.ca

Seeds of Retribution

VOLUME ONE

Germination

Robert B.W. Morton

Prologue
Trail of Death
1838

*I*t was more than the relentless searing rays of the sun beating down
on their necks and backs; more than the thick dust spiralling its
miserable, dancing weave up and around their heads, cutting into
their eyes and choking their nostrils; more than the churning emptiness
that tore at the internal tissues of their pleading stomachs; more than
wearisome joints that continued to drag on day after day over rolling
drifts, through rocky shallows, through bog and swamp, mud and clay;
for the Potawatomi were hearty people, well-versed in nature's torturous
elements. They had survived thousands of years at the heart of the continent's vast unforgiving wilderness—through drought and storm, blizzard
and locust, wolf, fire and famine. Their tenacity and endurance were
testaments to their bravery and above all to their understanding—their
mastery of their land. No, it was something more. It was the deep hole
carved into their hearts. It was Whiteman's larceny—a stolen spirit that
gripped their heads and shoulders and pushed them down, so they walked
as if lowly corpses floating along a death trail. The connection between

body and spirit cut and the path they trod was as empty as their hollow stomachs.

Harassed and hated, the destiny of the Indian in the central areas culminated in a forced march west, far away from newly settled areas; far away from the Whiteman. Black smoke rising high into the autumn sky delivered a raw pungent odour—the definitive signal of surrender. Plans were made to guarantee their final withdrawal. Soldiers burned everything; there would be no returning. Almost a thousand Potawatomi gathered their meagre belongings and began a western trek on foot and cart—a distance of six hundred and sixty miles would be covered in two months.

Dr. Jerolaman bent over the languid body; his left arm reaching up high grabbing onto the iron braces in a futile effort to attain stability. The wagon continued to jolt him left then right, without mercy. With his free hand he steadied the young native at his knees; the task was a useless endeavour.

He knew that no manner of moist cloth delicately caressing her parched lips would save this young girl, yet he remained vigilant. The space inside the canvas canopy was meant to shield the sick and dying from the blasting heat and offer respite from the dust and wind, but they suffered the cramped confines of a man-made furnace—the canvas created an airless coffin—the unforgiving heat compressed into a hot vise that squeezed the life from everyone within.

Her body rolled in unison with the jolting rhythm of the wagon wheels over rocks and ruts. Her dry mouth, cracked and blood-caked, gaped open. The desperate sucking of her lungs: shallow. Then, a faint and final delicate expiration as she quietly, thankfully, yielded to her desperate plight.

Dr. Jerolaman lifted his hand away from her burning forehead, gently easing her mouth closed. Another small grave would be dug tonight when the soldiers allowed the caravan to stop. The toll was now averaging two deaths a day—the Potawatomi accepted defeat—many would never realize their new home in Kansas. It was of no consequence—better to die on the trail than within the cold restrictions of Whiteman's reservation.

Eight years before The March, before they were relegated to abandon their homes, somewhere in the swamps south-west of Chicago, a very small band of Potawatomi women toiled in their herb garden. Rising Sun looked skyward. She could smell the approaching storm. The clouds would bring more than rain this time. She collected her tools and gestured to the others to follow her back to the tent. A night like no other was approaching rapidly, with a threat so vital that she scowled at the swirling blackness high above her, reluctant to believe the icy minacious shivers she felt rising up in her old bones. How could she have not foreseen this?

"For everything there is a season:
A time to kill and a time to heal."

Ecclesiastes III, 3:3

PART 1

Chicago
1830

1

obert Tumblety was dead, that was certain. The messenger couldn't have been more contrite: a body—bloated, slimy and very dead, pulled from the lake only an hour earlier, was identified as the boy all right. The body had been savagely brutalized. To any observer it was quite obvious that possibly every bone in his body was broken. Shards of pointed bone pierced through the skin on every section of his arms and legs. The appendages were twisted and mangled in so many awkward directions that it was impossible to recognize front from back. Large black contusions spread across the entire body—seen vividly through the gaping tears of his shirt and trousers.

There was no blood visible as the long night in the cold churning waters of the lake had washed away all signs of the life liquid. Every artery, every vein and corpuscle had been thoroughly drained. Although the back of his skull had been clearly bashed open, allowing so much brain tissue there to ooze out, his face surprisingly remained virtually untouched. The ghoulish puffy visage dropped back, his open mouth reaching up to the ceiling in a silent scream—a pale, plea for mercy, for justice.

Margaret was sixteen, pregnant and unwed. Her betrothed was lying lifeless in a puddle in the Sheriff's office; her greatest fear had come to pass. The horrifying words had hissed through His lips only a moment ago as He had relayed the message to her and her mother sitting there together so relaxed on the Chinese sofa in the great drawing room. His short oratory was sublime—he announced it as if to remind them to bring muffins and cakes to Sunday's Social. There was no remorse, no care, no sensitivity in his words and perhaps in the corner of his eye lurked just a small glimmer of vindication— Margaret saw it; she knew instantly what He had done. Remaining frozen to the sofa, her hand clutching her mother's arm tighter and tighter, she stared with cool hatred into her father's eyes. The only sound in that great hollow room was the pounding of her heart and the muscle's increased rhythm began shooting blood at a furious rate to her head and to her hands matching the increased pressure; she uncontrollably began to squeeze and squeeze, never removing her icy stare from His face.

Then in the next instant she released her grip and rose up in a fury. Margaret raced for the door pushing her way past her father to the threshold with the solitary mindset of escape, nothing else. He clumsily attempted to restrain her with an outstretched arm, but she was slick with her exit.

Her reluctant surge forward into the night seemed to be provoked by an invisible hand that pushed from behind forcing its way through any physical barrier of flesh or bone, into her soul, wrenching like a digging corkscrew up through her body and into her head, pounding out through her eyes without mercy, without reason. It was crazy, irrational, but she could not afford the luxury of rationality...not tonight. Margaret secretly knew about tonight's inevitable exodus from her father's mansion, it had been slowly festering in some deep corner of her soul like a rotten boil, infected and sour—ready to burst any time—but she didn't know how or when it would avail itself. She regretted leaving her mother in this abrupt manner, but now He had forced her hand with His 'message', passed to her so politely—His cordiality made her sick with disgust.

The daily rigours of existence necessary to sustain sanity were choking her and she was quickly suffocating no different than a trapped animal caught in a snare under the frozen ice of Lake Michigan. Intelligence and common sense had screamed escape so many times in the past, yet it wasn't until tonight...tonight when news of the unimaginable reached her, that courage finally raised its proud head and in response, her screams rang out loud in tandem chorus with the pounding of her fists against the great wooden door of her prison; she blasted into the black freedom of the night.

The dark anvil clouds that filled the prairie skies far to the west had threatened to deliver their precious tender all day; the crack of thunder and vicious flashes of lightning filled the void with its ominous power. Torrential rain began to fall upon the dry landscape so thirsty for the sweet nectar. The old women of the swamps had been singing anthems of rain for weeks and now, finally, they would witness the welcomed results of their vigil. Unbridled tears coalesced with the pelting rain from the storm on her face as she raised a delicate, shaking hand to her eye—a fruitless attempt to brace against the relentless elements of God's wrath. With maternal grace and care, Margaret's other hand carefully caressed the underside of her swollen belly, as if to comfort her unborn baby and encourage its safety even as it lay asleep and unaware of the tempest erupting around it.

Margaret's attempt at racing through the muddy street was quickly reduced to trudging, painstakingly, through a viscous mixture of thick mud and horse manure. She headed southwest to a corner of town visited by only a desperate few. Often failing to avoid water-filled potholes, mule or animal dung, she struggled on, stopping to turn her gaze behind her only once. There was no one pursuing as she suspected. *He would not come after me*, she thought. She knew that any attempt by her spineless mother would be immediately thwarted without hesitation, with the quick flick of a strong backhand, no doubt compounded by His typical coarse verbal threats. She was gone and nothing less than the combined forces of heaven and hell colliding together in one great final barrage against her could reverse her decision. Looking up into the great black maelstrom that blanketed the sky, she thought that she was quite possibly facing the very nemesis that could force her home. However, the grizzly image of Robert's limp, broken body floating face down, tossing about on the crashing waves of the lake quickly eliminated any doubts and offered her the encouragement she needed to press on.

The pain in her head continued to pound in powerful swells ebbing and flowing, matching the rhythm of the powerful din exploding around her in what seemed to be every direction. The night was erupting as God's great fusillade bombarded his poor deserving sinners—retribution for past crimes. No one was out tonight, not a person, not a horse. Even the stockyard dogs had found refuge under the corral planks and boards, escaping as best they could from the storm. Margaret was alone, anxious and scared. The baby was not due for another three weeks, but instinct told her that something was wrong. The pains were now coming closer together. She had cast herself out, yet even the overwhelming terror of the unknown here in the bleak abyss of the vast prairie frontier on the edge of Chicago's town line, was to Margaret, almost a type of macabre sanctuary compared to what waited for her back at that dreadful house.

No, she could never return, not now, not after what He did. She hated Him all the more for the disastrous choice He forced her to make tonight, and for jeopardizing her baby's life in this way. Her vigil would proceed, without Robert, without anyone; she would not return, she could not return.

Without warning, another sharp, striking pain in her abdomen, clenching tight like a steel fist punching through a stone wall, forced her to her knees. Mud shot like violent, stinging spears into her eyes and hair; the putrid mixture dripped from her chin and ears. Both hands stretched out to break her fall, but the ground offered no resistance, they sunk deep into the mud-soaked street, layered as it was with animal excrement and urine at the edge of the stockyard. The abysmal concoction saturated with the powerful stench of ammonia, forced Margaret's eyes to wince and her lips curled into a twisted grimace.

Raising her head slightly, Margaret tried to focus on the blurred shadows floating in the distance, framed by the jagged wooden rails of the corral fence. The relentless rain continued to drop a veil of grey over the town, and, combined with the overwhelming odour, her tears of pain and futility screened her view casting doubts on what now moved towards her with such slow stealth on the opposite side of the fence. Convinced she might die tonight, as any manner of beast might be looming there ready to spring on her frail, vulnerable form, pressed even as she was, down deep next to the vile grime of nature's purges, Margaret held on to hope and prayed for strength. "Please God, not like this. Help my baby." She whispered a short prayer in desperation. She knew about the dogs that scraped out a living here at these stockyards, feeding off the butchered remains of cattle and pigs. Although they were relentlessly beaten and tormented by the cowboys and the old Indian women, their emaciated figures became irrepressible apparitions that haunted the corrals and sheds, ever ready to make quick work of a lingering body alive or dead—the buzzards of the flesh heaps. Their teeth were razor sharp and Margaret would have no defence against their vicious attack. Her hands and arms would be snatched first as she would try in vain to pound away their advances. She imagined her stomach ripped open and the evil beasts ravaging her unborn child as gleaming white fangs soon turned black with her blood in the dark shadows of the storm. As these ghastly visions began tearing at her brain, Margaret felt a sharp grip tighten around her arm as the terror finally arrived! Thinking this was the first bite of what was to be the final agonizing moments of her life, she released a scream so loud the Lord's heavenly cacophony repelled in response, and her voice alone shattered nature's vast, angry shroud above.

Shashona then reached a second time under the rail with her other hand and gently cupped Margaret's dirty face. Their eyes met for only an instant, then Margaret slipped into a peaceful slumber. Within moments Little Raven arrived at Shashona's side, fell to her knees in the mud and stretched out her arms to assist her mother. "Who is it Mother? Do you know her?"

"Hush child. Help me pull her through the fence." Together the two Indian women struggled with Margaret's limp appendages and immediately became wary of her precious belly. Careful not to disturb her unborn baby in any way, they slowly freed her from the other side of the mangled boards of the corral fence and pulled her through.

When Shashona finally cradled Margaret gently in her arms and looked down at the angelic soft features of her tiny face, splattered as it was with rainwater and mud, she cautiously combed the black strands of wet hair from her sleeping eyes and answered Little Raven's question. "Yes child, I know her. She is your sister."

2

Margaret's mother, Kate, fell to her knees on the threshold of the great stone archway which framed the main entrance to the huge mansion. Folding her hands to her eyes, she wept uncontrollably, "My baby, my baby," and whispered her daughter's name—a soft, sweet echo of her love for her child, over and over.

"Get up you great fool, she's gone, the rain is soaking the carpet!" Charles Smithson showed not a fraction of remorse for his actions tonight, nor an ounce of sympathy for his wife, now desperate with grief, cowering at the doorstep, crying for Margaret's return.

"She got what she deserved, and by God if you don't get up off that floor, I'll throw you out there with her and the two of you can wallow in the mud together like the two great pigs you are!" Charles stood over his wife arms akimbo, feet apart in his favourite dominant pose, flailing his diatribe like a master's whip over a submissive slave, wet spittle spewing from the corners of his mouth, salivating like a stockyard dog over a rotting animal carcass.

Kate turned her head slowly to meet the focussed, evil gaze of her husband and allowed her hands to slide slowly down her face to her lips which quivered in anxious tension. Her submissive behaviour all these years had allowed Charles to become the monster she now saw before her. Impulsively and without thought of consequence, she began to formulate the words in her head and unexpectedly they finally reached the edge of her tongue and remained poised behind her lips ready to strike. So many times in the past her words had lingered in this position unable to make the final forward thrust—unable to reciprocate his acerbic attacks. Her young defenceless daughter was gone and towering over her stood the man responsible for all her grief and now possibly, the loss of her only child. Tonight her words would not be restrained. Sixteen years of suppressed loathing came rolling forth: first like feathered steam slipping out from between tight pressurized filaments as her teeth remained tightly clenched together, then more like thunder slowly rising from deep within her soul and rumbling up through the back of her throat, exploding and crashing like a freight train pounding through a rock wall, spewing boulders out from its path and tossing them down the canyon wall. One hand curled from a cup over her mouth to a gesticulating fist with an extended accusatory index finger pointed squarely at the man's dark, brooding eyes. Kate then rotated on her knees, turning her back to the open door and pounding rain. The wind tortured and dislodged the tightly twisted hair bun at the back of her head, wet strands of black hair began to whip across her face striking out in arcs behind her head creating a frightening image of Medusa herself about to cast a spell on an unsuspecting adversary who dared to threaten her. For a fraction of an instant the unholy sight gave Charles reason to take pause.

"You...you evil monster. You have no love for anyone. You hate everything and destroy everything you touch! You think you are so powerful—you are weak! You are a coward who bullies women and children. You are not a man; you are a snake...a slime! You are repulsive and disgusting, and you will be cast out. Your day of reckoning will arrive soon enough and no one will save you. The flaming fires of hell will burn you forever! God will punish..." But before Kate could finish her sobering verbal outburst, a flashing fist sailed across her face and crashed into her mouth, dislodging teeth, splitting her lower lip in two and splashing a stream of blood to the wall.

The powerful blow lifted Kate from her penitent position on the floor, she flew into the heavy doorjamb, crumpling there like a dirty pile of wet laundry waiting for the unfortunate laundress. The rain pooled on the carpet and Kate's blood silently, smoothly, curled into circular designs as it mixed with the splashing rainwater, and blended rhythmically with the Persian weave, creating paisley curls swirling with casual indifference to the brutal origins of its scarlet hue.

Charles stared down at his work still clenching his huge fist, poised in a pugilist's stance, daring an absurd counter strike. The creases in his brow seemed to squeeze tighter, reaching deeper. His eyes, recessed deep into his face, tightened into tiny dark green marbles. His focus remained fixed and unwavering on the motionless form at his feet. An eerie silence enshrouded the great house save for the relentless rain playing its continuous wet symphony on the stone steps leading up to the monolithic doors of the mansion. Charles hesitated. *What if I killed her? This murder might not be as easily explained,* he thought to himself. His head lifted, he stared out through the door and deep into the night for anyone who may have witnessed the horrific results of his rage. He looked for Margaret; but understandably, not a soul lurked in any direction. He would have to hide the body. *Another body floating by the docks on Lake Michigan tonight would raise suspicion.* But his anxiety was shallow and brief; it passed in a less than an instant. He reached down to his wife touching her shoulder. A weak groan slipped softly from between her broken lips. Then Charles noticed a foot on the carpet—it slid forward so slightly. *She's not dead.*

He quickly sprang into action. Charles grabbed Kate by the wrist whipping her across the carpet away from the door, then with one great swinging motion he flung the great door across the threshold; it slammed shut, crashing in a shuddering explosion that reverberated throughout the house. The sound of the slamming door roared like the blast of a canon through the halls echoing up to the rafters. Every stone answered in a great hollow bellow, every windowpane crackled, shaking as if in sympathetic response to the evil deed which befell here within their protective walls tonight. The great house now stood paralyzed, helpless, unable to offer comfort to the pathetic victim lying there, as Charles stepped closer...and even closer. He stepped over the motionless heap and stood astride her curled torso. With one foot on either side of Kate's crumpled body, he reached across to the door quickly driving the iron bolt into the jamb with a loud crack, then replacing his hands to his hips, satisfied, remaining square in his stance, like a master over his property.

Charles was shaking. He was angry. His wrath would not be contained. He was a man void of any reason or logic. His emotions were erupting, reaching the very limit of human tolerance. Grabbing his wife by the ankles, he dragged her from the massive foyer through the serpentine stone hallways to the kitchen; her dress pulling up over her hips, her head bumping and thumping on the cold, unforgiving stones. Kate regained a slight level of consciousness, enough to recognize her plight, envisioning the events that might follow should she reach the kitchen under his commanding grip. She began to scream. "You great brute, release me!" Although with her front teeth loose as they were, and her lips so swollen and cut, the articulation of her words were less than coherent. In any event Charles was not about to be deterred by her pleas or anyone else's. Kate's screams continued to echo off the great stone walls, from curtain to tapestry, from doorway to lintel, until finally he dropped her at the foot of the big chopping block in the kitchen. Her head was pounding, her face soaked in blood; she sobbed holding her hand to her ripped lip, attempting to console the pain there.

Charles stood solid over her—a sentinel over fresh prey. "Now we shall see the monster you married...my dear wife." He mimicked her words to him. Kate gasped in terror, frightened of the inevitable bloody encore that was to follow.

3

Rising Sun and Nootkana squeezed tightly together, one behind the other inside the tent, the door flap flipping wildly in their faces; they cautiously peered out into the storm. Trying her best to prevent the rain from entering, Nootkana beckoned with the wave of her hand when she saw the black outline of the lone figures reaching the edge of the compound, bending over like two pathetic wood gatherers bringing home the day's load, bracing in a curled dark knot against the power of the wind and rain. When they finally reached the tent with Margaret in their arms, the entrance flap to the tent was opened—they were greeted by Rising Sun's accusatory gaze. Her ugly face was as stiff as stone; her arms were folded below her breasts on her stomach each fist tightly grasping the opposite bicep. She looked at Margaret, then to Little Raven, and then finally turned her eyes to Shashona. "Remove her clothes." She directed with one finger lifting up from her hand, her arms not moving from their crossed position, in simultaneous rhythm with a slight upward gesture of her chin. No one was going to enter her tent covered in mud and cow shit.

Lowering Margaret down, they propped her up in a vertical position, her head resting on Shashona's shoulder, her shoes sinking into the slippery soil; Shashona and Little Raven began to carefully remove Margaret's dress. Reaching down with both arms, grabbing the mud-soaked hem—together they pulled the garment up to her chest. They then bent Margaret forward pulling the dress over her dangling arms—finally, her head slid through the neck. Lastly, they pulled the stubborn sleeves over her wrists and hands—she was free of the heavy, mud-soiled dress that had become as tight as a restricting straight jacket as it shrank, sticking tight to her skin, burdened with the heavy layers of water and mud collected from the storm. She drooped lazily like a wet rag doll in her soggy, white cotton shift; Shashona held her up by the waist. The relief afforded by the removal of the dress and cumbersome weight, seemed to release Margaret from her sleep—she slowly began to regain consciousness—she instinctively stood erect and more firmly on her legs. With her arms about her two busy assistants on either side of her, she aided as best she could with their next task. Raising her arms up, with one quick pull, her damp undergarment was whipped over her head. Margaret's immediate reaction to the cold wind of the storm and her raw nakedness, was to wrap her arms quickly around her chest for warmth, as much as for modesty. Her skin quickly became covered in goose pimples, her nipples protruded stiff and firm in the cold. She stood now naked, save for her pantaloons and her high lace shoes.

Little Raven bent down and began to unlace her right shoe, Shashona did the same to her other shoe. "Help my baby...please help me," Margaret pleaded.

"Hush child," Shashona reassured her. "We will clean you now." Margaret was sobbing quietly but was eager to surrender to her plight, now so grateful that no dogs had attempted to devour any part of her, or drag her through the stockyard like a piece of cow carcass—a fortunate prize for the evening scavengers in this forsaken hole of a settlement. She tentatively looked up towards the tent. Two curious faces peeked out from behind the tent flap; without a hint of emotion, they watched the little pregnant girl strip in the rain storm, small drips of water silently slipping down their noses, their eyelashes blinking repeatedly from the rain pouring on their head and faces, like shimmering black threads dancing to the rhythm of the incessant rain. Rising Sun looked down to Margaret's swollen belly, glistening and gathering rainwater in small puddles below her folded arms, and knew the difficult ordeal that was at hand. Nootkana, tucked in tight beside her, viewed the scene in child-like awe, as she felt sorrow for the girl and yet, also a strange sense of intrigue for this mysterious visitor tonight, who offered such an unusual pallid profile in the dark recesses of the storm's embrace.

When the difficult and cumbersome task of unlacing Margaret's muddy shoes was completed, they were carelessly tossed aside along with her lace stockings; Shashona pulled the pantaloons down to her ankles and Margaret delicately stepped out of them. For a moment Margaret's pale, naked body reflected the pure beauty and innocence of a Botticelli Venus, as she cupped one hand over her breast, the other between her legs under her round, extrusive belly, her black hair swinging in long, wet strands about her head as the wind continued to toss and aggravate around her. Her skin reflected a glossy white sheen; the rainwater beaded in tiny pools on her soft, cold form. The silhouette presented, appeared chiselled from smooth alabaster and the curves of motherhood radiated in their purest form; a sight so out of place here in the dismal mire of the stockyard, Nootkana stared in wondrous disbelief through the blowing cowhide flap of the tent, motionless in admiration and amazement. She had never seen anything as beautiful as this young mother, and she had never seen so many useless garments come from one person at one time. She wondered how white women could walk at all.

The twinkle of a small, silver, heart-shaped locket resting firmly within the short cleavage of the girl's breasts was not lost to Nootkana and she turned her head to see if Rising Sun shared the same discovery. She had.

Margaret suddenly screamed and doubled over with pain. Without hesitation, Shashona quickly picked her up and cradled her in her arms as Little Raven wiped her feet with a cloth tossed out to her from Nootkana. "Bring her inside," —a stern order from Rising Sun as she whipped back the clumsy, leather door flap— Nootkana graciously held out her arms to receive the little, wet, naked package. The two women exchanged the precious bundle from one set of arms to the other; Nootkana gently set her on the table inside. Rising Sun immediately wrapped a warm blanket about Margaret's shoulders motioning to the two at the door. "Remove your clothes." Shashona and Little Raven would have to leave their muddy clothes outside before entering. They exchanged a quick mutual glance, frowned in exasperation, then commenced the bothersome task.

The tent, the largest of three, owned and operated by the little band of women, would serve nicely as a delivery room. It was a modified A-frame with a flattened roof of four feet or so at the peak for extra width. A small iron, wood stove was quietly crackling in the corner producing a generous amount of heat; a small volume of smoke was silently sneaking outward from a hidden crack in the metal pipe near the exit hole at the ceiling, filling the space with a cloud of fine grey haze, pungent in its odour and translucent in its airy composition. It floated in and about the cramped quarters like a welcomed ghost weaving its course of silent, silk threads from pipe to board, pot to bowl. An oil lantern on the table was flickering, casting a dull glow with just enough light to highlight the immediate objects in its direct path. The space inside was surprisingly generous, the room was dry and warm. Rising Sun went right to work.

The cache of lotions, potions, herbs and medicines were close at hand on the rough piece of lumber used as a countertop, precariously balanced on a series of wooden crates along a side wall. As this tent was the kitchen tent, all the utensils were displayed on the coarse wooden table where Margaret now sat: pots, kettle, bowls, and a wide assortment of spoons—wooden and metal—and a great selection of knives. The dark corners, out of view, contained Rising Sun's proud collection of jars, bottles, pouches and baskets of weeds, berries, vegetables and plants—all the ingredients needed for her daily labours. Above, swinging on the top poles by thin leather strings, were strips of animal flesh in various stages of decay: chicken, pheasant, pork and dog—to be used for soup or medicines when required. A large cast iron cauldron was sitting on the floor in the far corner still smoking from the day's recipe, its fumes rose up and caught Margaret off guard. She turned her head, searching for the origins of the foreign odour and was about to cough as she raised her hand to her nose, when Rising Sun blurted her disapproval. "You should not be here."

Startled by the sudden, crackly voice, splitting the momentary silence, Margaret responded. "I am Margaret..." she started.

"I know who you are," interjected Rising Sun, cutting off the completion of her introduction. "You must go home." She finalized her command.

"I cannot return to my home. I am having my baby...he is coming too soon. Please help me." Margaret was sobbing and became desperate with her pleading. The pain rose again and sharply stabbed at the entrance to her womb; she screamed in terror.

Nootkana folded her arms around Margaret's narrow shoulders in comfort and then Rising Sun moved in close between Margaret's legs to gain a better angle of observation. She gently parted the legs and carefully moved her hand down to the opening. She then rotated Margaret's body towards the lantern for better illumination. A very short manual manipulation followed—her head returned, popping up from between Margaret's bare knees, like a prairie dog searching for trouble on the horizon, her eyes shooting an incredulous stare into Margaret's teary countenance. She was about to scold Margaret, when her chastising was interrupted by two wet, naked bodies clumsily falling through the entrance flap in one great, wet explosion of slippery skin and whipping hair, like two saturated logs of driftwood washing up on the beach after a tidal wave—the precious, private moment: gone. Rising Sun, hesitating, held her words in reaction to the outburst. Shashona's great sodden breasts came bouncing into the tent leading the intrusion, followed behind by the tiny figure of her daughter, Little Raven. They had disrobed, cleaned off, and were ready to address Rising Sun's predictable scrutiny, polished and scrubbed as they were.

As the two figures came to an abrupt halt and stood motionless, all eyes quickly turned back to Rising Sun. "There's no baby. You go home now." Her words were alarming and Margaret reached down between her legs in shocking disbelief, as if searching for her baby's head, which she assumed would be protruding there.

The wind howled twisting the buffalo skins that wrapped about the poles overhead, threatening to tear the little tent from its moorings. Shashona and Little Raven looked up with trepidation at the violence whipping about the shaking structure. They had finished securing the straps tightly only a few moments ago, when they had spied Margaret at the corral fence; then left their job to aid with her muddy predicament. They wondered now if they had completed their task to the full level of Rising Sun's tough, demanding standards. Their bent forms were sharing a praying stance as they each held their fists together in a tight, knotted clutch to their lips and nose, their elbows squeezed hard against their chest, attempting desperately to regain some warmth. Shivering, they nervously lifted their eyes to the roof, praying the tent would not sail away in the storm. They appeared as a forlorn, pathetic pair of lost urchins begging for a handout; their nakedness a testament to their lowly, desperate station in life.

Nootkana left the tight hold she had on Margaret. Searching through a box in a shadowy corner for a towel, she passed one to Shashona who immediately began to dry Little Raven's thick, tousled hair. Temporarily satisfied with the tenuous integrity of the straps, the damp duo departed to the same corner soon emerging, dressed in plain, patterned dresses, typically worn by the pioneer woman of the day, happy of the little warmth they provided. Traditional Indian garb had long since been abandoned by these women living so close to the Whiteman. However, unlike Margaret, cumbersome undergarments were never worn.

As she completed the buttons on the front of her dress, and turned to the centre of the room, Shashona pointed at the floor below the table, under Margaret's feet. "Her water!" she exclaimed. Rising Sun followed the angle of Shashona's directive and spied the fluid dripping there.

"Fetch me a bottle, quick," demanded Rising Sun, as not an ounce of the precious liquid was to be lost. Amniotic fluid was life's elixir—a necessary ingredient used in many of Rising Sun's medicines and potions. Nootkana quickly snatched a bottle from the table—passing it to Rising Sun, she placed it between Margaret's legs at the opening to her vagina; with a slight push of her finger up and in, the water came gushing out. The little bottle was filled in an instant.

The opening to the womb remained tight, but as Margaret instinctively now started to push, a split opened, blood began to spill forward. Rising Sun encouraged the baby with a gentle insertion of two fingers into the cervix. Margaret screamed in agony. Rising Sun responded with a demand, "Don't push!"

Shashona gave her young daughter a pot. "Fill this with water and put it on the stove." The women seemed to know what to do now without direction—a mat was placed out on the floor beside the table—Shashona and Nootkana gingerly lifted Margaret from the table and placed her on the floor, making her comfortable with a blanket and pillow. Rising Sun searched her stores on the board behind her for a special tonic: partridgeberry to loosen the cervix and encourage the baby to exit the womb, wormwood to ease the pain.

Little Raven placed the pot on the stove, Rising Sun dropped in two knives for cleaning, then washed her hands thoroughly, wiping them with a clean towel. The Potawatomi women seemed to have an innate understanding of the crucial element of cleanliness before endeavouring to commence a surgical or medical procedure, long before the concept of sterilization was ever introduced to the western world. If the baby would not come naturally, a surgical extrication would be necessary—she would be properly prepared.

Wiping the blood from the inside of her legs, Little Raven looked into Margaret's eyes for the first time—they were a similar, dark, emerald green; an immediate, inexplicable recognition passed between them. Margaret reached out for Little Raven's hand, as Little

Raven bent down on her knees. They gently touched in the dim light of the smoky tent. Her eyes fell with a tender gaze onto Margaret's face, searching the lines and creases for evidence of familiarity—a connection. She gently wiped Margaret's damp brow with her hand; she whispered in her ear. "My mother says we are sisters."

Shashona bent down close beside her daughter, adding words of enlightenment. "You share the same father," she explained. "Charles Smithson has visited this tent more than once."

"That evil man; don't call Him my father." Margaret blurted out. "I am Margaret Tumblety. My husband is Robert Francis Tumblety— or at least he would have been—and I will not be associated in any way with that murderer." The bold expression of hatred brought on more cramps; Margaret cried out in anguish.

"Hush child and lie still." Shashona begged. "You will have your child tonight. Do not think of Him now."

"You have...been...with my father?" Margaret hesitantly asked Shashona.

"Not by choice," answered Shashona. She tenderly wiped Margaret's wet brow with a cloth. "He came to this tent many times—before he was such a big man—when the cowboys believed they could have Indian women whenever they wanted. We were not given the chance to disobey; there are no men here to protect us. They have all left.

Rising Sun passed a cup of the potion to Shashona and the mixture was offered down to Margaret. "Drink this child." She softly lifted Margaret's head up with her left hand, placing the cup to her lips with the other. Margaret delicately sipped swallowing a generous amount and responded with a frown—the potion was bitter and vile. Her head was carefully returned to the pillow, where she seemed to calm down almost immediately, yet it would only be a short respite.

"Little Raven is his daughter; you share her eyes," Shashona continued. "All my other children have gone; Little Raven remains with me."

The storm continued to rage. The flaps smashed against the sides of the tent with greater fury than ever; the thunder crashed as if heaven itself was ready to explode and release all manner of creature that had been securely bound within God's great hands from the very beginning of time. Flashes of lightening illuminated the sky so brightly that morning's golden rays of sunlight would recoil with envy. The rain beat in vicious torrents against the tent and its small company inside huddled ever closer together in fear and disbelief. *Would this storm ever end?* thought Nootkana, sadly reviewing Margaret's inevitable circumstance, as she watched Rising Sun pick up the knives from the boiling pot with a pair of wooden sticks like a Chinese chef preparing soup.

Between sips of the medicine, horrific screaming bouts and short, reassuring moments of calm, Rising Sun saw no change in the dilation of the cervix even after a half an hour...only blood, and more blood, as the baby continued its relentless attack on freedom; she knew the only solution for the removal of this child would be at the end of a merciful sharp knife.

A heavy dose of a crude analgesic in the form of alcohol and wormwood was given to Margaret throughout the last fifteen minutes of her ordeal, and now, the continued loss of blood from her uterus gave Rising Sun no choice: she would have to cut the baby out.

4

Charles Smithson aggravated very little over his quandary. Kate lay beaten and bloody at his feet—her temperament sour, belligerent. He would tolerate no more arguments from this woman. The verbal bashing tonight between him and the two women of his house was over. Whatever he did, he had to do, and there would be no going back. No 'mick' dock worker was going to marry his daughter—pregnant or not—and that would be the final word! He assumed that over the course of a few days Margaret would return home to have her baby; her female rantings subsiding, her senses returning, and a restoration to normal—if life in this house could ever be referred to in such an arbitrary manner—would follow, even at the risk of his bloody brutality being exposed. He also considered that, with time, Margaret would drop her ridiculous infatuation with Robert Tumblety, his death would be forgotten.

Charles would consider a resolve when and if Margaret returned. For now, Kate's immediate future became his prime concern.

Kate turned her head lifting her gaze up to her husband. This small task, so simple in its gesture, so slight in its motion, yet costing every ounce of energy left in her broken body, seemed to her like a promise of persistent determination she must present to her husband, demonstrating her indifference to his cowardice; hopefully demeaning his victory and expressing a pride that would thwart his righteousness. In all the years of marriage to him she had never shown even the slightest hint of courage, never a rude remark, nor a hostile glare. She now felt she had no more to fear. *What more could he do to me?* she thought. She would not reveal her fear to him— he would only revel in it. Her only weapon left: tenacity and pride. Kate barely opened her lips, swallowing some blood, with a wry smile slowly creeping up the corners of her blood-caked mouth, she quietly directed an accusation at her husband. "You killed him. I know it... she knows it...and soon...everyone in this stinking town will know it."

Not in the least impressed by her futile attempt at a continuous effort to antagonize him with her hollow threats, Charles bent at the knees and cautiously...slowly, descended like a venomous spider over his helpless victim caught in a sticky web. Leaning forward, he placed his mouth within inches of her bloody face. Kate reluctantly received the hot pulsations of his vile breath in full force as it blasted in rapid bursts on her nose and mouth. Big and strong as he was, Charles had expended a tremendous amount of energy dragging her through the house to this cold, isolated corner of the kitchen and he was struggling to catch his breath. Rancid body odour wafted up from his damp shirt like the stale lining of an outhouse shed; Kate cringed in response to the smell. He grabbed the wet strands of hair draping down her face with his left hand and twisted it tightly between the fat fingers of his huge fist; then with the index finger of his right hand he inserted his fingernail into the bloody slice on Kate's mouth, twisting and digging, like a clumsy lab assistant examining the wound of a dead animal during dissection. Kate screamed—Charles smiled, gladly receiving the predictable reaction as a reward for his cruel torture.

Pulling hard on her hair, he snapped her head back with a quick flick of his wrist and stared deep into her eyes; the distance between their eyeballs—no more than a whisper. His sour breath released the words into her face with delicate, torturing cruelty, "And who's going to tell everybody, my dear wife... you?"

His eyes were so close—they seemed to be burning into her soul. Kate could hear his wicked heart rapidly pounding through his chest. She knew his tolerance level was breaching, but she hesitated for only a second. "I will tell them," she bravely responded in a low volume growl. Attempting to conceal her trepidation, Kate stared right back into Charles' eyes. His grip on her hair tightened—regardless, she continued, "Margaret will go to your precious Mr. Ogden tonight and you will be surrounded by a lynch mob by morning. Your best friends will hang you...your days as any kind of a man in this town, are over."

Charles pushed Kate's head hard into the leg of the chopping table in frustration and stared long and hard into her weary accusatory expression. "You have no idea what I am capable of my dear. You will be speaking to no one!" Frank Ogden and Charles Smithson had arrived together as business partners twenty years ago from Boston, hoping to develop a stepping-off station for pioneers heading west. Together they became very wealthy as landowners and merchants. Frank Ogden was elected sheriff as well as owning and operating the hotel and saloon. It was in his saloon where Charles first met Kate Winslow. She was small, beautiful and voluptuous with brazen eyes and an enchanting smile. She was ambitious—a destitute saloon girl with few prospects, seeking a better life; Frank introduced her to Charles hoping to aid in the improvement of her station in life. Charles was smitten immediately. Frank had maintained a close family bond with Kate and Charles over the years, as they both climbed to great heights on Chicago's social ladder. Unfortunately, Charles always held Kate's previous, questionable career-choice up as contemptible leverage whenever he required increased levels of subservient behaviour from his wife. Kate assumed Frank would come to her rescue once he discovered the truth about tonight. His mandate was peace and the good welfare of the citizens of Chicago and security for the thousands of pioneers heading west from this mid-western outpost, as well as amassing as much profit as possible.

Charles Smithson owned the Mercantile and the dockyards on Lake Michigan—receiving the logs from the north as they arrived by ship and boom, to be loaded onto long horse-drawn carts waiting for the short trip to his lumber mill. His store served all the patrons in the Chicago area and outfitted all pioneers heading west to homestead. All buildings in town were constructed of lumber from his mills or stone from his quarries. Anyone who was not heading west and resided full time in Chicago, worked for either Ogden or Smithson—their monopoly on the land and the people grew into a tight stranglehold; it was well understood that any impertinence or disregard in relation to their authority would end in swift tragedy. Frank's unshakable code of duty concerning Robert's murder is what Kate was depending on tonight—Charles' contrariety in that respect, if left unabated, would be her downfall.

Charles regarded his battered wife at his feet, he knew a quick solution was necessary—she would not be allowed to leave the house to expose this crime or any other. The death of Robert Tumblety on the docks tonight could in no way be linked to him—he would make certain of it. The broken relationship between Tumblety and his daughter was no secret in this town, nor was his vehement outspoken response to her pregnancy. It was a shameful embarrassment. His daughter was a whore—there was no doubt in his mind. Dockworkers had witnessed vicious threats passing between Charles and Robert on previous occasions; they knew Robert's persistent rebuke of Smithson's challenge would lead to nothing but inescapable disaster. Ogden in no way condoned illegal strategies to sustain their commercial ventures. An upstanding man, Frank Ogden could be trusted to follow proper procedure, and would never stoop to murder to eliminate a vexing problem. He was a hard and intense man—more than one drunken cowboy had been thrown out of town at the hands of his deputies. Crude scaffolds in the town square had bared witness to many a hanging by the order of Frank Ogden, but his methods of justice were tempered by law and were understood and accepted by the people who elected him. His actions were never the result of sedition or vengeance. Charles would not have Frank as a confidant in this matter, and he knew it. No, he would first have to deal with Kate himself then, consider Margaret and her possible compliance in this short conspiracy to turn him over to Ogden, if and when she returned.

The men Charles hired to smash in Robert's head and throw his poor, young body into the lake could be trusted, he assumed, as they knew of Smithson's long list of wilful and dangerous cohorts who would leap at the chance to make a few extra dollars to hunt them down if they crossed him. Besides they'd received their fair share for tonight's cowardly work.

Charles glanced around the kitchen, searching for a solution: rope or shackles perhaps—maybe a box or a device to restrain her but keep her alive. He then spied a pair of two newly cut axe handles in the corner, sanded but not yet notched for the heavy steel blade that would crown their heavier top end. They were oak, solid and heavy—at least four feet in length—he had ordered them for the new double-headed axe blades that would be arriving from Boston in the next shipment. Rising from Kate's position on the floor, he took a few steps to the corner and picked one up. The twin handles had been inconspicuously leaning against the countertop in the farthest corner of the kitchen—their presence almost going unnoticed—their purpose unassuming and strangely cold, almost forbidden. It felt good in his hand. He swung it back and forth to check the weight. He slid his hand up and down the handle with amorous affection; the smooth texture of the wood curved so delicately in the palm of his hand—the weight perfectly balanced. His eyes seemed to twinkle with delight as a tiny, wicked curl developed at the corners of his mouth, not quite a smile, yet definitely a cruel expression of the warm elation quickly picking up speed as it swam through the pounding vessels of his cold blood.

He turned to Kate and for a frightening second, their eyes met. The horror of the dark image before her forced her to recoil in terror. His great figure was dark, menacing, and seemed giant-like in relation to her lowly supine position on the floor. He stood not unlike a medieval marauder from an ancient battlefield, his stance with feet wide apart, war axe in hand, and with brooding temperament, stood gallantly poised for the final blow to finish off a beaten adversary. She would not have been surprised if he had raised his axe handle high in the air, with his neck stretched back and face lifted to the ceiling, released a vociferous war cry summoning all the evil visages from hell to rally to his side.

Charles took a step towards Kate. Realizing her life hung precariously at the end of the next two steps he would take, she quickly found the strength to bolt up and crawl forward on her knees. A scream exploded from her mouth; her breathing was short and quick as she gasped for air. *He couldn't possibly...*she argued with her senses and all that was holy. "Holy Mother of God, he's gone crazy, please help me." Kate pleaded with her invisible saints hoping Charles would not complete the horrible task he was threatening.

Quickly scrambling across the stone tiles of the kitchen floor on her hands and knees, Kate nervously twisted her neck back to peer over her shoulder checking her husband's position. He hadn't moved. Charles was not concerned with Kate's attempt at escape. She had nowhere to go. He knew she was trapped and remained pitifully at his mercy. She fell into the hallway but before she could crawl another inch a grip as tight as a vise clasped around her ankle. Kate screamed in terror. She began kicking her legs and flailing her arms in useless abandon. Charles effortlessly pulled her back into the kitchen dropping her once again at the foot of the chopping block; before she could roll over entirely to face him, he raised the axe handle high in the air over her vulnerable form, in striking position.

5

The saloon girls that had reluctantly arrived at the Indian encampment to receive the deft midwife talents of Rising Sun in the past, usually assumed the traditional squatting position for birth, as natural gravity was considered the best way for the baby to be encouraged to exit the comfy confines of its precious womb. In the case of an abortion, crude potions were used to loosen the attachment to the uterine wall, and after a significant waiting period the girl would vomit, then be placed on her back so an instrument of Rising Sun's own design, could be carefully inserted to root out the fetus if it refused to slide out on its own accord.

Margaret would not be standing or squatting for her procedure tonight as the baby was refusing all aid, including gravity, to exit her womb. As she lay there, still and complacent—the calming features of Rising Sun's potion slowly taking effect—Little Raven wiped the perspiration from her brow, taking the time to look closer at the locket that had fallen behind her neck; its presence vitally aware to everyone in the tent. It had become caught in the twisted wet hair behind the girl's head. She reached for it, loosened the chain, pulling it closer. Margaret looked up, "Open it," she whispered. Little Raven cautiously snapped the little clasp holding the two halves together— two faces were revealed to her: a handsome young man on the right side and Margaret's likeness on the other. "That is Robert. He was to be my husband."

"He is very handsome," responded Little Raven. Without asking, her eyes were searching for more information. With her thumb and forefinger, Little Raven rubbed the engraved surface: roses and Irish knots, so delicately entwined, and so tiny; the craftsmanship almost unbelievably pure and perfect. In the centre: a heart-shaped ruby. This was a precious thing that Little Raven could never have imagined, let alone viewed or touched. She was amazed and remained captivated by its beauty, not unlike a child who could finally, miraculously, hold a star in the palm of her hand for the first time after viewing it for so many dreamy nights in the dark heavenly sky above. Everything she owned was wooden or made from coarse fabric. She had no adornments, save a beaded necklace of ochre clay and a few frayed leather fringes dangling loosely from her wrist as a crude bracelet.

"We met by chance when walking home from Ogden's last spring. The Minstrel Show had played that night and the dockworkers listened from outside. They couldn't afford tickets I suppose. When they turned to watch us pass by after the performance, Father grabbed my arm and dragged me along assuming their gaze alone could infect me. From that moment on, I passed by as often as possible whenever I went into town hoping to catch another look at Robert. He was the handsomest. We would meet secretly after that. Mother

knew and scolded me. She said Father would not be impressed, but…
He…wasn't impressed with…anything I did anyway."

Margaret's eyes were drooping and her words began to slur.
Little Raven looked up and realized Shashona was standing over the
boiling pot of water ready to dig out Rising Sun's operating knives.
The extraction was imminent, as the blood loss had been continuous;
there was still no sign of any contraction. In order to save this baby,
Rising Sun would have to go to work immediately.

"Did your father fight with him?" asked Little Raven.

"Yes…desperately. The situation became intolerable. I couldn't
leave the house; I was forbidden to do anything. Mother did nothing
for me. She was a coward—as bad as Him. It was as if I was locked in
a jail. That big house became my prison."

Margaret lifted her left hand and held it out to Little Raven.
"This is my engagement ring." This simple act seemed to take every
ounce of effort Margaret had left. Little Raven held her hand—it was
so small, so cold, as if there was no blood left to circulate there—she
looked closely at the tiny silver band on her ring finger.

"What does it mean?" asked Little Raven. Shashona and
Nootkana moved closer. This meagre collection of jewellery was a
great prize for this little band of women, as they knew full well that its
value could bring them considerable food for the approaching winter.
The necklace had been obvious, but this ring was a delightful surprise.
Nootkana, in particular, considered the sale of the locket and ring
almost a reprieve from the horrendous sexual exploits she would have
to endure at Rising Sun's request in order to meet the needs of the
winter months. The cowboys would be coming around soon enough
and Rising Sun always took full advantage of any opportunity, even at
the displeasure and defiance of Shashona and Nootkana. Rising Sun
was too old and ugly for the cowboys now, and Shashona would not

allow her daughter to participate—she was seventeen, she considered her too young. She continued to oppose Rising Sun in this matter; but for how long, she didn't know. The income from the locket and ring would help her daughter's case for a time; this was a great relief. Of course if Margaret lived, the locket would remain around her neck and the ring would remain on her finger—a consideration sliding surreptitiously between the mindfolds of the attending women no doubt.

The importance of the visual games being exchanged between the Indian women, as Margaret spoke, was lost to her. They continued to look on with eager curiosity.

The design on the ring was a heart with two hands embracing it from each side; above: a crown. "It's an Irish Claddagh ring. The heart is love; the hands friendship, and the crown loyalty," Margaret explained, her powers of cognition fading away so that her words were only slight whispers. "Robert's mother gave them to him when he left Ireland...his most precious things in all the world, and...he gave...them...to me." Her words died away, Rising Sun stepped in with a knife in her hand.

6

bottle. A solitary bottle. The sideboard at the far end of the cavernous room was empty save for a long, single bottle. The gentle curve of its profile was almost lost in the shadows; its existence almost entirely forgotten. Its position: the farthest corner of the expansive kitchen. The Tiffany lampshade above—so high, almost buried in the dark corners of the ceiling rafters, its oil flame cast such a dim glow—it illuminated nothing, allowing any number of things to remain hidden in the large stone-clad room, their identities a mystery to all but the kitchen staff. But the dark object, shy and reserved in its solitude, was definitely a whiskey bottle, and Charles recognized it even though he glanced away from his gruesome task for only the slightest breath of a moment. Then in the same instant he returned his focus to the broken body of his wife at his feet. He lowered the axe handle over Kate's head, but so slowly and gently, that the wooden handle became an extension of his straightened arm and the swing was reduced to a cautiously placed touch, like a wand delicately floating down from its lofty height to land softly, not unlike the kiss of a butterfly wing, tickling the corner of Kate's eyebrow.

As gentle as it was, Kate jerked sporadically at the moment of its touch and opened her eyes in shock. The axe handle was frozen within a position of such immediate proximity to her eyes that her field of vision was completely filled with nothing but the horror of its wide, thick breadth—a solid block of oak—intimidating in the prospect of its raw power, held as it was, in the tight fist of her predictable husband. Kate's swollen eyes quickly came into focus and she gasped at the sight, her muscles tightening.

A taunting smile escaped from Charles' mouth as he stepped over Kate's body. She recoiled in response, but the anticipated blow did not arrive and Charles stepped lively to the sideboard, intent on retrieving the bottle he now remembered from the earlier activities of this miserable evening.

Not realizing she was receiving a short reprieve, Kate remained frozen in her curled position on the floor, leaning slightly up against the leg of the chopping table. The blood on her face was beginning to dry into caked blotches on her face. Watching him walk away, her eyes drooped in a pathetic expression of exhaustion and surrender.

Jameson Whiskey was Charles' favourite—its flavour was so much more sophisticated to the palette than the local sour mash bourbon and whiskey the cowboys drank at Ogden's saloon. A considerable amount of the golden liquid had been consumed earlier, yet luckily half of the contents remained.

So cocky was his stride, so confidant his manner, that he gave his wife a false impression of security as he teased her with his cruel stroll across the stone tiles of the kitchen floor, carrying the axe handle over his shoulder as if heading to the lake with a fishing pole for a leisurely afternoon of quiet repose.

Charles carefully placed his weapon on the counter, reached for the bottle, raised it to his mouth and, with the cork squeezed tightly between his teeth, he bit down hard, popped it out and spit it on the floor. Turning to Kate he raised the bottle in a mocking toast, "To you my dear wife." He celebrated with a winsome laugh, placing the bottle to his lips, he swallowed a generous amount with two large gulps. The taste was exhilarating, the burn soothing, like a cool, refreshing blast to his dry throat.

Only a few hundred yards away at the edge of town, Kate's daughter Margaret lay on a bed of horse blankets on the warm dirt floor inside a smoky tent. The storm continued to rage—the incessant rain pelting the sides of the buffalo-hide walls without respite. Rising Sun stood above Margaret, the sharp imposing implement in hand, preparing to retrieve the baby from its sweet warm sanctuary. Shashona raised the coal oil lantern high; Little Raven knelt at Margaret's head tenderly holding her hand.

Margaret's thoughts, clouded with a powerful concoction of wormwood for the pain and licorice root and broom snakewood to loosen the placenta, began to drift to the docks where ghostly, transparent visions of Robert appeared as grey shadows—his hollow voice calling her. Rising Sun's potion dulled the pain and planted swirling images in her brain where nebulous apparitions rotated and gyrated with smooth abandon around the docks folding in and out of the fog and rain. Margaret could see her father's men as they danced around Robert in a twirling orgy of anger and violence, raising their clubs high, swinging with powerful strokes, lifting and pushing Robert's body with each swing. Robert jerked and swayed in partnership with the bloody murderers in a macabre devil's dance, his raised hands useless in defence.

Charles took another gulp from the bottle; holding the tart solution at the back of his throat, he regarded Kate, coolly considering his task as he raised one eyebrow in eerie calculation. Squeezing one eye closed—then the other in alternating blinks, he playfully tested the focus of the light through the bottle, holding it up in front of his face before the lamp. The dim light of the coal oil lamp, hanging above the long wooden table in the centre of the kitchen, reflected a sour bronze tint into Charles' eye as he held the bottle there for a few moments continuing to peer through the glass cylinder—he was hesitating. He gently swallowed, slowly appreciating the full value of the rich flavour of Irish peat and rye as it slid down his gullet. He then replaced the bottle to its position on the counter, picked up the axe handle and turned to Kate.

The thunder crashed in wicked bursts overhead; the rain slashed the sides of the tent in angry repeating barrages as Nootkana and Little Raven knelt at Margaret's head, holding her arms down tight. Nootkana propped a folded blanket under Margaret's hips to raise her cervix higher and held her knees up and open. Rising Sun gestured to Shashona to raise the lantern high and steady. She then dropped to her knees between Margaret's spread legs; the long blade of her knife glistening in the flickering flame of the lantern's dull light.

Margaret reached out to save Robert as he searched through the curtain of rain and fog with an outstretched hand to his love. The shadows hid the faces of his tormentors yet Margaret found Robert's eyes—they were flooded in tears of loss and regret as they fell upon Margaret's gaze in futile desperation.

Rising Sun's knife entered the vagina and reached the stubborn walls of the cervix. With a gentile slice, she cut into the opening.

Blood poured forth layering a thick, red, slippery covering on her arms and hands.

Charles stood over Kate raising the axe handle high. Kate held her hands over her face to shield her head from the blow. A powerful chop sliced through the air over Kate's tense, coiled figure smashing into her right shin! Kate released a torrential stream of aching screeches, as another blow fell and another, and yet another!

Blood spewed forth from Margaret's vagina as Rising Sun reached in with her left hand searching for the baby's head. She began to pull. The opening was still too small for her hands. Using the knife once again she continued to cut away the restrictions of the cervical opening making it wide enough to wrench the baby through. The sky outside illuminated with a flash, and the thunder that followed exploded like a cannonball shot from a nearby field gun shaking the tent, forcing Shashona's arm to waver and Rising Sun scolded in her deep, raspy voice, "Hold the lantern steady girl!"

Margaret held Robert's hand as he began to fall at the end of the dock, his face sombre, lonely and destitute—complacent in his fateful resolve. From within the fog, clubs arched and flashed above Robert's head like a Chinese fan whipping and churning, flashing like a strobe in the white light of the exploding tempest.

The axe handle reached up and drove down again and again. Kate's legs became crumpled, twisted lumps of bloody flesh, broken and ripped. The excruciating pain finally and mercifully rendered her unconscious—a small salvation. Charles' eyes bulged with uncontrolled insanity at the horrific scene at his feet; he was breathing in rapid short bursts from the violent workout.

The thunder roared, the axe handle pounded down, the knife sliced through, a hand reached out. The night: a theatre of horror as Kate lay broken; Margaret, bloody and still, her hand slipping from Robert's as he slid slowly, silently from the dock into the stormy waters of Lake Michigan. She drifted into sleep—barely hanging on to life.

Kate lay motionless in a bloody pool on the kitchen floor of the great house; her legs bent and broken; her flesh torn and raw.

Margaret's dream faded to a warm echo as Rising Sun, with one last careful tug, pulled the baby free and quickly handed him to Nootkana. Then, without hesitation, she ripped out the placenta and cut the cord, as more blood spewed forth and soaked her face and chest.

Instantly and without warning, the storm finally began to subside—only a light breeze now whistled by the door flap of the tent; a few last drops of rain quietly dripped into the muddy puddles by the entrance.

Charles stood in a stoic pose—the bloody weapon in his hand was lowered to the floor—it hung there heavy, dripping with Kate's blood like the dead weight of a brass pendulum of a broken clock, void now of its perpetual swing. His eyes slowly calmed; his pupils began to focus. Lowering his gaze, he viewed the unholy, vile scene at his feet. He remained detached, emoting none of the frenzied emotions of his uncontrolled attack. His shoulders began to slump—he regained his composure.

Nootkana wiped the blood from the baby's eyes and wrapped him in a clean blanket. Francis began to scream and the world shuddered in response.

Morning's soft light gently peaked over the horizon to the east and danced and sparkled on the surface of the broken ripples curling over the great blue lake. The new sky was painted with a palette of warm, pastel tones of azure and fuchsia, and although the quiet dawn was a welcomed relief after such a turbulent night, it would be a day like no other—for a new life had arrived like no other, violently pulled into a world like no other—a testament to the baby's tormented life yet to be endured.

7

The bony black claw of a shrivelled prairie chicken leg hung precariously by a thin, withered leather string high up in the damp, dark crotch of the ceiling poles; its dead skin, broken and cracked, flaking off in crispy layers, was threatening to break free and descend directly into Margaret's eye as she lay wrapped in her blanket on the floor below.

Rising Sun's potion was wearing off and Margaret was slowly gaining some clarity as her eyes opened slightly and she began to focus on her surroundings. The claw was the first thing brought to her attention and she was having difficulty discerning its identity.

A bright shard of morning light stabbed the gloomy tent's interior as Nootkana opened the door flap and graciously welcomed the new day inside. All eyes turned to the opening and immediately everyone inside instinctively raised their hands to their eyes for protection, wincing at the shocking brightness. The sky was blue; the ground was saturated in water; the air: fresh and clean—the sweetness of its purity was not unlike a cleansing elixir as it filled the lungs with its glorious bouquet and brought with it a redeeming renewal to heart and temperament. The vile stench of the stockyard for now was heavily diluted, and that alone was a gift, even if only for a few short hours until the heat of the sun dried up the puddles and more animals completed their stinking business, as they did day in and day out.

Margaret moaned and shifted. The towels folded up between her legs were bulky, damp and uncomfortable. The pain there stabbed her like a thousand porcupine quills and she reacted by folding into a tight curl; then released a loud groan through clenched teeth as she bit down hard, repressing a scream.

Rising Sun had done her best with the wounds, sewing the cuts with horsehair threads and covering the area with a lotion of echinacea root to prevent infection. But she knew the amount of blood loss was so great that in order to survive this night's ordeal, the frail child would need the constitution of a lumberjack.

"My baby" Margaret whispered to Little Raven who had yet to move from her kneeling position at the girl's head.

"Your baby is fine. He is a boy. You must rest." Little Raven answered and instructed her caring message to Margaret in a soft consoling voice, brushing her damp brow with a tender touch of her delicate fingers. Little Raven peered down into Margaret's face with concern and listened to her soft whispers.

"Bring me my baby," commanded Margaret as best she could in her weakened condition. Each vowel emitted from her dry lips triggered a pain originating from deep between her legs but then travelled in a violent gunshot pattern up through her torso ripping into an explosion in her head all within a fraction of a second. She pressed her teeth tight together and held back another scream.

"Drink this child." Rising Sun brought a tin cup to Little Raven who held it to Margaret's lips.

"This will help the pain," explained Little Raven as she gently held Margaret's head up from behind with her hand and steadied the cup to her mouth.

Shashona brought the warm bundle over and squatted beside Margaret. Laying the baby on her chest, all eyes fell to the tiny mother and child. Margaret carefully lifted the edge of the blanket away from the child's face and peeked in. The hint of a weak smile gradually grew in the corners of her mouth but stopped short before reaching its full extent, as she viewed her child for the first and only time. It lasted for only a few seconds. Margaret looked up and consciously gave each one of her nurses a grateful moment of her appreciation, each in turn, from one to the other and back again, saying nothing but looking deep into their eyes—conveying a heartfelt message of thanks for her gift. The exchange was received and understood: a silent bond between sisters—a spiritual connection.

"His name is Francis...Francis Robert Tumblety." Margaret felt she could trust these native women and she found comfort in that resolve: her baby would be cared for. "Promise you'll give my boy my locket and ring... tell him of me." Little Raven nodded silently. Margaret's hand holding the blanket on the baby's head slowly slipped to her side and her head softly turned away.

Rising Sun pulled back the blanket at Margaret's legs and found the bulky towels deeply saturated in dark red blood. The crude stitches had held nothing back.

Far from the tent, in a quiet place below a great sycamore tree, beyond view, to the south, Margaret's body was laid to rest in a shallow grave, deep enough to keep the dogs and coyotes away, but shallow enough to give Shashona and Little Raven little grief in their task. They were grateful: the soil was wet and easy to remove. There was no marker, save a bulky stone hidden in the grass.

Little Raven looked down and opened her hand. She quietly reflected upon the little silver locket and Claddagh ring in her hand. Its possession would be difficult to keep; there were no secrets from Rising Sun, but she knew this might be the only connection the boy would ever have to his past and she had made a vow. Little Raven decided that if he was a gift then she would call him 'Mingaswen'—the Potawatomi word for gift. Some day she might be able to reveal to him the truth about his name and about his mother and father, but for now he would become a member of the Potawatomi, and surviving in this swamp with his adoptive Indian family would be enough challenge for the boy.

Little Mingaswen, quietly sleeping in Little Raven's arms, cared not for the solitude of the place nor could he appreciate the horror of the first moments of his life.

He was asleep; his violent birth—the first seed.

8

Charles bent down; he laid the axe handle on the floor beside Kate's tangled body. Reaching under, he lifted her limp body up with both arms. Turning, he left the kitchen. Following the long hallway to the great foyer; he stopped at the bottom of the grand staircase. Raising his chin, he considered the lofty route before him. The morning sun, rising above the cold, blue waves on Lake Michigan, shot rays of golden light through the arched stained glass windows that lined the grand stairwell, facing the eastern horizon. Charles realized the dreadful night had finally ended and the storm's anger had ceased.

The bright light of the sunrise pierced the glass crystals dangling from the chandelier, which hung majestically from the centre of the foyer's high ceiling, distributing a range of every colour and tone of blue, red and yellow, as it refracted rectangular and teardrop shapes, painting the front walls and doorway with a wide assortment of miniature rainbows. Charles casually reviewed the colourful display without concern, as he cautiously lifted each foot up, then down, slowly climbing the winding staircase—his wife Kate in his arms, a trail of blood painting a polka-dot line on the carpeted steps at his feet, as a continuous red drip trickled down from her battered limbs.

Finally reaching the top of the great stairwell, Charles followed the corridor to the end. He was breathing heavily. Kicking the door hard at the bottom to make the opening wider for his cumbersome load, Charles entered the master bedroom and stood before the bed. The smooth line of the silk, oriental-patterned duvet, covering the mattress, and the untouched shams on the pillows at the head, perfectly defined a bed that had not been slept in, and Charles suddenly remembered, *the servants would be arriving any time.* He didn't panic, but it was a situation that had not occurred to him until now.

With uncharacteristic gentleness, he placed Kate upon the bed, standing for a moment with his hands remaining outstretched, frozen and unsure. Her body was limp, her clothes bloody and dishevelled. Charles regarded the blood on his hands with incredulity and disdain; he had not realized that Kate's blood had splattered up the axe handle onto his hands and arms during the beating. He turned them over, and over again; rubbing them together hard as if to erase the deed, as much as the stain—then moved quickly to the dressing table on the opposite wall. He poured cold water from the tall porcelain vase into the basin and washed his hands. He pressed the thumb of his right hand into the centre of his left palm and squeezed his fingers from behind, then stroked forward to the end of his middle finger over and over—as if trying to press out the blood. He repeated this technique on the other hand and squeezed each finger in turn. He washed for several minutes then turned to the motionless figure on the bed, still holding the blood-stained towel in his hands. Rather than concern, his face expressed the features of exhaustion: mouth drooping, eyes warn and puffy.

Lifting his head, his eyes darted left and right, quickly surveying the dark room. He dropped the towel on the bed and moved to the window. He drew the heavy curtains open with one powerful pull from the centre of his chest, each arm flinging in opposite directions. The morning light crashing through the window, illuminated more than the huge bedroom; it revealed the true extent of the damage Charles had inflicted. He squeezed his eyes tight and waited for his pupils to adjust to the bright sunlight. As his eyes focussed, the ghastly image slowly began to appear before him.

One would truly wonder if the person on his bed had recently been hauled in off the battlefield, as the extent of Kate's injuries were so severe, it's doubtful that the blast of a cannonball could have done worse. The flesh on the tops of her shins had been completely ripped off exposing the white of her bones. The bones were so broken and bent that no straight line remained. The skin remaining on her shin was red and raw; her flesh and muscle was hanging in lumpy pockets. The discolouration included shades from black and purple to bright red. The blood loss was great as the entire area was painted with thick, dark blood; it continued to ooze out from throughout the area. He took the towel from the bed and wrapped her legs together—attempting to stop the bleeding—a crude and temporary procedure, but he had to reach the lower level of the house before his staff arrived in the kitchen. He then left quickly out the door and down the staircase to meet them before they arrived for their daily chores.

He would close the house temporarily due to a contagious sickness, and he would attend to his wife himself: no doctors. Charles needed time to think things through.

He locked the doors and began cleaning the stone tiles on the kitchen floor. He displayed a conscious disconnection from his duties, as he pulled the mop forward and back, and forward again. The blood seemed to be everywhere—sticking like a red blanket; its dark viscous coating left behind to identify the place where his raw anger had met her delicate destiny.

9

*I*n the following days Charles conducted his business in the usual routine manner. There were questions concerning his wife of course, but he managed to convince everyone that Kate was suffering from a contagious illness and could receive no visitors. He tended to his wife himself with little compassion and without results that included any signs of recovery. He had dismissed his staff entirely.

Within ten days, Kate's fever escalated to a point where she would not regain consciousness and all attempts by Charles to revive her remained futile. Her legs were so swollen and discoloured, they were barely identifiable for what they were—or used to be. The rancid odour of gangrene wafted up into Charles' face when he pulled back the covers to check on Kate's condition; his body cringed with repulsion and he quickly covered his face with his hand. Without immediate attention; he knew his wife would die. Her skin was split wide open in so many locations on her legs from her knees down to her ankles. The flesh was raw and inflamed, running with yellow and green puss. The stench was overwhelming and Charles staggered back checking his balance by grabbing a corner of the duvet, preventing a clumsy fall to the floor.

Frank Ogden had enquired about Kate's state of health as well as other prominent townspeople who showed their concern over Kate's quarantine, and Charles' excuses were wearing thin. Kate would soon die if he did not take quick action.

He would make one final attempt at saving her, or kill her now, bury her and be done with her; he had to decide.

10

Shashona held Mingaswen close to her breast as her milk continued to flow with the help of Rising Sun's herbal mixture of raspberry leaves, stinging nettle and oatstraw, as well as a mild drink of red clover blossoms, and the infant responded with the soft cooing and gentle breaths of comfort.

Activity at the camp returned quickly to a peaceful but busy tranquility after the storm and the tragic birth. Little Raven and Nootkana were ordered to gather specific weeds and herbs from the prairie grasses, as new concoctions were formulated and new batches of soap began to cook in the pot over the fires. Sheep wool was boiled with salt to produce lanolin. The soft creamy oil would be used to keep Shashona's nipples moist and to prevent cracks.

Gazing into the western sky, Rising Sun knew the cool breezes of autumn gently teasing the whiskers on her chin, would bring winter's cold grip soon enough and there must be money set aside for the necessary provisions to guide the little band through the harsh winter months. Soap and herbal remedies would be sold to the people of Chicago and to the pioneers passing through on their way west to a new life of hopes and dreams, visually expressed by nature's great panoramic vista of the open freedoms of the vast prairie skies and expansive grasses reaching out far before them to their future.

As the sun set and the lights began to flicker in the widows of the hotel on the main street—the dancehall girls began to squeal—a combination of tinny fiddle and banjo rhythms released a lively cadence that reverberated through the windows echoing down the streets to the Smithson Manor House. Muddy boots pounded a steady thump on the floorboards as the cowboys and dockworkers answered the lively sounds in their own graceless way: holding their glasses high—celebrating in the din with loud bellows and boisterous choruses. The men in the streets and alleyways turned their attention to the saloon and began to drift in that direction. Charles, watching closely from the kitchen windows of his house, stood vigilant like a hidden sentinel observing their movements with clever intention.

Standing at the threshold of the open kitchen door at the rear of his great house, Charles studied the shadows darting about in the alleyway. A dark, folded blanket made of heavy fabric, lay in a pile on the floor behind him. It was not easy to discern its purpose, but quite possibly a load of dirty horse blankets had been piled haphazardly for quick distribution to the horse stables or to the laundry. Charles remained at the door with one hand clasping the latch, the other holding onto the great wooden trim framing the opening for balance.

Dissecting the dark with sharp glances, he peered into the alley searching for someone or something. The sounds of the night broke into disjointed fragments with borderless divisions where the shuffle of steps in the dirt drifted away to meet the eerie howl of the stockyard dog's lonely dirge, blending in weak discords with distant banjo rhythms. A muted sound space opened, and Charles reacted with a swift turn of his neck, responding to a faint, muffled moan that gently filled the momentary, silent void; it resonated from deep within the coarse folds of the horse blanket at his feet. It softly faded away and he quickly returned his attention to the dark alleyway.

When he was convinced that his route was clear, Charles picked up the blanket carefully, so as not to reveal its abhorrent contents, balancing the awkward load between his arms. He stepped down into the alley; then he twisted a quarter turn to gently close the kitchen door with a push of his shoulder behind him. His step was then lively, without pause, as he followed the cart tracks in the alley, and headed directly to the stockyards, dodging in and out of shadows. His pace was smart but cautious, in that he was wary of the ubiquitous piles of manure and mud that clung to the cracks and crevasses of every corner and notch within the inky contours of the dirt trail. He was desperate to keep his boots free of the despicable muck—although the task was almost impossible. At times his darting steps were almost comparable to that of a ballet dancer on tip-toe: an absolutely absurd vision, and totally irreverent in relation to the clandestine industry in which he was now deeply entrenched.

Little Raven was first to spy the bulky shadow as it rounded the corner of the corral gate and quickly grew in size as it approached the tent.

"A cowboy is coming for Nootkana," Little Raven whispered to Shashona. She lifted the flap and peered into the tent. Little Mingaswen was sleeping in blankets on the floor. Shashona, Nootkana and Rising Sun were sitting at the table carefully picking the last pieces of dry skin from a prairie chicken's foot in the dim, flickering glow of a coal oil lantern, shovelling it into their mouths with great enthusiasm. All eyes turned to the direction of the soft words. With the disclosure of this information, Nootkana's mouth drooped to a disappointing frown; a fragile piece of chicken skin sticking there by a thread.

Rising Sun snapped her head and curled her brow. With cautious incredulity, she completed a quick survey of the tent and the people at her table. She stopped and stared at the skin protruding out from between Nootkana's lips and at the grease dripping from her chin. "Wipe your face!" she commanded.

Nootkana was not impressed with the possibility of surrendering to the sexual needs of a drunken cowboy tonight. Yet she understood her plight, and turned her hand over and dragged it across her lips twice quickly, then dropped it to her lap and wiped it on her dress. Hopefully her appearance was worth the ten cents she might earn tonight.

Little Raven stepped back and Charles Smithson filled the gap in the tent wall with his imposing figure and stern countenance. Without invitation he stepped into the tent holding his bundle above the table.

"Remove the lamp," he demanded. Shashona responded immediately, grabbing the lantern away. Realizing he was about to drop the blanket, Rising Sun and Nootkana cleared the chicken bones and bits of half-eaten bread on the table with two swipes of their arms—everything dropped to the ground. Charles laid the blanket on the table and stepped back. Rising Sun approached and bent her head down close to the blanket. With one sniff, she understood; the undeniable odour quickly resolving any mystery it may have been harbouring. *He wants me to bury it,* she thought.

"Do what you can," Charles coolly ordered, then continued, "I'll return tomorrow." He then turned and left the tent; his dark figure folding into the shadows of the night, he disappeared.

Pulling back the heavy blanket folds, Rising Sun exposed the battered body. Kate was alive but suffering greatly from the symptoms of advanced infection. Her face was pale; her skin soaked in perspiration—her fever, high; she was delirious and weak—her chances of recovery: remote.

The others winced and immediately cupped their hands to their faces covering their noses and mouths in a vain attempt to repress the overpowering odour. The gangrene on Kate's legs had been allowed to advance without restriction for ten days and the discolouration and putrid smell was no less than that of rotting cattle corpses lying about in the dumps adjacent to the slaughter sheds.

"We can do nothing for her," explained Rising Sun.

"Cut them off," suggested Shashona. "She might live."

Rising Sun responded by offering a simple nod while examining the injuries. Nootkana, relieved that she would not have to service a cowboy tonight after all, found the knives and Little Raven took a pot outside to place over the fire pit.

Shashona tied the wire handle of the lantern to a cord hanging from the centre pole at the ceiling. Still the illumination in the tent was poor. Rising Sun aimed to work fast.

Little Raven gently held Kate's head and wiped her brow. Shashona and Nootkana held her legs and arms.

Rising Sun tied a leather strap in a crude but efficient tourniquet above each of Kate's knees cutting off the blood flow. She then reached for a slim knife that would be used as a scalpel. Skin was then expertly sliced and peeled back at the knee so the stumps could be covered after the operation. She then reached back into the pot that

Little Raven brought in from the fire and retrieved the biggest knife. This buffalo blade was twelve inches long and three inches wide, with a double-edged point at the tip for cutting buffalo sinew. The top edge of the knife was flat and wide. The cutting edge was thin, fine and as sharp as a barber's razor. It was truly more of a cleaver than a knife and would be more than sufficient for the job at hand.

Rising Sun placed the blade in position just below her cuts with her left hand and raised a heavy hatchet in her right. Turning the hatchet to the heal side she dropped it like a hammer and struck the top edge of the knife blade with a powerful stroke that sent the blade through the flesh and bone, down to the table in one merciful flashing chop! Immediately upon completing the amputation, Rising Sun placed the blade over the other leg and hammered it through without hesitation.

The action was so fast and true that less than a few seconds passed for the whole ordeal. With a quick brush of her arm, Rising Sun cleared the table of the repulsive remnants—they dropped to the ground and rolled in the dirt. She tossed her head to the left in a quick nod to Shashona indicating the direction for her to dispose of them with haste. Shashona quickly complied, retrieving the limbs, placing them outside the tent. Then with equal fury Rising Sun began sewing the large blood vessels up and burning the ends of the smaller ones with a hot knife. She then sewed the skin flaps she had prepared over the ends of the stumps with horse hair threads and a thick needle. She released the tourniquets. Blood loss was minimal and quickly contained. Her work was as deft and sure as any field surgeon in any army.

Kate had raised her head and expressed discomfort for only a moment during the first amputation and then quickly slipped back into total unconsciousness.

The stumps were carefully wrapped in clear cloths soaked in a diluted formula of coal tar. The release of carbolic acid from the residue included properties that offered valuable prevention from infections. If Kate died, it wouldn't be from any surgical procedure administered by Rising Sun; they would be the result of symptoms already present when Kate arrived at the tent.

Nootkana and Shashona carefully laid Kate on the floor on a bed of blankets in a corner of the tent where her daughter had given birth and died only ten days previously.

Mingaswen woke with a cry and Shashona lifted him to her breast.

Only time would tell, if Kate would survive; or whether she would soon lie beside her daughter among the prairie flowers, beneath the great sycamore, beyond the corral boards.

11

Charles did not return the next day, nor the next. On the third day Kate died of the complications from gangrene and blood loss, but not before regaining consciousness for a short time—just long enough to hold Mingaswen to her chest. "He is Francis. He is your grandson," Little Raven whispered to Kate.

One word lingered on Kate's lips as she began to fade—the life slowly draining from her body, "Margaret..." a soft, sweet plea for atonement.

"Your daughter was too young; she was not strong," answered Little Raven. "She was my sister. My little brother will be safe with me. Francis will stay with me," she explained. Although she understood that little Mingaswen was truly her nephew, Little Raven would always refer to him as her brother. The bond of sister and brother being closest to mother and child, this was the heart-felt connection she wanted to maintain.

It was difficult to know if Kate understood Little Raven's words. She did not react in any way. Her stare remained frozen; the heat from her fever now turning ice cold in a matter of seconds. Little Raven lifted Mingaswen up and placed him in Shashona's arms.

Within a few moments of her passing, the great dark form of Charles Smithson appeared at the entrance flap—a visual path to his wife was cleared, as Little Raven and Shashona stepped smartly aside.

Looking down he acknowledged Kate's death by placing his hands on his hips and pressing his lips tightly together. His questioning frown related to his new concern, which dealt with the disposal of the body—the loss of his wife: an inconvenience.

"The infection was too great," explained Rising Sun.

"We did all we could," added Nootkana. The atmosphere in the tent was sombre, and uneasy; the women were cautious of Charles' next command. They did not trust the man, and understandably so. His reaction would be unpredictable. The women assumed the worst—possibly a violent display of angry emotion resulting in a beating or, conceivably, the death of one or more of the Indian women. He was not wearing a gun, but his fists were weapons, true enough—his violent reputation was well known and feared; besides, only one look at the body on the blanket was enough to validate their trepidation. However, Charles stood steadfast on his feet continuing to stare down at his wife's corpse.

At no time did he enquire about his daughter Margaret, who had been missing all these days without a trace, since that horrible storm. Frank Ogden initially believed Charles, when he was informed incorrectly, that Margaret had travelled east to Boston to stay with relatives after the discovery of Robert's death. His tragic death was considered an accident, and the issue had been quickly dropped. Now

Ogden was not so sure; Smithson wanted to ensure the death of his wife would remain outside the margins of suspicion.

Charles realized, correctly, that a proper funeral was necessary and would have to be arranged to satisfy the hungry fascination of the town folk and the people of Kate's church. She had been Ogden's good friend; for this reason alone, Smithson would have to do the right thing. Her death would have to be announced and properly certified; however, a viewing of the body by a medical examiner would never be allowed by Charles. Her death would be the result of some contagion, consumption, or fever or some such illness. He would see to it. Immediate internment would be necessary for the sake of the town, perhaps to prevent an epidemic of some sort, and he doubted if there would be any resistance.

Charles bent down and picked up the body, sure to wrap it carefully in the blanket so nothing suspicious was exposed. The sun was setting and Charles knew enough of Chicago's back alleys from the stockyards to his house; he had no reason to believe that his furtive activities would be discovered as he slithered between the shadows with the body of his deceased wife draped in his arms. He left the tent.

The Indian women did not linger. Shashona and Little Raven were relieved that another grave would not be necessary. The rotting legs deposited three days ago in a tiny hole would quickly decompose alone without the rest of Kate's remains, unless the dogs discovered them as their location was so very close to the surface—then they would be dug up and shared, their final destination: atop a bone pile whose discarded members, although not originally human, would be just as white and just as bare. The Potawatomi women thought they would never see Charles again, and that possibility was a great comfort. They, of course, could not have been more horribly wrong.

A tiny parcel wrapped tightly in a blanket slept silently behind some boxes in a dark recess of the tent. The existence of his grandson was never revealed to Charles as Shashona kept Mingaswen well out of view. Safety was her prime motivation, although even the slightest chance of thwarting Charles' power by harbouring this secret gave the women some claim of restitution for his past crimes. It was a courageous move, but they were resolute in their decision.

A large contingent came out to the ceremony and Kate's body was buried in the churchyard of The First United Methodist Church in central Chicago. Charles returned to the bleak cavernous silence of his great house—a great concern weighing on his brain: the shipment from Boston was late.

Little Raven carried her little brother out to the grassy fields bordering the trails that lead to the open prairie about a thousand miles to the west. The cool western winds brushed the soft skin on Mingaswen's face and his cheeks glowed bright red.

Rising Sun stirred a pot of soap keeping one sharp eye on the pair standing alone against the autumn wind. She wondered about the locket and the ring—about the usefulness of this boy who had come to stay, and share her food.

12

Frank Ogden reached down to brush the dirt from his boot tips. Custom silver triangular trim accentuated the toes, reflecting light into the eyes of all who stood before him, a sharp contrast to the deep black of the leather uppers. But no one stood before him this morning, only the silent weedy mounds under which lay the rotting corpses of Chicago's nameless dead. This was the town cemetery, only a short ride and ferry trip across the Chicago River at Deerborn Street, north from the Methodist Church where Kate's recent funeral had taken place and the location of her grave site among Chicago's elite. Holding the reigns tight in his left hand as the head of his prized black stallion jerked and pulled, his eyes scanned the haunted patch of lumps and scraggy bushes of the desolate place so loosely termed a cemetery. He knew Robert Tumblety's grave was here because he had overpaid a digger twenty-five cents to cart his dead body out and bury it here the day after the great storm.

There were few markers: a pathetic limp stick here and there, a broken cross, mostly just a rock or a few stones to identify a grave site—this small piece of lonely dirt, this sad pile of wind-blown rocky soil was pathetic internment property belonging to the forsaken— those with no connections, no names, no past. Squinting into the sun, Frank Ogden squeezed his mouth tight shaking his head in exasperation. He had specifically instructed the placement of a marker with the letters 'RT' inscribed upon it, yet he saw no indication complying to his request. Ogden cared not a single once for Tumblety, yet the boy's death had triggered some concerns. He was not naturally suspicious, but there were too many factors for him to ignore: the boy's deep affection for the girl, her pregnancy, Smithson's wrath and well-known despicable disposition, Margaret's mysterious disappearance on the same night, and now Kate's death. He held the reigns tight leading his horse forward through the dirt piles, searching. *There must be a fresh one, its only been two weeks.* The weeds grow with such voracity, that even the most recent digs become concealed within a matter of hours. The ground would have been saturated after the storm—muddy and easy to dig—*perhaps twenty-five cents bought Tumblety a shallow grave and the dogs or coyotes finished him off.*

Dressed in his Sunday best, the inept survey comprised of just a stone or two being kicked, a small bush being stepped on; he was not prepared to soil his boots or tarnish his silver searching for a half-eaten body in this desolate corner of Chicago. He would however seek out Smithson, perhaps tomorrow...or soon, anyway. *Kate's poor body after all, had only laid in the ground a few hours and Charles was no doubt still distraught.*

13

*A*nother week passed—Smithson had ignored Frank Ogden's invitation to visit him at the saloon or town office yet again—however, the time had come; facing Charles Smithson was never a pleasant experience, but they were, after all, partners in some regard; Chicago's future depended upon a continued balance between these two men. Together they had introduced the infrastructure necessary for the development of a town that would satisfy the needs of the expanding west: property management, building resources, daily necessities—food, clothing, shelter, employment—law and security. True, their perspectives dealing with styles of procurement and scruples in general differed greatly, but Frank Ogden had to admit, he was growing rich due to the ambitious efforts of Charles Smithson and his business concerns—perhaps he resisted this admittance on most occasions and that is why, most likely, he regretted having to confront Smithson today, face-to-face on the matter of Tumblety and his daughter.

Smithson stood at the edge of the landing closely watching his men—they were jumping from log to log controlling the rolling timbers floating on the lake, with great iron hooks—governing the boom and their unpredictable displacements and fickle behaviour. The hooks pulled the logs forward and chains wrapped around the trunks in a furious display of strength and skill; horses on shore hauled them in—then, with an incredible combination of dynamic manipulation and perseverance, they were lifted to the wagons—using knowledge and equipment borrowed from ship rigging and artillery: ropes, blocks and tackle, leverage and brute strength. Horses did all the heavy hauling and Smithson watched the handlers closely—without skilled horse handlers, the logs would never find their way to his sawmill.

The task was daunting: thousands of pounds of unyielding timber, sharp grappling hooks, unwieldy chains, miles of rope, freezing water, and trampling hooves—delicately balanced with human strength and ingenuity—a recipe for great success or swift disaster. The men who lost their hands and feet from twisting chains, squeezing timber and crushing wagon wheels, spent their remaining days at Ogden's saloon drinking sour mash whisky, living on meagre handouts at the discretion of Ogden and a few generous lumbermen who kindly offered a penny or two for bread and bacon—their days as a longshoreman or lumberjack: over. There was a solemn place for the other less lucky men, in a weedy plot of land north of town across the river; Ogden's visit there last week, still weighed heavy on his mind.

Frank Ogden approached the dock—the great, wide expanse of Smithson's back blocking the view to the lake—his rapid, deliberate advancement hastening his arrival to the objective. "Looks like a good haul Charles," Ogden yelled out from behind.

Smithson, recognizing the voice immediately, turned swiftly and shot an incredulous stare directly into Ogden's face. There had been talk—he reckoned this confrontation was inevitable. *Why couldn't he just leave it?* Ogden's handgun was holstered and hung conveniently in view on his hip. To pull it would mean someone had said too much— whiskey had loosened a tongue in the saloon—Ogden was here to serve justice.

Smithson raised his hands to his hips—he would have none of it—he was intimidated by no one. He wore no gun—he didn't need to. "It's a good haul, but I need more horses, these are overworked and beating them only kills them." That was a keen deflection, but Frank had started it with his note about the lumber haul—so he answered cordially in kind, no need to antagonize.

They both turned and checked the teams pulling the logs from the shore—great black Percherons—straining and stretching with their massive loads up the steep embankment to the waiting wagons. Smithson needed twenty teams to complete the work—the ice, in a matter of six months, would dam the Lake and impede any further delivery of lumber, then all loads would be carried by team and wagon through the deep and unforgiving snow on windy treacherous trails, through frozen temperatures, a system that would double the time to delivery. He had only three teams—their life expectancy reduced to three or four years as a result of this hard labour. The timber species included pine and spruce for building and furniture, hemlock—from whose bark was extracted tannin for leather tanning, a new industry developing directly in relation to the stockyards, and fir for solid house construction.

Smithson was about to lament his misgivings about the lack of good draft horses in Chicago and Percherons from France, although the best, were so rare...when Ogden interjected.

"Too bad about young Tumblety," Ogden slipped it out; it balanced like a great iron anvil over Smithson's head, laying there on a precipitous ledge ready to drop.

"Not my concern", Smithson snapped back, his eyes widening, his focus however, never shifting from his horses. *So he IS here to pursue this thing.*

"I know you and the boy were at odds, so you'll not be missing him that's for sure." Ogden was pressing, but Smithson would not take the bait.

"If these guys want to beat each other up, it's not my concern. Close your saloon and keep the whiskey out of the hands of my men and you'll see less trouble." Smithson threw the issue right back into Ogden's face—his response: direct, aggressive. Standing just in front of Frank Ogden and a bit to the right, Charles could not see Ogden's hand or gun—if perhaps he was about to make a move—he wasn't. He waited for a response...silence. Then, the chains from the wagons snapped and clanged, the men yelled, "Hey ya!! Git up there!" The great horses dug in and pulled.

There was a hesitating moment when Ogden reconsidered his position, then he let it pass. "Yes, whiskey...its true. Still, a thorn removed from your side Charles." Smithson did not reply—he studied the timber and watched the boom, swelling and crashing against the dock. Redirecting, he continued, "So your daughter headed east Charles?"

"Yes, Boston, I suspect. Took the stage east, next day after the storm. I haven't heard from her." Charles Smithson had no idea about the whereabouts of his daughter, but heading east's a good an explanation as any other and he'd used it continually for more than three weeks now.

Frank Ogden kicked the dirt at his feet, he beckoned the nerve to remain tight in his gut, he promised himself he wouldn't touch his gun, but his next comments could provoke a reaction that might trigger a sudden move from Smithson and he would have to be wary. "There's no record of Margaret boarding a stage east Charles—she did not leave on any stage in any direction from here. I have all the passenger lists." Charles was too tough to show Ogden that this information affected him anyway. He said nothing, he remained steadfast and continued to maintain focus on the business at hand. Ogden continued, "How do you think she left Charles?"

Smithson's answer was evasive, he parried nonchalantly, "Maybe she boarded a wagon to avoid me tracing her. I don't know. I've got wagons heading east every day with lumber for Detroit. She wanted to get away from me, from Chicago, from her mother as soon as possible. She's gone that's all I know." His tone now irritable, Charles was just about done with Ogden and Frank could feel it. He began to jostle his feet and shift his head nervously, back and forth from the dock to the wagons; he wanted to remove himself from this meeting as soon as possible. There was a chance Ogden would receive little or no more information.

Frank Ogden was the sheriff and his job did include following up questionable activities taking place in his town: missing barrels of whiskey, cheating gamblers, drunken dockworkers misbehaving around saloon girls, and certainly dead bodies washing up on the docks. But continuing to press Charles Smithson about Robert Tumblety, a man no one admitted really knowing or caring about, was dangerous territory, Ogden decided to leave it for another time. "I'm sorry about Kate, Charles; curious ailment."

"Kate was sick—unfortunate—but it's over." Smithson stepped forward and began shouting directives at the teamsters as a huge log became stuck behind a wagon. Ogden turned and walked away. He would have to consider a different approach if he was to proceed further.

Charles Smithson would have to enforce his harsh demands on his men to ensure mouths would remain shut, and perhaps a visit to those old Indians at the swamp south of the stockyards might be in order again. *I should have killed all three when I had the chance.*

PART 2

Chicago
1834-1847

14

Rising Sun raised her arm straight up above her head focussing on the neck held tightly between the fingers of her left hand. The hatchet was dirty, covered with the rusty brown stains of dried blood collected over many years; it reflected no light from the sun—a pale yellow split opened in the sky between the dark water below and the thick grey clouds above on the eastern horizon behind her. The corner of the iron head blocked the early rays—its bold shape pausing for just a slight moment at the top of the swing. The imposing profile cast a long black, pointed shadow, spiking across the dirt before her over the boards and out to the prairie grasses—just for an instant. The edge of the small axe however, was clean and razor sharp—she couldn't tolerate a dull tool. The morning was new, and fresh. She had no trouble catching a victim today; the pen was dry and dusty. Her lips were pressed tightly together, causing the creases above her mouth to sink deeper into her face resembling the dark skin of a dried prune. Her eyebrows squeezed close together in concentration forcing so many wrinkles to converge there that her face seemed to disappear and then was cruelly replaced by a tightly twisted rag of brown weathered leather. The long grey strands of hair drifting down from the sides of her head, hung dangerously close to the angle of her strike.

She held her breath. With one clean, fast descent, the blade sliced through the air and sunk deep into the tree stump with a dull thwack! The chicken's head went flying, the blood spurted out in every direction. The animal jumped off the stump, out of her grasp— she let it go. It spun with spasmodic jerks throwing blood everywhere as it tried in vain to prolong its already extinguished life.

This was the part Ming liked the best. He chased and jumped at the chicken trying desperately to catch it. This was his job; his part to play in the morning's chore—and he loved it. Finally grabbing the chicken, he held onto the legs as it hung upside down out in front of him. He watched the dead chicken with curious fascination as the final jerks shot blood out in regular rapid pulses from its severed neck and tugged violently on his two tiny outstretched arms. He was enthralled by blood and the thin line between life and death even at his tender age of only four years.

"Bring me the bird, Boy," commanded Rising Sun; Ming quickly brought the chicken over. Mingaswen watched carefully as she grabbed it and turned it over. Using a thin-bladed knife she slashed it from gullet to ass; the guts fell forward to the ground. Shashona stood ready to receive the bird; Rising Sun cut out the heart and gizzard; the only organs that concerned her. She held the bird aloft, Shashona snatched it and threw it in a pot of hot water that was hanging over a fire by the tent. The chicken would simmer for a while before it was retrieved; then the feathers would be plucked and the legs cut off. It was an easier task to remove the feathers from a semi-cooked chicken.

The stockyard dogs stood a distance away, on the other side of the fence boards, they knew better than to try to steal the chicken guts while Rising Sun was still present. She would beat them to death if she could. More than one courageous, foolish dog had found its way to her dining table after a short scrap with Rising Sun and her assorted collection of deadly sticks and hatchets. Actually dog was considered a treat, almost a delicacy by the Indian woman of the swamps, but they never went looking for a dog meal intentionally.

Shashona picked up the gooey entrails from the ground and placed them in the folds of her dress just above her knees and headed to the fence; Ming following close behind. She gathered the useless organs up in her two hands—with one great heave she tossed them over—they fell a good distance away, so the vicious dogs converging on the slimy feast would not jeopardize the safety of the boy or her, as they stood so close to the action. The dogs growled and fought for only a moment—dust flew, fangs glistened, then in a flash, every bit was devoured—not a fraction left, not a feather, not a drop of blood. Ming stood on the bottom fence board watching with unwavering intensity; his little face peering through the fence at the wild scene, smiling with excitement. The mangy beasts sniffed the ground, then raised their bloody noses to the air above hoping to catch the scent of another sailing, savoury gift from Shashona. Then, quickly realizing the futility of their hesitation, and with heads bowed, tails tucked low, they turned and skulked away as quickly as they had arrived, seemingly from nowhere, back to nowhere, licking their lips as they trod. Shashona waved her hand at them, "Go on!" she scolded, "filthy dogs, numosh!"

Shashona wiped her hands on a clean portion of her dress then took Ming's hands in hers, checking for blood and then wiped them on his trousers.

Mingaswen arrived at the stewing pot looking for Little Raven; she had become his closest ally among the Indian women—and truly his sister—most of his days would be spent in her good care. It was Little Raven that began calling him Ming; the others referred to him only as "Boy, or Gigabe." But she was not there and a basket, instead, was dropped in his hands with direction from Nootkana. "She is there waiting for you." She pointed to the patch of bushes far in the distance.

Little Raven had finished her morning ablutions in the bushes and was preparing for a search today for special plants according to Rising Sun's insufferable orders. Mingaswen looked up and scoured the horizon to the west. He smiled when he saw Little Raven's hand waving to him. He left the encampment in a furry, no salutations— not a word; he rushed to meet his sister outside the boundaries of the corrals.

The route from the small encampment out to the range was no longer so easy and swift a manoeuvre as it once was. The stockyard corrals were growing. Mingaswen would have to weave a crooked path through boards and sheds, bone piles and manure to reach the opening to the range beyond the city limits.

The location of the little encampment had been moved now four times: once each spring since little Mingaswen's birth. As Fort Deerborn now became officially Chicago, the swampy land around Lake Michigan was being developed with housing construction and industry and the stockyards were being pushed farther and farther to the south-west away from the centre of town. The boards of the corrals weaved a curious path around the tents and enclosed them between pens and sheds, making mobility tedious and tiresome for the little band. The land generously left to the Indians was shrinking; their presence quickly becoming intolerable to many citizens; the need for their potions, soap and medical services less and less necessary.

Nootkana raised her hand over her eyes to cut the sun's glare and watched with envy as they wondered out farther to the west, through the prairie grasses, to a place far from the camp, far from intruding eyes.

"Get the chicken" was Rising Sun's order, and with that curt directive, Nootkana quickly dropped her hand and spun around. Her business today included toiling over the camp's needs, not dreaming of wandering among the berry bushes and weeds with careless abandon and selfish desires. Stomping past Rising Sun, they exchanged repugnant glares.

The Potawatomi Indians were mild-mannered people that lived in close bond with the earth. The natural balance of all things alive and dead was not greeted with awe or fear—it simply, was. Day to day survival dealt with eating, shitting, fornicating, giving birth and dying. Any problems or concerns in any of these areas were always solved with remedies from the earth. It was the earth that brought the malady—it would be the earth that took it away. Nootkana and Little Raven understood the value and the secret of every root, every herb and every technique used in every cure for every human ailment, from a fever to a breech birth. Rising Sun and Shashona had taught them everything, and now little Ming would receive the necessary lessons from Little Raven.

Together they bent down and studied the plants at their feet. Ming was eager and picked every little plant, presenting it to his sister, waiting to receive the congratulations she showered on him for his tiny accomplishments. He was learning fast, receiving life lessons and skills that he would retain securing his position as a valuable member of the family; lessons and skills that would follow him throughout his life and journeys well past his time in Chicago.

The potions and concoctions were stored in the tents, at first in clay pots and leather pouches, then eventually in glass bottles and jars as more contact with the Whiteman ushered in the use of more modern storage containers. But the ingredients never wavered from their earthly origins. Skunk cabbage for phlegm and asthma; pulverized dried root of mullein for respiratory ailments; tea of arnica for back pain; gentian and horsemint for inflation and fever; creosote bush, pleurisy root and wormroot for lung infection. The women were also experts in birth and abortion, copulation and fertility. Boiled leaves of partridgeberry were used to bring on delivery if the baby was late, and American licorice and broom snakewood was taken to help loosen a stubborn placenta from the uterine wall after a difficult delivery. Ragleaf bahia for contraception, horny goat weed for fertility and American mistletoe for abortion. All herbs and berries from the surrounding forest and prairie found a place on the medicine shelves of the Potawatomi women, including poison, if there was a need.

The Indian women were also adept surgeons. If herbs were too slow or not in season, a knife was used to cut open a cervix when a baby refused to leave the womb. Mingaswen's birth was not the first time Rising Sun was forced to use such methods. If inflammation and infection persisted in a wound, amputation was delivered swiftly and cleanly to save a life; there was no discussion about necessity or consequences—the limb was removed. Kate's surgery was necessary. Rising Sun received no discussion from the women as her methods were time-proven and her skills were never in doubt: sharp, clean blades, swift action, a necessary amount of skin retained around the wound to cover the stump—anaesthetics administered if available—

stitches of horsehair closed the wound and proper herbs were used to prevent further infection.

The pathways of the human circulatory and respiratory system were no mystery to these intelligent, gifted people. These potions and medicines had been applied by Native American Indians for centuries and their place in Indian culture was solid and well understood. These people took all the necessary precautions to stay clean and they understood infection and the inevitable results, even if they had never studied bacteria under a microscope, and therefore suffered in no way from Whitman's diseases of influenza, smallpox or typhus which originated in the dirty clothes and on the crushed, sweating, filthy bodies of hundreds and even thousands of immigrants as they crowded aboard ships on their way to seek a new life in the Americas. They brought new diseases to North America, but no cures. Because doctors were in short supply in Chicago at this time, herbal remedies from the Potawatomi women were sought out by settlers and businessmen alike. The Indians became a necessary source for livestock butchering methods and hide tanning, to the treatment of typhus infection and the practical secrets of midwifery. Unfortunately, over time many thousands of Native American Indians would also fall victim to Whiteman's diseases.

Bottled herbs and medicines were sold for money, and goods were purchased by the Indians when needed: knives, oil lamps, fabrics and clothes, and eventually food. The Indian medicine women developed a make-shift trading post at the stockyards where businessmen and cowboys could spend some money and receive the secrets of health. Whitewomen would never venture to such a place; their husbands would pick up any order they required. For them it was considered a frightening place of witches and wild dogs, of horrendous odours and god-awful sights. They never knew if they might see an Indian crapping in the field or butchering a dog for supper. If a cowboy spied a young, pretty native girl at the tents and thought maybe a remedy was required to satisfy a particular sexual need, for only 10 cents, a quick copulation was allowed. The older medicine women would copulate for less. This type of fornication was not considered sinful or immoral to the Indians. They understood sexual needs, and even though they found the Whiteman to be ugly and stupid, they would comply. They, in fact, found the idea of paying for a sexual remedy, very humorous, as they were experts at masturbation, which was a free remedy available to all, anytime.

They sold medicines, potions and soap to the homesteaders and townsfolk, and kept a small herd of sheep for wool and lanolin, a milking cow, chickens, and a few pigs. They performed abortions for the prostitutes and delivered babies when no doctor would come. They were the last bastion of medical hope for the Whiteman in a cruel, primitive environment.

Shashona was now fifty-four years of age and the hard prairie lifestyle was beginning to take its toll. Her hair was turning grey and heavy creases were forming around her eyes and mouth. The dark brown of her eyes however, could not hide the sparkle of the life she projected with each smile—each laugh. She was the warm heart of the little quartet, as she always found humour in the day-to-day chores and toiling lifestyle of collecting, stirring, cooking, mixing and otherwise preparing meals and potions. Her figure, once curvaceous and firm, and the envy of every woman in the camp, would happily receive the focus of every lewd stare from young brave to elder. Now her waist extended out in generous mid-rolls, her buttocks ballooned and her great breasts swung low. A matronly figure to be sure, but Shashona was far from unfit, as she could outlast any of the others from sunup to sundown collecting wood or herbs, milking the cow or chasing down a dog for supper during the cold, desperate days of winter. She enjoyed the search for berries and weeds; whatever the list of difficult ingredients Rising Sun would give her. By the end of the day her basket was overflowing and she was proud to do her part for the family. It was Shashona that would become Ming's nurse, as Rising Sun could always encourage her milk to come, even years after the birth of her most recent child, Little Raven. Rising Sun would use a special drink of root of antegin that provoked a hormone to begin lactation even for the driest of breasts. Shashona's gift was humour and the deft skills of midwifery. Having had eight children of her own; she was well-versed in the necessary ordeals associated with child-bearing.

Nootkana was the second youngest and, at twenty-four, would now become every cowboy's favourite. Rising Sun had taken her in when her family died years ago. Starvation had wiped out an entire band north of Michigan during a very severe winter during their southern trek. Only two survivors arrived in the swamps: Rising Sun and Nootkana, then a bony infant in her arms.

Her hair was thick; a beautiful full, rich ebony mane—shiny and flowing. Her cheeks were high and firm as if carved from stone. The texture of her skin was as smooth as the spring pedals on the prairie roses, bearing not a mark, not a wrinkle, nor a crack; her colour: sweet, creamy coffee. The world of dirt, mud, cow shit and decaying animal carcasses, seemed to change, unbelievably, into a land of delight and wonder when Nootkana opened her perfect lips into a smile. Her teeth were white and even; her eyes bright and sparkling. Her waist was small; her legs were long and evenly tapered; her breasts were high, round and full. No man could resist Nootkana and every cowboy on Friday night after payday, was eager to spend a small portion of their wages on her fine features. Rising Sun always stood by with a heavy club as Nootkana bent over the table, her skirts raised, her delicate, female folds exposed. Any cowboy attempting to hurt her in any way would receive a swift crack on the back of the head. The copulation would be smooth, quick and painless. Shashona's misfortune at the hands of that brutish Whiteman, so many years ago, would never happen again; Rising Sun would see to it. Nootkana would not suffer the same violent terror—copulation for money: yes—rape: no. Unfortunately, this philosophy would not apply to Mingaswen—her desperate needs altered her reason, and she wanted that jewelry— besides Ming was a Whiteman, not Potawatomi.

Nootkana mixed the ingredients for soap: lye from wood ashes, glycerine from cow fat, beef kidney fat, vegetable oil, salt for hardening, sugar for lather and sweet wild lavender and hyacinth for aroma. The sticky solution was closely supervised by Rising Sun, any deviation from her tried and true recipe would bring about a severe tongue lashing and fierce reprimand at the end of a wagging, bent, bony finger. Her compliance with Rising Sun's directives was never heartfelt as she was a simple girl who preferred to walk in the prairie sunshine or wade peacefully in the cool waters of a chortling brook. She was immature and hated the dreadful chores demanded by Rising Sun. Nootkana could never retain any semblance of composure when ordered to spend the day bent over a hot, boiling pot of lye as the stinking, rising steam devoured her face and hair, quickly turning her clear, youthful countenance into a red prune, dripping with oily perspiration. The thick, grey smoke and ashes reaching up from the burning coals, beneath the black pot, would stick in dirty ashen layers on her clothes and hair. Casting quick, evil glances over her shoulder at her impatient keeper, Nootkana surmised correctly, that jealousy was at the root of Rising Sun's cruel intentions. Rising Sun's protection had limits—rape was one thing, vanity quite another. However, Nootkana was not ready for her own, precious beauty to wither away so quickly, as it obviously had for Rising Sun over countless years of stirring and grinding the putrid mixture. Continual whining and complaining, would usually invite a welcomed rescue from Shashona; and off she would run with Little Raven to some special hideaway they had found together, far from the foul odours and miasma of the encampment. Rising Sun's sharp, resentful eyes didn't miss the flash of an arrogant smile escaping from the corner of Nootkana's lips, obviously meant for her, as she took Little Raven in one hand and little Ming in the other, then playfully dashed out of sight through the berry bushes. This was a scene that would play over and over again, to the delight of Shashona's light-hearted encouragement and to the detriment of all Rising Sun's wasted, wilful endeavours.

Nootkana's ultimate capitulation to the sexual needs of the insatiable cowboys was also never well received by her or any other member of the little family, save Rising Sun. The little cash they received in exchange, however, was desperately required to sustain them through the harsh, hungry winters and Rising Sun's and Shashona's days with the cowboys were rapidly closing.

Rising Sun, as the eldest, held her position with unwavering strength and righteousness. Her true age was unknown and un-important. She was the matriarch. She gave the orders every day and insisted they be carried out with rigorous detail and proficien-cy. Herbs and berries would be gathered, fires kept hot, chickens fed or butchered and soap and potions created in their prospective cauldrons. When stirring her concoctions, her dark profile truly portrayed the common theme of a witch at her craft: long stringy hair unkempt and blowing into her scraggy face. Her nose, broken and bent, hooked forward from her face predominant and intrusive; never a hint of a smile, never a glint of humour or sincerity. Rising Sun was the mother and sole leader of this band: she was "Ne'ni."

Little Raven became the close guardian of little Ming and protector of his secret. Four years had passed and now at 21 years of age, her position in the band was changing. Rising Sun looked to her young figure and pretty face with evil manipulation and device. She may have to sacrifice her virginity to the cause, but with age and maturity, Little Raven had also developed strength and tenacity. She would fight her own battles now, with her mother as her constant partner and she was well prepared to confront Rising Sun on her own terms. The hiding place of the locket and ring were never revealed to the others, yet she knew their existence was residing deep within the recesses of Rising Sun's scrutinizing mind. When her greed to have them became desperate, she would be unstoppable and this attitude was well understood by Little Raven. Nootkana remained resentful as the bond intensified between the two as she quickly became weary of eager cowboys and cold meagre winters—the ring and locket would bring ease to her detested predicament.

Rising Sun squeezed her eyes closed to an eerie slit; cleverly contemplating Ming's tiny backside and considered a plan as he raced through the grass, to meet with Little Raven. The boy would earn his keep she thought.

Little Raven was crouching low in the grasses—Ming hurriedly approached—she reached out with one hand to beckon his arrival but encouraged a more stealthful gate, as she raised a finger to her lips, "Shh!" Ming stopped and bent down, closely sharing the space beside her.

"Listen." Ming looked into her eyes for direction and listened intently. Nothing. Then…a rustle, a faint squeal—then the grasses shook only a few steps away. Together they crawled towards the sound silently inching their way, Ming in the lead, his eyes and ears alert. Together they found the snare and the little squirrel struggling for its life, its leg hopelessly tangled in the wire. Ming smiled triumphantly and without further direction grabbed a fist-sized rock, raised it high above his head and smashed it down hard, the little animal's head exploded; blood and brains whipping furiously out in all directions soaking the grass around it. Ming released its leg and held the prize aloft, his face beaming with a wide excited grin. Little Raven responded, "Let's find another."

15

A brisk autumn wind circled and rushed eastward across the prairie painting its white, crispy lattice work on the tops of thistles. Tall yellow grass tips bent down heavy with the weight of the early frost, and the ground so often mushy and viscous, dried and compressed into a firm crust throughout the night, betraying the soft underbelly and giving a pedestrian false confidence that would vanish by midday. The pots and jars of pickled roots and vegetables were carefully sealed and placed on the sideboard. Baskets on the floor were fully laden with every herb and weed gathered; berries were dried and stored in sacks. Dried meat from prairie chicken, squirrel and gopher hung by stiff leather strings at the highest points of the ceiling poles: a lumpy veil of dead flesh dripping as a shredded curtain trimming the ridge point in a continuous horizontal winter menu of tasty meat.

The air was thick with heavy, noxious odours wafting in from the stockyards. Each board of the corral was continually screeching, painfully stretching and pressing across the posts, each receiving the full weight of the crunching animals endlessly jostling for position within the crowded stalls; each one overloaded, filled to capacity— each animal growing fatter slowly and, reluctantly, inevitably, navigating a tightly compressed, manure-encrusted route to their bloody destiny. The cattle groaned and howled throughout the day and all through the night without reprieve. There would be not a moment of silence now until after the butchering was finished. It would commence when the sheds were frozen solid and end when spring melted the frigid soil to slimy mud again. Roundup was over and, with the thousands of head of cattle, the cowboys arrived eager to spend their wages.

The rancorous inner linings of Rising Sun's heart could not be so easily described by one word, but evil was undoubtedly the prime motivator of her intentions. As well, black offered no range in tone, and the colour, although grievous and dark, claiming the deepest section of her cruel heart, it could not expose the depth she was willing to crawl to secure her power and control over Little Raven and that boy.

She looked to the corrals, to the desperate moans of the defeated cattle, to the riotous hoops and hollers of the men, so gloriously elated over the termination of their laborious travails. She wanted that ring and necklace, and she would have it. A cowboy would come and she would get her money and retain her control. She watched and waited, and waited, and watched.

Fred Barnett was young and his first cattle drive had finally, gratefully, ended. He was tall and lanky. His teeth were too big for his mouth; his hair was red, oily and ragged, protruding wildly out in every direction from under his ragged hat; his working attire: rough and beaten, still thickly laden with the trail's dust and sweat; his odour—rank. Coins from his wages were pouring out on the bar at Ogden's saloon and were quickly grabbed up by the barkeep as fast as each shot of whiskey was poured. Far from home, surrounded by veteran cowboys he fell easy prey to jokes and chastisement. The girls upstairs were busy and he was cordially instructed by his devious trail mates about an Indian encampment just south of town where he should christen his first successful drive—opportunity there they say, was wondrous and sublime. Assurances concluded with hard slaps on the back, and Fred was directed out to the street and helpfully pointed in the correct direction.

It wasn't hesitation that timed his slow gait, it was alcohol. But sexual determination trumped inebriation and disorientation—after several crooked deviations and fumbled footfalls, Fred wandered into Rising Sun's tent.

His intent was obvious and the absence of Nootkana and the others offered Rising Sun the evil opportunity she had harboured for so long. "Boy!" she called Ming in from the fire, and innocently he obeyed.

Instantly upon his entrance, Ming was violently grabbed by Rising Sun and held against the sideboard, jars spilling to the floor without concern, as Fred looked on, somewhat confused. She whipped Ming's trousers down with a quick flick of her hand while holding him steady with the other. Ming struggled. Scared and confused, he was in no way aware of the peril of his situation.

"I don't want the boy!" exclaimed Fred.

"You'll take the boy, there's no one else," was Rising Sun's stern remark. With some hesitation Fred stood bewildered in his drunken fog, but began to fumble with his belt buckle, a curious but familiar tingle and tightness emerging from within. Was this the wondrous experience he was told about? Rising Sun held the boy forward hard into the sideboard with one hand, spreading his legs apart with her knees, then flipped around to aid Fred with his buttons with the other. Ming struggled and screamed. "Hush boy!" With impassioned difficulty she twisted all six front buttons—his trousers finally exploded open. Pants, belt and underwear cascaded together in unceremonious fashion, collecting in a crumpled pile about his ankles, settling on his shit-encrusted boots. His huge penis thankfully released and now fully exposed, stood out strong and direct taking aim at the tiny pink anus innocently presented before him.

It's quite possible that Rising Sun had not used her lower facial muscles in over forty years as traditionally her expression never changed no matter the circumstances—delighted, discouraged, determined or depressed—all the lines and wrinkles remained steadfast, lips pursed and tight, eyes dull and unfocused. Perhaps the lack of use over so many tough years of pain and hardship had rendered her muscles useless and engaging them in any animated emotion was impossible. However, when her head dropped down to appreciate the huge male organ rising up between the tiny white cheeks of the little victim pressed firmly prostrate across the narrow board, her eyebrows uncharacteristically rose in two perfectly curved arcs reaching skyward forcing her brow into a series of long even rolls from her eyebrows to her grey hairline. A single dry throaty expulsion of air escaped from deep within her lungs in one understated tone, "Kcak! Too big! You will kill the boy!" A surprisingly sympathetic response from the old woman, and she quickly spun around to her shelves behind. "Let him go!" was her fast directive to the cowboy. But he bent at the knees and assumed the position, one hand pushing into the boy's back, the other directing the object of his wicked intentions. Rising Sun scolded, "Wait!" as she retrieved a small bottle of lanolin from her stores. She grabbed his hand away and released the boy, "Go!" she yelled to Ming, then began to quickly stroke the large member with the cream and he began to groan. Ming did not hesitate. He grabbed up his trousers and ran out faster than a terrified prairie squirrel being chased by a ravenous stockyard dog.

Only a few moments later, Rising Sun stood at the entrance to the tent; wiping her hands thoroughly on the hanging traces of her dress, watching Fred pick up the tempo of his stride as he headed back towards town fumbling with his belt buckle, desperately dipping around mud and manure. She raised her hands to her eyes and inspected them; convinced they were clean she curled her fingers into fists and firmly placed them on her hips swinging around to face the prairie grasses to the south in the direction of the hidden spot where the boy now sat with Little Raven—the grasses waving about their heads. Her eyes squinted in the setting sun and she tightened her lips. She was disappointed but never deterred. There would be another chance, and the boy would pay.

In time Little Raven returned with Ming whimpering at her side to face Rising Sun's sober miserable face, the entire dire episode securely retrieved; the details clear, the motives indisputable: Rising Sun would trade the boy's protection for the ring and the necklace. The right index finger of her hand pressing tightly into the centre of the palm of her left hand held up into Little Raven's watering eyes, clearly indicated where she wanted Little Raven to place the treasure. There was no need for words. Little Raven shook her head and grabbed Ming's arm, turned and retreated; that evil woman's indomitable wrath was left simmering silently within the dark shadows of her cold tent and even colder heart.

16

The next four years for Mingaswen, life desperately evolved at the edge of marginal existence: a delicate necessary balance of survival within the precarious, but predictable grinding spokes of two colliding eternal cycles: nature and man.

Daily tasks of foraging, hunting for berries; trapping small rodents, mixing potions from wild plants and natural elixirs; drying strips of meagre sinews from wild chickens and coyote carcasses; carefully planting beds of herbs and vegetables in the spring only to dig them up again in the fall; huddling together against winter's harshest elements and trenching spring's floods from their makeshift tents—harnessed strong traits of tenacity and survival, an appreciation for the land, an understanding of the bond to the earth shared by the members of his family—but Mingaswen was not an Indian. Ming suffered the steady decline of commitment and appreciation of the Potawatomi way of life—life in winter was stressful and at times unbearable. The cow was butchered and eaten, as well the sheep, the chickens, the pigs; stocks of bottled vegetables and dried meat dwindled; coal oil disappeared; wood piles faded away and the tent coverings ripped and blew away in the wind. Each winter was harsher than the previous, each spring was welcomed with more appreciation and jubilation, and with each season the desperation for survival worsened.

The people from Chicago rarely visited the encampment anymore as modern products were now more attainable: soap, medicines and medical treatments—although abortions performed by Rising Sun were scarce, her tent was the sole location for such a procedure, as well as herbal medications for many common ailments. A full-time doctor now resided in Chicago: Dr. George Jerolaman, twenty-seven, young and fresh, from Indiana; he could not condone medical relief afforded by the Potawatomi; yet he often turned a blind eye to those procuring Indian elixirs to solve ailments he could not claim victory over. He was not, however sympathetic to patients who became violently ill after consuming toxic herbal concoctions purchased from '*those damn Indians*'—he was quite adamant about it. Some said his father was killed by Indians, and he continued to harbour a deep resentment. He was soon to learn about the true plight of the Potawatomi, and develop a keen empathy, however—his medical skills and endurances would be tested beyond his capabilities—all would be challenged to supreme limits—many would not survive.

Cowboys still arrived every fall with herds of thousands of cattle, the numbers rising every season—Ming's home in conjunction was necessarily uprooted—the detestable disruption was tantamount to persecution—tolerance from Chicago: totally absent—extinction was looming perilously close; stress level in the little family was breaching. Little Raven was not always able to block Rising Sun's vicious agenda, and Ming unfortunately fell victim to sodomy for cash more than once. He became, understandably, more withdrawn and nervous, hateful and vengeful—not understanding the action or the insensitivity so harshly imposed upon him. His trust dissolved. Continually approached about the desperately needed income from the necklace and ring, Little Raven fell dangerously close to surrendering for Ming's sake, but somehow managed to keep the tiny legacy safe—guilt ripping at her conscience daily—Nootkana reluctantly filling the gap. By this time Little Raven was expected to offer her services as she was no longer 'too young' and the need was great—Shashona, however, her mother and protector, wouldn't allow the cowboys near her—forever retaining an unwavering hatred from her youth—she had been sexually abused by Whitemen so many times. Animosity continued to climb to overwhelming levels, splitting the band in half: Rising Sun and Nootkana on one side—Shashona, Little Raven and Ming, on the other. Continuing along this volatile path for another winter would mean separation and disbandment— each side seeking survival in their own way.

The solution and ultimately salvation, needed to bring the two clashing cycles together—nature's unrelenting cruelty and man's encroachment on Indian land—arrived unexpectedly in the fall of 1838. Potawatomi not abiding by extraction regulations stipulated in the 1830 Indian Removal Act, were surrounded at Twin Lakes, Indiana—south-east of Chicago—by armed militiamen, and began a forced march on foot south-west to Kansas. Two men from the caravan would visit Chicago, and everything would change forever.

Richard Deacon (Deek) had nothing much. He could plough, and dig; he could cut down trees and wrangle a mule to rip out a stump. He could turn sod and plant crops—but there was nothing for him in Plymouth now. His parents were gone with fever, the crops were invaded with thistles and ragweed, knapweed, swallowwort and brome, the ox was lame, nothing seemed right anymore. Deek was very tall and stronger than most, but never as wise; he had a good horse and he could ride. He was restless—they wanted volunteers. He didn't think about it much, he never did. He would go south to Kansas with the Army. The Potawatomi meant nothing to him. He could join a drive travelling north next fall and return if he wanted; there was always room for another cowboy on the trail.

Lieutenant William Marks received his orders and there was no doubt about his duty: round up all Indians and arrest them, hold them at Meyers Lake, south of Plymouth Indiana, then move them all south 660 miles to Kansas at gunpoint, on foot and in wagons. Hire a militia of 200 men, buy horses, wagons and food. Clear the land of all Indians and make the land safe for the Whiteman.

But the Potawatomi were sick and tired and distressed as they sat in the dirt, many with their hands bound; many confused, angry and agitated. They had been ripped from their homes, from their harvests, without trial, without reason; Treaty rights destroyed. The cowboys hired as militiamen were tormentors; they were mean and vulgar, they worked for $6.00 a month and a Potawatomi life meant nothing to them. The trek would be plagued with illness, fights, belligerence and desertions. Lieutenant Marks had a difficult task ahead and he knew it.

Marks selected Deek to guide him to Chicago, 100 miles to the west, as he said he knew the trail well, and promised to cover the distance in 3 days. Marks could not begin the trek without a doctor, and Chicago was the only centre close enough to locate and hire such an important member of his portentous party. They left with instructions for the members of his ragtag militia: to mind the prisoners and expect their return with a doctor in about 1 week. "Try not to kill any Indians."

The trip was uneventful enough and after a dusty 3 day sojourn, Deek sat in Ogden's Saloon drinking whiskey as if perhaps the supply might be depleted within the hour, with two unemployed cowhands recently off the trail, and who's pockets were quickly losing their weight due to a similar endeavour. Deek scratched the whiskers on his face and wiped the dirt from his brow. He smelled bad. He talked to the men at the bar. They enjoyed Deek's humorous banter about Indians and doctors, and were keen to enquire about a chance to join a troop of militiamen travelling south to Kansas for $6.00 a month. When Lieutenant Marks arrived back at the Saloon with Frank Ogden and the reluctant Doctor Jeroloman, it was these two intrepid cowboys that quickly rose up, eager to accompany them back to Twin Lakes, if positions in his militia were still available. Deek was never seen again, and Marks didn't enquire; he had his Doctor and his orders. They would head out in the morning with or without Deek.

How Rising Sun knew of the round-up wasn't certain, but her ardent encouragement and fierce commands warned of trouble— Nootkana and Shashona followed her out, without question, to a hiding place west of the stockyards—a heavily treed area, a safe area—no militiamen would find them, they would not join the trail south. Little Raven and Ming were left in camp to retrieve water and food—then follow along shortly. They stayed too long.

Deek was drunk but managed to follow the crude instructions— they were simple enough: south of town, down past the stockyards, past the feedlots, and watch for the smoke rising up from a small stinking fire and you'll find some Indians to take back to Indiana. Ogden and Smithson were well aware of the Removal Declaration, but Smithson had made it clear to Ogden that His Potawatomi were not to be touched as his daughter and her Indian family were to be protected from the order. His first intention was to remove Little Raven away from the band—to keep her safe with him and let the others travel west, but a plan to accomplish this and include an explanation eluded him—he'd had no time—Marks had arrived so suddenly. Lieutenant Marks remained ignorant of their existence; the cowboys never mentioned the Indians or Deek again. Doctor George Jerolaman joined a hopeless, doomed caravan against his wishes; and Ming's life would now change forever as Deek slowly, precariously, carved a circuitous path around the corral boards following a thin grey line of wispy, odorous smoke as it cautiously rose above the broad leather backs of the struggling beasts in the immediate distance, indicating the exact location of his bloody destiny; and he headed straight for it…off balance, but straight.

The camp was vacant. There were no Indians, he had been duped and his upper lip curled with anger. He kicked the stones under the fire and pushed over the pot hanging there, its gooey contents splashing, searing and steaming. He staggered and swivelled; searching and finally, desperately, reaching out—he flipped up the hide and entered the closest tent. Little Raven, startled, muffled a cry of fear with her arm as she quickly raised it to her mouth. Deek was caught off guard by Little Raven's beauty, her long thick ebony hair, her wide bright green eyes and the curvaceous contours of her slim figure. Instantly without thinking, Deek savagely wrapped his arms around her body—slamming her face down into the sideboard across the small space. He was not considering arresting Indians for the trek south.

She let out a shriek as Deek twisted her arm back. He was powerful—driven by lust and drink. The glass jars crashed to the ground, the metal plates clanged and spun out across the sideboard, her arm reached forward attempting to gain a hold so she could attain leverage to push away, but Deek was heavy—his arm strength too powerful. Little Raven screamed—Ming turned abruptly, facing the direction of the wild shrieks—he raced from the supply tent adjacent.

The angle of the bodies and the spread of the legs where all too familiar—he was well aware of the situation about to unfold. "No Ming, no! Get out!" Little Raven screamed. Without hesitating, Ming grabbed the buffalo skinner from the sideboard and raised it high above his head ready to strike. Deek remained poised in position, his trousers down at his boots, one hand gripped her wrist and pressed down hard into her back, the other—greedily filled with the silky strands of thick black hair—pulling tight, like the reins on a horse—her head snapped back. He bent his knees forcing his hips into her buttocks, but was suddenly stopped before he could reach his goal—twelve inches of cold steel rammed up under his vest, tight and deep into his right kidney—he screamed in pain, his back arching, his head flinging back at the painful impact. Ming had recalculated correctly in an instant—he reversed his grip from overhand to underhand knowing he would never have the power to jab through the leather vest and shirt, through rib and muscle—he switched and ran the knife through with an underhand strike, slicing through soft tissue into Deek's vulnerable organs.

Deek stepped back to face his assailant releasing Little Raven— his arms reached forward to grab Ming, his legs locked by his trousers, his balance jeopardized by the trauma—he stood tall over Ming ready to bring him down. Ming remained steadfast in his stance, the long knife gripped solid in his fist—lunging forward, he carved into Deek's inner thigh cutting the femoral artery down to the bone. Deek began to topple forward—Ming withdrew the blade, then with a back-handed slice, cut into Deek's throat—a wide gash from left to right, deep through to the neck bone—a single, rapid swish of steel—Deek crashed to the dirt at Ming's feet.

Little Raven lifted from her position on the sideboard—turning to Ming, she gasped—there was so much blood on his face, his features were totally lost. The huge knife still in his hand, his fist totally soaked in Deek's blood, his feet well apart, Ming looked down with a fierce expression as if he might be ready to continue the fight if necessary. A massive pool of blood quickly soaked into the dirt—Ming adjusted his stance—the sticky, russet fluid swelled past—silently disappearing.

17

Ming watched as Rising Sun cut the last of Richard Deacon's bones. His bloody clothes were smouldering on the fire and the dogs circled impatiently, their noses raised high searching, sniffing and growling. Ming wandered north through the fences—he needed breathing space from Deek and his blood, from the tent...from the brutal reality. It was September and the men were hammering boards; the cattle shifted and scurried uneasy in the feed lots. Thousands of miles without any barrier, and now: prison. They had arrived lean and tough, now they would eat ceaselessly and fatten until December when the killing would begin. He stepped up onto the bottom rail and closely regarded the doomed animals. He considered their plight: eating, jostling, long horns swishing, hooves digging, always carefully scrutinizing their new angled, rigid boundaries and wary of their captors, fearing destiny. Could they know? They had travelled hard, following the dusty trail north, suffered the endless scowls and pitiless calls of the cowboy for miles and miles, week after week, only to arrive here, to be squeezed and tortured until the butcher's knife came down.

The wagons with the Indians had moved on, the Army had not waited for news of Deek, there was no search or investigation; no one cared; no one else ever ventured down to their tents. The remains of his body were lost to the insufferable dogs and the dirt, within minutes; the rising cloud of grey smoke held no scent of his clothes. Nothing remained. Rising Sun did not look up when Ming returned; she could not connect with his eyes, he was now a man. There were no orders for him and no chores. Finally, her cruel threats were over. The women allowed Ming to come and go as he pleased. Ming began to wear a knife on his belt and his stance was no longer timid, his attitude no longer childish. The time for him to find his own way was fast approaching. He would wait for the slaughter.

For sixty-one days, a pathetic, lingering, winding trail snaked along a dusty plain for almost seven hundred miles—stretching and weaving, drifting and knotting, bending, tripping, limping—the ragged group of dis-heartened Potawatomi—860 displaced prisoners—marched at gunpoint from Twin Lakes, Indiana to Osawtomie, Kansas. Some rode on wagons, some on horseback, most walked—all suffered torment, fatigue, illness and unjustified abuse—the victims of Whiteman's larceny: everything was stolen from them: their homes, their crops, their dignity—their pride; and for some...their lives. Dr. Jerolaman was young and inexperienced—the daily suffering and gradual, cruel decline of the people he was ordered to serve was an impossible task. He administered his dwindling reserves for fever, dehydration, exhaustion, starvation, and typhoid. Still, forty-two people died, mostly children. At four in the afternoon after trekking eight hours through drought conditions, the caravan would stop and the single meal for the day would be served, the ill tended to; the dead buried. Fifty soldiers stood sentry throughout the night—unaware of the few young braves that would silently fade away through their thin picket lines, softer than a whisper, running on to freedom—racing to secret places where no militiaman could find them, where no fences could corral them, contain them, bury them—where they could rebuild their dignity—become Potawatomi again.

Jerolaman was forced to gain a new perspective of Potawatomi medicine as the women administered their natural, herbal remedies in conjunction with his poor reserves—he learned and appreciated the intelligence and perseverance of these brave, gentle people. When he eventually returned to Logansport, Indiana to settle and build a practice, that winter, he became a strong endorser of Indian herbal medicine, and a champion of the Indian dilemma as it hopelessly played out through the remainder of his life. His time on The Trail—never forgotten; his lessons dutifully retained.

In Chicago, a small band of Potawatomi remained, slipping under the detection of Lieutenant Marks and his militiamen—safe from death on The Trail...for now.

18

By December the prairie was covered in thick, heavy snow, the paths through the stockyards were frosty and firm; the pens were bursting with livestock; the interminable concert of groans and howls from the cattle radiated throughout the day and night without end. The frigid air over Chicago was layered with the moaning remonstrations of the beasts—their plea for freedom: a death knell infused with the rancid odour of their manure and blood. The butchering was well under way. Ming followed a path through and around the boards: a labyrinth of Smithson timber; he headed for the killing sheds. As he approached, someone was lifting a wheelbarrow full of severed steer limbs and pushing it out the back along a ruddy track to the bone pile. Ming stopped close to a tall man who was supervising the operation. "I can do that," he quietly declared to Bill Morrison, the top hand for waste removal.

Bill turned to the small voice and responded, "And who might you be?" Placing one hand on his hip and wiping his brow with the other; he sized up Ming, looking up and down, confused about his sudden appearance.

"I am Mingaswen...Ming."

"What kind of Chink name is that?" Ming had his long black hair pulled back behind in a tail, tied with a leather string, not braided, but the Chinese similarity was a reasonable guess considering his hair and name. But his eyes were round and green and his complexion brown. "I am Potawatomi, not Chink." Ming answered proudly, with more than hint of indignation.

"Well we don't hire no Chinks around here, so we'll call you Mick, a good Irish name. Pick up that wheelbarrow and haul it out Mick." Bill and the boys stood watching as they had no doubt the contents of the overflowing wheelbarrow filled with severed legs, hooves, heads and tails, swimming in a slimy sawdust pastry of blood and guts would crash to the ground, the entire gruesome medley sliding across the frozen dirt.

Ming reached down, placed his hands firmly on the handles and squeezed his grip tight. Bending at his knees, he lifted square and true. There was a slight shift to the left but he checked it and began moving his legs forward—one short step, then another.

"There's our little Mick!" the boys cheered. "A good Irishman!" They removed their hats and laughed, surprised at Ming's success. Ming broke a smile over his tightly clenched teeth—eyes firm in concentration—he remained careful of every dip and hole.

"Back to work lads." Bill ordered, and their short respite ended.

The cart was much heavier than Ming had anticipated and within seconds the pain began to stab—first in his back and arms, then his legs. He could see the bone pile ahead only a few yards beyond the shed door; the narrow path in the snow was well-marked—red—from spilled blood and lined with bits of bone and organs. The crew tried to catch a glimpse of this strange little boy that wanted to work so hard like a man; they wanted to laugh when he failed at negotiating the wheelbarrow along the crusty path; they were betting on a disaster when the load would dump and O'Brien would come out screaming and swearing.

Ming was sure he wouldn't make it, tripping on ruts and bone fragments, stones and frozen turds. But he was a man now. He lifted, pushed and stretched every muscle. Sid stood to the side, his haul poured out, his wheelbarrow still tipped up and over the pile. The dogs were close, but they would keep their distance until Sid turned to leave; they'd been rapped in the head with a board on more than one occasion. Sid turned and spied Ming. A very tall young man, he couldn't have been more than twenty years of age, thin whiskers, bony shoulders, stooping posture. He watched Ming with wary concern, hoping he would not be responsible for cleaning up the mess once it was dumped prematurely, and this little boy was running back through the corral boards, splashing through the red snow, defeated and scared.

Sid squared his wheelbarrow and passed Ming on the path on his way back. "I'm not picking up your mistakes boy," a cool firm reminder as he pushed past. Ming made it to the pile, turned his wheelbarrow sideways and pushed it over. Sid watched over his shoulder, surprised but pleased, as his job would not be made any more difficult today.

Sid and Ming returned to the slaughter shed and rubbed their freezing hands together to recover some warmth; the relief Ming felt when he dropped his wheelbarrow was euphoric, and he stretched his fingers out and in to regain circulation.

The barn used for a slaughter house was crude: just sheds really, solid, vertical studs holding up a central ridge beam, a roof covered in wooden shingles; the sides—clapboard spruce. There was no attempt at closing gaping sides to keep out the bitter winds of December as the carcasses had to be kept frozen. Two very wide sections open to the roof allowed livestock to enter and waste to exit. The sheds were a place of murder and looked and smelled like death. The chutes were filled with terrified, manure-encrusted, moaning bovine beasts, tightly squeezed between the wooden confines of their temporary imprisonment: a compressed conduit of wailing, condemned flesh, verbally protesting their inevitable bloody destiny; ever jostling for freedom. The crew stood on the rails poking and smacking their sticks over the hind quarters; whistling and yelling, "Get on there, move it…hey, ya!"

The floor consisted of a lumpy mixture of snow, mud, blood, manure and sawdust; Ming collected the gooey meld immediately on the soles of his moccasins. It was thick and viscous and made walking very difficult and painful. In the corners—all the corners— below, above and anywhere where beams and boards met and were nailed together, a sticky residue of animal entrails, bloody mud and cow manure mixed to form a hard plaster-type of re-enforcement mortar—a place where flies would congregate in the thousands in the summer, driving men wild with frustration as they cleaned and repaired the sheds making the place ready for the arrival of next season's reluctant occupants.

Ming's acute olfactory senses picked up the atrocious odours— there was no denying the purpose of this place. The cattle continually dropped their manure all along the chute line, as they fought and struggled, raising their necks and heads up high to prevent their long horns from locking between the rail boards. They howled and moaned until the finale, when the rear board slammed down behind their hind quarters—the great hammer smashing into their skull forcing them to their knees; to their bellies. Four powerful men with huge, sharp knives ripped into the hide as another slit the animal's throat. Chains were secured around its hind legs and hooves, then with amazing speed and agility, the animal was raised aloft by a series of turnbuckles and ropes—two men heaving together pulling with all their strength as if pulling a 24 pounder back from the edge of the ramparts into loading position. A quick dissection followed where great rivers of deep red blood squirted, splashing to the floor, sticking to the shovelful of sawdust thrown there moments before by Sid or Bill, who stood by waiting to procure the next load. The gut was ripped open and the organs exploded forth in a great putrid torrent: an anatomical waterfall—slimy and bloody; the stink: thick and raw, catching in Ming's throat—a choking thrust—he winced, turning his head momentarily, then whipping it back, not wanting to miss even a second of the procedure. Within minutes head, guts, tail and legs all sloshed together into a repulsive, ponderous pile at Sid's feet, and he began to dig in with his shovel. The carcass swung overhead on great hooks, the heart, lungs and liver were set aside on a butcher slab, the hide thrown over a special rail in behind; everything else—waste. Sid bent over the odious compilation and began to work; everything had to be cleared away quickly as another sorrowful candidate was entering the final stages of his predicament.

The splash of the organs and entrails sprayed Ming; he wiped the back of his hand across his face to remove the wet sticky fluid, but in fact the effort only smeared the rancid recipe, painting a grotesque design worthy of any Potawatomi brave ready to set out on the hunt. Sid filled his quota, his senses remaining numb as more than a few winters had desensitized his reactions to the scene; he lifted the heavy wheelbarrow and steered for the path to the bone pile—his gate: a determined stride worthy of a young man whose cerebral attentions drifted far from the stinking stockyards—to Ogden's saloon and a hearty pint of beer—it called to him with every repulsive, despicable load.

The system was not a well-organized machine—it was relatively slow and cumbersome, even awkward; but the foundations were laid for the development of a smoother operation that would be introduced in the very near future, as the demand for beef and pork increased from season to season—necessarily, in order to satisfy the needs of the rapidly exploding eastern populations. Ming might have witnessed the Chicago Stockyards becoming the biggest and busiest in North America—a phenomenon...but he wouldn't stay that long.

Ming moved closer. He observed everything—he was keenly aware of the process: move the cattle, kill them, remove the hide and organs, send them out and slice the meat into long strips and hang them to freeze and tenderize. There was a rhythm; there was an understood process, but it was far from perfect. When operating smoothly, when all crew members knew and understood their jobs, then the livestock were contained, the waste did not overflow, the cutting was true and rapid, good meat was hung and quality could be reasonably ensured. But a steer could jump the chute, horns could jam under a board or stick into a man's ribs; the whipping blades of the butchers could slice a hand off in an instant, a slip on the scummy floor could result in a face full of stinking manure and shitty entrails, and a faulty swing from the hammer could mean the loss of a limb or a crushed skull. The Irishmen of the stockyards were hardworking, vigilant men, wary of strangers entering their special death house and possibly disrupting their crude but orderly system; the work was reliable and lucrative; they were, understandably, concerned about anything that might upset the balance. As a young visitor, Ming didn't appear as a threat and they paid him no mind—the trip with the wheelbarrow was humorous and offered a brief moment of levity to a dreary day in the sheds.

Ming, however did not consider himself a visitor and his load to the bone pile was not a joke; he was a man—he had proven it, only three months ago. There was no fear in his face, he did not shy away from blood or knives, he would not whine like a baby. There was no work for him at the encampment; the days of drunken cowboy visitors were over; there would be no more cruel starving winters—he was here to work.

Pat O'Brien was the foreman: tall and stocky, a full bushy handlebar moustache, a wool cap over his head and ears, a full-length leather apron over his coat—dyed with red splotches from years of exposure to the business—thick gloves on his hands. His stance was firm and he blocked Ming from moving his wheelbarrow towards the next load. With hands resting on his hips, chin deep in his chest, he grumbled through his whiskers, "Why are you stealing my wheelbarrow, little chief?" Ming stopped and looked up—he saw O'Brien; he knew his chance at earning Whiteman's money might be over.

"I am not stealing, I am working. Clear the path so I can pick up another load," was Ming's arrogant response.

"Do you know who I am little chief?" O'Brien asked assuming Ming would run off now knowing the game was over—he was, after all, chastising the boss.

"No, but if you don't move the bones will pile up in here and the killing will become too slow." Ming answered as if he was already a full-time Irish stockyard hand knowing and understanding the vital consistency required for the smooth operation of the slaughter. It was risky but Ming wanted to work—sitting around Rising Sun's fire pit or picking berries with Nootkana and Little Raven now seemed like women's work—he had killed a man, felt the living flesh at the end of his knife, had stood his ground; he couldn't go back. O'Brien recognized the serious resolve in Ming's eyes—they stared at each other—Ming had threatened and O'Brien was challenged. The butchering stopped, the hammer held its poise, the crew regarded the scenario with trepidation, O'Brien finally spoke.

"Well I guess I better move. I wouldn't want to slow up production." O'Brien stepped aside—Ming moved his wheelbarrow in and began shovelling—removing his cap, scratching his head, O'Brien was definitely perplexed. "What are you looking at? Get back to work!" And the hammer came down, the knives began to slash, a few laughs escaped from a few mouths.

Four more loads to the bone pile and back. Sid didn't seem to mind, the fact that another wheelbarrow was working meant that he could relax somewhat—the urgency to keep up with the slaughter was reduced and Ming had not dropped even one load. Ming however had reached the end of his endurance—he was desperately tired, in great pain and very cold. He dropped his wheelbarrow in the shed and checked his hands; they were raw, blistered and frozen, but he was ready to continue. O'Brien had watched the entire ordeal play out; he knew the day for Ming was over. "Let me see those hands." Turning them over, O'Brien appreciated the effort and the fortitude of this little boy; he was impressed. He placed a ten-cent piece in Ming's palm and told him to go home, he had done enough today.

On the trail home Ming opened his hand and looked closely at the coin; it was dirty on the edges and shiny in the middle, he had no idea of its value but to him it was a fortune and more importantly he had earned it outright through hard work; he felt proud. He knew exactly what to do with it, there was no doubt in his mind. When he entered the camp, Rising Sun was stirring a soapy concoction in her great cauldron over a smokey fire—stringy grey tips of her long hair hung down teasing the slimy surface of her tedious enterprise. The closer she stooped over the fire the warmer she remained; snow gently floated down above her head meeting the flakey ashes drifting up. The cold wind picked up; December would be another long miserable month. She sensed his arrival but would not look up. Ming tapped his closed fist on her arm—she turned—he opened his fist and offered her the coin. Without acknowledging him, she took it. Ming turned and walked away.

19

*B*y March Ming had shovelled tons of bloody animal waste, hauled hundreds of miserable loads to the bone pile, kicked pugnacious dogs, sharpened dull knives, hung hides, and planted almost twenty dollar's worth of coins into Rising Sun's greedy palm. The furtive evil glances between Little Raven and Rising Sun had stopped; the animosity had dissolved. With cash in the camp throughout the winter months there was no need to be concerned with selling jewelry—Little Raven became content; Ming's lofty promotion in the family had been justified—Rising Sun had reached a satisfactory, but unspoken resolve as well. Mr. O'Brien didn't allow Ming to work every day; other cowboys willing to do the dirtiest job in the stockyards had come and gone. Warm spring breezes softened the ground around the sheds; melt water dripped from the eves, forming long pointed icicles diving vertically from the roof to the snow drifts below, fringing the buildings with shiny glass candy canes. Muddy canals trenching along winding paths between fences carved and twisted, draining the runoff; mud mixed with manure everywhere created a viscous swamp. The dogs continually dug around the bone pile searching for scraps; the softer ground now allowed for greater success in their desperate, ceaseless excavations; bones buried for months under snow and waste, now emerged like spring crocuses reaching skyward for the sun's renewing rays. The corrals were almost empty; the stockyards were so quiet the silence was almost eerie. Ming arrived every day ready to work.

"Let me see those hands." O'Brien regarded Ming and shook his head, "You're a fine sight for sure." He was thick with mud; cake-infused with dried blood and entrails. Splashes of the vile grunge streaked his little face—his pathetic worn countenance was tired and worrisome. O'Brien reached down, taking Ming's hands, turning them over to check the damage. They were worn right down with blisters on every finger, the palms were ripped and battered. "Look at me boy," O'Brien demanded still holding Ming's hands gently knowing full well the boy was suffering great pain from his shoulders to his toes. O'Brien could be a task master, true enough; he could swear and yell—his demands in the slaughter house could be strict, his attitude fierce—but he was not void of compassion.

Ming looked up. "Come home with me today lad and the Mrs.' will wash you up and feed you a proper meal." O'Brien could only imagine life with the Potawatomi—the boy was thin, his clothes were rags; he was never really clean. There was pride in Ming's eyes and the question perhaps overstepped a boundary—it was an impulsive gesture; O'Brien meant no disrespect.

Ming pulled his hands away. This was an unusual request and he was reluctant to oblige. "I can wash myself!" was his belligerent response.

"I know you can, but a short visit won't hurt you none, now will it? And besides you've eaten your share of dog this winter. Come on now lad." Truthfully he didn't realize the comment reflected insensitivity and bigotry—O'Brien gave Ming a huge bright smile—all his teeth pleasantly displayed though his huge moustache, attempting to seal the deal. They both stood facing each other in stubborn silence. "Are you afraid Mick?" This taunting question was asked with full knowledge of Ming's temperament, which, throughout the season's tough demands, and right up to this point, definitely included no hint of fear from this resilient young boy.

"No I am not afraid."

"Well then follow me, and I'll pay you another nickel." O'Brien turned, leaving the vile stench and the dark shadows of the shed. Ming followed a few paces behind—they walked into town one behind the other—Ming's focus remaining steadfast upon the dirt and mud at his feet, his posture submissive.

"Good God!" was the loud and terse exclamation blurted out at Ming upon her first glance at the boy. Mrs. O'Brien shook her head, "I have never seen the likes of this."

"Well this is Mick and he's come for supper." Ming's existence and his history at the slaughterhouse was not unknown in the O'Brien household—Pat O'Brien had spoken of the boy many times before, to his wife and daughter, yet his sudden appearance at her door left the woman somewhat unbalanced—she wasn't exactly sure how to proceed. O'Brien made no explanation or excuses; he removed his boots, slid past his wife without another word, entered the kitchen and drifted into the parlour following a well-worn routine bravely executed a thousand times before. His technique was based on the assumption that all would end well if he removed himself from the situation, leaving Mrs. O'Brien's good nature and Godly charity to intervene; and he was correct. Mrs. Siobhan O'Brien was somewhat rotund in her middle age—a full matronly figure; her hair streaked now with lines of silver, throughout warm tones of brown and auburn, always pulled back in a tight bun; her stature short, never without an apron, always cheery, but it was strict rules and regulations that kept her household clean and orderly. Finally, after a short but firm visual inspection—a swift calculation, and then an expeditious summation: "Take everything off!"

"What?" That order caught Ming off guard; his back stiffened abruptly.

"Remove it all for God's sake, and heaven help us, what has he been doing to you?"

Ming stood frozen in his muddy moccasins, convinced full-well that whatever this lady was assuming—it would not be happening to him; his clothes would remain where they were and if eating in this house meant removing clothes, he would leave now…hungry. Shannon O'Brien, a girl of thirteen, peered around the corner, eyes bulging, a wide grin stretching her mouth to its limits—she suppressed a giggle, then ran to prepare a bath—the order from her mother snapping out was answered with immediate diligence.

For a few lingering moments, Ming observed the little porch in which he stood. He regarded the stout door frame, the thick walls and high ceiling; the floor was solid wood, there was no dirt, windows were glass—the thought of a permanent structure offered mixed emotions: an instantaneous feeling of security—yet a hint of confinement. This house would not blow over in a wind storm; moving it every season would be impossible—too big, too heavy. He cautiously minded the only exit he could see—the one behind him—just in case. It was the first time he had ever entered such a building—a Whiteman's building. The slaughter sheds were wooden structures, but they were crude and open to the elements. Here was a house—small intimate secure spaces inside—no wind challenging the walls' integrity, no holes or slits in the roof allowing the rain its relentless search and attack; the heavy wooden door closed tight and firm in a wide frame behind him—he jerked, concerned of its power. He listened...there were no crying animals. He smelled: no wafting odours from the corrals. The inviting aromas from the kitchen were rich: baking bread, roasting stew, jams and jellies cooking on the stove—sweet fragrances—appetizing, warm...comforting.

Mrs. O'Brien reached down and attempted to remove Ming's shirt—he resisted. Slowly raising his dirty little face to hers—his worried expression innocently searching for trust in her eyes—she responded with a bright smile and a tiny nod—Ming surrendered.

Pat O'Brien's situation and procedures were not generally reclusive at this time of day—supper was typically served before him at the head of the table immediately upon the conclusion of a thorough washing—however this evening's schedule was decidedly interrupted and supper would be delayed—he slouched in his chair in the parlour and lit a pipe, truly mirroring post-supper ministrations, however not begrudgingly, he would be patient. Once Ming was seated in the large steel tub, Mrs. O'Brien began to scrub—the effort was firm and resounding, repetitive and diligent, but not rough or cruel. The months of thick dirt and odours began to dissipate and a shiny clean boy slowly emerged—the shockingly pale white skin covering his thin bony figure was an unexpected revelation and Mrs. O'Brien caught Shannon's eye looking, sharing a similar discovery when she lifted a hand up beckoning for a towel. This prized bit of information would be cleverly retained until the boy headed out—but first, supper.

Temporary clothes covered Ming while his belongings swayed in the evening sun; the wind offering a thorough final freshening— the rags blowing like well-worn battle flags of a militia regiment so gratefully home from the fray. The shirt and trousers he wore were O'Brien's from slimmer days: big, bulky, loose, but they received no distain from Ming—he stood by a chair in the dining room, the position directed by Shannon, and he pondered. Mr. O'Brien, having finished his wash, entered and sat down followed by Shannon. "All washed are ye lad? Well sit down, sit down." Pat O'Brien never considered for a moment that Ming had never eaten at a dining table let alone never sat in a chair. Ming watched and copied—in fact Ming's entire first visit to the O'Brien's would consist of repetitive mimicry—he would replay each move after his hosts' initial manoeuvre: napkin, praying, crossing, passing, spooning, eating, dipping, wiping—not under- standing but obliging. He was truly mesmerized by the activities: the odd words during Grace, the fingers flying up and about in a magical formula: touching the forehead then crossing the chest—he tried clumsily, and they smiled—*what a good Catholic he will be*—spooning the stew to the mouth and slurping every bit in...and what a taste! Dipping the bread into the bowl, wiping the gravy, filling his cheeks with the most delicious meal of his life—it was a glorious repast, and he was so satisfied. "Was it good lad?"

Ming responded with a smile, then released a deep full belch, "Oh yes, thank you." At first eyes rolled and mouths dropped open— the rude and vulgar noise was wholly unacceptable—but then, Mr. O'Brien smiled and everyone shared a laugh at the little boy who didn't know any better. There was so much to learn, and Ming was in the correct house to learn it all.

2nd Corinthians was read aloud around the fireplace—Ming sat at Shannon's feet watching her lips move gently to the rhythm of the foreign words, "Whoever sows sparingly will also reap sparingly, and whoever sows generously will also reap generously." Mrs. O'Brien rejoiced in her charity tonight and was well on her way—directing this boy's salvation—when Mr. O'Brien interrupted and suggested it was indeed late.

Ming's tiny silhouette disappeared around the corner, as the clouds rolled in, the wind picked up. Mrs. O'Brien stepped in from the porch, hands placed firmly on her hips, face squared to her husband, "That boy's no Indian!"

Ming dashed around the buildings in town, dodging between dark shadow and glistening moonlight, past the Mercantile, in front of the Saloon—the boys were hollerin' and the banjos were plunkin', past stables and feed, past wagons and carriages—teams of forlorn horses with heads hanging low, munching on feed bags, dropping their stinkin' dung to the street—until the stockyard boards rose up forcing him to turn and follow a well-known path through and down to the bone piles. The spring air was fresh—it felt so good on his clean face, as if new skin was receiving rejuvenation after being buried for so long. The sky was clear, his stomach was full, new emotions and sensitivities swirled in his blood; the elation was invigorating—like nothing he had felt…since the day he stood over that cowboy holding fragile life at the end of a knife blade. The camp was quiet; a familiar thin line of smoke was dancing and wavering to a simple cadence in a soft breeze above a pathetic fire pit where only a few ashes fought for a final flicker of life beneath a black chicken bone. His bed—a blanket over straw deep within a recess of the storage tent—offered no interest for him; restless, he returned to the night, to the stars, to the moon glow that hid behind wispy racing clouds. He listened to the coyotes cry; the crickets singing in the tall grass. His heart pounded in his chest. Little Raven arrived after a time and sat beside him—she said nothing—she could smell the soap in his hair and in his clothes—she could smell…Whiteman. She knew; she said nothing.

Life for the Potawatomi was measured in seasons: planting, gathering, preparing and hoarding, waiting through winter, then beginning again—against rain, flood, drought, wind and torment. Life for the Chicagoan was measured by the Drive: arrival, feeding, butchering, repairing and expanding. Ming's life for the next nine years took many turns and twists, the spinning cycles ever crashing and colliding; Chicago's encroachment ever persistent—the stockyard's continuous advancement becoming voluminous: more lumber, more buildings and bridges, more cowboys, more business, more livestock—the last Potawatomi family slipping away to mere shadows on the southern fringes of the swampy outskirts. Cowboys, farmers, lumberjacks and teamsters too drunk or too poor to qualify to receive the virtues of the town girls still found their way occasionally to Rising Sun's tent and Nootkana's reluctant backside. Ming hated them and hated Rising Sun's repulsive enterprise; he would race from the camp ensconcing himself in tall grasses in the summer or snow drifts in the winter, far from the grunts and yelps.

Potawatomi medicine would become Ming's forte, as gathering, mixing, procuring and administering all medicines, lotions and all manner of concoctions became second nature to him. He would assist during abortions, births and amputations, during fevers of typhus, wrap bandages and apply lotions for infection. The few doctors that arrived in Chicago rarely treated sick or wounded cowboys, or dockyard workers; pregnant girls whether from the saloon or from upstanding families, had two choices: leave Chicago or visit an Indian medicine woman. Ming worked at the stockyard more regularly and his personage was commonplace in town, retrieving parts from the Mercantile for Mr. O'Brien or purchasing goods for his family. Mrs.

O'Brien cut his hair—his clothes were typical of a stockyard worker, yet he still received slanderous comments and half stares: "Half-breed"—his time in town now doubling his time at the encampment.

Every Sunday after Mrs. O'Brien and Shannon returned home from church, Ming would visit for supper, but more importantly for lessons. Mrs. O'Brien taught the scriptures and Shannon taught everything else. Ming learned to read and write, apply mathematics for basic calculations at the Mercantile, weights and measures for salt, flour and tea. Ming read Dickens from the newspapers from Boston, learned of faraway lands, science and machinery; he observed and retained every scrap of information from every book and newspaper in the O'Brien house; he taught the butchers how to be more efficient in their cuts, he designed a fast and safe sharpening system for knives; he rarely lifted another wheelbarrow, except when short-staffed, but organized the slaughterhouse for increased efficiency and better storage; but he was never 'one of them'—he received no pay increase; he received respect from Mr. O'Brien and no one else. For a time, Ming built the tents stronger, they lasted longer, the walls were dryer, the smoke filtered away above the roof, food was better and more plentiful; yet he began to resent his plight—trapped between two conflicting worlds: respecting Potawatomi culture, appreciating his survival skills, while simultaneously, temporarily, basking in Whiteman's comforts, but never understanding their arrogance, greed or disrespect.

Nektoshe arrived—an Appaloosa pony, lost on the prairies, she wandered into their campsite one day and stayed; Ming persuaded Rising Sun not to butcher the animal but instead convinced her of the gifts it could bring. All provisions were assembled and moved on a litter Ming built for transporting, and physical repositioning of the Potawatomi homestead each year was made considerably easier, in spite of Ogden's Deputies—they, however, remained terrifying: violent, vulgar, impatient—an unwelcome annual assault on their home, their culture and their dignity. They grabbed Nootkana from behind and squeezed her breasts, they pushed Little Raven to the ground and called her half-breed whore; they kicked the horse and threw stones; they punched Ming and laughed when he fell into mud and horse shit. Ogden wanted the Potawatomi out of his town; the short distance the camp moved each spring was never far enough— but Smithson continued to thwart Ogden's regulations—he wanted Little Raven spared. Ogden's wishes would earn fruition soon enough.

Ming gained insight over time—dealing with cowboys and butchers, as he did daily—and about Whiteman; he fashioned an adolescent perspective regarding Chicago, Frank Ogden and Charles Smithson—much of it carried in disrespect and distrust—the day arrived, however, when he came face to face with a truth he could not ignore. A task for Mr. Morrison brought him near the docks.

Ming stared stunned and ashamed, the huge Percheron valiantly fighting, the massive tree impossibly heavy, sunk deep into the earth, resisting, immovable—ever victorious—the huge figure of Smithson standing over the scene, whip in hand—ever masterful, ever seditious—the sight too ghastly to be real. Ming felt the horse's cries, felt the sting of the whip as it slashed through the hide, but he could not move, his feet were encased in lead, his body frozen, horrified. The whip flashed back and forth with such speed and power, the snap and slice cutting the air into bloody strips inter-layered with imperceptible screaming orders, matching the deep, vicious wounds on the animal's hind quarters—his soulful cries: eerie harmonizing— desperate yelps of surrender from its frothing lips. Then…nothing.

Charles Smithson stood back, his shirt soiled in sweat, chest heaving—gasping for air, the whip lying behind him in the dirt in preparation—a quiet snake curled, limp but poised—its tail gripped tightly by the huge hand. The horse lay still in its harness, on the ground—once a proud massive black warrior—now a bloody inconvenience in the dirt; his teammate still standing, frightened and exhausted, waited for the next flailing attack.

"Cut him loose." Smithson finally spoke—his men jumped from their silent sentinel, releasing the bloody carcass from its leather strappings. Ming wanted to grab that whip. He would give that man such a lesson—it would be the last lesson of his life. Reaching up his back under his shirt, Ming grabbed the handle of his knife that was cradled in the small of his back hanging in a leather sheath... he walked closer to the man. Smithson's broad dark shoulders rose up before him; each step was carefully determined and calculated: not too fast, not so direct. Everyone at the dock turned their focus to the dead horse—the space around Smithson widened, he stood vulnerable, exposed. Ming gripped the handle of his knife tighter; he flipped the leather tie open on the sheath with his thumb, the knife dropped a little; he stepped closer. Just as he reached the wide expanse of the man's great shoulders, just as his courage reached a climax, Ming jerked on the knife...it jammed—someone's hand pressed down on his back, another landed hard on his arm. "It's a sad thing when that happens to be sure," whispered Pat O'Brien into Ming's ear, startling him and freezing him in his tracks. "Come with me Mick, you don't want to see any more of this."

Ming and O'Brien sat in the parlour; the familiar pipe aroma swirling about his head and throughout the room was relaxing and satisfying. O'Brien sat back deep into his favourite chair; Ming leaned forward legs akimbo on the floor, cradling his head in his hands. O'Brien spoke slowly, softly. "Look at my house Mick, this pipe, my wife and daughter, the life I have made for them. It comes at a cost. Do you think you are the first one who wanted to draw a knife on Smithson? He operates the docks, the quarries, and a major share of the stockyards; he answers to no one and everyone answers to him. I want to keep my house so I stay quiet. Ogden answers to him, and there you have it, we are tied."

Raising his head, staring into the fireplace, Ming responded, "I am not tied."

"No but you'd be dead if you pulled that knife." O'Brien was dealing with a young man, not a daughter; a young man who might not be so easily convinced; a young man who was not his son; a young man who necessarily balanced two cultures on his narrow shoulders daily—all too often a precarious task, and becoming more difficult for him as the years progressed. "If you want to stay in this town, if you want to work, you will let it go Mick." That was all the advice O'Brien had.

Ming left, satisfaction eluding him, but a slim sense of understanding settled on the outskirts of his young mind—enough at least to leave that brute of a man to deal with bloody horses and heavy lumber at a place far from his sad little corner of Chicago…for now.

June 1847, another season climaxed. Ming was seventeen years old, a veteran of nine years in the stockyards; a veteran of Ogden's unrelenting persecution, including the stories of the forced removal of the Potawatomi to Kansas; of Smithson's indisputable terrorism—the strangle-hold on the people of Chicago; continued harassment by irritating, irascible cowboys—the clear and frightening memory of their sadistic sexual violations forced on him as a young boy and the subsequent recurring nightmares—of Rising Sun's mundane herb collecting, medicines and bloody surgeries—her continued obsessive abuse of Nootkana; nine years of Shannon O'Brien's lessons and Mrs. O'Brien's Sunday suppers; nine years reading the Boston

Globe, Dickens, Corinthians and Revelations; the annual vexatious relocation of the Potawatomi camp farther to the south deep into the swamps.

Little Raven was now Lil and her relationship with Ming was close, as close as a sister and brother could be—she gave Ming a spiritual grounding—the only true closeness he had ever experienced from another person, and he cherished it—they still spent private times together in the tall grass dreaming together: for her a soft bed, new clothes and mild winters, for him: punishment for cowboys and perhaps new adventures far from Chicago. Nootkana and Shashona were grateful for Ming's leadership; his monetary contributions— they gave him respect, and he appreciated their companionship— they were predictable, their rituals dependable. The little band—his Potawatomi family—small and often destitute, crude and simple— meant security for Ming; he went home to them every night.

Rising Sun remained steadfast in her duties—tolerant. Ming remained restless.

Everything was about to change...forever.

20

here was that rock? It seemed so gigantic, obscure—out of place, in the spring, sitting alone on the dirt, but now the tall blades of summer grass reached around from every corner entirely hiding it. Even the wind, as it carved its flowing designs and patterns across the surface of the thick green blanket, would not reveal its location—its hiding place remained safe, deep within the dark, soft roots of the clever prairie weave. The last of the new corrals were far behind him. Pressing his teeth hard together in a ridiculous attempt to hold it in with his mouth, he ran farther and farther south into the tall prairie grasses away from the slaughter sheds, away from the tents and the stinking slime, away from the insufferable dogs and the sucking sludge of the swamps.

The pressure in his bladder was now unbearable; but Ming wanted to find that rock. The early morning sun sparkled on the dew, delicately clinging to the tops of the cattails; the shiny spider webs strung between them were laced with water droplets precariously floating like translucent pearls on silky strands. Ming began to break through the grass at a desperate pace crunching the weeds beneath his boots, driving the tall green blades to the sides with flashes of whipping arms and hands tearing the webs apart—the spiders sailing through the air dangerously swinging by a sorrowful single life line. *Where was it?* He was beginning to panic! He reached down spreading the grass apart in every direction. His hands were soaked in dew. He kicked and pleaded; he scraped and screamed, the pain in his bladder ready to burst! Finally, forgivingly, the toe of his boot drove into the evil rock—with one giant leap he gained immediate balance at the top, spun around to face the corrals, reached down and unbuttoned the bottom two buttons of this trousers, pulled it out, drew back the foreskin, arched his back and with a throaty gasp released a torrent of urine to the sky!

The relief was especially euphoric as he had held it for so long and he had raced out so far. The arc was high and smooth. Out it shot: five feet, six feet—he knew the distance would be great because he had saved it up all morning. He pissed on the hundreds of steers he had butchered over the past nine seasons; he pissed on all the buckets of blood and the thousands of cartfuls of cow and pig guts he had painfully carried out to the bone piles; he pissed on Ogden and Smithson and on all the soldiers that forced the Potawatomi to their death; he pissed on all the stinking cowboys that forced their way into the tents at night and grunted and groaned over Nootkana as they had their way—disgusting pigs; he pissed on the loathsome, stupid cowboys that had split the cheeks of his ass open and violated him, so that the unbearable pain and repulsion remained, locked deep within his soul forever; he pissed on Rising Sun's moronic, ugly, wrinkled face and her tedious demands and putrid cauldrons of rancid, smoking soap. He pissed on Chicago and the whole world; and he pissed and pissed. It felt so good in so many ways.

With each condemnation the watery arc grew higher, the distance reached farther; his power was rising to an exhilarating climax. He bowed his back into an impossible reverse curve that questioned the very laws of human anatomy and its natural tolerances. He pushed and pushed, destroying his enemies and releasing years of suppressed hatred and frustration. He squeezed his teeth tight when thinking of those cowboys; he cursed them again and again, and aimed his piss right down their pathetic mouths; he split their brains open and pissed on the bloody mass; he buried them in his piss. And yet it still was not enough. It would never be enough.

A thieving wind whipped across and eclipsed his beautiful stream. The sticky yellow spray sparkled on the tops of the foxtails and stinkweed blooms; splashed on his boots and trouser leg. The spiders scurried for shelter—their daily tenacious endeavours forced now to recommence as their silky traps snapped apart at the seams. A curled smirk coiled on his lips; a contemptuous scowl. He shoved it back in, buttoned his trousers and jumped down from the rock. He headed back.

He studied the campsite from a safe distance not wanting to attract attention; that same stupid, slender grey spiral of smoke encouraged to rise, provoked by Nootkana's stupid stick twisting and poking in yesterday's ashes, gave testimony to the sad start of the morning's rituals. Ming was tall, a slender figure with broad shoulders, but he knew how to stand on the bottom rail and dig his side into the corner post so as to blend in with the corral. He hid and watched. It would be the last time.

Ming no longer indulged in the needed care demanded by the camp—he was tired, discontented…irritated. The old buffalo skins were tattered and ripped; the top hole for the stove pipe would have to be wiped with pine grease again—the rain water discovering a new route in with every shower. The tent poles were bent and cracked; the roof was tilted and sagging; the site was strewn with broken boxes, ripped fence boards, cans, weeds, smashed bottles, dog shit and chicken feathers, and rotting bones—bones everywhere, a desert of drying rotting bones. There was nothing admirable about living as a Potawatomi at the edge of the stockyards in the Chicago swamps, and Ming wanted to race into town away from Rising Sun's malodorous boiling concoctions, away from the destitute scavenger life he had grown up with, to the comforts of Mrs. O'Brien's home with sweet jellies and fresh bread and soft chairs, and newspapers, and solid unflapping walls.

He stepped down and followed the rails far around away from the tents. It was still early but there was work at the slaughter sheds. It was late spring—a time of repair and cleaning, and although there were always animals in the yards, the vast hoards of cattle would not arrive until the fall; they were on route from Kansas, Texas and New Mexico, thousands of miles to the south and west.

The cowboys would drive them hard all summer long. The strong odour of manure subsided at this time. Ming lifted his face to the sky and ran down the trail through the corrals—the twisting path, the broken boards, the moldy hay, the sagging sheds, until finally he felt he could really breathe; it lifted him; it renewed him.

That same sun casting a shimmering lacy veil across the wet blanket of spider webs, fusing them together into nature's crocheted mosaic, pierced Eunice Johnson's bedroom window a half mile north of that rock, disclosing a pathetic and tragic scene that would release Ming from his bondage and set him on a destined intrepid course of misery, the likes of which he could never have imagined.

21

That early white slice of morning light cut through a centre split in the heavy curtains and painted a bright stripe across her face—into her eyes, but did not awaken her; she was not asleep. Eunice had not slept all night.

Her body remained in a compressed curl; her knees held tight together by her arms up under her chin; her hair stuck in wet strings across her forehead; the pillow and bedclothes: damp with sweat. The rag in her mouth was still clenched tightly between her teeth, her eyelids drooping, her breathing intermittent—calmer now. She was exhausted.

A young girl—fifteen—with dark hair, blue eyes and rosy cheeks, round pouty lips and dimples so sweet, some said the fairest in Chicago—was now a colourless shadow; a lifeless deposit of tissues and fluids saturated with toxins, wrapped in a dishevelled contortion of wet cotton nightclothes and torn bed sheets. She was dying.

The fire in her stomach—a crooked branch of sharp rigid thorns churning and stabbing, had subsided and she lay still for the first time in hours. Her frantic wiping and continuous searching on the sheets and between her legs for the bloody spoils of the vulgar potion had stopped. There was no blood, there was no baby. Rising Sun's little brown bottle lay open-ended on the floor beside her bed—empty. She was instructed to take a small sip once daily for five days—she drank it all down in a hasty gulp, so desperate to rid her body of the unwanted intruder.

One final cramp—a long twisting punch, and she rolled to her back; her eyes freezing: two watery slits on a puffy pale countenance—her torture over.

The Sheriff's men took no time rushing through the stockyards; dragging the four Indian women to the jailhouse. Mrs. Johnson's choking wails demanded justice and she would not be denied!

22

The normal traffic congestion for mid-day was decidedly low on the south side of Main Street and Ming noted a general shift to the north from those people walking on the boardwalks and those riding horses or carriages, plodding their way up the street through the mud.

There was excited activity in town and although he had only a few moments to retrieve the hardware order for Mr. O'Brien, Ming turned his attention to mid-town and joined the rest of the crowd as they headed towards the hotel, where a permanent stage had been erected in the centre of the street for special events.

Several important people had made it their duty to visit Chicago lately, as railroad and canal projects were at the heart of huge construction initiatives to bring the city into a level of modernization that could rival New York and Boston. Ming assumed the unannounced meeting probably dealt with hiring work crews, or the introduction of new industrialists from the East or perhaps from Ireland or England, who would inspire the crowd with their rhetorical speeches of hope and future success, and their explanations of how Chicago would become the centre of American development in the mid-west. The conclusion of the ceremony usually included colourful flags, roaring applause and often marching music from a band. Ming had seen something similar before, and he assumed the fuss today was a result of festive activities of a comparable sort.

As Ming reached the centre of town close to the hotel, he unwillingly became caught up in a powerful force, as the street had taken on a life of its own. The wave of people was gushing now more rapidly towards a low gravity point at the centre of town from all directions, as if the pipes containing the water of humanity had been released and the contents had come pouring forth from every hydrant seeking to quell a blazing fire. Everyone was rushing frantically and Ming was caught in the deluge.

But there was no boisterous welcome as expected upon his arrival; no cheers, or banners or speeches. Ming saw none of the usual hoopla associated with civic pride or political ceremony. The men on the scaffold did not wear the long dark frock coats—the typical administrator's garb—or tall black stove pipe hats; and the people of Chicago, squeezing in tight up to the edge of the platform to witness the spectacle, were unusually quiet, sombre and lacking in any sort of enthusiasm. They were instead, surprisingly pensive; even apprehensive.

The platform was raised eight feet above the street—no one would be blocked from the view: it was so high. Two large vertical posts at either side reached a height of another eight feet above the deck of the platform and were connected by a horizontal beam stretching a distance of ten feet across from side to side. Each post was supported by two diagonal boards on each side of the platform to secure the heavy wood and prevent it from shifting.

Three wooden chairs from the saloon across the street, usually reserved for dignitaries, sat empty in an orderly row; their vacancy normally significant, as they would be filled at any moment, to the crowd's great approval and pleasure, by important speech makers or perhaps Frank Ogden himself in his new official capacity as Mayor. But the chairs today would not be filled with the bottoms of arrogant, self-righteous politicians or rich industrialists ready to spout their rhetoric, because above each one hung a rope of heavy twisted hemp, the end of which was bound and tied into a thick noose. The sight of three empty ropes swaying above the crowd, their profile casting a grim, dark silhouette against the noon sky, meant only one thing: execution; and it was imminent!

Young Ming was unaware of any criminals that were waiting execution in the jail, but that wasn't unusual. Since the rapid growth of Chicago began when the town was officially incorporated in 1834, many people drifting through were not always intent on following the letter of the law—and many opportunities existed for the fringe element in the West.

No one could keep track of all the outlaws that passed through Chicago—certainly not Ming. But an execution was a topic of common gossip and Mr. Morrison, O'Brien and the boys in the slaughter house hadn't referred to a hanging in any of their daily exchanges with Ming throughout the morning's chores. It would be highly unlikely that such an important event could have slipped by their attention.

Ming, understandably, was taken by surprise when he approached the scaffold and saw the ropes hanging there in bold view, waiting for their unlucky customers. He squirmed his way in as deep as possible to a distance of a depth of five people or so away from the lip of the wooden deck, when he felt a tug on his shirtsleeve and he turned sharply to address the culprit.

"You must leave here at once Mingaswen. Something has happened!" Little Raven was frantic.

Ming could see that she had been crying. Her hair was dishevelled and her dress was torn at the collar. A bruise was beginning to swell under her eye. Ming took both hands and reached out holding Little Raven's forearms near the wrists.

"Lil, what has happened? What is it?" he demanded, a worried expression growing stronger across his eyes; his brow pressed tight to the middle of his forehead curled in puzzlement.

"They've arrested..." but her words were cut short as a loud collective gasp escaped from the crowd. Little Raven and Ming turned their eyes in response to the scaffold—Nootkana arrived on the top step.

No words would come to him; he was almost faint with shock. Ming might very well have fallen over if he had not been pinned vertical by the crowd pressed tight to him on all sides.

Behind Nootkana, Shashona and then, lastly, Rising Sun arrived, to stand on the platform followed by a Deputy, the Sheriff and finally Frank Ogden.

Their necks were bent forward—their faces covered by the long strands of hair falling from their lowered heads. Iron bracelets bound their wrists behind them as they were pushed to their position—each standing behind one of the vacant chairs.

Ming turned to Little Raven in alarm. "What is this? Why are they arrested? What is happening?" His words blurted out in rapid succession like bullets shot from a revolver at close range, landing full in her face. She closed her mouth—she could not answer; she only looked at him with water-filled eyes and shook her head.

"You must tell me! Tell me!" Ming shook Little Raven as if he might shake the explanation from her with the quick violent jerks of his arms. He squeezed tighter, starring into her face, until she finally spoke.

"They...arrested us this morning. The Johnson girl died and Ogden is wanting their death. He's calling it murder" she explained.

"But what about a trial? Have they had a trial?" he asked her, looking over his shoulder towards the scaffold.

A Deputy was assisting Nootkana as she stepped up onto the chair.

A man in a long dark coat and a broad-brimmed hat stepped onto the platform. Another gasp circulated among the people cramming ever tighter up against the structure on all sides. He was late and went straight to work. His face was lean with long lines cutting deep into his pale cheeks on either side of his mouth. Above his lip, a long black moustache curved out and down—the ends almost reaching to the bottom of his prominent chin. His long nose above was hooked and chiselled to a sharp point; the nostrils underneath were long and extended fully from the inside to the pointy extent of the obtrusive beak, from which protruded great black hairy bushes long enough to reach his moustache and disguise the point from where they ended and the others began. His black eyes: tiny beads buried deep into his face—were surrounded by deep, cavernous facial cracks at the sides and below, and by thick, black, bushy eyebrows above. The man's facial features and eerie body gestures were so fierce and intimidating that a stage hand at the theatre could not have designed a more convincing costume for the evil villain playing in any penny production, and the crowd played right along as they hesitantly began to hiss and boo when he dared to glance their way.

As he tested each noose with a pull and a twist of his hands, his long, bony fingers manipulated the knots like the hands of a great skeleton in some macabre horror show.

Shashona was assisted to step up onto her chair.

"They don't try Indians" replied Little Raven.

"But this is wrong! I must stop it!" Ming jostled with Little Raven attempting to break her grip on his shirtsleeve as he turned to push his way through the crowd.

"You can't, you can't! They will kill you!" She tried to keep her voice to a whisper so as not to attract attention. She pulled him back to face her.

The hangman's hat was flat on the top with a wide brim all around and black to match every article of clothing on his tall, lanky body. His long, black hair was neatly pulled together with a leather string and fell in a narrow queue running ten to twelve inches down the centre of his coat at the back. The only inconsistency in the uniform blackness of his overall appearance was the bony whiteness of his hands and a vertical silver streak of hair that cut the sinewy strands of the black tail reaching down his upper back into a black and white-striped flag resembling the rear end of a skunk.

He did not speak, and now deliberately refused to make eye contact with any member of his critical audience for fear of inciting more cat calls. He did not refer to Ogden or to Armstrong, the new Sheriff, for any encouragement or acknowledgement in terms of the correctness of his duties.

Rising Sun stepped up onto the third chair.

Ming pushed forward but it was impossible to get any closer. The fascination of watching three Indians hang today was too great an attraction—no one would shift, for fear they would lose their spot.

"You can't stop them! You can't!" Little Raven tried to plead with Ming. "They will have their way. Don't give them an excuse to hang you too!"

"Hang me? Hang me? Why do they want to hang me? What have I done?" Ming's response was angry and incredulous. He couldn't understand Little Raven's threat. His questioning eyes stared soulfully into Lil's face, hungry for answers.

"Because you are Potawatomi; because you stay at the camp— you mix medicines with the Indians—because you were ordered out like all the Indians and did not leave."

"This can't be happening; it's not possible!" Ming searched the scaffold for a clue. He was looking for a mistake. He watched Ogden standing to the side reading the charges in silence to himself. He watched a Deputy checking the bracelets which bound their hands securely from behind. He followed the bony fingers of the hangman as he reached up and pulled the noose down over each head and wrenched it tight to their necks; each in turn.

He couldn't find the mistake. He didn't know what words to yell out in defiance that would freeze every player on the stage above, eclipsing the tragedy about to unfold and forcing their exit from the platform of death.

Above him he watched helplessly at the three women that, with Little Raven, represented the only family he ever knew.

They stood timidly on their chairs; their clothes: tattered rags, compared to the fancy fashions of the Chicagoans at their feet. Shashona's head bowed low, her hair hanging down; she was crying as her shoulders were rising and lowering in jerky fashion with each sob.

She would not look up or make a sound to challenge her accusers. Nootkana was visibly shaking uncontrollably, her knees weak—the Sheriff was watching her closely, concerned that she might fall from her capricious position prematurely, beginning the proceedings before the appointed signal. Her head as well, hung low, seeking no mercy from the men on the deck, nor sympathy from the curious crowd at her feet.

Contrary to the others, Rising Sun stood tall and straight—as proud as her spindly, narrow shape could manage. Her face was raised to the sun; her eyes searching the horizon over the heads of the leering onlookers. She was calm and resolute. Her spirit was already wandering over the prairie grasses. She was communicating with the spirits of her Potawatomi ancestors. She began to chant—an Indian death song—low and solemn. It wasn't for the sake of the people watching—it was for the spirits that were waiting for her—that would welcome her to her new home.

The hangman approached each woman; at this point he would usually place a black hood over the head of the prisoner, but there would be no hoods for Indians. He pulled each rope tight to their necks.

The features on Ming's face became stiff and firm; his eyes glassy. He bit down hard and ground his teeth together—the muscles on the sides of his cheeks stood out hard in square lumps on his face, with each press of his jaw. He turned to watch.

The Chicagoans would witness something very unusual today. The scaffolding had trap doors built into the deck that were hinged and designed to release below the feet of the prisoners with the simple pull of a lever. The ropes would hang slack until the drop, then snap tight at their full extension—the distance cleverly calculated by the hangman—thus breaking the necks of the prisoner and hopefully, humanely, offering a quick instant death; no choking. The dead bodies would hang below behind a drape—hidden from view. Typically, boys would run to the drape with curious abandonment and pull it across exposing the morbid sight to the crowd—girls would scream at their delight, women would faint, glorious wonderment would seal the final act; the deputies would chase them all away—the execution becoming a carnival side-show. The satisfying event would be relayed over and over again in the saloon at the lumber yard and at church on Sunday.

The chairs on the deck of the platform and the three Indian women standing upon them, shaking, the chair legs wobbling; woeful faces and stringy hair hanging low, no black hoods to render dignity—this was not typical. The trap doors were still broken from the last hanging and there was no time for repairs—this side-show would offer a sight so extremely gruesome, few would dare to speak of it in church, few would ever forget.

Little Raven took both hands and wrapped them around Ming's arm and laid her face into his shoulder. She was weeping: soft, soulful breaths—her tears soaking into his shirt. It was her only family as well, and it was dissolving before her eyes in an unbelievable scene of horror and pain.

Ming's blood turned to stone—he was frozen in place; looking up—the sight was at times barely visible through the curtain of water saturating his eyes, the tears pouring in relentless streams down his face. Nootkana's shaking was a continuous pulsating jerking—she could barely balance on the chair; her knees were wobbling, the crowd prepared for her to fall forward. Urine trickled down below her dress sliding down the inside of her leg catching on her moccasin and flowing to the deck. Her head shook with each wailing cry.

The evil man in black had maintained a patient steady stance behind Nootkana—finally receiving a subtle nod from Ogden, he raised his boot, then drove a deliberate hard kick to the rear leg of the chair—it slipped forward; Nootkana lost her balance and fell back; she began to swing. He kicked the chair again, Nootkana was fully released; the rope tightening around her neck, choking, squeezing. She squirmed and twisted fighting for air—kicking her legs in sporadic abandon. Little Raven screamed. Loud gasps ruffled throughout the audience; some ladies fell into the arms of bystanders, appearing faint. Ming released a throaty yell.

Frank Ogden felt the momentary anxious pull of compassion, although remaining transfixed at the abhorrent spectacle, his leg released a reflexive twinge—a jerk—as if perhaps he was about to move with an autonomic motion towards the struggling woman, without thinking, without conscious decision—his body alone, separate from his brain, was about to engage in rescuing the poor victim as she struggled for air, as she fought for her life. He pressed down hard in his boots, he squeezed his fists tightly, he checked his balance and recovered. Glancing right to the crowd, apprehensive about their scrutiny should they see his flinching, he regained composure. Ogden had witnessed many hangings, but the bodies had swayed below the deck out of sight, black hoods had shielded the grotesque tortured faces and muffled the desperate pleas of life's remaining moments.

Ming cried aloud, "No!" Lil continued to press her face into Ming's shoulder as the hangman moved to Shashona's chair. Again with a forceful kick Shashona's stance was awkwardly discharged and she twisted around losing balance. Another kick and the chair fell forward—she began to swing freely, the space about her filling with flailing legs and jerking spasms as her body fought for life—a desperate death dance wrapped in futility. The rope turned her neck upward, her face tightened, her mouth stretched wide, her tongue protruding —the slit between her lips sucking and gaging, desperate for air, without success. Urine flowed down her legs and puddled on the deck near the edge; the crowd shifted back. The spasms slowed, but the swing continued…gently, back and forth and a bit sideways.

Ming looked away having seen enough, but then he slowly returned his gaze—it became a glaring stare directly into Ogden's face. The hatred was building along with a plan. He envisioned a moment after the crowd dispersed where he would attack Ogden, bring him down and stab him repeatedly with his knife, over and over until the street ran red with his stinking blood. He could feel his body inching closer and closer to the platform—he would try to reach around to grab his knife.

Rising Sun stood patiently upon the last chair; the crowd remained quiet—the dead bodies drifted lazily above them—the tension in the rope squeaking tight with each extension upon the wooden beam high above their heads. The tall man in black lifted his boot and with one hard kick the chair under Rising Sun's feet tumbled over; the roped stretched—she dropped, and without a struggle her limp body began to drift with the others. Little Raven felt the tension in Ming's shoulders; she raised her head just enough to see the horrible sight—then together they turned and followed a path through the slow exodus: the sombre shuffle of a hundred boots in the street inched their way to the boardwalk. The sun was dipping lower behind the scaffolding; three black silhouettes remained alone, silently cutting a row of dark vertical slits into Chicago's skyline; the breeze gently playing with the tattered fabric of their skirts—the halting image slicing the horizon like a trio of vicious claw marks against a pale sky. Some patrons chose to turn for one last look as they arrived on the boardwalk in front of the saloon, others cleared the streets. Arm in arm the women walked with bowed heads home to more familiar surroundings, to a place of solace, to a place free of guilt.

A Deputy moved forward, a knife blade gleaming in his hand—the ropes were cut, the bodies dropped to the deck like sacks of potatoes, with a muffled thump; any semblance of humanity had long since left—a limp pile of soiled clothes remained. Frank Ogden raced down the steps and scurried to his office across the street in the courthouse, his eyes never leaving the contours of the ruts at his feet. He had finished with the scene; he was visibly shaken. The hangman and Armstrong quickly followed leaving two Deputies to carry away the bodies.

Lil could feel Ming's tug as he attempted to twist away from her grip on his arm. She knew his intentions. "No, you cannot. It's over!"

"It will never be over; I will kill him now!" Ming pulled hard to free himself from Little Raven's grip, but she remained adamant.

"Come with me now, I have much to tell you; you must come, they will kill you." She felt Ming begin to relax a little. He stopped, turned, facing her. He held her arms in his fists and stared into her eyes.

"What do you have to tell me? What do you know?" Ming was angry and impatient; he was on the edge, he was ready to kill; not a fraction of tolerance remained, holding him back was unthinkable—he wanted to feel the handle of his knife in his hand, he wanted to feel Ogden squirm at the end of his blade. He dared Lil to stop him. His eyes focused tight and slashed right and left across her face searching for a reason.

Frank Ogden entered his office and slammed the door behind him; a great hulking black figure sat at his desk. "A fine job, Frank."

Charles Smithson sat back in the chair precariously balancing on two rear legs, the shadows of the dark room hiding his face, the heels of his huge boots, crossed one over the other, were barely secured on the edge of the desk; the shit-encrusted soles pointed directly into Ogden's face.

"It was disgusting."

"Nonsense, it was beautiful."

"Get your boots off my desk." Smithson slowly, reluctantly, complied rocking forward landing square, placing his hands on the desk—his face came into the light, it was unusually jovial.

"You're getting soft Frank. They were Indians."

"What do you want?" Ogden could think of nothing worse at this time then to begin fencing with Smithson.

"I know you will be cleaning out that Indian encampment now that this business is finished. I want to remind you to leave the girl alone, she's not to be touched, I will deal with her in my own time." His words were direct, not commanding, but Ogden knew when Smithson's suggestions carried a parcel of threat.

"What do you care about an Indian?"

"And there's a boy there, one of their bastards. He's been working for O'Brien. I don't care what you do with him, just don't touch the girl."

"Get out." Smithson rose giving Ogden a slight jolt at his shoulder when passing just to reinforce his order.

"We'll talk later Frank, after those stinking bodies are in the ground."

Overwhelmed by a sense of urgency, Little Raven pulled Ming through the lingering crowds determined to reach the campsite before more trouble followed from the Sheriff's men. Ming remained stubborn and returned her unrelenting demands with jerks and

shakes of his hand and arm, until finally he broke free; they stopped—
facing each other at the entrance to the stockyards. Little Raven's face
was awash with tears, her hair dripping in sweat, she was breathing
rapidly, her stance was firm but her expression was weak—her eyes
were pleading to Ming for his acquiescence—she reached out to him
with both hands together. Ming stood before her, adamant, hands
on his hips, his chest rapidly rising and falling with each breath, he
was not a child to be dragged, to be disciplined for misbehaviour.
Confusion spiralled around his head: the horrific vision of his dead
family—a deep wound freshly cut; Little Raven's erratic behaviour
savagely compounding his anxiety; his knife blade and violent
thoughts of revenge still keenly balanced on the forefront of his consciousness. "What are you doing?"

"Please Ming, follow me home. I will explain everything, you
must trust me." For a moment Ming lifted his eyes to a place far away,
south, and then beyond. He relented; Ogden could wait.

They turned together and walked the rest of the way, in silence.
They found the little camp the same as they had left it: a sad series of
broken tents, a forsaken refuse at the edge of the stockyards, humble,
dishevelled...vulnerable. The pony, tethered to a broken post, raised
her head in a muffled whinny when she saw them; the chickens
scurried and ran in every direction. But something *was* different.
Ming entered the big kitchen tent. The utensils placed upon the table
were displayed in no particular order, the roots and dried meat hung
on the ceiling poles above, no different than any other day. A warm
wind blew through a slit in the hides—Ming raised his face to the
sharp line of dipping sunlight that pierced the flapping tear—the
white shard danced upon the wooden table at his knee changing its
fickle pattern with each flip of the fabric. The thought of repairing
another cursed rip crossed his mind, then vanished in a flash. The

tent was empty. They were alone. "Why didn't they hang you? Why did they let you go?"

Little Raven gathered her thoughts and her courage. "They arrested us and I was dragged to the jail with the others, but Smithson was there, and he told the Sheriff to release me. He wouldn't allow them to hurt me."

"But why?" Ming stared into Lil's eyes trying to understand, and then she looked down, she couldn't say the words while looking into his eyes.

"Because…he is my father." The words cut though Ming and he froze, he slumped to the table and sat before he fell.

"What?" His response was quiet, a whisper, he wasn't sure if he understood what he had heard, yet it was plain and clear.

"I am a half-breed. Shashona was my mother, Charles Smithson is…my father." She continued whipping the words out in rapid order; perhaps they wouldn't hurt as much if she spoke fast. "For now, he wants me alive. I might be the only family he has left, and perhaps that gives him some sense of ownership, I don't know. But all Indians were to be moved south and Ogden has his orders. That means they will arrest you or expel you. They think you are Potawatomi; you will never be safe here."

Ming listened intently, then his brow curled and he composed his thoughts. "Look at me Lil." Little Raven raised her eyes slowly, she knew the question before it was asked.

"But I am Potawatomi."

"Smithson had another daughter, not a half-breed. He was married, his wife was Kate, she was White. His daughter was Margaret, my half-sister. She had a child, a White child…you, Ming. You are not Potawatomi, you are Whiteman." Little Raven might well have reached into her quiver and pulled out an arrow, placed it in her bow and released it directly into Ming's heart—there would have been no difference. Ming remained on the table, frozen in shock.

"Smithson...is..."

"Charles Smithson is your grandfather." You must pack everything now, everything you need and you must leave Mingaswen, there is no other way. You are not safe here." Little Raven tried desperately to divert from the issue, continuing to plead with Ming, but he remained firm on the table as if impaled to the spot. His mind continued to spin.

"You are not my sister?"

"I am your Aunt. But that doesn't matter Ming. Gather your things, you can take the pony, leave now before the Sheriff's men arrive. They will destroy this camp." Ming was not concerned, he was listening to her words as they echoed over and over again within the churning folds of his mind, *Charles Smithson is your grandfather, your grandfather, your grandfather.*

"Charles Smithson is not my grandfather; you cannot be right." Ming was unable to believe her words, he was not ready to accept her confession. "I will kill them both, Ogden and Smithson. I will be back shortly." Ming rose to leave, Little Raven grabbed his arm and swung him around.

"Oh you are so brave, you are so right, such a killer! Go then, kill them all! That's what you are, a murderer. You killed a cowboy with your knife, now you will kill everybody that gets in your way. What a brave man, what a Potawatomi brave! You will not live to see another sunrise; you will die like the rest of your family. You will swing high above the people by a rope on the platform; the great Indian brave. You are a fool, and I am tired of discussing it. I am finished. Go and die! The rest of us are all dead. You go and die!"

Ming stood at the opening of the tent facing south, the sky on the horizon to his right in the west was blazing with sheets of red and orange, clouds above were stretched in thin bright bands, the lines reaching across without beginning or end: ribbons of gold, fuchsia and violet folding and slipping—the patterns ever-changing, the colour palette first diluted, then rich and full, only to fade again; the final composition: an eternal mystery. He stood tall, obdurate—a lone sentry carefully scanning his post—squeezing his knife tightly in his fist, staring to the west, facing a destiny; torrents of confusing questions flooding and clouding his mind. Lil slowly advanced and caressed his arm with her hands together pulling him to her, cautiously attempting consolation; she said nothing. He remained vigilant, searching...searching.

Bill Armstrong was tall and slim, his legs were skinny and crooked, a new Sheriff—he took his orders as much from Smithson as he did from Ogden—he had no reservation about hanging Indians or destroying their camp. Identified by a faint limp in his right leg, the results of an encounter with a wagon and a team of horses while in Smithson's employ, his current position easily secured by acclimation—no one dared question Smithson's directive—Armstrong had a reputation of getting the job done. A man possessing few cordial attributes: cruel, belligerent—but also obedient when he felt so motivated (the trait most appreciated by Smithson)—he was never ambitious. The task, tedious and bothersome at best, would be carried out by his Deputies. Armstrong was more concerned with the shine on his boots, the cut of his clothes—tight and dark—and the cocky angle of his hat dipping low on his forehead, when the ladies strolled by. A short visit to Ogden's saloon would be followed by a rousing display of immaturity, reckless abandonment and stupidity as three inebriated Deputies would ride down to destroy the Potawatomi encampment and burn it to the ground. Armstrong would stay behind and reap the accolades from Smithson when the job was finished.

Pat O'Brien was a member of that sombre collective that had only moments ago experienced a vile and torturous public execution—he too walked away in silence, lost in thought, confused and disheartened, unsure of the part he played in the macabre display. He did not return to the slaughter sheds; he turned and followed the back alleys, swung through narrow back streets, shuffled through shadowed cloisters in Chicago's reclusive darker neighbourhoods. He was attempting to wash off the shame, but it remained stuck to him like slimy old grease congealed in the bottom corners of a frying pan after the pork was long gone. He remained enshrouded in the sticky residue when he finally found the courage to enter his home to face his incriminating wife, the only person who had warned him not to go, not to join the pathetic assemblage of wicked sensationalists, and not to bring the experience home with him—and yet here he was. With only a few short words Siobhan O'Brien managed to add without hesitation, a thicker layer to the already burdensome glutinous cloak weighing heavily on her husband's shoulders. "Well, did you enjoy it?" Stepping around her, head hanging low on his chest, O'Brien drifted through the kitchen to the parlour; he slumped in his chair. He did not respond, there were no words available to justify his actions or what he had witnessed. "Did they hang the boy too?" Mrs. O'Brien wiped her hands on her apron, standing at the archway into the parlour, she was prepared for disastrous news of Mick.

"No." O'Brien continued staring blindly into the cold ashes of the fireplace, there seemed to be no strength in his body; to raise his head would have taken the strong muscles of integrity which had all but dissolved.

"Thank God; and Little Raven?"

"No, she was not there. They hung three, it was an immoral display, a…mistake." O'Brien bent forward and dropped his face into his hands; he wept.

Mrs. O'Brien approached her husband, with a mild touch to his bowed head—a series of tender caresses—she spoke softly, "They will find them and kill them."

"I know."

Ming turned to Little Raven, relaxing the grip around the handle of his knife, "Where would we go?" Still confused and overwhelmed, Ming, relenting, was ready to listen. He replaced the knife and secured it in its sheath on his back under his shirt.

"Come in and sit down, I will help you gather some things."

A few bottles of medicine, laudanum, camphor, herbal remedies, Rising Sun's amputation knives, some dried meat, an extra shirt, a pan for cooking, flint and small snares for trapping, a blanket—they shoved everything into a leather bag. Lil handed Ming a pouch, it jingled—all the money she had saved from his wages, soap and medicine sales—she offered to him. "You will need this."

Ming threw a blanket on Nektoshe, then secured the leather bag to a rope tied to the pony's neck. Together they rode out to the sycamore—not a glance to the rear. The soft grass around the base of the great tree had always been their special place, and now for the last time they sat together.

"Listen to me Ming, I have much to tell you." The sun was setting, a soft pink glow reflected on Lil's face, the breeze from the west was warm, cicadas buzzed high in the branches; time was running short, Little Raven spoke clearly, her words were precise, she was careful and sensitive. Ming wondered how everything seemed the same: the sky, the prairie grass, quietly sitting with Lil under the tree; Shashona might call for supper. Little Raven spoke of his mother Margaret and his Father Robert, of his violent birth and his mother's remorseful death, of his grandmother Kate and Smithson. "This is sacred ground Ming; your mother is buried here. Look." Little Raven began to dig under a rock; the rock was hidden under the grass; Ming knew it well.

Three of Armstrong's Deputies diligent in their quest for liquor, where now embarking on another; the order was to finish the job tonight; they rode south through the stockyards searching for a small cluster of animal-hide tents they had only heard about.

As if O'Brien and his wife composed a solution together, without a word spoken, they now stood together in the parlour and held out their hands to each other, touching and nodding. Pat O'Brien dashed out into the evening, he would bring them home, there was no other choice.

The stockyard corrals had turned into a labyrinth, so many turns and blind alleys, the Deputies returned to the north-end more than once without finding their prize. They whipped their horses around and started again. The urgency of their deviant task seemed to be diminishing in equal amounts with the rapid elimination of the amber liquid left in their bottles; but miraculously, as the pace of the horses slowed from a trot to a shuffle, the end of the puzzle appeared, the open fields emerged—steering their horses along the fence line they spotted their miserable reward.

Little Raven gently pulled something from under the rock and carefully brushed away the dirt; she held the little leather pouch up to Ming's face. Ming raised up on his knees bending in close to view the tiny item Little Raven held with such delicacy. Pulling on the draw string, the opening spread just wide enough for her fingers to reach inside; she pulled out the ring. "This was your mother's. It was to be her wedding ring." She described the Irish design and what it meant; Ming held it close to his eyes turning it over and over. She reached in again and withdrew the thin silver chain, the heart-shaped locket swung freely, she caught it and gently pried it open. Ming's eyes widened as Lil explained about the two faded images: his father and his mother. He thought they looked so young and so beautiful. "These are your parents. Your name is Francis Tumblety." The sun's radiance was soft and weak in the last moments of sunset. Francis turned the locket towards the fading light, straining to gain every chance of recognition.

"Francis?"

O'Brien raced to the stockyards, carefully retaining strong footholds, cutting sharply around the corrals, dodging between shadows and broken boards, watching and listening for the Sheriff's men, praying he might arrive in time.

Hoops and hollering broke the evening's stillness, crackling sparks and shooting flames reached high into the darkness; flimsy animal skins and spindly tent poles quickly succumbed to the slashing flames. The horses reared and whinnied protesting the cruel tugs and twists on their bits, the cutting spur slices to their flanks. Lil and Francis turned, rising up to see the final, fateful moments of their home disappearing, dissolving into the night air—a whiff of smoke, a flickering ember, dusty clouds kicked up by scattering hooves—a forgotten patch of dirt swallowed and buried within the shallow creases of a sorrowful thought.

O'Brien stood transfixed by the scene, hiding behind a corner post at the edge of the corral; he was too late. The horses rode past him as he slid down adjacent to the lowest board dipping out of sight; the riders, barely acknowledging each others's presence, gave no notice of O'Brien, sauntered past throwing their bottles behind, smashing them in the dust and ashes.

Lil faced Francis with pleading eyes, "You must go Ming!"

It seemed as though within the matter of a few desperate minutes Francis had lost his family and home, had become the sole patriarch of what remained, as well as instantly transforming into a Whiteman whose embarrassing name was Francis Tumblety. He was being forced into immediate exile, was desperate to save his sister who was now his aunt, and was consumed by the overwhelming desire to kill his grandfather, as well as the town's mayor. The fragile grip of Lil's hand on his arm and the pathetic, eager reflection on her face offered no resolve. "What should I do?"

"East, travel east as far as you can go. Don't look back. Return when you can. Get as far away as possible."

"What about you Lil? Won't you come with me? You can't stay here. It's not safe. We will go together." Francis held the little leather pouch tight in his hand searching Little Raven's face for direction.

"No. He will not hurt me. A Whiteman travelling alone has a better chance than an Indian. I will be safe. You must go, they will be looking for you." Little Raven pushed Francis toward the pony and beckoned him to mount. Not convinced Francis sat upon Nektoshe considering the night and the east. He could ride out and return at anytime. There was no need to panic; no need to solve all these concerns in one night. There would be time.

"I will return." Francis pulled the pony hard and rode away. Continuing to plead with Lil was futile and he was tired of it. He was confused and angry. The pungent odours rising from the remains of his home caught in his nostrils; he curled his nose; he gritted his teeth. The sun's final signature split the eastern sky into thin grey strips that frayed and spread wide across the horizon; his head remained forward, his chin high and defiant. Francis disappeared into the night. Little Raven left the soft grass beneath the dipping branches of the sycamore tree; her heart heavy—a mournful sigh quietly easing from her chest—she instinctively followed a well-worn path home.

A dark silhouette stood beside the overturned iron caldron; a final slim line of silky residue spiking up from beneath its lip, the few embers below valiantly attempting to survive. He stood alone staring out to the prairie watching Little Raven approach. "I am Pat O'Brien, where is Mick?"

"I know who you are. He is gone."

23

The ideological and business gaps separating Ogden and Smithson—although initially there were very few—began to widen over time, extending beyond cordial accommodating spaces and familiar tolerances, growing into trenches and eventually chasms and finally canyons. Similarly the original ties that drew them together—so strong and grandiose at one time, as they dreamed of Fort Deerborn's future—loosened then drooped, frayed, tore and finally dissolved. Frank Ogden could never come to terms over the failed investigation involving Tumblety's death or the confusing circumstances surrounding Kate's 'illness'; and although it was his duty and responsibility by law to round up and arrest any Indians that did not comply with relocation orders, he did not sanction the execution of the Potawatomi women without a proper trial—Smithson wanted them dead and they would have been killed one way or the other, he made that very clear. The guilt weighing heavily on his mind was not so much the death of the Indians as much as his failure to thwart Smithson's power over him, and the associated injustice; and that distinction also caused him tremendous grief. He concluded that he quite possibly was not the righteous man he thought he was after all, and therefore he relinquished his position as Mayor not long after the execution. There was also the possibility that if Ogden stayed in Chicago more than another few days, it was very likely that he might shoot Charles Smithson, as he had considered this on more than one occasion. Some say he wandered north into Rupert's Land above Superior; perhaps he was killed by Hurons or mauled by a bear. Others say he travelled south and eventually found solace trapping in the Utah territory. Some say Ogden, Utah—the town near where he resided and trapped— actually received its name from him, awarded by the locals who came to admire him, for whatever reasons.

Charles Smithson, on the other hand would excel far beyond his own expectations and eclipse all previous enterprising endeavours. He bought the hotel and saloon from Ogden; he ventured into railroads and shipping on the Great Lakes; redeveloped and amal- gamated the stockyards—eliminating the labyrinth-style jumble of many small ventures in the swamps into one large well organized grid work of efficient production—and became a prime stakeholder. His reputation as a cruel and seditious taskmaster was never in doubt however—public whippings and hangings increased—he maintained his tight grip on the Sheriff's office and the courts. Chicago was growing and developing at great speed as investors and their money were readily welcomed at Smithson's request and encouragement.

Charles Smithson was well aware of Pat O'Brien's generosity and his wife's reputation for charity. Little Raven was seen accompany- ing Mrs. O'Brien into town on a few occasions, and he was satisfied for now knowing his daughter was safe and resided in a comfortable home. In time he would deal with her in his own way. Whatever his plans might be, she could not refuse him, no one could refuse him. There was no sign or mention of the little Indian boy that lived at the Potawatomi encampment, and when asked, O'Brien told Smithson that he had probably run away after the hanging. Smithson gave it no more consideration.

Mrs. Myra Johnson was accompanied by her husband and a very large contingent from her church three days after the hanging. They laid Eunice in a plot in the very beautiful cemetery of the Chicago First Baptist Church. Frank Ogden was present—it would be the last social commitment in his capacity as Mayor. Although Ogden was very conscientious about maintaining a very low profile—bowing his head deep into his chest, staring at his silver tips, holding his best Sunday hat in his hands—there was a brief moment of eye contact as they raised their heads together. Mrs. Johnson glanced in his direction with watery eyes, her handkerchief held close to her face. Frank Ogden returned the glance for less than a minute. The message relayed by the sorrowful expression was no longer filled with hate or vengeance. Ogden wondered if Mrs. Johnson now realized that the deaths of three Potawatomi Indian women from the swamps could not return her daughter. He wondered if it crossed her mind.

North, across the river, three bodies were dropped into an unmarked hole near the graves of drifters and criminals, in close proximity to where Ogden had ordered Tumblety's body to be buried so many years before. Although no margins outlining the gravesite were delineated in any way, by a fence or rocks or wooden pegs, Armstrong's men knew to dig the hole far from the other plots; they were not to be inclusive or even adjacent; no marker. They were Indians.

PART 3

Kingston, Rochester, Boston
1847-1854

24

*T*here was no doubt in his mind, he was a man. He had committed murder with his bare hands when he was just a child, slicing him to bits with a knife; he had lifted and carried his share of animal entrails day after day through snow and bitter cold winds bringing home money to feed his family without complaint or remorse; he could hunt and trap, feed himself, identify any berry, track any animal; he could read any book, Dickens or the Bible (especially Corinthians), discuss politics, repair a wagon wheel, add sums and correctly weigh any amount of seed or flour. He could perform an abortion, supervise a birth or amputate a limb, stay a fever. There was a confidence about Francis—there was never any concern about surviving alone away from Chicago, even as he began to enter strange country—yet his preoccupation with vengeance settled somewhere inside like a dormant nettle ready to sting if he twisted or tensed up, those men coming to mind—threatening to obscure his focus; he needed to remain sharp, wary that his path might be plagued with uncertainty and treachery—he could trust nobody. He wondered about Whitemen and how he might compare. There were few Whitemen he respected—Mr. Morrison and Pat O'Brien—but scanning his brain for others left him blank. Whitemen were crippled; they were rude, stupid, drunk most of the time, cruel to their animals, they rarely had anything interesting to say, appreciated nothing other than stupid screechy music from the saloon and watching people hang from ropes in the centre of town. They were always leering at girls and grabbing their dresses; they would rape anything with an open hole: woman or boy without a second thought. Lil said he would be a murderer, but the killing of Smithson and Ogden to him seemed justified; they were meant to die—and he would see to it. Sneaking back, skulking through Chicago streets, a blade ready in his hand, striking them down in the dark—that was murderous. Stirring the fire at his feet, his thoughts gathering, plans developing, he envisioned facing them directly perhaps, confronting them—*would that be Whiteman's way?* The ring and necklace slipped about between his fingers and rested in the palms of his hand. He viewed the faces over and over. He thought he could never be called 'Francis'.

Francis had ridden his pony through bush land south of the main road that followed a route east to Upper Canada. In thirty days he arrived at a horse-drawn ferry; he paid ten cents to cross from Detroit to Sandwich on the British side. Nektoshe couldn't suffer more than ten miles a day; her pace was slow but steady; Francis gave her some days off to refresh—riding was such a luxury, continuing on foot would be a sad alternative. The well-worn trail to Detroit might invite inquisitive travellers to stop; he preferred to remain hidden, away from Smithson's employees who might be on route to Boston.

Rock cuts were blasted and bridges were built; the beds for rail ties were laid adjacent to the trail daily; but the railroad to Detroit would not be completed for another five years—the route was busy. Francis stayed clear of the workers shacks; listened and watched for men in the bushes shirking duties or taking a crap.

Francis watched for Redcoats. The war between Britain and America was over but the resentment lingered; British soldiers lined The King's Highway from Sandwich to Kingston along the northern shores of Lake Erie and Lake Ontario. All Americans were considered spies, and they were being arrested and hanged. Strong fortifications and garrisons maintained full regiments of infantry and artillery along the entire route prepared to repel any American invasion from the south. Many settlements maintained a militia unit; all residents were suspicious of strangers—Francis stayed off the highway.

The weather was intensely humid that summer—walls of saturated lush green foliage, a tunnel surrounding him as if submerged in a blanket soaked in hungry vegetation, grabbing and pulling—the sticky sweat dripping from his head and face never seemed to stop running. Branches from poplar, maple and birch trees hung low in the bush wiping their broad leaves against Nektoshe's neck and flanks—Francis reached out with both hands repelling the branches in every direction fencing with the long blades as they whipped and stabbed; cicadas buzzed their incessant shrill sirens above, anxious squirrels scattered about on the forest floor, contented fat bullfrogs sang a continuous throaty drone in the soggy shallows. Francis and Nektoshe laboured through dense patches and a scant few open pastures with the ever-present welcoming cool breezes drifting north across from the great lake on their right. The black flies dug in deep under his skin leaving his face at times a red mask of blood as he smacked and swatted the annoying insects day in and day out. His arms and neck were swollen and itchy with red lumps, the inevitable response to swarms of blood-sucking mosquitoes. At night the clouds would billow and fold creating huge great anvils of dense wet air; massive volumes of thunder rumbled and clashed, great spears of lightning flashed, lighting the sky for hundreds of miles. The torrent of rain impeded any further movement through the forest and he halted; raising his face to the storm's powerful tyranny, the blasting fresh water washed his face, repelled the mosquitoes; he felt relieved, refreshed. There would be no fire tonight.

Mile after mile of dense forest, day after day of choking humid air, thousands of insects, thin meagre squirrel meat for supper—so careful, so cautious not to be seen, not to arouse suspicion, to continue east, always east, following the great shoreline—until one night.

25

The potatoes were rotten, the people were starving, the government had abandoned them—there was no hope. Over one million Irish emigrants sailed to Canada in the summer of 1847 landing at Grosse Isle in the St. Lawrence River in Quebec, Lower Canada. Many died on board during the journey, their vessels termed 'coffin ships'; many died upon arrival—five thousand perished on Grosse Isle alone due to fever, famine and other related illnesses. When the facilities in Quebec became overcrowded, the disease-infected, starving Irish were sent up the St. Lawrence River to Kingston to die. Millions of Irish emigrated to the United States, to Boston, New York, Philadelphia and Baltimore; still millions of others arrived in London and settled particularly, in Whitechapel—the plight they were so desperate to flee from only intensifying.

The chest wasn't big: probably two feet long and eighteen inches deep; wooden with worn leather straps. It's numerous scrapes and scratches revealed a history—one of lengthy trips, long voyages and the associated stresses of being lifted, thrown, dragged and stored for many years—from its European origins no doubt, finally to Emmitsburg, Maryland where it now resided and sat empty in the centre of Sister Hieronymo's room. Although the trip would be long and tedious, and scores of necessary provisions would accompany the Sisters on their trek, this particular chest alone would hold their only allotment of personal items. Inside two thin vertical wooden sleeves separated the trunk into three distinct sections—one for each patron; one small compartment for each Sister: a tiny piece of privacy, of ownership; the contents within identifying the scant composition of items laying carefully and neatly arranged and stacked, of the individual to whom they belonged. These sole possessions of the three Sisters from Maryland of the Catholic Convent of the Daughters of Charity equalled the slimmest requisite, as all their earthly items were relinquished when they vowed to become Brides of Jesus in a Holy Alliance.

Sister Hieronymo without hesitation was answering a request from Rochester, New York. A new hospital—St. Mary's—required her expertise as nurse and supervisor. Construction was under way, and with an experienced nursing staff the hospital could begin receiving patients.

Joining her were Sister Martha and Sister Felicia; young but fully qualified. They arrived and quietly deposited their belongings in the section designated to them. Undergarments, soap and rosaries, a bible and writing paper, perhaps a family picture and a scarf for winter weather. Sister Hieronymo added scalpels, camphor, bandages and laudanum as well as a few other bottles of medicine: iodine and liniments and extract of willow bark.

The journey would include a fifty mile coach trip across wooded land north east to Harrisburg in Pennsylvania; followed by a long river boat voyage on the Susquehanna River against the current to Williamsport—a 250 mile trip on a relatively smooth course. The final leg of the trip would be the longest and most difficult: Williamsport overland to Rochester, approximately 260 miles through dense forest, deep valleys and swampy bogs—at an average of 50 miles a day the final section would take 5 to 6 days—if they were lucky. The Sisters, if not of a hardy disposition initially, would learn to adapt or die trying—the trip would indeed be a challenge for anyone.

Upon arrival in early July their story relayed to Father Bernard O'Reilly included escapades involving attacking Iroquois Indians who stole a pair of horses, bandits who confiscated a watch and a ring from the drivers, (the Sisters had nothing of value to any bandit) a lost mail bag that flew off the boat on wild rapids on the Susquehanna, and drunken cowboys that shot up the carriage house in Mansfield while the Sisters were having supper in the new Mann's Hotel. They were, without question so very happy to have arrived safely.

Father O'Reilly was a jolly old sort—short, rotund and truly happy with a round soft face, adoring twinkling eyes, and although affable in every way, when he offered his full smile, his mouth stretching wide to the very limits of acceptable facial proportions, he immediately let his guests down. The few teeth remaining in his head were brown and totally rotten—the sight was ghastly and Sister Hieronymo was nearly knocked off balance, her own smile vanishing immediately upon receiving the vile expression. Father O'Reilly had not been following a serious dental regimen and he had paid for it—in the most extreme way. Initially she thought perhaps he was suffering with scurvy, as she had seen the raw symptoms of that grievous illness in Maryland—so many sailors arriving from long whaling voyages, their mouths ripped and bleeding, gums red and raw, terrible extensive infections in their mouths and throats—but that was due to barren supplies after the rapid consumption of fruits and vegetables on an over-extended voyage. Father O'Reilly was living in a lush, rich region of long hot summers and bountiful precipitation on the southern banks of Lake Ontario. The area was an Eden of fruit: blueberries, raspberries, plums, apples, peaches, and any assortment of every variety of vegetable anyone wanted to grow—it was a farmer's paradise. Sister Hieronymo always assiduous, had made her quick assessment: the good Father was indulging in copious quantities of wondrous varieties of food no doubt considering the proportions of his capacious waste line, however the institution of cleanliness and its sacred relationship to Godliness had been disregarded to the greatest extent—and the horrendous odour emanating from his mouth, the brown slime secreting from between the few lonely remaining stubs of enamel on his soft black gums was enough to knock any sea-hardy sailor to the deck. Furthermore, she thought correctly, that perhaps massive volumes of tobacco might also be a contributing factor in the gross deterioration of his oral health—smoking it or chewing it—it mattered not. She quickly backed up at the sight and smell, her sudden response nearly smashing the two Sisters behind to the floor. Sister Hieronymo was thoroughly unimpressed—she shot the good Father a powerful indignant glare; unconcerned, he adamantly retained his gapping empty, oral salutation, welcoming them whole-heartedly.

Father O'Reilly extended his hand and directed the Sisters into his parlour in the adjacent rectory house. They stepped cautiously over dirt piles, stones, pyramids of beautiful red brick and wheel-barrows of fresh mortar—the crew however delegated with the task of working with these building materials, was not anywhere within viewing distance, save for Dancy. Dancy, an old negro servant, and full-time resident of the rectory, bent and crippled, was ordered to pick up the trunk from the road and drag or carry it inside. Two other wooden boxes containing coal oil lamps, pots and pans, blankets and mostly kitchen utensils, were left. The Sisters gave him no considera-tion, and followed Father O'Reilly inside.

Beckoning the Sisters to sit at the large, elegant dining table in the grand salon, the hand-carved scrollwork flowing around the legs and trimming the edges of the imposing piece, impeccably cleaned and polished—these details not missed by Sister Hieronymo's scrupulous eye—Father O'Reilly's oratory, obviously well-prepared and finally ready to discharge now that the Sisters had thankfully arrived—was suddenly and somewhat violently interrupted, as sister Hieronymo vigorously raised her hand to his face in a curt gesture of arrest. "Where can we wash?"

Father O'Reilly jerked his neck back and withdrew his tongue into that slimy brown cavity with shock—he was not used to being inter-rupted; he stared at the Sister with bulging eyes and raised eyebrows. The Sisters stood in a solemn orderly line one beside the other facing the man, their black habits soiled in dirt and dust, their faces tightly squeezed all around by binding headgear caked with layers of trail residue and sweat. Sisters Felicia and Martha obviously exhausted and spent from their arduous journey, hung forward appearing ready to collapse, their drooping eyes pleading for respite; the question was decidedly appropriate. Father O'Reilly took a moment, dug down deep, sucked in a reasonable amount of air, then responded. "Yes." His jolly demeanour quickly returning, the error in his lack of social graces accepted, he led the dusty trio to the bathroom.

The rectory was beautiful; huge vaulted ceilings with shiny oak beams, tall arched windows encased exquisite stained glass panes depicting scenes of the Passion, imported rosewood furniture all about—tables, chairs, hutch and side table—every piece spotless, and dust-free, not a speck of dirt on the maple wooden floors, a testament to cleanliness and fastidiousness. It appeared the sacred pact was highly regarded in some respects after all. Father O'Reilly then approached the door to the bathroom located down a tiny hall behind the kitchen at the rear of the building. The doorframe creaked, dirt fell to the floor from the joints above as the belligerent door finally surrendered and opened; the Sisters peaked in. There was a large bathtub in the centre of the room and a window clouded with smudge of some kind on the far wall, but some light filtered through—enough to ascertain the number of visitors who had used the facilities within the last month or so: few to none—the details of the cleanliness pact appeared deceptively selective. Sister Hieronymo nudged the Sisters inside and made a final demand, "Bring buckets of hot water, three clean bedsheets and the trunk." She closed the door.

The Sisters washed the tub thoroughly, then themselves and finally their habits and undergarments. Dancy was ordered to draw a rope across two willow trees and hung their clothes out to dry; the Sisters wrapped the bedsheets about themselves, sat on the edge of the tub, enjoyed the fresh breeze blowing through the newly cleaned window and waited. Father O'Reilly also waited; he did not at any time assume to approach the bathroom or enquire in anyway about their progress or needs.

The evening meal served on a hand-embroidered linen cloth spread evenly upon the entire length of the huge dining table, arrived on silver plates, from the hands of Dancy, the ever-present humble servant, who now, estimated Sister Hieronymo, must be builder, grounds-keeper, cleaner, cook and waiter—but obviously did not over-extend his duties to include bathing. He offered the most

generous, mouth-watering, aroma-filled, joyous, sumptuous meal
anyone had every experienced, including, most of all, three travel-
weary Sisters, shiny and clean and very hungry, as they now were. A
massive roast turkey, potatoes, squash, turnips, fresh steaming bread
and hot slippery butter; grapes, cheese, apricots and apple pie. Bottles
of wine from the Father's private collection were lined up proudly
on the table, the glasses before the Sisters were shimmering lead
crystal—the sparkly vessels waiting patiently for the sweet nectar to
fill their yearning voids. Sister Hieronymo was not clairvoyant but
the fat jolly face and wide round waistline belonging to her accommodating host revealed an honest source that was becoming most clear.

The Sisters declined the wine but indulged in the meal with
great gusto and enthusiasm—albeit with the most decent margins of
decorum. Sisters Martha and Felicia stole side glances hoping to solve
the mystery of Father O'Reilly's eating technique—satisfied that it
was a system of mostly sucking and swallowing with a rare amount
of chewing, they struggled not to giggle. As the potatoes were passed
around again, Father O'Reilly began to initiate his oratory for the
second time, assuming his timing was more acceptable—the Sisters
washed, their stomachs filled. The fact was, St. Mary's Church was
in the final Stages of completion, and with continued perseverance
Christmas Mass would be held on time; the Hospital, however was a
very different case. St. Mary's Hospital was far from ready and in fact
the Sisters medical services would not be required for some time; they
were welcomed to visit for as long as they wished of course, however
Father O'Reilly had another suggestion to offer.

Boats filled with starving, sick Irish immigrants restricted
entrance in Montreal, were slowly being transported to Kingston in
Upper Canada. Sheds built along the harbour sequestered these poor
dying souls (men, women and children) with no hope. There were

few supplies, medicines, food or facilities to care for them. A request received from the Kingston Parish implored St. Mary's in Rochester to offer aid if at all possible, in any way possible. Father O'Reilly was ready with food and blankets; his request was then extended to Sister Hieronymo. Would it be possible for the good Sisters to travel a little bit further to Upper Canada to offer their services for the Irish famine victims suffering in Kingston?

Their first night in Rochester not yet concluded, supper barely finished, the wonderful amenities of the rectory warmly enveloped around their tired but slowly rebounding bodies—Sisters Martha and Felicia felt a heavy spiritual weight crash on their shoulders—the thought of leaving the comforts of upper-class accommodation, bountiful meals and limitless bathing, to begin another difficult sojourn across miles of open water to British landholdings in a foreign land, was unbearable. If, up until now, the Sisters retained a silent, stoic disposition—as if words escaping from their tiny lip-clenched mouths would be considered blasphemy—this question, casually disclosed from the good Father, left them comatose.

Sister Hieronymo, also caught off guard, hesitated, then finished stuffing a generous piece of apple pie into her protruding cheeks.

26

Finally, Francis could find enough dry wood for a fire; he settled down in a small clearing among tall birches, a clear brook nearby afforded water for Nektoshe and she drank heartily. The sun had set, the night was clear, a vast canopy of wispy leaves above tossed and brushed a soft melody of gentle whispers weaving in and out. Stars twinkled intermittently between the swishing leaves in the few open spaces above, smoke rose up twisting through the thick foliage searching for the open dark sky so out of reach.

The smoke would be a welcomed deterrent for the miserable mosquitoes, if even for just a few hours. Francis knew of many natural repellents for insects, especially mosquitoes, but the ingredients required weren't readily available. The best would be a mixture of garlic and crushed lavender, also sunflower oil and witch hazel would perform well, thyme oil would also suffice. Apple cider vinegar rubbed on his arms and neck would take away the itch, but mud would have to do. He scooped up damp dirt from the edges of the brook and mixed it with clover and grass to give it strength. He washed the sweat and blood from his face then applied it—face, neck and arms. He took a moment to wash Nektoshe's eyes, wiping away the crusty dead bugs gathered there. Within the moist, cool soil by the brook Francis dugout the roots of trillium flowers, storing them in his bag; ground up and dried they would yield antiseptic qualities always considered beneficial. He then withdrew his extra shirt and decided tomorrow he would pull it over his head, cutting slits for visibility, therefore most vulnerable areas would be protected. The bandana he had been using did not sit firm in his face, it slipped down continually due to the sweat. He would have to devise a way to keep his shirt sleeves wrapped tight around his arms, even as the tree branches viciously attacked them with incessant consistency.

Supper was dried squirrel meat from a previous catch, a few raspberries and mushroom caps. Francis listened carefully to the woods as he pried open the locket, the faces of his parents always granted a special moment of introspection—*who were they? Who am I?*

Although the night offered a time of serenity and contemplation, the tiny camp levelled out between fallen trunks, tall birches, wavy slim grass shoots and golden rod deep within the shadows of the dark forest far from the King's Highway, it was anything but silent. Francis often took this time however to linger between the sounds of the forest and the voices in his head, always vigilant of a sound that might not belong—he could not afford to miss the stealth of a predator, be it animal or human. The crickets and frogs played a continuous chorus of chirps and bellows coalescing into a great harmonious drone—a covert blanket, turning the immediate area into a security zone, as the music would instantly halt if someone or something passed by.

Francis didn't wholly depend on the invisible assistance, however a sudden break in the collective nocturnal voices gave him fair warning; his senses were well-tuned to the modulations. The leaves above brushed their sweet tempo, the voices below added tenor tweets and bass thumps and burps; the final glowing embers crackled, poplar sap would pop and hiss; his mind would lift and float, his eyes ever-fixed to the faces in the locket.

He knew of three mothers and one sister; he had never enquired of his father when he was young. The Potawatomi traditionally shared all things: food, shelter and children. It was common for a child to refer to all women elders as Mother, 'Neneyem', or 'Ne'ni'. The O'Brien home was the first and only time Francis became aware of the Whiteman's family traditions. He saw a mother, a father, a daughter and he accepted the standards, but wasn't concerned about a comparison to his own situation, as he was Potawatomi—as a young boy the differences were not worth questioning, they just 'were'. Now everything was decidedly different.

He had a mother and a father, he was a Whiteman—the word still sat on the edges of his mind like the syrup on a plate of pancakes freshly served up by Mrs. O'Brien—sticky, ready to slide off and be wiped away, yet sweet and warm with wonderful satisfaction as it slid down the gullet emitting delicious tastes, graciously accepted and appreciated—yet he could not say the word aloud. The years of Sundays spent at the O'Brien's was truly an enlightening and joyous time—greatly appreciated—but at the time he considered himself a lucky visitor, an Indian receiving generous hospitality (the O'Brien's knew otherwise). It's true the final days in Chicago were filled with doubt and dissatisfaction. There was a guilt gnawing at his soul—he had withdrawn respect for his family; he had revelled in the attention from the O'Briens, from their love, their compassion—it was spoiling him. The ring and necklace were pushing him on, away from the past, to answers perhaps, but the vision of the execution continually pulled him back—back to Little Raven, back to Ogden and Smithson—there was a void, something was left incomplete, his heart had been torn. In spirit he was Potawatomi; he became a Whiteman when there was a need, a convenience—it troubled him. He reconsidered who he was every evening when he took out the locket and the ring.

The crickets stopped. He put the little leather pouch away and pulled his knife. The trail was travelled by British troops wary of Americans, as well as pirates and bandits; Indians who would steal his horse slitting his throat without a second thought. To find water and food a traveller would have to enter the forest adjacent to the trail. A lone traveller wondering down the King's Highway or hiding in the birch forests was easy prey for a greedy thief or belligerent soldier; an easy meal for a wolf or cougar. The rotting corpse meant a rare find for hungry scavengers, a pair of free boots or perhaps a saddle bag with a knife, black powder or flint. The crickets returned to their evening choruses, Francis held the knife steady in one hand and poked at the fire with a stick in the other. He ruthlessly tortured the glowing embers, his eyes and ears keen, sharp. The last dots of orange and red vanished. *A few pokes and then death. Once alive, bright and dancing, hot with energy—now grey dust, smouldering, choking—dead. I can create it—I can destroy it.* Smithson's face appeared to him among the black coals and smoking ashes, a wicked countenance, an evil smirking affectation. He jabbed his stick hard into the eye of his scratchy artwork.

A twig snapped, the frogs and crickets fell silent. Paws or feet gently touched down—an intermittent rhythm—something approached. Francis steadied his blade forward, piercing the dark void—he remained silent, still, patient—prepared. There it was again, only a few feet away. Francis rose, stood tall by the fire, clasping his buffalo skinner, all his muscles tightening—he froze. His senses acute and focussed; his eyes darted left and right into the trees. Then…nothing.

His visitor, it seemed was reacting similarly—frozen in position, waiting, listening, searching the shadows with eyes and ears, with instinct. Waiting. Finally, an odour of tobacco. *This was no lone wolf.* Two more steps. Francis remained rigid, rooted to the grass under his boots. He squeezed his brow in concentration. He was ready.

"Hello friend. I am alone like you." Francis strained his eyes into the darkness, through the shadows of the birches, dissecting the space for the source. The shadow moved; Francis watched the deceptive edges as darkness slipped from empty space to became form: human above the neck—below: thick fur. *A beast of some sort—part human, part bear!* "I am Magwah. I am Huron. I travel alone."

27

Although the Erie Canal had finally been completed from Albany to Buffalo, and was considered the greatest American achievement since the Revolutionary War—the trade and business quadrupling across the continent within months of its completion, and Rochester became "The Young Lion of the West"—it, unfortunately, was inadequate. The depth was too shallow and the width was too narrow. Continuous expansion and rebuilding were underway seemingly within months and continued uninterrupted throughout its entire history. A very long and important section cut right through the heart of Rochester; particularly impressive was the aqueduct across the Genesee River, built by convicts from Auburn Prison. The prisoners, canal labourers, Irish famine victims and scores and droves of pilgrims travelling westward seeking work on the canal or chasing dreams of a better life in America in the cities or on the frontier, over time and sometimes immediately, required desperate medical assistance due to the high rate of typhus, cholera, malaria, scarlet fever, small pox, consumption and outright starvation and poverty. The solution for these destitute people was the Almshouse set up on South Street initially by the new Rochester Female Charitable Society, which collected and distributed necessary provisions, clothing, bedding and food for the sick, poor and needy. The small structure that was erected in 1826 became sorely over-burdened by the time the three sisters from Maryland arrived, and when Sister Hieronymo visited Buffalo Street in the city's core, she witnessed the first stages of the City Hospital that would replace the Almshouse—however it wouldn't be completed for many years.

The good Sister could not give Father O'Reilly the response he required regarding Kingston on that first night, but after visiting the Almshouse on the following day, she had her answer. The Sisters belonged to a very strict order that put charity first above all else, absolutely, and although the needy in Kingston were undoubtedly in dire distress, Rochester required a severe dose of heavenly assistance from the community and from The Sisters of Charity that now resided within its boundaries. They went to work immediately. The Sisters returned to St. Mary's Rectory very late on that second day— Father O'Reilly would receive his education directly.

The hot summer sun had finally, thankfully, set leaving the streets dry and dusty again, yet the dampness in the air weighed heavy—a burdensome thickness, invisible yet so powerful—workmen struggled to breathe in the ditches along the canal. Humidity brought the insects; the mosquitos at times swarmed in great voluminous clouds so dense the sunlight vanished; the air black with swirling, buzzing vermin biting, stinging, aggravating, turning men into screaming lunatics as they smacked and jerked desperate to maintain grip on their shovel, careful not to drop their pick on their boot. The mosquitos and black flies caked around their eyes, dug deep into their hair; but to relinquish a tool to fight the insects might result in a hasty dismissal from a lucrative canal job—the supervisors watched, intolerant, their vigilance steely—many workers remained resilient; some did not. The Almshouse was full of sick, exhausted Irishmen who had given up the battle with the canal, the pick axe; the insects.

Humid air began to rise and cool by evening, huge grey clouds expanded and spread wide across the Rochester sky—it would rain—the Sisters picked up their pace as they rounded the corner to St. Mary's challenging the first drops, racing back to Father O'Reilly after a rude awakening at the Almshouse.

Dancy stood at the door, hat in hand, bowing deep "Evnin' Miss. Evnin' Miss. Evnin' Miss," each Sister brushing past, through the great oak door, escaping the deluge behind as the sky cracked and the flashes burst across the night sky. They gave Dancy no heed. "Supper Miss?" Dancy had waited supper as instructed by Father O'Reilly; they were long overdue.

Sister Hieronymo did not answer Dancy, but instead demanded the good Father's whereabouts. Dancy remained in a subservient position—face deep within his chest—lifting a hand slightly, he gestured in the direction of the parlour. The Sister turned her head following the reticent indication in response. Sisters Martha and Felicia were ordered to remain in the dining room; they sat with great relief and released loud sighs in tandem. That was a mistake. The instant the critical air was released from between their pouting lips the gross error was keenly acknowledged and they jerked around with wide panicking eyes. Sister Hieronymo had not a speck of tolerance from complaining Sisters who had given their life to Jesus and charity; the sighs were expressions of disrespect and blasphemy; there was no time for exhaustion or complacency. Her scowling expression forecast eminent discipline: an evening of lectures and lessons on indulgence and diligence, followed by prayer...and more prayer. The Sisters sat up straight; eyes now regretful and apologetic; Sister Hieronymo entered the parlour.

"Rats, Father."

"Rats, Sister?"

"The devil's unholy pestilence."

"Yes Sister."

Sister Hieronymo stood before Father O'Reilly—his glass of brandy in one hand, pipe in the other, expansive buttocks comfortably slung in the bottom of his immense leather chair, supper slowly digesting, wide smile stretching across his chubby cherub face, rotten teeth perfectly exposed and offending—she was ready, yet cautious, he was the parish priest after all, and a certain amount respect was in order. "You are familiar with the Almshouse Father?"

"Yes Sister." He raised his glass. "Brandy Sister?"

"Certainly not!" His smile quickly shrunk. "The very largest contingent of starving, sick Irish people are barely surviving in a cruel corner of your town's property not fifteen minutes from your church...and...your chair." She fought the strong urge to raise and point a finger in his smug face. Father O'Reilly looked down quizzically at his chair. "We have cleaned, washed and treated men, women and children—babies with half eaten toes chewed off by filthy rats—sweating, fever victims of typhus and plague, burned garbage and dumped human waste, swept rat filth, re-stuffed straw beds filled with lice and ants and insects of every kind—flying, crawling, digging, slithering—washed muddy blankets, ripped rotting shreds of clothes off the backs of dying crippled canal workers, poured thin useless watery soup down dry wanting throats of children so thin and emaciated the skin on their backs peeled off to the touch," she took a breath, "buried three corpses that had been stinking for a week, rebuilt collapsing tents holding the overflow of men that can find no room inside, baked bread in the useless, tiny kitchen, chopped wood and stoked the fires, carried more water than flows in that stinking canal," she hesitated, "there's more arriving every day, nowhere to house them, no medicine or food, not enough help…and certainly not enough prayer from anybody in a position to offer such a holy gesture." Her eyes wide and accusing; she stopped. Father O'Reilly remained frozen, staring, gapping. She glared into his face. "And close your mouth!" She abruptly retreated to the dining room. "Dancy bring hot water to the bathroom!"

In time the Sisters washed and returned to the dining table. Sisters Martha and Felicia desperately controlling their exhaustion, fighting to keep their eyes open, their ears still stinging from the lecture in the bathroom, raised shaking hands to their mouths and carefully slurped in the wonderful hot stew prepared by Dancy. Father O'Reilly sat at the head, careful to leave his brandy in the parlour—*it seems to offend her*—the only sounds included slurping stew and pounding rain, the candles in the grand candelabra above flickered and glowed; he tried to choose his words carefully. "You… will not be…travelling to Kingston then?"

"We shall travel to Kingston when we have done as much as we can for the people here." Sister Hieronymo's eyes remained steadfast on her bowl; she slurped along with Sisters Martha and Felicia; Father O'Reilly returned to the parlour; he sipped his brandy. He smiled.

28

The strange raspy voice cut through the night sharpening all senses; Francis tensed his legs ready to spring away—to escape if necessary, to kill if necessary. The indiscriminate outline began to refocus into two legs covered in buckskin with moccasin boots barely visible below. The rest of his body was covered—a composite layering of wolf, beaver, lynx and muskrat. Over his shoulder Magwah slung a musket and powder horn; a knife was sheathed in his belt—a large leather pouch hung at his waist. Under his fur hat, long black strands of hair cascaded down his shoulders: a disarray of tangled filaments weaving in and around the animal hides, accentuated with a small leaf here and a tiny twig or two there. Francis considered to most forest creatures he would be indiscernible as a human—he would have great potential for invisibility if crouched down low to the forest floor, his face buried in his furs, which undoubtedly was his intent. It was very difficult to see his eyes, but they were set deep into his face and stared directly into Francis' own cautious glare.

"You are welcome friend." Francis motioned with his hand to the tiny red embers of his dying fire.

"My trap lines are bare and my furs are sold. I am travelling home for the summer. I have come far south, now I go east," the big Indian explained as he crouched down to the fire. In cooperation with mutual respect, Francis also bent down so their heads aligned at the same level. The elimination of a height advantage immediately reduced the tension, Francis began to relax a little, his fist still tightly clenched around the handle of his knife. Magwah was twice the width of Francis, but without his furry garments Francis doubted that his weight would be little more than his own. His age was unapparent— a rugged complexion but few deep creases—there was a definite aura of experience about him; he was reserved, wise. His odour was of the woods: pungent, damp—there was no human scent, save tobacco— and that was enough to give it all away. It clung to his furs mixing with the smoke of past campfires, fusing together beaver blood and the sour, slimy stink of swamp water—the aromas of a forest on a trek, following him wherever he might travel.

They sat quietly together for a few moments pretending to ponder over the remains of the fire; Francis caught Magwah quickly glancing up and then down again; he had focussed on Nektoshe. *So that's what he's after.* The pony would be a real prize for the Indian— Francis prepared for a struggle.

"Do you have a smoke?"

"No."

"Do you go to the Great Thunder?"

"I go east. I do not know the Great Thunder." Francis continued to watch the Indian closely. He assumed the conversation over the dead fire was strictly a diversion before the race for Nektoshe. His knife was steady, he was ready. Magwah reached for a stick lying by his side, he poked at the fire, he raised his eyes to the knife in Francis' fist. Francis suppressed the urge to flinch.

"A great blanket of water crashes over the cliff. The thunder explodes day and night, from month to month. From there I travel north."

"I will stay on the east trail. I have no smokes, no food." Finally it came.

"You have a fine pony. Will you trade?" Magwah's gaze was continual and intense on the fire—the dusty ashes, the annoying poke of his stick—he did not look into Francis' face when asking.

"No." A long quiet pause hung heavy in the space between them. Two moths flitted over the fire, dodging about, their tiny brown wings dancing and darting above the smoke, averting collision at every intricate, silent manoeuvre, then vanished. Francis and Magwah watched.

Together they slowly rose. Magwah looked to the pony, then glanced at the long blade of Francis' knife. "Travel well my friend." Magwah turned and disappeared into the forest.

In ten days, Francis reached an old fort at the entrance to the Niagara River on Lake Erie. Although Fort Erie had been abandoned by the British by 1823, armed scouts from Niagara and Fort George down river from the falls still patrolled the area as the crossing from Buffalo was narrow—Americans could easily enter Upper Canada, and they did...regularly. Francis could not hear the roar of the falls from his location at the mouth of the river, but he could see the current was extremely fast, and beyond a misty cloud hung like liquid vapour—a dense, white haze covering the horizon to the north. Francis rode Nektoshe along the river breathing in the fresh scent of clear rushing water, a welcomed renewal from the closeness of the unforgiving forest. Two soldiers approached, muskets at the ready. Francis stopped and dismounted as commanded.

The stone walls of the fort had crumbled, yet the enduring immensity of the edifice was overwhelming. A huge star-shaped fortification digging deep into the ground covering many acres, remained dispassionate, yet proud: a sober reminder of the bloody war between two powerful countries so closely aligned together at this crucial geographical crossroads. The soldiers had been lounging on the grass against the outside perimeter; they jumped to their feet when Nektoshe approached and challenged Francis directly.

The soldiers were young, younger than Francis; their red uniforms hung loosely around their shoulders, not a wisp of hair on their smooth chins—but their slim, long triangular bayonets were sharp enough—glinting in the sun, the points were razor sharp and threatening—flashing in Francis' face.

"What is your purpose here?"

Francis had to think quickly, he had never confronted soldiers; although they were not physically imposing, they were armed—unpredictable. "I am travelling to Great Thunder."

"What?" The soldiers were not familiar with the Indian name given to the falls. They looked at each other in confusion.

"The great falls." Francis hoped Magwah was correct, it was all he could think of, as he had no real purpose other than escaping Smithson and Chicago.

"Give me your bag." The tallest soldier reached out and demanded Francis respond. The other held his musket on a direct bead to

Francis' forehead. "You have medicines and surgery knives; are you a doctor?" He continued rummaging through the bag as he spoke.

Francis, almost without considering the lie, gave the soldier the answer he desired. "Yes."

"You are heading to Kingston to assist with the fever victims?" Once again, not knowing of Kingston or any fever victims, Francis without hesitation answered quickly assuming the response would remove any doubts about his purpose or personage. "Yes. I am travelling east. Is this correct?"

"Follow us." The tall soldier returned the bag, Francis was ordered to lead his pony alongside the soldiers following the river. "You don't look like a doctor." They kept their muskets at the ready.

"I have been travelling a long way." There were no more words exchanged, however Francis wasn't confident about his lie. His face was washed, but his clothes and pony, he knew, just didn't suit the typical image one might expect for a travelling doctor with any sort of reputation.

The encampment at Niagara Falls was busy. The Regiment had rows and rows of tents lined up all along the grasses below the town nearest the cliff; soldiers and visitors were mingling and scurrying about—the falls was a tourist attraction. A town had grown up around the falls and businesses, streets and carriages were bustling everywhere. The largest congregation of course crowded along the edge of the cliff. Francis walked ahead of his captors towards the roaring din; the mist fell gently and welcomingly on his face as they approached the edge. The Regiment's headquarters was a small wooden blockhouse, no stockade, no guards—Francis was directed to halt in the street and to stand square and still before a poor young boy on his knees. *This is a serious place.* The young soldier's head and hands were securely locked within wooden stocks which were placed solidly on the ground before the entrance to the blockhouse. His hair was long and dirty, his face bloody, his uniform disheveled— he was exhausted and ill. To his left a tall beautiful black stallion stood quietly tied to a rail; an exquisite hand-crafted saddle rested on a blanket on his back displaying the British coat of arms in gold braid. *Definitely not* his *horse,* Francis thought looking down on the poor soldier.

"Water." A brittle, dry-throated plea barely escaped from between the young prisoner's mouth. He raised his face, yet only slightly as the stocks wouldn't allow a full vertical lift upward. Francis hesitated, he had no water; he then approached slightly, ready to assist when his guard stepped ahead quickly.

"I wouldn't give him anything, he's got another day in there and if you give him water the Lieutenant will replace him with you." Francis stood back.

"What did he do?"

"Asleep on duty…idiot."

The young offender attempted to adjust his balance; his britches were torn at the knees, his back bent forward with a terrible twist, he couldn't drop his head for fear of cutting off his breathing, he couldn't move up or straighten as the stocks were crushing down; his torture was perverse and cruel. Francis couldn't look away. He moved in closer again, then stopped suddenly.

"You. Come inside."

The tall soldier appeared at the blockhouse door and ordered Francis inside. The other soldier took tight hold of Nektoshe's rope. Francis left the stocks and the pathetic suffering wretch to his torture; better to follow orders, the British seemed to have little patience for disobedience.

The blockhouse was small and dark, just a desk and chair. The hooks on the wall behind held the officer's belt and sword. His shako hat was on the desk. To the right against the wall: a bed—just a small cot actually. The Lieutenant was young, his blond hair was pulled back in a tail; his uniform was a deep rich, red serge trimmed in gold piping and braid. "What is your name?"

"Francis Tumblety." The words almost stuck in his throat. It was the first time Francis had ever said his name out loud. It sounded so strange, it sounded so…stupid. It definitely didn't sound convincing, and the Lieutenant looked up into the eyes of his prisoner with scrutiny.

"You are a doctor?"

"I am a medical assistant."

The Lieutenant paused. "You have an Indian pony. Did you steal it?"

"No. It is my pony."

"Are you an Indian?"

'I am Potawatomi."

"What?"

"Potawatomi."

"I have never heard of that tribe. You don't look like an Indian and you don't look like a doctor."

Francis was getting nervous and the Lieutenant sensed it. If he was caught lying, the lightest punishment might be the stocks. He could be shot. "Where is your home?" Francis could not allow the Lieutenant to know he was an American; he had to answer fast and with confidence.

"Sandwich."

"Where is that?"

"West on the Detroit River."

"I know that area. There is a British garrison in Windsor."

"Yes. Sandwich is a small town just a bit west of Windsor on the river. There are many Potawatomi there." He lied.

"Are you a half-breed?"

Francis hesitated again. "Yes." He lied again. Francis was desperate to give this man the correct answers. He wanted to avoid those stocks on the street. He was sweating, he shifted weight from one foot to the next. He wiped his brow with his sleeve.

"You do not look well."

"I have travelled a long way."

"You are travelling to Kingston?"

Francis remembered what the soldier had said. "Yes. I am to assist with the fever victims." He had no idea what he was saying, but these people seemed to want to hear this answer. He continued to lie. He followed the Lieutenant's lead; he tried to look healthier…maybe doctorly, at least confident—he released a tiny smile and raised his eyebrows in an attempt to appear, possibly…optimistic?

The Lieutenant leaned back in his chair, stared deeply into the eyes of his prisoner, searching for a reason to release this rag-tag half-breed with the Indian potions and surgical knives, riding a stolen skinny pony. The silent moment of calculation was killing Francis, and it seemed like an eternity. Suddenly the chair crashed forward with a bang and the Lieutenant dismissed Francis. "You may camp north of town along the gorge. You are not welcome in the town. Stay one night only. You can reach Port Dalhousie tomorrow and catch a ferry to Toronto. If you stay any longer, I will lock you up. Get out."

"Yes Sir. Thank you, sir." Francis turned and left the building. He led Nektoshe to the falls.

Niagara Falls was a place where God displayed his magnificent architecture in unlimited majesty; all dimensions were measured on the grandest scale. A vast curving cliff rising to over two hundred feet forced the rushing river above to empty its powerful contents in a broad cascade, careening rapidly down, smashing on the rocks far below—its inevitable destiny. Thick plumes of cool mist flooded the air above and saturated the trees and grass in all directions. Sunlight trapped in the water droplets painted a sparkly rainbow that drifted high above the falls—bright then hazy, yet illusive as the breeze stole it away in an instant only to return again in the next; a gossamer veil, a tenacious spirit.

The roar of the rushing water above and the continuous explosions of crashing torrents below delivered a deafening pulse numbing the senses, leaving the human spirit tranquilized and dumbfounded. How insignificant was man now; the great power released was beyond any of man's trivial achievements. Francis stood mesmerized, his mind and spirit captured and controlled by the great wall of rushing water. Parasols and umbrellas dripped with the water from the mist; people laughed and played along the great cliff, inching ever closer to the deep gorge; tempting fate at the edge of Table Rock, a great nose of thin cliff jutting out over the falls—a perilous position, dangerously attractive. The visitors were sure to keep their distance from Francis and Nektoshe. The dirt and the smell were offensive. Critical glances and questioning expressions soon encouraged Francis to move along.

Slowly wandering north along the road adjacent to the gorge, Francis passed a market where tables of fresh fruit and drinks were available; he didn't approach but stopped at a well where a public hitching post secured a group of horses, their owners drifting about the scene enjoying the bright sunshine and cheery crowds, no doubt. Nektoshe lowered her head to drink at the trough provided there, Francis dipped his hands in for a drink. "Well Doctor, you better keep moving." The young soldier in the baggy red uniform that had captured Francis and accompanied him from Fort Erie to the blockhouse, appeared at this elbow, musket lowered, his position too close, it was purposely uncomfortable. "And I still don't think you're a doctor."

Francis was not intimidated—the Lieutenant had released him, he was complying with orders—this soldier's attitude was provoking a challenge, Francis could feel it—but he was in no position to riposte. There was a distinct disconnect between Francis and this new strange environment. He had always been somewhat alienated in Chicago even as he walked freely among the townspeople. He had been abused and ostracized, he never truly fit in; but as time went by, he assimilated: they tolerated him, he tolerated them. He was always the half-breed that worked in the stockyards—O'Brien's boy. He wore boots and trousers; he didn't dress like an Indian; Mrs. O'Brien kept his hair cut short. He wasn't a stranger in town; he knew his place and generally respected his ranking; however as time went on, the imposing knife hanging down the centre of his back gave him a strength, a confidence, a secret; he had killed a man—it's shiny steel blade delineated an understanding: it didn't matter that he didn't fit in. Francis made his own special place among the people of Chicago, among the hands at the stockyards, among the women of his family. No matter what clothes he wore, what attitude he harboured—there was always the knife. Even now walking among the visitors at Niagara Falls, the fancy-dressed ladies, the men dressed in their suits and top hats, the officers in their bright red uniforms so tight and imposing, the soldier standing next to him—a boy really—pressuring him with words, standing with a musket—his attitude so cocky, his smirk casual and impetuous—the knife was hidden, carefully hanging down his back. He was a stranger, he received rude glances, he didn't mind the separation, the discrimination—although in time he would beg to assimilate entirely. Francis smiled and answered. "Yes, I am moving north along the gorge." Francis grabbed Nektoshe's rope and began to leave the well.

"As you a doctor, Massa?" The tiny voice drifted up from behind the well. A small negro boy crouched there holding a water bucket, his wide eyes staring up, his tense stance ready to scramble if ordered to run.

"Why, do you need a doctor?"

"No Massa. Moses. She need a doctor." No shoes, a ragged shirt; the boy was so small Francis would have walked past if he hadn't spoken. He crouched low in the dirt within the deep shadow of the well.

"Who is Mosses?" The boy wasn't sure how to convince Francis to follow him, so he moved ahead and continued to announce his great concern for Moses by beckoning with his hands and wide smile, frantically looking behind hoping he was being followed, the bucket sloshing water, spilling its contents a slight amount with each step.

Francis watched a handsome couple dressed in their very best Sunday clothes, sitting on a bench, the Falls behind: the great backdrop—the mist dancing and frothing all about—a man adjusted a three-legged contraption before them. A huge wooden chest on the ground displaying the letters 'PLATT D. BABBITT PHOTOGRAPHER'. A table to his left offered interested customers a chance to view his work: postcards and photographs of Niagara Falls, as well as an opportunity to become some of the rare few to be first captured with this new technology, if they could hold still long enough and pay the extravagant price—twenty-five cents. People were watching, but not lining up. Francis searched for the negro boy; he spied him running into the woods farther down the road. A carriage whipped by, the passengers stiff and proud inside, the lady's frilly, pink umbrella held tight to the wind, paying no heed to Francis and his scrawny Indian pony. The beautiful horse was prancing ahead, a trotting gait almost pushing Francis and Nektoshe off the road.

Francis took a moment to view the wondrous sight for the final time. The roar of the rushing water had not diminished, the balloon of fine mist continued to fill the sky, the hazy rainbow colours shimmering from within, the mountains of thunderous water plummeted down with penetrating voracity just as it had when he arrived, just as it had for thousands of years, and thousands of years before that—*the Great Thunder explodes day and night, from month to month*. Francis was truly impressed, but he was ordered to move along; somewhere in the birch trees, deep within the maples, beyond the vast rows of military tents, past the critical glances, past the bustling onlookers, there was a little negro boy and his persistence had provoked a curious nerve.

The dark spaces between the trees seemed vacant, silent, yet there was movement—a rustle, a shadow tilting, then jerking upward, leaning forward to see. Francis stopped, his eyes adjusted, then the figures slowly began to emerge. Eight, maybe ten, no twelve dark people huddling close together under the tree branches, holding each other tight, whispering, sitting under the bushes, afraid to speak or move. "This a doctor for Moses." The little boy with the bucket stood beside a blanket on the forest floor, reassuring his friends. Francis stepped forward. Long rays of sunlight cut through the leaves exposing a face; bright flashes flickered and quivered, as the leaves silently shivered in the breeze above. Moses was sweating, shaking.

"She has a fever. Remove her blankets." No one moved. "I can help her, but you must remove the blankets and her dress. She is too hot." The hesitation was understandable. The boy had not answered a request for a doctor; he went to the well to fetch water, and returned with a stranger. "I am an Indian medicine man. Let me help."

In a very short time, tension relaxed; they welcomed and assisted Francis. The blankets and clothing were removed. Moses slept in her shift; cool water applied to her head and shoulders offered relief. The evening temperatures dropped and the fever began to abate. A campfire was lit, Army beans and bacon were served. Joseph was a tall man, strong; his eyes were very serious, suspicious—the oldest man and the group's spokesman. He explained about the six hundred mile journey they had suffered and the assistance they received from the British Army including food and blankets once they crossed the Niagara River at Fort Erie and rested, finally, under the secure protection of the government of the United Province of Canada. They were slaves who had escaped from their homes in Maryland; Moses was their leader.

Francis slept at their campfire that night; images of vicious dogs, mad slave hunters, whippings and beatings swirled in his mind—Joseph had revealed all—an unbelievable story. He had thought perhaps his understanding of Whiteman had at least gained some newfound toleration as the British soldiers' generosity to these destitute refugees instilled hope and comfort—however the heart of the Whiteman seemed to be as dark as ever—slavery had blazoned the shadows with the darkest tones of all.

The sun rose early enough, the woman sat up and looked with consternation to Francis. "Who are you?"

"I am Francis. I am a medical assistant. You were feverish. Your people allowed me to help." He still wasn't sure how to refer to himself, but medical assistant seemed more important than Indian medicine man, and perhaps more convincing.

"I am Harriet Tubman. We must continue to St. Catharines. Do you know it?"

"No. I am travelling to the ferry at Port Dalhousie, north."

"It is on the way."

"You are still sick."

"The soldiers will not allow us to stay any longer, we must continue." Francis watched the woman struggle to rise up attempting to regain her authority with Francis and with her group. A woman close to her raised a cup of water to her mouth. "We have come this far, we must go on. Get me my dress." Francis could see a strong determination in this woman's face; serious eyes that retained focus, reflecting a will of steel; beneath: a heart of unbridled passion. Her lower lip remained rigid in an angry pout; she would leave with or without Francis' permission.

"You can ride my horse."

"Thank you." Two women helped pull her dress down over her head. "Now get me up."

Nektoshe could maintain a good ten miles a day, if the forest was not too thick and the weather was forgiving; Francis assumed on this clear dirt road they might cover fifteen miles. Most of the slaves were barefoot, their stamina worn out; he may have over-estimated. When the sun set, Moses dismounted and Francis assumed they would camp for the night. He was wrong. "No, we will continue on until we reach St. Catharines."

"But how can they go on?"

"Faith, Mr. Tumblety. Do you believe in God, Francis?"

Francis hesitated. "I have read the bible."

Moses gave an incredulous smirk. "What have you read?"

Oh God, a test. Mrs. O'Brien had tested Francis. He was able to quote some passages, but it had been so long. There was a serious attempt to instill an understanding of Christianity—a belief in God, the teachings of Jesus, humanity, charity, benevolence—but the invisible saints and holy scriptures seemed to bite and linger at the edges of his curiosity rather than render a deep belief in his soul. Rising Sun and Little Raven taught a spirituality that encompassed the life around him: the land, the plants and animals, the weather; they unveiled a truth about nature and balance—how human beings were part of a great harmony. It had made sense to him...right up to the time he was brutally, repeatedly sodomized by drunken cowboys, and up to the moment when the Sheriff ordered the chairs kicked out from under his family's feet.

He thought about a passage that might impress Moses. "I have read Corinthians."

"Tell me."

"*Now the Lord is the Spirit, and where the Spirit of the Lord is, there is freedom.*"

"Oh yes, the New Testament speaks of freedom. Do you know Ephesians?"

"No."

"*Slaves be obedient to your human masters with fear and trembling, in sincerity of heart.*"

"The Bible speaks of slaves that way?"

"Yes. I prefer the Old Testament. Ecclesiastes: *There is a time to kill and a time to heal.*"

Francis sat with Harriet Tubman for a moment on the grass, they shared water and dried bacon. "I see you carry a pistol in your belt. Have you used it?"

"Not yet." She ordered the group to gather their things; they would move on. She told a young girl to ride Nektoshe. "Get up here girl."

"How far would you go for freedom?"

Moses gave Caroline a boost up then turned to Francis. "To the ends of the earth. Are you searching for freedom Francis?"

"I don't know. Why do they call you Moses?"

"Because I have released them from bondage and I am leading them to freedom."

They travelled throughout the night and all the next day without stopping; no one complained. Together they sang songs, spiritual songs—a ceaseless harmonious rhythm—fuelling them, binding them, delivering them:

"Wrestlin' Jacob seek de lord. An' I will not let de go.

An' I wrestle all night till de beak of day. An' I will not let de go.

Wrestle, Jacob. Jacob, day is a breakin'

Wrestle Jacob Lord. I will not let de go,

An' I will not let de go,

An' I will not let de go. An' I will not let de go.

Till Jesus bless my sool."

Francis sang the songs and wondered if he was searching for freedom.

There is a time to kill and a time to heal.

The church in St. Catharines was just a small log building on Henry street, constructed by black Americans who had reached freedom some years before. The clear resemblance to a church was meagre, but Bethal Chapel was now home; the new arrivals wept... and sang, and prayed thanking God for their safe deliverance. Francis curled up on the floor among his friends and slept soundly; his stomach growling, in cadence with twelve other empty stomachs.

The next day Reverend Hiram Wilson escorted the new refugees to his house, where clothes, food and baths were graciously provided. The end of July was wet; it seemed as though it rained every day.

There was no sun. The Reverend Wilson explained, "The bounty harvested from the earth requires heavy doses of rain as well as sun and the good Lord has provided both in great abundance here in St. Catharines; we are lucky in so many ways." A broad smile stretched across the Reverend's face as Francis received the directions to Port Dalhousie. Lunch and water were handed up in a bag as he sat upon Nektoshe, Moses stood at his side. "You are home now Harriet. You can be satisfied. Will you live here with the Reverend?"

"No, I will return to Maryland as soon as possible."

"What? Why? The slavers...they will hunt you down. You can't go back."

"I must return. There are many people that must be free. My duty is to them."

"How will you find them? How will you get through?" Francis couldn't believe she would return. He knew the chances of evading the slavers once was incredible—but to challenge them again was suicide.

"God will show me the way Francis. I have no doubt."

"Stay here Harriet. The Reverend has a school, you could teach."

"I suppose I am a type of teacher. I teach the good Lord's word and I teach how to be free. But my people need to be Here! They must follow me Here!" She hammered that final note up like a command from a general and pointed hard to the ground at her feet. She was adamant and perhaps a bit disappointed that Francis didn't seem to understand. "Good luck Francis, remember to put your faith in God. I hope you will find what you are looking for."

"Good bye Harriet." Francis gave Nektoshe a little kick and turned to the road.

"Bye Massa."

The little boy, Gabriel, who first appeared with the bucket at Niagara Falls, waved to Francis. "I am not your Massa, Gabriel. You have no Massa." Gabriel smiled and waved, still struggling with his new shoes; his first pair—they just didn't seem to fit right.

Preparations were being made at Lakeside Park in Port Dalhousie. Tables and banners set out; a tent in case of rain—a very real possibility—although the chance of poor weather discouraging attendance was low if not impossible. August 1st was Emancipation Day, and it would be celebrated most heartily by hundreds of people from all over the St. Catharines area. The British passed the Slavery Abolition Act in 1833; the day was celebrated throughout the British Empire and in northern American States. Francis could not attend; he was bound for Toronto; the little ferry was docked at the entrance to the Welland Canal. Ten cents for him and five cents for Nektoshe—he boarded and set sail.

The rain and the wind drove the waves high on Lake Ontario; the little steam engine punched through continually demanding passage, fighting for every inch. Nektoshe stumbled often—Francis gripped her rope tight for fear of her being washed overboard. The clouds were dark and thick, the rain unforgiving—striking like stinging bullets, cutting into faces, pelting heads like stones flying up from behind a carriage pulled by a startled horse. Passengers huddled down close to the deck squeezing between their boxes gripping the ropes that bound their belongings together. The distance across was about forty miles and on a good day the pilot promised Francis a trip of about four hours; however no straight line could be found, nor consistent speed be attained—until after about two hours when the sky began to clear and the waves began to subside. Seagulls above began to blurt their angry calls once again; the Toronto shoreline was clearly visible ahead. The sun's radiance exploded upon the waves—now so smooth—the pilot, filled with new confidence, pressed forward at full speed. The relief was welcomed by all aboard; everyone quickly rose, rushing, searching the horizon for Toronto; new expressions of thanks and consolation shone in their eyes; mothers relaxed their nervous grip on their children. The pilot gave Francis a wink and a nod. Francis decided this would be his first and only trip on a boat—it absolutely did not appeal to him. This conclusion, unfortunately, could not have been farther from the truth.

29

Toronto was busy, much busier than Chicago. The harbour was overloaded with ships and barges—so much cargo being unloaded, so many people urgently scrambling about, screaming—particularly on the far east side where Francis and Nektoshe docked at the bottom of Church Street—shipments were backed up, anger was mounting. A small woman in a long black dress was belting out orders to the dock hands and receiving no satisfaction in return. Upon her head was a black bonnet tightly secured around her face with stiff white fabric pressing her face into such a narrow shape, Francis wondered how she could breathe let alone scream. Sister Hieronymo wanted those boxes aboard, her patience had dissolved hours ago, she was a mile past the end of tolerance, intensity in her voice was peaking—surrender, however, was never a word associated with her disposition or included in her vocabulary. She wanted the cargo aboard now, and she would have it.

Standing anxiously nearby were Sisters Martha and Felicia, ducking and dodging loaders, swinging crates and sacks all around, overhead and in carts jamming, pulling, but in no way attending to the needs of the Sisters. The problem in question was their destination: Kingston. It was plagued and no dockworker would consider loading on that barge that had made a dozen or more return trips to 'that place'—"the depths of hell and horror," as one young man proclaimed spewing expletives and flashing a hand high in the air over Sister Hieronymo's face. Francis pulled Nektoshe tight weaving in and about the ruckus, watching intently at the show.

"These boxes must go to Kingston, this boat cannot leave without them, they are crucial!" The dock supervisor was insisting that the good Sister wait as, possibly, he could recruit assistance tomorrow, today was out of the question; it was too late—the barge was ready to sail with or without her supplies.

Without considering his reflex offer as perhaps reckless or at least impulsive, Francis came forward and announced that he would load the crates and boxes. "I can move them."

"Who are you?" Charlie MacDonald was a huge burly man with endless muscles on his arms and shoulders, handlebar moustache, hands as big as shovels; he was the loading foreman and his fighting stamina had just about breached, when Francis stepped forward holding his little pony by a rope proclaiming his foolish intensions.

Barges arriving from Kingston loaded with limestone blocks freshly cut from the quarries were stealing all the dockworkers. Mr. Gooderham's new distillery was the number one building enterprise in the Toronto harbour at this time and he was paying top dollar to get his limestone delivered. If it wasn't limestone, then thousands of wheat sacks from the American mid-west arriving daily were being unloaded ready to be carted to Gooderham's flour mills. Either way, between the plague, wheat and limestone as well as coordinating the stockyards, allocating space for fruits and vegetable crates, catching thieves and chasing dogs, Charlie MacDonald could not possibly entertain the needs of this bantering Sister—there were no extra hands and another ship just docked!

MacDonald turned to the feeble voice. "You'll not be paid by me!"

"That's fine." Francis turned his face to the barge and to the stern countenance of the tiny, frustrated nun with the resounding diatribe. Sister Hieronymo stood solid on her feet, hands upon her hips staring at Francis—a scruffy traveller holding a pony that appeared to be sucking in its last few breaths of air before keeling over. The Sisters did not suffer the fierce winds and angry waves of this morning's storm on the south shoreline, they had arrived yesterday from Rochester on a little steamer paddleboat with every donation they could manage from Father O'Reilly and his Parish—boxes and sacks of clothes and blankets, dried fruit and meat, jars of fruit preserves. Those items were loaded in the early morning when the barge from Kingston arrived and unloaded its huge cargo of harvest vegetables from the Kingston area, bound for the Toronto markets. The issue now facing the Sisters was to load the supplies, generously donated from the three different Toronto Parishes for the fever victims in Kingston, previously arranged by Father O'Reilly weeks ago. The Sisters had worked tirelessly for almost one month in Rochester and they were desperately late for their assignment in Kingston.

The boxes were so big and awkward a single person would be hard-pressed to manage without assistance. "If he can get your cargo aboard and you can ship out in the next twenty minutes, he's all yours. But lookn' at him I would not expect too much." MacDonald rushed away to the pig pens where a fight had broken out—a dog had grabbed a pig by the leg under the fence and was attempting to drag it home. The boy who brought the pig to market was being dragged along.

Sister Hieronymo stepped towards Francis and gave him a quick look-over. She was not concerned about his stature: skinny, or his appearance: dirty; she only wanted his compliance. "Well?"

"If you grab the other end, I can lift this box and carry it aboard." With a flashing glance and a hasty nod, Sisters Martha and Felicia were relegated to assist. Francis tied Nektoshe to a post near the bow of the barge, and the gruelling task began. Together the unlikely quartet completed their task admirably and within less than thirty minutes the barge was ready to depart. MacDonald kept a considerable distance from the action, but kept a close eye. He may have hidden a cruel desire to see a catastrophe, as boxes and crates smashed together, dropping off the gangway into the lake—he would laugh pompously, hands gesticulating with condemnation, shaking his head. He could then take a great story with him back to the Wheat Sheaf Tavern on King Street after work. The glasses would raise, the beer would flow; he would regain his title as strongest shoreman in Toronto with powerful feats of arm-wrestling, while exaggerating the mishap on the Kingston barge today when three nuns and a dirty vagabond dumped all their cargo into the lake. A story like that could earn him many beers over the next week. However disappointed he may have been with the surprising outcome, he was impressed with their success as they were ready to leave the dock, all goods on board, but he gave no indication.

Unfortunately, Francis faced a final duty before setting sail for Kingston. He had been contemplating it for some time and he knew it was inevitable. The room on board for passengers was very limited—it was a flat-bottomed boat after all, not a ship—walking around the cargo was impossible, there were no handrails for support. The idea of travelling by boat again was a discouragement, but the weather was favourable—calm water, no wind, blue sky—and the barge would sail close to shore most of the way. The trip to Kingston would take about fifteen hours; they would travel all night and arrive the next day. However, there was this one last thing and Francis was not eager to say goodbye to an old friend.

"Allow me five minutes. I will return." Francis gave the pilot an appreciative smile.

"Hurry up, I've got steam!" The pilot was not impressed with more delays. Francis raced down the gangway.

The Potawatomi love and appreciate all things living and passed. The Creator has a plan, a balance that includes understanding the needs of man and animals and their place in the Great Circle of Life. Nektoshe was there for Francis when he needed her and she was a good pony, a good companion. Francis had to go on now without her and her fate would rest in the hands of these people at the market on the docks of Toronto's shoreline. Francis wrapped his arms around Nektoshe's neck and whispered a prayer in her ear. He said "Bozho" (farewell) and gave the rope to a man at the corral where many ponies and horses stood—the unrelenting July heat burning their backs, the flies torturing their eyes without reprieve—there was no shade, no water trough. This man did not fully appreciate what was happening, yet he responded with a smile. "I will try to find her a good home."

"Thank you." Francis turned away, a tear fell from his eyes. "Ttha ge na tom ge." (So be it.) He raced up the gangway, the little paddle wheel began to spin, the barge headed east to Kingston, to the fever sheds.

30

*F*rancis bullied his way around wooden crates, over boxes and stubborn sacks, past the pilot house to the bow—the position occupied by the three Sisters—he thought proper introductions might be in order.

"Do you have family in Kingston?" Sister Hieronymo spoke first. Her arms were crossed, chin raised high, she searched the eastern horizon as if she were commandeering the boat. If she thought the proximity to an island was too close, or a deviant log was threatening, she would complete an about turn to face the pilot—she assumed the power of her deeply focused glare would be enough to warn him of impending doom. To her profound chagrin, he purposely ignored her. Sisters Martha and Felicia stood quietly by the apple barrels just to her right on the starboard side—their faces hidden from view, their tired, sour complexions covered by their habits, they were exhausted—they were always exhausted—it nearly drove Sister

Hieronymo crazy with exasperation. Everything nearly drove Sister Hieronymo crazy with exasperation.

"No Ma'am."

"I am not Ma'am, I am Sister Hieronymo. Why are you travelling to Kingston?"

"Sister what?"

"Her…on…eee…mo."

"Yes Ma'am."

"What's the matter with you?"

"Nothing Ma'am, I mean Sister Her on ee mo."

"Close enough. What's your name?"

"I am Francis. I thought I could help you in Kingston.

"I can't pay you."

'I am an Indian healer. I don't want money."

"How will you eat?"

'I don't know."

"What's the matter with you?"

Sister Martha started to giggle. Sister Felicia's shoulders began to shake up and down.

"Stop that noise. Come here and meet Francis. He's going to help us in Kingston."

Augustus Higgins was the pilot—not a true master of the lakes, not a salty old sailor or naval commander, but a farmer who had inherited an old steam barge when a friend died of cholera building the Welland canal—he thought he'd give it a go; that was thirteen years ago. He knew the lake well enough—well enough to slip by the rocks dangerously jutting out invisibly from the pointy ends of an island, or to dodge a nasty free-floater attempting to jam her paddles and leave her dead and stranded. It wasn't Higgins, it was his two stokers that gave the Sisters and Francis concern. Ralph and Johnny were ten and eleven years old respectively; by the time the sun set and the coal lamps were lit around the boat—swinging up high on poles clear enough for other ships to see—they were spent. They were so sure they could do the job, so insistent, so dedicated—Higgins reluctantly surrendered and agreed to accept their pathetic plea for employment. It might have been a hasty decision, but there was no one else—Gooderham's had taken every dock worker and labourer for miles around; Higgins couldn't compete with those wages.

Up to the point when Ralph finally collapsed, Francis had been deep in slumber on a sack of potatoes near the stern. There had been a moment of solace when he retrieved the little leather pouch from his pocket—the faces of his parents giving him a familiar comforting connection—he still wrestled with his new lineage, his name, his destiny—but a few moments free of crowds, heavy boxes, mosquitoes, smokey fires, runaway slaves, high winds and tossing waves—seemed a true luxury. He thought of Nektoshe and hoped she would not be butchered but perhaps live her final days carrying a little rich girl around a glorious wide acreage, sprinting in the sun, receiving amorous affection and nightly brushings—*foolish thoughts*. He watched the sky slowly fading then explode with a thousand vibrant colours; the stars one by one beginning to dot the open heavens, the final slit of orange and pink silently dipping into the wake behind him.

Sisters Martha and Felicia had settled down in Higgins' little tent he had erected on board just behind his wheelhouse. They had finished two jars of peaches and a loaf of bread in record time, then debated who would be first to use the ablution pail—the entire thought disgusted them—however worse situations jeopardizing their privacy and wholesomeness (both of which were barely hanging by a thread, yet they continually refused to give them up) had threatened their sanity in Rochester: including cleaning up dying old men suffering from dehydration, fever, boils and starvation; as well as cleaning out other peoples' ablution pails. Besides they had no choice. When that nasty bit of repugnant constitution concluded, they both stretched out as best as possible in the little tent on a woollen blanket and drifted off within minutes—the water being so calm, the sky so clear, the little steam engine chugging a soothing, repetitive rhythm… and they were so utterly exhausted.

After six or seven hours maintaining her valiant pose at the bow, Sister Hieronymo finally sat down on a crate immediately behind her, however the burden of her self-proclaimed duty had not abated: she remained ever vigilant. So when Johnny dropped his shovel attempting to revive his partner without success and ran to Higgins to report, Sister Hieronymo caught every nuance and retort shared between himself and an enraged boat master.

Francis was awake in an instant; he rushed to the wheel house to investigate. Johnny was not a negro, but the volume and layers of black coal dust on his face and neck, arms and over every inch of his trousers and shirt would seriously question that observation.

They carried Ralph away from the furnace and placed him carefully on the deck. He was breathing, just thoroughly exhausted. Sister Hieronymo wiped a damp cloth across his face. "When was the last time you ate?" Johnny did not respond. "Did you have any water?"

"No. We didn't have any supper today. We didn't eat yesterday either."

Francis immediately grabbed a shovel and began to stoke the furnace. The boiler would hold its steam long enough to sort this out. "Someones's got to maintain that furnace or you can forget about pulling into Kingston harbour tomorrow at any time." Higgins yelled out the door of the pilot house to Sister Hieronymo—he stuck his head out, angry at assuming those two children could do the job, angrier still at the assumptions the Sister was making about his character.

At least there was plentiful water—they were sailing on Lake Ontario after all; miles of fresh water in every direction. The Sister dipped a bucket overboard and hauled in a new supply by rope. She began to wash Ralph's face and offer a cup to his mouth. When he seemed settled, she left him and turned to the tent. "Get up! Bring me a blanket!"

"Lord give me strength." Sister Martha shot up like a shocked soldier when the sergeant announced the enemy was in sight. She smacked Sister Felicia on the back, whipped off the blanket and stood somewhat dazed before Sister Hieronymo waiting for her orders.

"Get me some bread; send Sister Felicia to the furnace." Her words were direct, there was no discussion, as usual. Francis removed his shirt and knife—he continued to dig into the coal pile as if his life depended on it—it didn't. Initially, shovelling coal was no worse than shovelling animal bones and entrails, he had grown up with a shovel in his hands; but this was different: the heat, the extreme heat from the summer sun and the intense blast from the furnace. There was no icy trail on which to balance a cart through winter's harsh weather, an additional painful frustration to the shovelling—but here on the boat, there would be no rest until she docked—that was many hours away. Endurance would be the measure this time.

Higgins kept his eye on the water. The moon, full, perfectly round and bright, began to inch up above the eastern horizon, its light radiating like a resplendent beacon—the path ahead was clearly illuminated. Higgins was resolved to relinquish the plight of the boys to the Sisters; he could see Francis was properly motivated; he was satisfied. Sister Felicia stepped into the furnace room.

"What do you want?"

"I don't know."

"Stand back, I don't want to hit you. Get out of the way."

Sister Felicia backed out of the room—lost, unsure and still half asleep. "Get back in there and pick up a shovel!" Together Francis and Sister Felicia shovelled coal; load after load—the heat was unbearable, the continuous back and arm strain—torturous. Sister Hieronymo and Sister Martha gently cared for the boys—they were washed and fed; they fell asleep on the blanket. After two hours Sister Hieronymo made her way across the deck to the furnace room. Sister Martha said a silent prayer. *"Please, please Lord."* But it was in vain; one look at Sister Felicia's face and habit was enough. The nun was a mountain of coal dust—her face, totally absorbed by the residue, had been replaced by a black mask that completely hid any features of her former self. She was crying; the amount in each shovel-full was less and less with each lift; she could barely raise the shovel to the furnace door any more.

"Sister Martha, get in here!"

"Please Lord." They changed places; Francis stayed continuing to work, the boys slept, Sister Felicia wiped her face and dropped down hard onto a sack of cabbages; Sister Martha picked up the shovel, Francis shook his head at the entire dismal scene. The routine repeated over and over again throughout the remainder of the trip until the next morning. Twice the little paddle wheeler pulled into shore to fill the boiler—the respite was received whole-heartedly and was greatly appreciated—but the efforts involving filling the boiler, relaying dozens of buckets from the pump to the boat—gave no one a moment to relax.

As the sun rose in their faces, Sister Hieronymo finally took her turn at the coal. Francis was exhausted; he leaned against the back of the furnace room, his eyes heavy with strain, clouded with layers of the black dust—he was barely standing; he dug in again demonstrating the procedure to Sister Hieronymo, who lifted a shovel-full and tossed it in with gusto—this being her first and only shift.

Five more hours stubbornly laboured on. Finally, Higgins yelled out a thankful cry. "Another hour, maybe two." Even with those wonderful words, Francis didn't move. The movements now: bending, lifting, shovelling, coughing, sweating, wiping—it was all accomplished without thought or consciousness; the moves were automatic, there was no mind process, just painful repetition. He dug in again.

The little steamer barge docked in Kingston at noon; there were many ashore who raced to meet her, offering warm welcomes and hearty assistance. The cargo was unloaded smoothly and safely, then arranged on shore according to purpose: food and clothes, or blankets and sheets, coal oil, and kitchen utensils, barrels of newly harvested fruits. Ralph and Johnny were handed over to an enthusiastic lady from the Female Benevolent Society—the fate of their future surely more optimistic than their past—but before they followed her into town, they both received wages from Mr. Higgins. "And you'll be paying them their wages, don't doubt it." Higgins was quick to oblige, the statement was not debatable; a long black finger pointed a dire threat in his face—Sister Hieronymo's final words to that boat master. She received no argument.

The little barge had sailed past the fever sheds—a crumpled stack of broken boards mixed about on the beach—all four sooty sailors stood and watched with somber amazement as their boat slowly slipped by, past Kingston centre harbour where the final construction phases were being added to a great Martello Tower in front of City Hall—out in the bay—the twenty-four pounder cannon clearly exposed on the top level. They sailed past the stone walls of Fort

Frontenac; soldiers of a Highland Regiment watched them closely from the ramparts—their feather bonnets blowing in the wind, their shiny bayonets glistening in the sun—to a dock reaching out into the swampy mouth of the Cataroqui River.

No boats or barges were allowed to dock before this point—farther west along the shoreline close to the sheds—that area was heavily restricted. Yet above the faded boards lining the roofs of the sheds, tall masts did appear, masts belonging to sailing schooners and steam ships—ships that had very recently arrived with a human cargo: casualties of the Great Famine—these ships alone were sequestered to the west side—theirs was a solitary mooring—these ships were quarantined—they carried plague. The fever ships had sailed up the St. Lawrence River from Grosse Isle east of Quebec City. Their fateful passengers had endured weeks, even months, on the Atlantic on larger ships that deposited them ashore, then returned to Ireland. Throughout the summer months of 1847 more than eight thousand sick passengers would be buried at sea, never reaching Canada. For those that survived, their story would only take another evil twist as they were turned away—refused sanctuary due to the contagious illness aboard. They were then boarded upon smaller vessels that could bypass the Lachine rapids at Montreal, through the canal, to Kingston; some to Toronto.

Kingston was a heavily fortified town. A series of four great stone bastions: Martello towers, faced the lake protecting the town, each with a huge cannon that could pivot 360 degrees to face an enemy from any direction; as well as two great stone fortifications: Fort Frederick and Fort Henry. Regiments stationed in Kingston included infantry, garrison and field artillery as well as sailors from the Royal Navy. Although Kingston had only recently lost its status as capital of Canada, it remained a strategic post as it guarded the waterway to Ottawa and the entrance to the interior of the country to the west. The towers and fortifications also protected the Queen's Navy. The town was growing rapidly; the activity on shore was vital and energetic.

Francis and the Sisters were instantly overwhelmed as they stepped ashore, however the level of exhaustion they suffered permitted only a semblance of participation in the unloading and distribution of their cargo—they needed baths and sleep before they could even consider the victims that they had come to help. Francis could not imagine selecting boating as a means of travel ever again—there were no redeeming qualities what so ever. Perhaps he would remain in Kingston until the spring, when he might finalize his plan to return to Chicago—an overland journey he reckoned. Lake Ontario would remain a wonderful vista, a beautiful panorama of shimmering water, seagulls drifting aloft, elegant sails tilting in the wind. He would watch from shore...solid, dependable earth, where he could walk or ride a horse without the need to balance over unsavoury waves or thrust black rocks into a blazing furnace in order to propel his body forward. Sisters Martha and Felicia, if allowed to comment on the subject, would have heartily reciprocated, absolutely. Sister Hieronymo had no opinion on the matter.

31

The bed was thick with goose feathers, the sheets: a soft luxurious blend of cotton and linen. The pillows were so firm and full, Francis sank his face in deep to a place from which he hoped he'd never have to arise. The gentle, easy crackle of the fire in the hearth and the friendly orange glow flickering on the ceiling above only added to the sublime level of comfort—he drifted to sleep within minutes. Mrs. Cartwright was careful to leave the window open in the guest bedroom—it would be another hot evening. The sun shining in was no disruption. Upon arriving to the grand house on Sydenham Street—a considerable walk from the harbour—Francis received the most gracious welcome which included a hot bath, a thoroughly bountiful meal; then he welcomed a restful night even though the hour had not struck three. The trip from Toronto had worn him out entirely; the difficult task tomorrow would arrive soon enough. He struggled with the wraps on his hands for a short time—the blisters throbbing, the open sores and cuts were painful. The wooden shovel handles had left their mark on all three stokers. The bandages were a nuisance, but the sheets were clean and Mrs. Cartwright intended to keep them that way.

Sisters Hieronymo, Martha and Felicia were given rooms in the small monastery associated with the newly completed Hotel Dieu Hospital on Brock Street; they would be sharing duties with two other Orders: the Sisters of the Religious Hospitals of St. Joseph and the Notre Dame Sisters as well as their hosts: the Hotel Dieu Sisters. The rooms were spartan—straw mattresses and no pillows (apparently Jesus never needed a pillow)—the meal was slim, however they quickly received a thankful, peaceful night after washing and attending chapel. All three sisters had to bandage their hands—the blisters from shovelling would take time to heal, although they were instructed and warned that their work commencing in the early morning would not be in any way jeopardized by their injuries. Their tasks were critical as the numbers of refugees arriving from Quebec were now reaching over two thousand per week.

Mrs. Harriet Cartwright had paid Augustus Higgins his charter fee—a ridiculous amount—collected from a diminishing account, that combined sources from the Catholic Dioceses and the town of Kingston. Higgins was very happy to cook up some fish on shore, then relax on deck in his little tent—his needs only included basic necessities; he stashed his income away for future prospects. His services would remain in high demand until well into the fall; he was happy, although recruiting dependable hands would continue to be challenging.

The lecture Francis received in the morning on the way to the fever sheds—down Sydenham Street to the corner, then West Street down to King and the shoreline—was split between the humanitarian and the political as it swerved back and forth between Mrs. Cartwright and the Mayor Thomas Kirkpatrick. The Mayor often dropped in at breakfast time to give Mrs. Cartwright a briefing of the current situation. Talk was cheap—but in local politics, it was a prerequisite. Kirkpatrick kept her well versed.

Mrs. Cartwright liked Francis right away—he was polite and thankful concerning his accommodation—wonderful supper and breakfast as well as freshly cleaned clothes—but he was also so unbiased: he really knew nothing of the issues strangling Kingston and her people, and he was so willing to listen. He had many questions, but no opinions...yet.

Harriet Cartwright had been very busy in Kingston establishing a solid foundation for the needs of the poor and destitute long before the boats arrived from Grosse Isle. The Female Benevolent Society as well as the Orphan's Home and the Widow's Friend Society were well underway and quickly overburdened. She supervised the Sister nurses to treat the ill, meals cooked and delivered, new clothes collected and old clothes burned as well as arranging bucket crews to distribute fresh water and remove human waste. The Mayor supervised the debarkation of the immigrants and the allocation of encampments away from the shoreline for the healthy and placement in a shed for the sick. He also administered procedures for removing the dead—a shallow mass grave across the street near the Kingston Hospital (it was filling rapidly)—and digging new latrines. His problems were mounting: funds were dwindling fast; the streets of Kingston were beginning to flood with ragged beggars pleading for meals and shelters—there was no plan in place to secure any kind of a future for them. Kirkpatrick complained about citizens' petitions involving the expulsion of the Irish, rotting corpses and horrendous odours, increased crime and derelict children wandering aimlessly at night frightening everybody. Solutions? He was 'working on it.'

Francis listened, however he wasn't sure why they were explaining anything to him—he had no power and no money. He nodded his head when he thought he should, followed them along to the shoreline, dreamed about soft pillows and warm blankets, then he woke up...fast. The sight shattering the morning's polite but detailed discussions, terminating the stroll, and smashing his face with a perverse sense of reality like a heavy sack of potatoes swinging from a hoist, was an immense putrid dump that included dozens of dilapidated wooden sheds, as far as he could see in both directions along the shoreline of Lake Ontario just west of downtown. Smokey fires squeezed between lumpy grey groups of thread-barren men and women huddling and sleeping; the most horrendous noxious odour swelled up throughout the deplorable temporary habitat and wafted ashore on the south winds—the Mayor stopped immediately. He reminded Mrs. Cartwright that if he was needed, he would be at City Hall, for most of the morning anyway. He turned and walked back up to King Street. Mrs. Cartwright turned to Francis, "Typical, like a frightened puppy."

Francis wondered how they could expect him to deal with any of this. He looked at Mrs. Cartwright with bewilderment, and she caught his worried expression immediately.

"I only expect you to do what you can Francis, anything will be a help. Perhaps you could start with repairing some of the sheds." She hesitated a bit waiting for a reply. "Sister Hieronymo said you were a very dependable young man."

Ah, Sister Hieronymo, so that's the origin of all this fine attention.

"I would like to see the sick Ma'am." Mrs. Cartwright was surprised; the sheds, desperately attempting to contain the suffering and the dying, were the last place volunteers wanted to visit.

"Very well. Be sure to wear protection, you don't want to succumb to the fever on your first day."

"I'll be fine." Francis moved into the centre of the area containing the rambling refugee village. Mrs. Cartwright passed by; she walked to the tables towards the town centre, where yesterday's cargo was finishing the final stages of distribution.

Francis was very curious about this epidemic.

He could see the masts and the sails of the schooners and steam boats up the shoreline towards Murney Tower; the new arrivals were unloaded there, then brought to the sheds on stretchers. Those who could walk were given a space on the grass to rest and receive water and food from the Sisters. There were so many sheds, some big and long, some very small—they had no common design, they had been erected fast by local volunteers, probably farmers and labourers, each one a little different than the other. They were not solid, they weren't waterproof; strong weather would undoubtedly send them sailing like a leaf in the wind. The roofs were mostly flat; there were dropped hinged boards over the windows that remained closed—but Francis could see ropes attached that could pull them up—this was encouraging. The doors were closed.

Some dead bodies were laid out in a somewhat orderly fashion next to various groups who stood nearby sharing a forlorn ghoulish posture—they were waiting for the wagon—their family at their feet, wrapped in sheets, stiff, sour; they were grieving, they were absolutely bereft, destitute. Many others sat or reclined near the small fires, adjacent to more bodies of the recently dead, not covered, not laying orderly or carefully—perhaps they died last night; perhaps they had no family left to care for their final journey. Others wandered hopelessly from the tables offering fruit, to the shed door—placing a hand there, but not daring to enter—back to the fire and a friend, then to the bushes behind, then to the lake, then back to the shed; a repetitious circle, a death stroll, a blind meandering without purpose; the sad final moments between a pitiful life and a sickening death. If they were not sick, they were starving; in any case—they were dying.

Francis moved from the path near the closest shed, over just slightly out of the way, as a horse behind pulled near. The cart came tumbling in, the great wheels banging and thumping on the rocks, the wooden carriage groaned and shook with every twist and bend. The horse was old, a dappled grey, small and weary, his head hanging low. He stopped at the first fire and immediately plopped a load of fresh manure (another foul odour to add to the noxious recipe). The driver remaining high on the buckboard slumped his shoulders and sighed. He had already transported two loads this morning and he was ready to go home. Tightly wrapped about his face was a scarf; a thin space was left between the peak of his hat and the bridge of his nose. He wasn't going to say anything, he didn't want to give orders—but although they knew he had arrived, no one moved. Francis decided he would begin here.

Sisters Martha and Felicia were already at work by the time Francis arrived at the first shed. They had been serving chicken broth to people at the fires and to those standing at the tables farther down towards town. Sister Hieronymo left the biggest shed, one of the first sheds built, it housed over sixty people; she marched towards the table. Sister Martha gave Sister Felicia a heads up with an elbow to her stomach and a whisper. "Here she comes. God save us."

"Go to the shed and clean them. They need their buckets removed and those that didn't use buckets need to be cleaned. Do you understand?"

"Yes Sister."

"And cover your faces."

"Yes Sister." Sisters Martha and Felicia hadn't entered a shed yet, their task had been to ladle soup into cups and bowls—breakfast for those who could stand in line; they had prayed for a continuous duty in this regard for a time that might endure throughout the remainder of their stay in Kingston. Pray as they might, they knew their good luck would end, and now that inevitability was before them.

The space was black and that alone would make anyone take pause, gain bearings—cautious trepidation as who knows what ghastly obstruction might be directly before them threatening their safety; but it wasn't the dark that reached out and gripped Sister Martha's body, wrenching it tight, squeezing her throat past any breathing point, freezing her feet solid so further forward movement became impossible—it was the smell. Sixty dying bodies covered in dirt, vomit, excrement and lice...curing, simmering, festering for over two months, compressed together in a tight wooden box without ventilation under intense heat—that grotesque odour had the power to stop an army of Sisters with or without their eternal dedication to Jesus Christ and all his saints. Sister Felicia slammed into the back of Sister Martha, her face buried in her cape. "Good God, save us all."

Another sister within, held up a coal oil lamp; she turned to the new visitors, "Cover your faces!"

The Sisters complied immediately bringing their scarves up over their faces. The smell unfortunately was not blocked out however, the scarves were for protection from the contagion. They went to work. The system they had developed as a team in Rochester came directly into use. Sister Martha would reach in and raise the patient, removing the old soiled clothes, wiping down the bodies, handing out the dirty clothes to Sister Felicia who threw them on the fire outside. She would then return with a clean bucket of water and a new cotton shift or some undergarment for the woman or girl, a shirt and trousers for a man or boy. Other Sisters were doing the same, then feeding water and soup. The procedure went on bed after bed, shed after shed, day after day. New volunteers from town would enter and carry out the dead, new patients would arrive, often two on a bed, some on the floor. It was hot, damp, humid, stuffy, dark; the work was disgusting and laborious; the smell: viciously malodorous and totally impossible.

Francis reached down, he struggled with a body; he was eventually assisted by a man who dropped his blanket and grabbed the feet. Within a few minutes the bodies at that fire were piled in the wagon and the pony turned—he slowly carried his load to the pit located a few hundred yards down King Street near Murney Tower and the Kingston Hospital. The sorry task would be repeated throughout the day and night.

The wooden door of the shed was not bolted, it shivered in the wind; Francis grabbed the latch and pulled.

On that first morning—her first shed, dealing with her first fever victims, taking her first break away from the stench and the filth, the first retrieval of the first bucket of water from the well outside— Sister Felicia first learned about Francis and her admiration for him. A committee comprising of Mayor Thomas Kirkpatrick, Mrs. Harriet Cartwright (supervisor of the sheds), Dr. James Sampson (the only registered doctor from the Kingston General Hospital that would visit the sheds), Chief of Police Samuel Shaw, and one other rather excited man who Sister Felicia didn't recognize, who seemed to be jumping up and down rather hysterically, waving his arms about as he exclaimed to all those in the group how impossible the whole matter was and how he had been offended—approached from the centre of town at a rapid pace past the well and past Sister Felicia, giving her presence no concern.

"I tell you he's mad. He's got to be stopped. He'll infect the whole town!"

Mr. Kirkpatrick answered the man by accusing Sister Hieronymo, who maintained the quick step of the group without effort, as speed was a fashion to which she was accustomed and approved without reservation. "Wasn't it you Sister that recommended this young man? If he's responsible for spreading this infection to the town, I will hold you personally liable!"

"Francis is totally dependable; I can't imagine what he's doing." Her retort was quite terse, she did not appreciate the accusation.

Sister Felicia heard Francis' name, she was shocked and confused. She left the bucket and tagged along behind the committee.

Francis had an axe in his hands; the strokes were powerful—great chunks of boards were splitting and flying about. A huge gaping hole emerged in the south-facing wall of the shed. Chief Shaw approached and demanded compliance. "Stop that right now! Stop I say! What are you doing? Are you mad? I shall arrest you immediately!"

All the window boards were wide open as was the door—the sun poured in, fresh air now channelled from the lake through the shed—a wonderful cool draft. The sick inside who hadn't moved for days sat up, blocking the bright sun from their eyes with their hands; they sucked in the fresh air with great hungry gulps.

Francis stopped, he dropped his axe, reviewed his work, he was satisfied. He looked the policeman in the eye. "Now they can breathe!"

"You fool you are releasing the contagion, the entire town will be infected within minutes we will all die!" Chief Shaw felt it was his duty as the head of the Kingston Police to take charge of this criminal.

"Please Francis, what have you done?" Sister Hieronymo was ashamed and so disheartened.

"You are the fool. These people didn't come here to die, they came to live. The illness is Typhus, it can't spread to the town. You must share their space, their bed or wear their clothes if you want the fever. You know nothing of ship fever. Let me show you."

"Arrest him Chief, he's mad!" Doctor Sampson urged the Police Chief by pointing a finger from the rear of the group—a safe cautious, distance away.

"Come with me." Francis stepped over the axe and encouraged the group to follow him around the shed and inside. At first they were not sure, but they followed. Francis pushed by them all, looking into Sister Felicia's face lastly. *She doubts me too.*

Entering the shed, everyone was sure to cover their faces. The Mayor and the Chief were very hesitant. "In there?"

"Do want to learn how to save these people?" Francis was not angry, but his tolerance level was truly dropping as he dealt with those in charge. He couldn't believe their ignorance. He selected a man, perhaps in his late twenties, half way down the isle in the shed. He bent down and gently raised him up, he carefully removed his shirt. "Look here." Francis exposed his chest and back—they were covered with hundreds of small red sores, possibly thousands of them.

"The plague! These sores are the mark of the plague, you idiot!" Doctor Sampson was quick to offer an instant diagnosis. He covered his face and eyes, turned his head. "Arrest him. Arrest him!"

"These sores are not symptoms of any plague; they are the cause of the fever. They are insect bites. The people on the ships have been carrying lice for months. The lice carry poison in their bite. Remove the lice and you remove the cause. Cool the sheds and you will reduce their fevers. Give them fresh water constantly and you will revive them."

"How do know this young man?" The Mayor spoke up.

"I have seen this before many times in Chicago. From cowboys months on the trail, from soldiers who never bathe. You cannot spread this disease through the air—but the insects can jump. All nurses must wash their hair every night. They must search each other for lice."

"But the dysentery?"

"Those people with bowel illness have typhoid, not typhus. Typhoid is from bad water or meat, especially pigs or horse meat. It's possible that some people here are suffering from both. But it's not the plague. It's from dirt. These people have lived in filth for too long. Filth breeds illness. You can see it. Clean these people, cut their hair, clean these sheds and you will stop the fever."

"This man is no doctor. Are you going to take his word over mine? He doesn't know what he's talking about. You must close those windows, seal up the shed, you must prevent the fever from spreading!" Dr. Sampson was on the edge of screaming at the Chief; he was absolutely astounded that Francis might be considered a voice of reason, a possible source of a solution. He was, after all, a doctor—this boy was a drifter, a vagabond from a barge.

"I have seen filth, and I have cleaned it. I don't know if it will stop the fever, but I believe cleaning these sheds and these people will offer relief." Sister Hieronymo wasn't concerned about the doctor's credentials, only the welfare of the people. Hers was a legacy of charity; she was not afraid of the fever, she was not afraid of open windows and cool breezes, she may not have been afraid of anything.

"I'll give you five days young man. If we can see serious improvement in this man's condition, we will use your methods in the other sheds. We will open them up." The Major was not particularly impressed with Francis and his assertions of the illness, nor was he convinced about the spread of the fever, but he appreciated Sister Hieronymo and the vigilant efforts all the Sisters were making in Kingston during this difficult time. He also needed any program that would look good politically. He could now at least report that a new approach for the eradication of the fever was being introduced.

"That man's a quack! You will suffer the consequences. All of you." Doctor Sampson turned, pushing past Sister Felicia, practically running to King Street, away from the miasma of the sheds.

The others turned to leave the shed. "This man will walk out of this shed in five days." Francis had no reservations about his boast.

"Five days, young man…then you'll be arrested." The Chief gave Francis that sour endorsement, then coughed, then retreated.

Francis stood beside his special patient. Sister Hieronymo and Sister Felicia approached. "I hope you know what you're doing Francis."

"I need scissors and a razor. I need a lotion of lanolin and honey. I need herbs: elderberry, juniper, echinacea; I need alcohol, gin is best or pure ethanol; I need vinegar. Can you get them for me?"

"Sister Teresa from the Hotel Dieu knows of a herbal shop in town, I can check." Sister Felicia stared with her mouth open, then offered the answer—it came blurting out before she realized she had spoken. She felt an unusual excitement as if a new hope and a new perspective might be possible now; she wanted to give Francis every chance.

Sister Hieronymo turned to her. "Close your mouth. Then go Sister." The Sister instructed Sister Felicia; she left the shed quickly. "I will bring you scissors and a razor. Be careful Francis. Trust nobody. There's more happening here than just a cure for the fever." Sister Hieronymo offered a wise summation of the impromptu meeting that just occurred.

"I know."

Francis looked down at his patient. His face was so pale, his eyes glassy and red, his breathing shallow. "What is your name?"

"I am Patrick Monaghan. I am from County Meath. My family is dead."

"You will live Mr. Monaghan."

32

Francis showed Sister Felicia how to mix the salve, how to grind the roots of the herbs, how to add the powder. He showed Sister Martha how to shave Mr. Monaghan's face and head, how to collect the hair, to deposit it into a bowl and throw it on the fire outside. His armpits were shaved as well as his groin. Francis showed the Sisters the lice and the gnats in the hair and on his scalp and in the bite wounds. They washed him with soap and hot water, then with gin as no other alcohol was located; he groaned gently as the gin burned. Francis applied the salve to the bites; Mr. Monaghan rested with a stomach full of beef stew and thick doughy bread with butter—the most he had eaten in six weeks. His mattress of old straw was thrown out and replaced. Francis showed the Sister the nests of lice and fleas in the moldy straw under the head of the bed. His new mattress was woollen blankets and a clean cotton sheet, no pillow. In the middle of his 'thank you', Mr. Monaghan fell asleep, the cool breeze from the lake soothed his body, the fever would begin to break by morning.

The other poor souls in the shed were not ignored, they received the same treatment. Sisters Martha and Felicia worked all day and well into the night with Francis. They continually wiped down the bodies with cool cloths and maintained a strict regimen of fresh water for each to drink every five or ten minutes. They each received three meals that first day, new beds and new haircuts—although Mr. Monaghan was the only one shaved completely bald. The Sisters searched for lice and fleas on each patient at every visit. They soaked them off with gin and vinegar.

When two relief Sisters from the Hotel Dieu arrived at seven o'clock, they were instructed as to the procedure and began to work immediately; they would stay throughout the night. Coal oil lanterns were lit, the window boards were closed half way as rain began to fall; Francis was satisfied and followed the Sisters outside. Sister Martha scurried along fast up to King Street (she was exhausted). Sister Felicia told her not to wait for her, she would be along presently. Francis took hold of Sister Felicia's hand; he held it toward the flickering glow of the fire light.

"Here let me look at that." Her bandages were horribly dislodged and her blisters exposed. "Wait a moment." Francis re-entered the shed and returned in a moment with a cup of the salve. "Hold your hand out." He carefully removed the bandages then softly applied the salve to her palms after dipping his fingers into the bowl. The salve was indeed soothing, it was cool, his fingers were gentle, yet firm—there was a confidence in the way he used them—he was careful, thorough. He rubbed both of his hands over hers with tender patience—she could feel his compassion. Sister Felicia looked into Francis' eyes as he worked, her heart began to flutter. She didn't want him to stop.

"There, that should help. Put some new bandages on them in the morning, let the wounds breathe tonight while you sleep." His words were soft. He smiled. Their eyes met for a moment. He watched small drops of rain fall on her eyelashes—tiny wet pearls balancing on delicate golden strands—they collected and pooled, then slipped slowly down to her cheek following the fine curves of her face. His eyes pursued the wet course to her lips. She pulled her hands away.

"Thank you."

"Could I walk you home?"

"Well...I..."

"How is your patient Francis?" Sister Hieronymo appeared suddenly.

"Oh...I think he is doing much better, they all will. Thank you for having confidence in me."

"We shall see Francis, we shall see. Time for chapel don't you think Sister?"

"Yes Sister." They turned abruptly. They began their walk back to the Hotel Dieu Hospital.

The house on Sydenham Street was filled with welcoming aromas of warm jellies brewing and fresh cut flowers; there was steaming bread directly from the oven on the table. The evening rain strummed a gentle rhythm on the windows, the fire in the hearth was aglow with yellow flames curling and snapping viciously around spruce logs. Francis couldn't imagine a better place of retreat after the difficult first day. Mrs. DuMaurier and Agnes Stinson, both members of the Female Benevolent Society assisted with Francis' wash and examined his hair carefully. They searched for insects, but found none. He then insisted they cut his hair—short but not extreme; he also shaved—facial hair was quickly giving his youthful skin and face a more mature masculine profile. Within the flash of a blade the young boy returned. Mrs. DuMaurier cupped his face in her hands, "Such a handsome lad." His clothes were replaced by fresh donations—a bit airy as they belonged to Frank Stinson (Agnes' brother, and not a small man)—his were washed immediately. Mrs. Cartwright ate with Francis and they discussed the results of the day's endeavours, Dr. Sampson's accusations and the Mayor's concerns. Francis enjoyed a wonderful meal, but remained somewhat tight-lipped about the bargain he struck concerning Mr. Monaghan. There was no doubt that his leadership in the sheds was greatly appreciated and he was often overwhelmed with a sense of duty as he moved from patient to patient—he recognized tasks that required attention and he complied without hesitation—the urge often took hold of him as if it was preordained; he didn't pause to question it. He did, however, decide that Dr. Sampson's behaviour was irrational—he didn't trust him.

The dark wooden beams on the ceiling above in the guest bedroom securing the building's structure, offered a sense of comfort to Francis; he recognized and appreciated the order and the balance—the strength. Yet when he laid back, as he counted the beams from the left then the right and measured the space between them with his eyes—it wasn't equal—the middle beam was not centred—he wished he could rise up and move them creating equal lines and spaces.

He closed his eyes and graciously embraced the few quiet moments before he would surrender his thoughts to sleep. A pair of sparkling blue eyes danced and played in the shadows of his mind; rivulets of rainwater dripped down and washed them away.

He drifted far above the smokey fires, above the stench and the death, above the pain and the suffering, to the west, to Chicago—to the stockyards, to Little Raven; to a simple time of delicate caresses and youthful wonder. He was on the prairie carefully selecting berries for Rising Sun—the warmth of midday painted a radiating glow on his upturned face as he ran and played in the tall grass. Little Raven's sinewy body swayed with the grass in a willowy dance, the thick black strands of her hair spinning around, her arms outstretched. Joining her was Nootkana and Rising Sun, then finally Shashona—their long arms swerving to the weaving rhythm blanketing the stocks of golden grass. Then the pulses abruptly stopped: three dark figures remained—black silhouettes against a vast brooding sky. Snaking ropes lashed firmly to the gallows, squeezed tightly around their necks; their bare feet swung in unison below, the grass tickled the bottoms of their soles on each pass. The thick nooses binding their necks forced their heads to tilt and twist. Their tongues, black and swollen, protruded like slippery slugs, their eyes bulged from their sockets, frozen in a blank unholy stare bearing down on Francis— crushing, judging—he couldn't breathe.

Francis woke with a startled jerk, he grabbed his neck, he pulled the rope. With both hands he tugged and strained, desperate to breathe. Finally opening his eyes, he bounced to his knees—the grizzly scene began to fade. The quiet shadows of Mrs. Cartwright's house returned, consoling his fear—he wiped the sweat from his brow—he dropped his hands, trying to regain focus. The threatening corners of the bedroom drifted away; the prairie grasses shrivelled and dissolved, ominous clouds broke up, the haunting faces of death dissolved—they shrank, lost to the dark recesses; the gallows folded away, the wooden lintels and beams straightened and spread out across the ceiling over his head. Francis turned his face to the window pane, to the rain gently dripping, each drop delicately discovering their own channel to follow down the glass to the sill—again and again. He began to cry.

The soft bristles of her hairbrush gently glided through, stroking her hair, massaging her scalp—it felt so good at the end of the day. The chances of any gnats sticking to her hair was slight as Sister Felicia had kept her cowl and veil on snuggly throughout the day; however she brushed enthusiastically—back, then forward—her short blonde hair flipping and folding, her waves coming alive again. She had concluded a thorough washing from head to toe in the small bathroom provided—one for twenty-five patrons on the basement floor. She had carried three buckets of hot water from the kitchen upstairs down two dark hallways and one spiny metal staircase; then filled the rest of the tiny steel tub with cold water from the hand pump in the little barren room. The process of filling the tub was slow and tiring especially after the long day—but so absolutely worth every effort. She had to wait for all the other nuns to finish first, wash, then redress, then chapel, then supper, then undress again. She sat on the edge of her bed in her shift, the heavy weight of exhaustion pressing down on her shoulders. Francis came to mind; his dark green eyes, his coy smile, that thick mane of raven black hair, but most of all the confident manner he possessed when managing the issues in the sheds: his compassion, his strength. Taking charge seemed to come natural to him. She thought perhaps he could do anything; he could certainly stand up to the Mayor and to the Chief—Dr. Sampson, definitely. Sister Hieronymo…well, maybe not Sister Hieronymo. She looked at her hands; she drew her fingers across her blisters and thought of how Francis had touched them so carefully. She thought of…

"He's a nice boy isn't he?"

Sister Martha was standing in the doorway, the dim light behind her from the hallway filtered through her night dress, the naked curves of her figure easily and clearly outlined.

"Who?"

"You know very well who. Francis, and you were thinking about him just now."

"I certainly was not." Sister Felicia tried to make her retort emphatic, but she was tired, it sounded weak and unconvincing.

"You better get your rosary out right now. You are enamoured and you are lying." Sister Martha approached and sat down beside her on the bed. She pushed her hip in close; reaching around she began to gently stroke her fingers through the golden weave of her hair. "I know you like him." Her voice was soft and tender, not critical.

"I do not."

"You have taken vows my little sister. Be very careful."

"Don't call me that. I am not your sister."

"You know I look out for you; I don't want you to do something you might regret. You should confide in me. We are good friends aren't we?" Sister Martha continued to stroke Sister Felicia's hair until she applied one stroke too many.

She pushed her hand away. "Stop. I am fine. You should return to your room."

Sister Martha left her side and stood in the doorway of the little bedroom facing Sister Felicia; she knew the naked fullness of her body was exposed from the soft glow of the oil lamp in the hallway behind her. She drew in a deep breath—her breasts pushed forward and up against the soft cotton of her gown, the imprint of her erect nipples firm and prominent. "Look at me." Sister Felicia looked up. "Be careful Sister. Remember I am always here for you." She left. Sister Felicia grabbed her rosary and began to pray.

33

S tepping off the boardwalk into a puddle, Bill Armstrong annoyingly glanced down; shaking his boot for a moment to deflect the mud—a daily unavoidable occurrence in this town (*at least it wasn't horse shit*)—he began a casual stroll across the street from Smithson's Mercantile to Handlebaum's Market.

It was early and Little Raven wanted the best selection for Mrs. O'Brien; she quickened her pace. Stepping up into the store, she stole a quick peripheral glance and spied the wide dark brim of Armstrong's hat dipping low over his eyes; his confident, limpy swagger and lanky posture was indisputable. He was approaching; her heart began to race. She kept her head low, she gripped her basket tight. Chicago bustled at this time of day, the town continued to grow daily: new settlers, new stores and businesses, a circus of horses and buggies in the streets. She could hide in the busy crowd.

A few onions, salt and chicory, perhaps a jar of pickled peppers. She picked up a soap and held it to her nose—the scent was lavender—it made her smile. Was it so long ago that she and Nootkana had stressed over a boiling caldron—the fumes eating away at their skin, the smoke infusing into the fabric of their clothes, sticking to their hair? Lil enjoyed the market and now that so many new people mingled in the shops, it wasn't difficult for her to become just another face, just another shopper filling her basket.

She had slowly become a member of the O'Brien family; gradually her world began to grow out and away from the harsh elements of the prairies to Whiteman's structured boundaries of streets and buildings; strolling pedestrians, running children, wagons and carts and the ever-present sounds: tinkling piano chords from the saloon, boisterous cowboys and dockworkers whooping and hollering on Friday nights; speeches and sideshows from businessmen and pan-handlers to naive suckers sequestered in tight circles about them. Lil was cautious to keep to herself, venturing into town was not a typical daily activity for her, but she so enjoyed the opportunity and usually accepted Mrs. O'Brien's proposal when asked.

Armstrong was not crossing the street to arrest a thief or break up a fight; he was not considering fashioning a dress from the fine patterned fabric wrapped in bolts—the colourful collection stacked neatly behind the counter—but he looked up at them anyway with a smile and a curious expression, fooling nobody. "He wants to see you."

Lil heard the voice, deep, direct and in no way could it have been meant for anyone else, as the vile odour of his breath wafted over her shoulder, slinking down and around her neck, like poison released from a festering slime pit. He hovered like a vulture examining his prey. She froze. He smiled.

Lil gently turned; she did not look at him. "What does he want?"

"Not my concern little lady. Best come with me."

"I cannot come now; I am on an errand."

"You'll come now." A tough cowboy fresh off the trail carrying a pistol in his belt would have a difficult time arguing with Bill Armstrong, Little Raven could offer no contest. She felt the brute strength of his powerful hand grab her elbow and pull. She was being directed out of the shop. She left her basket on the counter, raising her eyes in pathetic surrender to the proprietor standing behind.

"I hope to return soon."

"That's fine. I'll keep this here for you Ma'am." Mr. Handlebaum stepped back; he wanted no trouble in his store. Armstrong smiled and touched the brim of his hat—a mocking cordial salutation.

Charles Smithson started drinking early, soon after he rose, now it was almost ten o'clock, the bottle retained only an inch of whiskey. Standing at the window of his office in the Mercantile, he swirled it about, then poured that final instalment into his glass. Armstrong and the girl were heading across the street, he swallowed then turned to fetch another bottle from his cabinet behind the great desk. When Armstrong and Lil entered, he was sitting waiting, drink in hand, the vast oak surface of his massive desk spread before him like a barrier between good and evil—bulky, solid, immovable.

"Thank you, Sheriff." Lil stood before him, her head bowed so low he could see the tiny flower print decorating the top her bonnet. She held her fingers together tightly, waist high. "You can leave." Armstrong left the office. Little Raven and Charles Smithson were left alone. The loud metallic click of the door latch closing behind her was enough to stop her heart. "You have been living with Pat O'Brien these months, I know." Lil did not respond, she did not look up "Look at me!" He raised the

volume of his voice just enough to convince her of his temperament—
she wasn't here to receive advise about tomorrow's weather. Pressing
his fists into the desk, he rose up slowly like a monolithic Egyptian
obelisk being raised over the desert pulled by a thousand slaves—the
great pillar reaching the apex and slamming straight upright into the
sandstone foundation below—the wide broad lintel of his shoulders
dominating the structure, the massive image exuding power and
strength…and terror. She watched the man stand, she could feel her
status shrink little by little with every inch he gained—the scales
inversely tipped and unbalanced as they settled into place. This man
had the power to give life and to take it as quick as a snap of a bull
whip over the nervous haunches of a doomed workhorse. She noticed
he swerved uncontrollably, just a little—this was worse—he was
drunk.

"I could have hung you with the rest. You are here because I chose
to spare you."

"What do you want?"

"So suspicious, so…ungrateful." Smithson moved around to the
front of the desk and stood directly before her, towering over her.
She was visibly scared, her shoulders began to shake. There was no
one else in the world that could frighten her like this man; this huge,
unpredictable man…her father. "I only want to offer you a home, a
home with me. You should want that now, don't you?"

Little Raven raised her chin high in order to reach his eye level.
"Never."

Smithson grabbed her shoulder and squeezed. "You will do as
you're told." Little Raven began to scream—he slapped her face so
hard the sound caught in her throat, choking her. With both arms
he shook her back and forth—she whipped around like a wispy doll,
her spine made of straw. The continuous motion gave him a moment

of unbalance, he tipped a bit forward, he used her to head to catch his fall—it slammed into his chest. He reached in grabbing her chin pulling her face up to him—his alcohol stupor began to swirl the image around—he could see the face of Shashona. His other hand twisted her arm behind her back; he pushed her down hard onto his desk. Little Raven began to fight, to struggle—his trousers dropped to the floor, her dress pulled up to her waist. Charles used his power to overcome her, pressing her, raping her—again and again; her screams were controlled by a fierce hand gripping her mouth and nose. When he had finished they collapsed together on the floor—he, a massive, half-naked stinking tumour of a man—lifeless in his vile whisky coma; her, a pathetic, confused victim, violated, distressed... exhausted.

Lil pulled her clothes together, stood at the door to the office and peered outside. She attempted to adjust her bonnet, to style her mangled hair with her fingers—she began crossing the street in a slow, careful stroll—feigning composure—wiping the tears from her face, being sure to keep her head low, removing her face from view— then scurrying, then running, never looking back.

34

Another hot humid, summer day in Kingston; the breezes blowing in from Lake Ontario were cherished by everyone, but especially by those working at the shoreline—the ships continued to arrive, the sick passengers continued to unload, the task facing Mrs. Cartwright seemed insurmountable. The Sisters and town volunteers continued to show up every day, bodies continued to drop into mass graves near the harbour, Mayor Kirkpatrick continued to grieve (for their plight as well as his). Francis entered the shed to check on Mr. Monaghan, Sister Felicia greeted him immediately with a smile and a bit of a chuckle. "Your hair!"

"Yes. It was best to cut it for the sake of the lice." Francis rubbed his hand over his face and head.

"It looks good." (She was lying a bit—she liked it longer.)

"How is Mr. Monaghan today."

"Oh Francis, he is so much better." They both leaned over Mr. Monaghan. He was awake and eating porridge, smiling.

"Thank you. Thank you." The porridge dripped down his chin. Sister Felicia was quick to wipe it. Sister Hieronymo arrived at the door. "I need your help Francis. Can you assist with a birth?"

"Yes."

"Follow me." Francis carried his bag with Rising Sun's medical kit. He and Sister Felicia followed Sister Hieronymo down to a shed that housed women close to the ships near Murney tower.

It was difficult to estimate Mary Fionnagain's age, but that wasn't the main concern for Francis. When asked, she provided the more important fact—she was not a first time mother, and this Francis presumed would help him understand the situation. She couldn't push because she was sick and dehydrated, not because it was her first child as the Sisters presumed. She was so weak, she would faint and remain in that state for many minutes—the baby, although crowning, would not come. Francis had Sister Hieronymo stand her up beside the bed and support her back, two other Sisters assisted on both sides. When she finally became conscious after cold water was vigorously rubbed on her neck, she was told to squat—it would be the old Indian method, where gravity would do some of the work. The baby began to move, but a tear opened and Mary began to bleed. Francis ordered her to be replaced back on the bed, and Sister Felicia watched Francis perform a small surgery for the first time.

"I can stitch up a cut much better than a tear," he explained as Sister Felicia brought in his small knives from the pot boiling on the fire outside. "Be sure not to touch the blade with anything. Do not wipe it!" His directions were firm, and Sister Felicia followed them without question. He cut a wider slit and Mary was once again moved to the squatting position. The baby soon dropped and Francis caught it in a clean towel. The placenta was pulled out and the wound was stitched. Sister Felicia had never witnessed such a scene and she was overwhelmed. Francis instructed the Sisters to watch her closely for the next few days. He was confident the stitches would hold, but was ready for any inevitability, particularly infection. His instructions included that she must be kept clean at all costs, cloths and towels as well.

The baby was placed on her chest and Mary slept immediately. Because there was no breast milk, a warm supplement was concocted with cow's milk, however a wet nurse in one of the other sheds was located and the baby received a good start—its new world, although desperately wanting, included a community of loving mothers who shared the baby as their own. She was the first Canadian born Fionnagain from that family: Jenny Margaret Fionnagain.

As Francis washed his hands by the pot at the fire, Sister Felicia watched him closely—she followed in kind and copied his method: vicious hot water and severe soap scrubbing, over and over again. Her respect for his skills had absolutely soared, and there was no doubt in her mind that Francis was every bit a doctor as Dr. Sampson or any other that dared to venture down to this horrendous location. All the Sisters were impressed and chattering amongst themselves. She caught herself staring into his eyes—innocent wanderlust mixed with giddy emotion. Together they washed silently. Sister Hieronymo exiting the shed identified the exchange between them and interrupted with haste. "Come with me Sister."

"Yes Sister." They left together quickly to continue their work at adjacent sheds.

A sad group of young men gathered at the fire at the next shed, close to the grave sight, where another cartload of bodies had been recently lowered; their song could be heard clearly through the derelict village, around the clapboard, over the rooftops—it drifted then hung its mournful chords on the winds from the lake: a soulful anthem of the terrible Irish plight.

"Sad, sad is my fate in this weary exile

Dark, dark is the night cloud o'er lone Shanakyle

Where the murdered sleep silently

In the coffinless graves of poor Eireann."

Suddenly the tune was violently interrupted—the men at the fire scattered—Francis dropped the soap into the pot. A carriage raced up beside Francis—the horses were a beautiful chestnut, the harness and reins were shiny black leather with brass hardware and silver chains, the driver was resplendent in a fine red surge, four gold stripes were shining on his lower right sleeve. The tall soldier, his mouth barely visible, buried deep within his great beard and moustache, raised his body up above the seat, then pulled the horses tight to a crashing halt and yelled out, "I am looking for a doctor. Are you Francis Tumblety?"

How could this man possibly know my name?

"Yes sir."

The carriage ride to Fort Henry was completed with great speed and finesse—the Sergeant Major was undoubtedly a master handler. Francis jogged about inside the beautiful coach sitting opposite Lieutenant Bigsby, the officer sent to fetch a doctor for the Major. They sped past City Hall and the Market Place, down King to Fort Frontenac, across the causeway, past the Royal Naval Dockyards and up the hill to Point Henry. The Lieutenant explained that the garrison's commanding officer (Major Liam Enniskillen), was concerned about his son, who had recently taken very ill and it was assumed he had the fever. No doctor was available to attend; the regiment's doctor was very ill himself and was sequestered in the small stone field hospital outside the fort. There was no one else. Mayor Kirkpatrick had offered Francis' name, it was his last hope.

A massive stone modified pentagon surrounded by a huge dry ditch on all sides, covering 20 acres—yet Fort Henry was hidden—totally invisible to Francis, as the carriage crossed the swing bridge over the west flanking ditch, stopping at the entrance to the Advanced Battery. The entire main section of the fortification was cleverly sunk deep into the hill—only the ramparts reached the surface: an escarpment of heavy artillery facing the enemy on all sides; a powerful foreboding structure—an impenetrable, military threat.

Lieutenant Bigsby explained that although the men and officers were allowed to visit Kingston during their short monthly breaks—the taverns and brothels bustling with business depending on the British servicemen—there was a strict regulation concerning the fever and the sheds. The contagion must be contained to that part of the city only, it must not venture its way up to Fort Henry; and all necessary precautions were taken, including searching the men daily for symptoms. However Major Enniskillen's worst nightmare was now perhaps affirmed—his son was sick with fever. The greatest fear now entailed the mass spread of the disease throughout the regiment.

The sentry at the gate to the Advanced Battery waved the coach through. Francis and Lieutenant Bigsby stepped out, then followed the stone corridor down into the ditch, to the main entrance to the fort, stopping at the drawbridge where another sentry stood with his weapon at the ready. The Lieutenant returned the salute and they entered the fort. A huge expansive space opened up before Francis, flanked by massive limestone walls surrounding the area on all sides. The immensity of the structure was overwhelming—the power and durability was undeniable; rows of vaulted casements spanning the entire length of two levels secured the fortification's foundation and strength; ramparts sixty feet above them wrapped about the entire structure proudly displaying a bastion of cannon directed to every direction. On the space open before him Francis watched soldiers marching through their paces as a Sergeant yelled the orders. From above a gun crew trained on the 24 pounder guns on the east rampart—hauling at the ropes as the massive cannons slowly inched back to loading position, their cries reaching out to Deadman's Bay and shattering around the walls, "Heave! Heave!" Francis watched children play and mothers hanging clothes out to dry on tentative lines. Field guns received repair, lying in the dirt, their wooden carriages and limbers bracing against six pairs of hands stringently rubbing, pressing, shinning—and voices singing, "We'll tear our guns and run'em through, for England's got men of iron for their gun crew…" From a dark corner out of sight, the prancing lilt of fifes and the tap of drums echoed through—bandsmen practicing their tunes. Soldiers on break returned his stares, but gave him no mind.

They reached the Commandant's room under the East Battery, Francis waited patiently outside near the flagpole—a giant mainmast borrowed from a decommissioned ship no doubt, continuing her service from the sea to the land—the British colours tethered to a rope flying with wild whips and curls high above the ramparts: The Union Jack commanding attention from all compass points, denoting pride and guaranteeing security.

When instructed to enter, Francis cautiously stepped over the threshold, the casemate within revealing nothing, the room was dark, the details were difficult to recognize—then a voice spoke from somewhere deep within the shadows.

"The North Lancashires are a proud regiment Mr. Tumblety. We take our duty seriously."

"Yes Sir."

Major Enniskillen was a young man, clean shaven save for two long arms of wiry red beard framing his face on both sides of his cheeks; his moustache was thin; the tight collar of his uniform pinched his neck so deep creases forming there appeared to choke him. He sat firmly at his desk. He looked Francis directly in the eye. "Are you a doctor?"

The light filtered in from outside and Francis could finally see his face.

"No Sir. I use Indian herbal remedies." Francis was not nervous; the Major's eyes were not fierce or threatening, they were soft and concerned, his voice was calm. Francis knew he would not be here if this man were not very concerned for his son's health. "I will do what I can."

"I am a great believer in Indian remedies. Are you an American Mr. Tumblety?" This was a question Francis had not expected. He had told the Mayor that he had treated typhus in Chicago—this may have been the tip. "Do you know why the British Military occupies this fortification?" He did not wait for an answer. "To protect Kingston and the Province of Canada from invading Americans."

"Yes Sir." Francis did not know that America was threatening Canada; his history lessons were scant and barely included the pyramids of Egypt and the American Revolutionary War. Shannon O'Brien was not keen on British history and Francis had made no effort in any regard to expand the course of his lessons.

"I am from Sandwich, near Windsor on the Detroit River." This was information that had worked before, so Francis decided to use it again.

Major Enniskillen remained silent and wondered about the amount of time he might waste interrogating Francis. He stood up and decided to reduce his conclusions to a few simple words. "If you hurt my son in any way, you will be executed immediately."

"Yes Sir." Francis decided his impression of this man might be incorrect. He swallowed hard.

"Come with me."

The officer's quarters were located in a series of casemates in the lower west wall of the fort; they were occupied at this time by Major Enniskillen and Lieutenant Bigsby, their wives and children; the other officers of the 81st Regiment Of Foot (North Lancashire) and the Artillery officers had residences outside the fort in Kingston. Francis examined the boy thoroughly in the presence of his mother and father and concluded that there was no typhus as no insect bites were present. The illness was probably associated with bad food—a type of typhoid—and required a cleansing. Francis mixed a powerful herb to a gin base and predicted that after a series of bowel movements and fresh water, the fever would subside. He suggested that the food be carefully examined and the water be boiled thoroughly. Francis also suggested that all soldiers should be quarantined to the fort; the chance of typhus reaching his men and the inhabitants of the fort was very high. Major Enniskillen was not so sure a quarantine was necessary; however he would consider it.

Before Francis left Fort Henry, Major Enniskillen asked for another favour. He asked the Sergeant Major to wait while he entered the coach and sat opposite Francis so he might discuss something private.

"The construction of this fort and the defence systems in Kingston was supervised and carried out by a very capable man—a man that Kingston has grown to love and admire. Sir Richard has received the highest recognitions the Crown can render, he is a great soldier and a great friend. He retired from service less than a year ago and I fear he has developed an illness from which he might not recover." Major Enniskillen removed his shako and, holding it in his hands, he continued his quiet oratory that included a deep personal respect and admiration for Sir Richard Bonnycastle, and his fear that his death might be imminent. "Our regimental doctor has not been successful in terms of rendering a diagnosis or cure, nor has Dr. Sampson. Do you know Dr. Sampson?"

"Yes." Francis refrained from offering further comment on Dr. Sampson, he wasn't sure how his opinion would be received.

"If you could take some time to visit Sir Richard and perhaps administer any assistance you see fitting, particularly ascertain if he suffers from the fever—I would be very grateful."

"Yes Major, I could do that for you."

"Thank you, Mr. Tumblety, and I greatly appreciate your help with my son. My wife and I will be sure to follow your directions. My Sergeant Major will drive you to Sir Richard. Thank you and farewell." Major Enniskillen offered Francis his hand. It was the first time Francis had ever shaken a man's hand in friendship or otherwise, and it felt good. He appreciated the respect he was receiving.

"Thank you sir."

With the snap of a whip, the horses bolted forward, the coach dashed through the archway of the Advanced Battery; down the steep hill from Point Henry and across the causeway—the distance to Kingston proper was covered in a matter of minutes.

Sitting alone in the Major's carriage, passing people shopping in the market place, viewing the beautiful limestone houses and businesses lining the streets, peering into the windows of other carriages passing by, spying on the beautiful ladies and proper gentlemen within, Francis was feeling quite special. He was feeling as though he was an important doctor sent to attend an important patient—and in a way he was. The concept of assisting medically away from the fever sheds was most attractive, and for a short while he decided to enjoy it, why not, what harm could there be?

Portsmouth, a very tiny village on the outskirts of Kingston on the lake about three miles west from the town centre, was home to Sir Richard Bonnycastle. A beautiful custom house, built from carefully selected choice limestone blocks, recently completed with wide white pillars supporting a grand portico in front, green shutters bordering the tall windows on the front edifice—very opulent and very fitting for a retired Lieutenant Colonel of the Queen's Royal Engineers and Knight—was situated majestically within a quiet meadow just north of the harbour. Major Enniskillen's carriage pulled into the vaulted archway between the main house and the carriage house, unannounced.

Mrs. Bonnycastle welcomed the Sergeant Major and Francis; they were led directly to Sir Richard in the large front bedroom where an ashen grey man looking much older than his fifty-six years laid peacefully upon his pillow—the afternoon rays shining about playing a shimmering duet on the curtains: bright and lively, then soft and dark when the branches blew the leaves together blocking out the sun entirely from the window. Mrs. Bonnycastle introduced his visitors, Sir Richard attempted a smile, Francis was asked to stay, the others left.

The room was plastered white over the stones, a wide, elegant crown molding trimmed the walls at the ceiling and the floor in matching shades all around; his desk was a fine mahogany wood shined to perfection, adorned with brass candlesticks and matching ink wells. The bright red of his dress uniform trimmed in gold braid hung on an arm of the corner rack; his sword: properly displayed on the wall behind his desk. Portraits of Queen Victoria and Prince

Albert hung proudly in over-sized gilded frames over his bed; the
Royal Certificate of Knighthood and the emblem of the Royal Order
of the Garter hung at eye level at his feet—their positions clearly
visible at all times when he sat upright. Francis was impressed and
realized how almost rude his visit would be—not a fraction of association mutually shared between the Colonel and himself. He asked
Sir Richard if he could begin.

Francis carefully examined his back, behind his neck, then
pressed on his abdomen where the pain was most pronounced. Sir
Richard complied to all the scrutiny and answered Francis' questions
in a low raspy voice.

"You have no fever Sir, you are not suffering from typhus or
abdominal infection—you do not have dysentery; you have no insect
bites. You have not visited Kingston for many months and you have
not been anywhere near the fever sheds or on a ship." Francis was
sitting on a chair drawn around from the desk and spoke clearly and
softly—however directly, within a very close distance to the man's
face—the final observations were conveyed without hesitation and
with candor as requested. "You have severe pain in the area of your
liver; your eyes are yellowish, your facial colour is very pale. Your
blood I think is not healthy; you have no appetite and you are losing
weight rapidly. Do you agree Sir?"

Sir Richard looked at Francis with eyes that reflected little life,
with a sorrowful expression. With some difficulty he spoke through a
slim purplish line that crossed his face replacing his lips. "Yes."

"I think perhaps you have an organ failure, your liver most likely.
Perhaps a cancer. It is unlikely that I can cure you. I have however,
herbs that will dull the pain, although I see you have been taking
laudanum, and truly there is no substitute, other than alcohol or
opium." A few silent moments passed.

"How long?"

Francis drew in a great amount of air and held his breath for a moment. Here was a great soldier that had served gallantly for so many years; a man who supervised the defence of Kingston and Upper Canada; a solder who had been Knighted by Queen Victoria; a scholar and author; a great man loved and admired by his troops and the people of Kingston and Canada—and now a run-away, a coward who had fled from his enemies, a would-be doctor, a quack, an American, a liar—a murderer—a man who had never been to war or understood its implications, its horrors—was asked to predict the date of his death. Francis had been honest and direct as he agreed. He took another breath. He hesitated. He didn't deserve the responsibility or the honour.

"Please."

"A month, maybe two."

"Thank you." Sir Richard turned his head, relaxing on his pillow, his eyes addressed the view to his front—his Knighthood. "It's supreme irony Mr. Tumblety. I have built the greatest defence system in Canada here in Kingston for a great enemy that never arrived—now I face the enemy that will kill me and he is invisible, yet all-powerful, and I have no defence against him." He turned his head back to Francis, where he could see tears flowing down his face. "Do you understand irony Mr. Tumblety?"

"I think I understand Sir."

"Don't cry Mr. Tumblety. You are not dying."

"Sir I don't know war, but I know death." Francis no longer felt special, he no longer wished to be a doctor who had a bag of amputation knives and bottles of herbs and medicines, yet processed no cures when they were most needed. He felt helpless, perhaps he was a quack, he had no business talking to Sir Richard, he did not belong in his grand house or in his company. He hung his head, ashamed.

"Look at me Mr. Tumblety. You have no reason to be regretful, there's nothing anyone can do. You want to be a doctor Mr. Tumblety?"

"Yes Sir."

"You are young, your future lies before you. Your destiny resides in your courage and confidence."

"I have no courage. You don't know what I've done."

"I know that you have put my heart at ease, and that you are honest and intelligent. You have given me the respect I requested. These are not virtues to be so quickly dismissed."

Sir Richard raised his hand to Francis. Francis shook the hand of a man for the second time in his life, in friendship and goodwill—in each instance: between a British soldier and an American enemy. It may have been an ironic gesture; Francis could only accept the moment as a cruel lie. He wished it wasn't so.

"Good luck Mr. Tumblety. I hope you find what you are searching for."

"Good bye Sir Richard."

The Sergeant Major stopped the coach above the sheds on King Street, then sped away in a violent charge, the spokes of the wheels barely allowed to steady their spin—Francis considered the hasty exit a reflection of a distaste for his company or perhaps an impertinent comment on his inappropriate association with the Colonel; this he could understand. He began to consider the fast approaching winter weather and if he was to return to Chicago he would have to leave soon. Continued efforts assisting the fever victims was fast becoming tedious and discouraging; he was carrying a glum attitude of failure after his visit with Sir Richard Bonnycastle.

The destitute village of fever sheds spread haphazardly on the shore of Lake Ontario, cast a crooked profile against the sparking water before him. The boards were grey and rough, the angles were sharp and uneven—the clumsy buildings ran together as an inglorious dark clump—a ramshackle collection of unusable construction materials meant for discard but had inexplicably been spared. There was the familiar odour, Francis winced. He walked forward to the shed where Mr. Monaghan was recovering. Sister Felicia was serving soup to people from a pot simmering over a fire outside. Her beckoning blue eyes caught Francis off guard, her smile was wide and full of welcome—he forgot about Chicago in an instant.

"How is Mr. Monaghan?"

"He is doing so well Francis, go in and see."

Mr. Monaghan's fever was reduced to a mere fraction from the day before. He sat up on the edge of his bed slurping his soup. Francis had difficulty recognizing the words slopping out from between his lips as they competed with the space where potato pieces and pork chunks were shovelling in—however he assumed it included extensive praise and hearty 'thank-yous'.

Sisters Martha and Felicia accompanied Francis around to all the fever sheds that afternoon; many new immigrants had arrived, many bodies needed cleaning, many other bodies needed burying. Francis explained about Major Enniskillen's son at Fort Henry and about Sir Richard Bonnycastle, and about his grand trip in the fancy carriage—they were very appreciative about such a story— and jealous—however no sign divulging this sinful attribution was disclosed.

Mrs. Cartwright's dinner was exquisite as usual that evening, but rather than drifting off to sleep soon afterward—the beams above still annoyingly unevenly spaced, the pillows still soft and luxurious—

Francis could not seem to settle. He played with the locket and the ring, attempting to recognize detail in the fine renderings—such a difficulty without a flame flickering nearby—thoughts of Chicago and Sister Felicia floated in and out—but there was something gnawing at his concentration, something persistently clouding his fantasies. Fort Henry? Enniskillen? Bonnycastle? The winter perhaps and a very difficult journey through the snow, without Nektoshe... No! Sampson! It was Dr. Sampson! Tomorrow was five days, the deal was up! Francis jumped off the bed and dressed in a flash. He raced out of the house. Was he too late?

35

Chapel was particularly long and tedious, the Sisters had finished another sixteen hour day; the effort to balance on their knees, hold their hands together in prayer and concentrate piously was becoming a nightly torture rather than soulful worship, or orderly benediction. Sister Felicia was struggling to stay upright, and once her eyes closed in prayer, opening them again became a contest of will and she was inching closer to a perilous loss every night.

Sister Hieronymo was not oblivious to the toll the work was taking, she watched the Sisters carefully—her task included their physical and spiritual health as well as the continued welfare of the fever victims they attended every day—she also was keenly aware of their service to God and that included the Sisters' continued patronage and service to Him and their obedience to their Order and to their faith. She reminded them daily of how Jesus suffered for their sake—the work He asked of them now was pitifully small in comparison. Sister Felicia listened and observed faithfully, but it seemed as though her body was crying for a separate private sphere of tranquility; a place located somewhere beyond her control—at times she felt she might lose that control and fall headlong to the floor.

She prayed for guidance, but it was when she was deep inside her prayer that she felt most vulnerable—as if she might float away peacefully to a place where the air was clean and the spaces were green, and all the people were healthy, smiling...she caught herself before she toppled over. The jerk upright nearly knocked Sister Martha over. *Oh God, another lecture.* And indeed before she returned to her room Sister Hieronymo summoned her. The lecture was stringent and was viciously applied while Sister Felicia remained for another hour on her knees, this time on the stone floor of Sister Hieronymo's room. Included were reminders of her observations dealing with young Mr. Tumblety and strict adherence to vows and service to Jesus Christ her Saviour.

Sister Felicia could not bolt her door for total privacy—it was not allowed—but sitting on her bed back in her little room, she added a prayer that might keep Sister Martha away; solitude during these few precious moments before sleep, was the only time she truly relinquished her discipline to personal freedom. She fought the visions of his dark green eyes as they penetrated deep into her soul, she tried to push his hand away as it gently moved from her blisters to her arm, to her waist; she drifted away, she gently swayed and rocked in sublime surrender away from the sheds, from the odours, from the suffering—together in his arms, they reached a wonderful serenity. She didn't want to leave this beautiful dream, she didn't want to fight, to allow her faith to intervene; she welcomed this new clarity—she searched for it every night.

Was there a sound outside her door? Footsteps on the stones? She listened. It passed. She fell asleep, her dreams sailed with her.

36

"A little late for rounds Doctor." Francis stood undetected as Dr. Sampson held a cup to Mr. Monaghan's mouth. Francis was breathing hard after the race to the sheds, through the cobble streets, through the black night.

Startled, Sampson froze in the darkness. Francis recognized the silhouette of the doctor—the moonlight filtered through the broken boards of the hole he impetuously smashed four days previously—casting a silver-blue hue, creating sharp angled shadows over cots and blanket-clad patrons within. Monaghan was sitting up innocently ready to accept whatever Sampson was about to pour down his throat. The Hotel Dieu Sister watching the shed was dismissed by Sampson minutes ago, and left with her lamp. "What do you want?" Francis was the one person Sampson absolutely did not want to deal with at this moment—his surprising appearance was shocking; he froze in disbelief.

"Don't drink that Mr. Monaghan." His suspicions were correct. Sampson had skulked down to ensure Monaghan would not walk out of the shed, or perhaps not walk at all again. Francis grabbed the cup and lifted it to his nose. "Goldenseal." The mixture easily obtained from the little Chinese herbal shop on Princess St. contained enough toxins to rip Mr. Monaghan's kidneys apart; Francis detected the bitter odour instantly. The bleeding would begin within a few hours and without any way to repair the damage, he would bleed to death by midday.

"I am the doctor here, he needs that, give that to me." Dr. Sampson was indignant, and remained adamant. He had been caught; typically he would admit to nothing.

"I will keep this cup and its contents. I will allow you to leave doctor, and if you continue to deny your attempt to kill this man, I will force you to drink this tomorrow with the Mayor and the Chief as witnesses, they would enjoy seeing that I think. There are several people here watching, perhaps they will speak for you." Francis waited for a reaction. Heads slowly rose up from the cots, many eyes turned to the commotion. Doctor Sampson left, his pace quick, his head low.

"Well Mr. Monaghan, I hope you can still trust me."

"Was there something bad in that cup?"

"Yes Sir. You can go back to sleep. I will visit you in the morning."

"Thank you."

Mrs. Cartwright, Mayor Kirkpatrick and Police Chief Shaw stood beside the empty bed in the shed on the morning of the fifth day as agreed. An empty bed meant only one thing: Mr. Monaghan, the subject of their inspection was, no doubt, laying among hundreds more decomposing corpses covered in quicklime, rotting in pathetic unison, a sad and disquieting legacy to an unforgettable event in Irish and Canadian history. Chief Shaw shook his head. He had passed by

Francis, Sisters Hieronymo and Felicia on the way into the shed—
they were standing together at the soup pot. The little trio of inves-
tigators were sadly vindicated as they realized the consequences of
Francis' actions, and the fate of the sheds and the poor sick people
ensconced within, as the contagion had obviously been allowed to
infiltrate throughout the town for almost a week due to the incorrect
regulations stipulated by Francis.

The Chief was a burly man, strong, tough and had a reputation
for accepting no nonsense. He had been arresting Irish beggars and
drunken soldiers every day for months; his jails were filled. The new
penitentiary on King St. west near the village of Portsmouth, was
overburdened—however nothing would suit him more than adding
an impertinent young quack to its lists.

"Get him in here." Chief Shaw directed his orders to anyone
standing by. No one moved; however the need was unnecessary—
Francis entered the shed at the very same moment. "You are in a lot
of trouble son." Chief Shaw wanted an explanation.

"Mr. Monaghan will no longer occupy that bed Sir, if that's what
you're asking?" Francis' attitude seemed casual, not anxious or fearful
as one might suspect from a man about to be carried off to prison.

"I can see that. You are an impudent rascal and you shall be
arrested immediately." The Chief's moustache was flinching, his
temper was rising, he was about to reach for his pistol.

"Perhaps we could do this outside." Francis made the suggestion,
leaving the shed without waiting for a response; the others followed
in kind. The Chief considered that perhaps Mr. Tumblety might be
ready to bolt. He was ready; he picked up a close position at his heels,
his pistol tightly clasped in his fist.

"Before you arrest me you might want to try the soup being
served today." Francis stood at the pot, the contents boiling, a fine

bouquet of beef and potatoes swirling about within the steam above; a short line of customers patiently waiting, tattered blankets hanging about bony shoulders, tail-ends dragging in the dirt at their feet, their bowls at the ready—they stopped to watch the strangers who had broken tradition and ventured into forbidden areas at the shoreline.

"Don't be ridiculous." The question was absurd. The very last thing Chief Shaw would be doing this morning was sampling the stew concocted from vegetable and barnyard scraps, cooked into submission for the destitute Irish derelicts who had infiltrated his town, most of whom, upon completing their fill, would undoubtedly rip about in Kingston proper, stinking, stealing, begging and puking their way into his prisons.

"Here Sir, try a sip, it's very good." Patrick Monaghan dipped his ladle in and offered a small cup to the Chief. "Here you are Sir, it's very tasty, I can assure you." Sisters Hieronymo and Felicia couldn't help but respond with the widest of smiles as the Chief, the Mayor and Mrs. Cartwright took a deeper, more scrutinizing look at the man with the ladle.

"Mr. Monaghan will no longer require a bed in the sheds." Francis was cocky with his announcement and his recalcitrant attitude was not appreciated by the Chief. The Mayor however was seriously impressed.

"You are the same man who lay dying here only a few days ago?" The Mayor stood transfixed. "This is wonderful. A great debt of thanks is owing to you young man." Francis would have stayed to enjoy his redemption, to watch the Chief's expression sour, his jowls squirm, his great moustache flip about—but unfortunately the little pantomime was interrupted—Sister Martha arrived at full speed as if crossing the finishing line of a world race. She pulled Sister Hieronymo aside.

"That little boy is much worse; I fear he is dying."

Francis gave no thought to Doctor Sampson, he assumed correctly that the issue of the goldenseal was over, and the chances of continued dealings with that man were slim—he concentrated on his investigation of the little foot belonging to the tiniest of patients. The boy lay quietly, his fever tipping the uppermost levels of capacity before a human collapsed into total coma. His mother, Mary O'Shaughnessy sat tentatively at his side, gently caressing the boy's wee hand. Michael was the last child, all the others had died: three on the trip across, and two in the sheds. Mr. O'Shaughnessy had left the sheds weeks ago and had not returned. Mary could not control the tears; she admitted that if God took Michael, he would take her too as there would be nothing more for her here in Canada or anywhere else for that matter. The Sisters had spent some time trying to reassure Mary without success, as well, the infection in the foot had not improved in spite of all their attempts.

"You should have shown me this much sooner." Francis cautiously examined an old wound on the boy's ankle that had not healed for many weeks; the gangrene had now eaten its way to his calf. The emaciated state of most of the fever victims was so high, the chances of fighting infection was reduced to the slightest of margins. Children were particularly susceptible. He was not hopeful.

Sister Felicia bent down close to Francis and whispered his ear. "Is there nothing you can do?"

"I can remove it." Francis looked into her eyes. There was an immediate exchange of understanding, of concern. "I will need your help."

Sister Hieronymo was directed to remove Mary away from her son; a special area was set aside for the procedure: a table was brought in, sheets were rigged up to surround the area, the instruments required were removed from Francis' bag and displayed upon the table. Sister Felicia dropped two knives in fresh boiling water, clean towels and bandages arrived from Hotel Dieu Sisters. Francis had assisted with an amputation in Chicago—a young cowboy who had ripped his arm and hand apart in a fall—Rising Sun's methods were clear, the details perfectly configured in his mind.

Sister Felicia, at Francis' side, watched as the sedative was mixed—she gave the boy a sip, then another, then a final one. Francis applied the tourniquet. She handed Francis the slim knife that cut back the skin, then passed him the knife for the bone. The cuts were true, fast, smooth. The tiny foot and lower portion of his leg was removed, there was very little blood. She watched the skillful hands sew up the blood vessels and the skin over the stump, apply the carbolic acid and clean bandages. The Sister was truly enthralled by the whole procedure and so impressed with Francis' skill. She learned how to wrap the bandage, how to thoroughly clean the knives, how to remain calm and relaxed. Watching Francis, she knew she would have to remain on her knees for more than an hour and pray for guidance tonight.

37

The summer, so hot and humid in Kingston, had finally surrendered to the cool and thankful lower temperatures of autumn. The number of boats arriving from Grosse Isle diminished daily to a point where only one boat arrived in October. The sheds were emptying, so many surviving immigrants had left to seek a future elsewhere in Ontario, some left for destinations in the west, now that the contagion was slowly fading away. More than one thousand four hundred people had died, their bodies filling a series of shallow pits near the Kingston Hospital. Many of the sheds had been dismantled, the wood burned. Mrs. Cartwright had organized her associations into committees that found placements for orphaned children, classrooms for school-aged children, employment for labourers fit to work on farms or factories; many single surviving mothers began to toil in the laundries and chicken factories—killing, plucking, wrapping. Francis, the Sisters and many volunteers had treated thousands of sick immigrants throughout the summer and now into the fall.

Foundations for future plans remained arbitrary for Francis. He assumed he would remain in Kingston for the winter, continuing to work with the Kingston Hospital in some capacity, perhaps as an assistant or labourer—but Dr. Sampson put a halt to that. *'No quack would ever be allowed to work in this hospital.'* There was the Chinese herb shop—he could gather herbs and make medicines, perhaps offer his services to those who allowed an alternative to regular medicine; perhaps work in the abattoir (although that type of employment would never be considered until all others failed.) He thought perhaps he would find a wife, build a house, have an apple orchard—but then when would he return to Chicago? Little Raven and Charles Smithson often slipped away to a deeper corner of his mind when his focus centred on the fever victims or Sister Felicia, or a future in Canada. The autumn winds—brisk and cool—the swish of yellow grasses along the roads to Glenburnie or Brewer's Mills on errands for fruits or vegetables, would draw them back, and plans of returning and finishing the job would come rushing through, his senses aroused, his knife-hand ready. But there was a discouraging realization: perhaps he was being foolish—this above all else depressed him. The focus on the past was dimming, he was no longer so desperate for revenge—other concerns often obscured his thoughts.

The supply of fresh fruit was dwindling along the shoreline, many immigrants were still depending on the benevolent contributions of the Kingston community for survival. Sister Felicia agreed to accompany Francis—they seemed to do almost everything together now: cleaning, burning, caring—the trip for fruit would be a welcomed break from Kingston.

The route to the apple orchard was scenic—it was early fall, some leaves on the birches and poplars were turning yellow, the maple leaves, red. The trail twisted and curved; its surface: a composite of pits and ruts—the buckboard jumped and swayed, the riders were bounced up and down—holding tight to the side irons was more than a caution. Two large fruit barrels and a stack of baskets threatened to shake their way off the wagon more than once. Francis pulled the reins in tight, keeping the little horse under control. After an hour the sun reached its pinnacle, not as hot as July or August (thankfully), but glorious, warm and beautiful. A few thin strands of white ribbons crisscrossed the sky slipping and sliding—schooner sails drifting on easy seas. Large grey limestone rocks jutted out from the side embankments; the bedrock was so close to the surface. Joseph MacKendry was an old Scott whose apple-picking days were over— he cared not for the apples—picking them, selling them or eating them—they would rot or be collected by anyone driving out this far from Kingston.

Conversation was limited to the weather, state of the trail and the stink of the horse droppings that were considerable and frequent— they laughed as their shared experiences in that department could attest to a much deeper appreciation—the stink would receive little to no notice in Kingston. The secret thoughts pleasantly swimming about in their daydreams were unknowingly similar. They privately reminisced about the times they had shared: lifting crates to the barge from Toronto, stoking coal until their hands bled, cleaning and shaving fever victims, the birth of the baby, the amputation of the little foot, working for hours in the sheds for the sake of strangers who deserved to live. There was no need to verbalize these thoughts, when they shared a glance, they knew; this was a connection they would always have—they had been a team now for more than three months—there was no denying it, even if it was never discussed. They never discussed it.

Sister Felicia spent no time considering the choices on the ground—they had not rotted yet, but why select those when fresh ones still remained on the branches? She reached up and picked the nicest, roundest apples—red and firm—collecting them in the generous folds of her long habit cape—until Francis dropped a basket at her feet, then she dumped them in. Francis worked on the branches of another tree close by. The baskets filled quickly, as did the barrels—there was so much fruit—similar trips could be made for a week and still apples would remain on the branches.

Their load completed, a large percentage of the afternoon yet to be embraced, Sister Felicia offered Francis a choice selection—they sat together with a canteen of water and an apple each, under a shady tree—its branches hanging low, the rolling hills to Kingston spread out far and lazy before them—a view so welcomed in its autumn shades of rust and orange. Also welcomed was the distance disclosed by the wide panorama—it was so far from those dismal fever sheds. There was a taste of freedom, a release, a relaxation—the air was fresh; they were alone.

Francis held his apple to his face; as he slowly bit down hard; he looked at Sister Felicia—to her eyes, then to her head—the tight white cowling framing her face and the black veil draped on top.

"Do you ever take that off?"

"Yes. Every night."

"Why do you wear it?" Francis crunched hard and chewed, the sound was loud, juice dripped from the corners of his mouth. Sister Felicia thought at first the question might be rude and perhaps she shouldn't answer, but she decided it was a fair question after all.

"We wear these clothes because they are modest, and not fashionable—we prefer not to attract attention."

"But it does attract attention. Isn't it hot?"

"Yes."

"Then why don't you take it off?"

"Because it wouldn't be proper." Now she was thinking his questions were becoming inappropriate."

"Did you ever see Sister Her...na...mo without her habit?"

"It's Her...on...y...mo. It's not her real name you know."

"Really? What's her real name?"

"I don't know. All nuns select a new name when they take their final vows. They choose from a list. The names are from the Bible or from Saints, or religious people from history."

This was very interesting information and Francis wondered if he should continue. Sister Felicia chewed her apple and faced the sun, her blue eyes sparkled—Francis noticed. She was not annoyed, however this was the first time they had ever really shared a conversation that didn't deal with Kingston or dying Irish immigrants—it was refreshing.

"Why would she choose a dumb name like that?"

"It's not dumb."

"No, sorry." Francis was thinking. "So Felicia is not your real name?"

"No."

There was a pause. Francis' eyebrows raised up appreciating this fascinating new information. Francis thought she would tell him; she didn't. Now he figured he'd have to ask.

"What's your real name."

"I shouldn't tell you.'

"It's a secret?"

"No, I just don't use it anymore."

Francis waited. She swallowed and wiped the juice from her mouth. She paused and looked Francis in the eye.

"Sarah. Sarah MacDonald."

A large lump of apple lodged between his teeth and cheek made his face balloon out like a squirrel collecting nuts for winter. He froze in that position for a moment then spit it out—the apple flew across the grass like a shot from a pistol. He began to laugh. Then he bent over and laughed hard.

"I didn't tell you so you would laugh. Stop laughing! What's so funny? My name is not funny!" Now she was perturbed. This was not the reaction she was expecting. She attempted to rise up and walk away. Francis stopped and touched her arm.

"Sit down, sit down. I'm sorry. No your name is not funny. It's beautiful. It's wonderful. Sarah. Sarah MacDonald. It's so...so..."

"What? Dumb?"

"No. It's...so normal. It makes you normal, like me. You are not so special. Sarah, you are...I'm so glad to know you...Sarah." He couldn't think of anything else to say to explain his behaviour: it surprised him just as it had her.

Sister Felicia wasn't sure how to accept the word 'normal'. She shouldn't have told him.

"You can't call me Sarah you know." She felt embarrassed, exposed. "I'm just a farm girl from Maryland. I'm not special. I don't know why you think I'm special."

"Because you wear this outfit and you have vows and you have a different name. And what are vows anyway?"

"We make a promise to be charitable, benevolent and chaste."

"And you can't have boyfriends." That was a statement not a question, and the conversation was definitely getting way too personal, and Francis couldn't believe he said it, and he wished he hadn't, but there it was.

"That's what chaste is."

"Never heard of chaste."

"Why is your dress black?"

"Does it matter?" She raised her voice. She was reaching irritability, maybe anger.

"No. Just curious. Can't you ever wear another colour?"

"No. I am in mourning?"

"Mourning? Who died?"

She sighed, exasperated. "Jesus Christ, my Saviour."

"What does that mean?"

"Francis, I don't want to talk about this anymore. I think we should be heading back." Sister Felicia was anxious about digging deeper into any more personal areas. She wished she could confide in him, tell him everything: why did she become a nun, what does it mean to be a nun, why she couldn't speak to him openly and honestly. She wanted to remain his friend, she wanted him to understand, but she thought the details of her personal life and religious commitment would be too difficult for him to understand. She was wrong.

The return trip to Kingston was quiet, but Sister Felicia did ask one question. "You are not angry with me Francis?"

Francis thought for a moment, smacked the horse with the reins, then smiled. "I could never be angry with you Sarah."

She rolled her eyes; another sigh.

Sister Hieronymo approached Sister Felicia and Francis as they struggled with the apple baskets. Sister Martha carried them to the area beside the tables, she watched them giggle, she listened to whispers, she shook her head; she groaned loudly with each lift and bend, but was unable to steal their attention. Sister Hieronymo read them the letter from Father O'Reilly; it described his concern about the approaching winter—the lake would freeze—they were needed back in Rochester; Dancy had died. She was making provision for a crossing within two weeks; an entrepreneur from Rochester was refitting a canal steamer in the Royal Dockyard—he was planning to be home before the freeze-up—Sister Hieronymo would be aboard.

There was a short eye exchange between Francis and Sister Felicia, they were sure not to signal concern to Sister Hieronymo, however Sister Martha was quick to observe—a wide vindictive smile spread across her sour face, then a sarcastic pout—both meant for Sister Felicia—its purpose duly noted, and unappreciated.

The following two weeks were busy enough for Francis as he concerned himself with disassembling sheds, assisting Mrs. Cartwright with chores at home and visiting the Chinese herb shop on several occasions to check their stock and to bolster his own dwindling supply. Mrs. Cartwright and the members of her committees continued to concentrate particularly on assisting single mothers with employment positions; but the overwhelming responsibility she shouldered now was the relocation of the hundreds of orphans who had arrived without their parents, or who had watched their parents drop without ceremony into the mass graves, leaving them alone and abandoned. Her mission now centred on the plight of these children, as many were sent to homes within Kingston proper and to families in the surrounding areas. Francis' final duties with the fever victims would end with these poor unfortunates.

Francis hoped sleep would overtake him in a speedy manner— he was tired and the task tomorrow would begin at dawn. Mrs. Cartwright had relayed the instructions with care—the names of the children were listed in a manifest to be given directly to Abigail Fairfield; she would be waiting at Ham House on Main Street in the little village of Bath about sixteen miles west on the shoreline of Lake Ontario. Someone from the MacKinnon farm would be there to meet him, and for now they would be housed in the Academy School until homes could be found for them. This would be the seventh trip Francis had taken with a wagonload of orphaned children—all the locations previously within a five or six mile radius from Kingston— but now Mrs. Cartwright was desperately forced to find homes farther distant as all resources in the Kingston area were exhausted.

But sleep did not come easy—the trip in the morning was a concern of course—he had no idea about the location of Bath, only the directions provided, but he reckoned he could find it well enough; no…pressing thoughts preventing sleep had been clouding his mind for almost two weeks since the letter arrived from Father O'Reilly. In two days, Sarah would be leaving for Rochester. Although they had not discussed the inevitable departure, casual discrete looks and smiles were shared and warmly exchanged. Sister Martha had cornered Francis one afternoon while he carried a load of broken boards from the dismantled sheds to a fire—she had no problem expressing her thoughts, "And you will never see her again." The message was clearly received—those particular words and her glum face had remained frozen and vivid among so many others, sharing a dark space within a crowded corner of his consciousness: Chicago, winter's bitter winds, future employment, Sarah MacDonald.

Finally succumbing to sleep, Francis immediately fell into an abyss—a dark slimy hole filled with corpses, their flesh tattered and raw, falling like torn ragged meat dripping from naked bones, reaching up from their grave, pulling at this face—his desperate attempts to escape: futile. Hollow eye sockets in barren skulls, dark and haunting—their horror: repelling, their evil: torturing—slowly evolving into the heinous eyes of Charles Smithson. He scrambled across the bone piles of the slaughter house, slipping, falling, churning down deep into the cavernous pit, falling...falling. Torrents of black blood from butchered cattle sprayed across his face, stinking manure smashed up his legs. Francis' heart began to race, his body writhed violently from side to side. Ghostly figures dressed in long black shrouds turned their accusing fingers to him; he searched for Sarah; he found her—but...no...it was Sister Martha that drove her accusing stare deep into his eyes. He reached back and withdrew his knife—the blade sliced through the black robes of her habit; she fell into a thousand pieces dissolving out of sight to the bottom of the endless void.

Once again Francis awoke in a sweat, his surroundings unfamiliar, his thoughts confused. Once again he attempted to resume sleep, apprehensive of returning dreams, unsure of their meaning, unsure of the morning. He imagined the face and the blue eyes of Sarah, her warm smile, her soft words. He slipped his mother's claddagh ring around his little finger and fondled the heart-shaped pendant of her necklace. Bony grey fingers of naked branches so rich with colour only a week ago, now stripped and bare, tapped on the window pane—their repetitive rhythm annoying and foreboding; howling north-east winds echoed a lament for the onset of winter and for the cold bodies of the dead sleeping eternally in their lonely earthy chasms.

Grey clouds covered the town, a thick mist hung heavy in the cold morning air—Francis followed the narrow streets down to the shoreline with instinctive accuracy as the fog was too thick to recognize any familiar landmarks. Mr. Hamilton was waiting, his horse and wagon usually ready to load the dead, was prepared for the journey to Bath instead. Sister Felicia and Sister Hieronymo stood patiently by, eleven tiny urchins huddled together grasping greedily to a single blanket, clinging to whatever measure of warmth they could render. The tally had been taken, all orphans were accounted for, the ledger given to Sister Felicia—they began to load into the wagon. Francis was relieved to know that Sister Hieronymo would remain behind, Sister Felicia would accompany him; the children's care would be her prime responsibility; the horse, wagon and route would be his.

Morning's light was stubborn to arrive, as it did, the wagon became deeply buried in shadows, flanked by Kingston's tall, stately buildings on each side of the street engulfing the tiny travellers like a stone tunnel. They would follow Princess Street out of town until it became Bath Road—a bumpy, dirty route west for sixteen miles. The horse was old, the wagon derelict; without a major mishap or stopping, the distance might be covered in three hours. The children were clothed well enough. Mrs. Cartwright had seen to the barest essentials: shirts, pants, sweaters, coats—some had shoes or boots, some were barefoot. Five boys and six girls all between the ages of five and twelve, all parentless, all hungry, depressed, and although constant washing of faces had become Sister Martha's priority, it seemed as though some tenacious shades of dirt had fused into a lasting dull brown tone—all shiny cheeks, rosy and pink, had long disappeared—the colour of pathos was irreversible.

With a few stops and no major breakdowns, they arrived at Ham House on Main Street in Bath before noon. Mrs. Rebecca Ham had rented the building to Mr. Hawley, it was now a tavern, and a very welcomed carriage stop along the Kings Highway as it followed the shoreline of Lake Ontario. Mrs. Abigail Fairfield was waiting and assisted the children as they unloaded from the old wagon and then reloaded into Mr. MacKinnon's new wagon—the short ride to the

Academy School was only a few blocks north. The goodbye waves from the wagon were really just a spiritless raise of a few hands; just another forgetful interruption along an endless string of disappointing tribulations.

Pleasantries were exchanged and Mr. Hawley invited Sister Felicia and Francis in for lunch; Mrs. Fairfield accompanied Mr. MacKinnon to the Academy School. Mr. Hawley didn't offer any comments about the fever or the orphans—he served ham and eggs, bread and beans; they were left alone (it was unusual to have a nun as a customer—he was visibly uncomfortable). The tavern was serving very few patrons at that time, only two older men at the fireplace at the back corner. They turned, glancing with curious interest for only a moment, then continued their checkers and beer, pipe smoke wrapped like a foggy blanket about their heads, floated up to the rafters.

With so many thoughts secretly swirling about in their heads; each wondered who should talk first. Sister Hieronymo would not have condoned Sister Felicia's patronage in the Ham House tavern by any means, and that notion alone gave Sister Felicia a special excitement; the other sensations she was experiencing related to the intimate setting at the table, the dull light from the beams above which cast a soft ambiance, and the closeness of Francis—she considered if they both leaned forward across the table, their noses would touch. *Stupid thought.*

"Who is Dancy?" Francis remembered the name from Sister Hieronymo's letter. He didn't really care, but the name had stuck and he was searching for something to say.

"He was Father O'Reilly's servant in Rochester at St. Mary's. He did all the cooking and cleaning, all the chores. Father O'Reilly will be looking for a replacement." She looked at Francis hoping her cue might relay the response she hoped for. He said nothing. Francis tore a fat chunk of bread from the loaf and took a sip of tea. She watched him. She wanted to see him watching her.

Francis understood. The food was delicious, the bread was fluffy and fresh; he could feel her eyes upon him, he didn't want to look up. "I can't go to Rochester. I have to return to Chicago in the spring."

"Can't you return to Chicago from Rochester? You could stay and help us at the Almshouse until the spring. The new hospital will need doctors.

"I am not a doctor."

"You are more of a doctor than you think."

"I can't go to Rochester."

The afternoon sun had broken through the persistent cloud cover. The cold, misty shroud fighting against them throughout most of their trip had vanished, the day would be warm after all. Standing by the wagon, ready to board, Francis hesitated. He looked south to the lake and breathed in the beautiful fresh air—they were so far from Kingston, there was only fresh air and colourful leaves twisting in the breeze all around them. "Would you like to stroll by the lake before we return?" Sister Felicia nodded and joined him. They walked down the lane between rows of maple and birch trees, the russet and amber colours flickered playfully in the sunlight. The autumn air was clean—full of rich aromas—they laughingly kicked their way through the fallen leaves at their feet; their pace was slow, carefree.

Sister Felicia sat on a rock cut, the waves delicately breaking on the water's edge just below her feet, she was strongly resisting an urge. Francis had removed his boots—he stood a few feet out in the shallow water throwing stones to the horizon. Turning to the side Francis picked up the faint echo of distant honking high above somewhere in the clouds—the sky was crisscrossed with thin black chevrons—thousands of geese flying south.

She was thinking only of herself; she knew it was wrong; she knew she should suppress her temptations, but she wanted him to return to Rochester with her.

"Come here I want to show you something."

Each toss of a stone was like a question he threw towards fate: *What should I do? Where should I go? How do I know what is the right thing?*

"Sit here. Hold out your hand." Francis sat down on the little limestone ledge beside her and held his hand out. Sarah reached up and removed a pin from her veil and placed it in his hand. She handed him the veil, then reached for more pins; she reached behind and unlaced the white hood that covered her head. Francis watched in fascination and wonder as Sarah's golden hair burst forth, her entire face and neck exposed—free and naked before him. He could say nothing."I wanted you to see me before I left." Sarah ran her fingers through her hair, attempting to rebuild the flatness of bondage.

Francis stretched his hand out slowly and touched the side of her face, he patted her hair gently. "You are blonde."

"Yes. Not what you expected?"

"You are beautiful Sarah." He slid in closer so his face was inches away, he looked longingly into her eyes; he searched her face, her lips.

Sarah spoke softly, "You...shouldn't call me...Sarah." They kissed, a soft, tender, short kiss. They weren't sure, they weren't thinking. It was Francis' first kiss, he was overwhelmed. He kissed her again, there was no description for the feeling, it was so new, so precious. He couldn't stop looking at her face.

"Should we do this?" Francis thought perhaps he had broken a very serious rule.

"No."

"Then… why?"

"Because we might never see each other again."

"Does that matter so much to you?"

"We work well together Francis."

He smiled into her eyes. "We're not working now."

Sarah turned her head away, embarrassed. "Don't."

"I can't go to Rochester. I can't cross that lake again."

"Is that why?"

"I'm not going to stoke a furnace for sixteen hours across that lake."

"Mr. Heinstein's got a canal steamer, not a barge. He has a full crew. You won't be stoking. He says at ten miles per hour, we might get across in ten hours. If the weather's good."

"It's not just that." Francis didn't continue. Sarah did not want to barter any longer. The fact was, she didn't know what she wanted. She considered revealing herself as she did, was a mistake, the kiss was a mistake, her feelings were a mistake. She just wanted to head back.

"Here, help me put this back on." Francis handed her the pins. She replaced her head covering and her veil. They returned to the village centre.

The journey back to Kingston was quiet, although they shared a few conversations. Francis wanted to kiss her again, but he knew she could not have a boyfriend. The kisses would remain a secret (as would the affection)—perhaps this was the problem: he would be sharing time with her constantly in Rochester, yet they could never be any more than working partners. The wind picked up, the dead leaves so resplendent in their rich colours blew in great billows across their path, it carried a chill that caught the travellers in the face and neck, enveloping like a restricting harness gripping over their bodies—their muscles tensed tightly. Sarah wrapped her arms about herself, they had brought no coats. When Francis suggested she cover up with the old blanket in the wagon—she refused.

Mr. Hamilton was not at the sheds when they arrived, there were three bodies waiting for disposal however—Francis knew the job would be his. Sister Hieronymo welcomed them back and asked about the exchange. She instructed Sister Felicia to return to the monastery to prepare for tomorrow's trip. There didn't seem to be a moment to offer a proper farewell. Francis agreed to see them off in the morning. He collected the bodies. Sister Felicia turned with her head low and walked briskly back up to King Street.

Francis worked until very late at the shoreline, serving food, attending to the sick, busting up boards, burying the bodies (Mr. Hamilton never did return for his horse and wagon). It was deep into the evening when he entered Mrs. Cartwright's home, she had saved supper for him as usual. She looked at Francis with puzzlement a few times while he ate alone, quietly at the table in the kitchen—he was staring stoically ahead as if in a trance, lost in thought. She attempted to break his mood only once when she mentioned how sad she would be to say goodbye to the Sisters from Rochester tomorrow. Francis had responded with a single word. "Yes."

He fought with his guilt: losing focus of what he thought was his main objective—revenge and rescue; grappling with false aspirations—attempting to become a doctor; losing control over his emotions—the useless feelings for a girl that could never be his. He would not follow Sarah to Rochester. He fell asleep with these thoughts and determinations crisscrossing in his mind, Little Raven's tiny leather pouch in his hand.

The wooden trunk, packed so long ago in Maryland, still shared equally by all three Sisters, was re-filled—the contents inside now occupying a space no greater than the size initially used. The single box however was all that would accompany the Sisters on the return trip to Rochester, as they had no donations to bring back—their mission fulfilled. They would carry a lunch: some fruits and bread, some water; they were promised that their services aboard Mr. Heinstein's boat would not include manual labour, and they were thankful for that.

Sister Martha brought her few items to the trunk that Sister Hieronymo had placed in the hallway outside her door. Supper and chapel finished, she stooped down beside Sister Felicia—they packed together. They whispered.

"You will miss him."

"Yes, won't you?"

"No, not particularly."

"You are a nun, a Sister of the Holy Order of the Sisters of Charity. Your heart is sworn to Jesus our Saviour. Where did you think this was heading?" Sister Martha's tone was rising above a whisper, Sister Hieronymo was only few feet away in her room.

"I don't know."

"It's for the best. You must remember your vows Sarah."

"Don't call me that."

"Isn't that what he calls you?"

"No."

"Don't lie to me. I know he does." She was angry. She sighed deeply taking a breath, checking her volume, watching the sliver of light piercing the hallway from the door—it was open, just a tiny narrow split—a whisker, yet a threatening space, so powerful; they stopped for a moment, they listened.

"You don't know anything."

"I know if he leaves with us tomorrow, you will be very sorry, and Sister will know everything."

"You have nothing to tell her. You should return to your room."

"Just remember, I will not allow you to throw away everything for the sake of a young quack who thinks he's a doctor. He has no faith, no future. He will destroy you."

"You mean he will destroy us...you are jealous."

Sister Martha squeezed her lips tightly together, she wanted so desperately to scream, to make her understand. "Forget him. I will make you regret it." She turned and left, a frown upon her face, not confidant in the success of her argument, but sure of her threats.

"And he's not a quack." She surprised herself with that impulsive response. *Too loud.* She quickly covered her mouth, shifting her eyes to the door afraid her final retort would expose their conspiracy; it didn't.

Mr. Heinstein did not stipulate that his boat would depart at the crack of dawn ("Early, but not before the sun.")—the Sisters were grateful for that—they had time for breakfast, chapel, and to offer farewells. His two sons, young and eager, were casting off when Francis reached the dock. He had time to throw the ropes and assist—he pushed the boat along as it reversed its way out. The space between the wharf and the boat slowly grew wider, and wider, Francis followed along to guide it straight. Sister Felicia watched, her hand ready to wave—she held it tentatively at her waist, waiting to catch his eye. Sisters Martha and Hieronymo waving to the small group of Sisters from the Hotel Dieu Hospital, carefully dodged the bow line as Francis tossed it aboard. He looked, their eyes met, the space between the dock and destiny growing wider and wider. He looked up then down at the gap, then up again—his foot suddenly shot out and he was spanning that space with a frenzied leap; he was smacked hard in the face with his own incredulity—he had jumped on board!

Sister Felicia tried hard not to grab hold with both arms and hold him tight—she instead, offered a hand to steady his landing.

"I guess I changed my mind."

"I guess you did."

The expression from Sister Hieronymo's face was blank, non-descriptive. Sister Martha's shocking glare burned a deep hole into the back of Sister Felicia's habit—her piercing eyes switched from anger to evil. Sister Felicia shivered as if she could feel it.

Sister Hieronymo finally spoke. "See Mr. Heinstein in the engine room."

"Yes Sister."

Clearing the end of the dock, Jacob Heinstein grabbed the wheel and spun hard turning the long canal boat—her bow now faced forward; he switched the gears. The shiny white limestone blocks and broad red roof of Murney tower near the Kingston Hospital began to shrink in the distance, as did the huge mound of dirt adjacent—the Irish people buried beneath, surrendering to the slow decaying savagery of nature, became the final sight and last thought of Kingston for Francis. He stepped forward to meet Mr. Heinstein.

Sister Felicia watched Francis make his way to the wheelhouse; she smiled. He had arrived at the dock with his bag over his shoulder, everything he owned—maybe that leap wasn't so impulsive.

38

Mrs. O'Brien sensed something, Lil just wasn't herself: peering tentatively through the curtains watching the street, sitting alone in the parlour, her head always turning away, her eyes vacant. She often replied with single syllable responses—she wasn't cordial, she wasn't right. Shannon asked Lil to confide in her, and at times she thought she had broken through—but there was a truth, a secret she withheld. Shannon had accepted the fact that she would be a spinster—she was twenty-one years old now, and although there had been a few romances, no engagements were forthcoming. She surmised her beliefs and strict ways concerning men and God were too restrictive for most suitors. Her mother had repeatedly reminded her to be patient, the right man would come along. But there remained a frustration.

Lil was supported by two women who continued to hold benevolence at the heart of their faith—and in time they would open their house up to more destitute and needy people—ostensibly Irish men who laboured in the stockyards or the quarries, or had just lost their way over difficult times and dissolving dreams. But for now they were very concerned for Lil—she had not left the house for weeks; a weary pattern of pacing followed by private ensconcement to a chair in the parlour was leaving curious doubts about her emotional well-being. Shannon hoped the relationship between her and Lil would become closer, although Lil was thirteen years older, a sister for personal confidences was at times preferred to a mother's constant hovering and prying. Her private thoughts about men and marriage where on the tip of her tongue most evenings, however there never seemed to be the right moment to open up or perhaps even discuss anything other than the weather, the stockyards or Mr. O'Brien's supper. But now Shannon realized it was Lil who needed a friend, a confidant—but again she failed at all attempts.

The shadow of a tall man flashed by the parlour window; Lil frantically ran to the kitchen. "He's here!"

"Who's here?" Siobhan O'Brien's hands were deep in bread dough, Shannon was at the oven.

"That man!" Lil was terrified, looking for a corner in which to hide.

"What man? Shannon, go to the door."

Shannon opened the front door and received Pastor Adams who had come by as he said he would to drop off the names of men who needed assistance—they were sleeping in the streets—the sheriff was threatening to arrest them. Irish labourers from the Erie Canal in New York and from Toronto and Kingston, were heading west hoping to forge a new life, arriving often unprepared: expired funds, dwindling provisions—Chicago became a dumping ground. The Chicago First Methodist Church was overflowing, they were now approaching the members of the Catholic Parish to assist—Mrs. O'Brien was more than happy to comply—although solutions were not promising.

"It was Pastor Adams. Here are the names."

Shannon put the list on the counter. She stood before Lil who had squeezed herself tight into the corner. With a burst of surrender she rose up, turned and held Shannon tight—she began to cry without restraint. "Oh, I thought he had come for me."

"You are fine now." Shannon continued to hold Lil, her figure was slight and small in comparison to her own. For Lil it was only the second time she had received such affection; her mother Shashona, and now Shannon O'Brien. The warmth and comfort were undeniable—she had been so despondent. Mrs. O'Brien gave Shannon a nod signalling that they should move to the parlour where perhaps Lil could compose herself. The two women walked slowly together, Shannon's arm still tightly wrapped about Lil's waist. Mrs. O'Brien remained deeply entrenched in the day's baking, confident that with time and patience, a resolution would be forthcoming.

It all came pouring forth: the birth of Francis, the death of her half-sister Margaret (Francis' mother) on that fateful stormy night, the wrath of Charles Smithson and the horrific fact that he was her father, and finally the rape—so difficult to relate, yet the confession was a dire requisite for her sanity. The revelation securely passed to Shannon was subsequently revealed to her mother—how could it not? Shannon did not wait for the inevitable inquisition; she obliged her mother directly after supper and after Lil and Mr. O'Brien had retired to bed.

Lil's emotional disposition would not be reversed in one night, in one confession, but for the present the calming effect of Shannon's words and the new close bond they began to develop offered the solution she required. Within a few days her confidence began to slowly build. She no longer lingered at the curtains, however even the shortest sojourn to town remained impossible.

Sheriff Armstrong was relegated to enquire at the O'Brien home—it was an eventuality that the O'Briens predicted knowing Smithson's tenacious demeanour. The man was turned away twice, Lil sequestered away in a room on the second floor—he would not enter—she remained an illusive predicament for Smithson, an awkward and annoying nuisance for Armstrong.

Charles Smithson eventually considered an alternate route around the situation; Armstrong visited the section of the stockyards where Pat O'Brien retained his position as supervisor.

"He doesn't like the way this stockyard is being handled." Armstrong stood back as hanging bloody sections of beef swung around the rails above his head. O'Brien knew the voice, but when he turned to face the man, he was still overcome with fear—the man was tall, broad in the shoulders, his face dark and sinister, partly hidden in the shadows of the shed—a very large gun rested firmly in the black holster on his right leg, another pistol in his belt.

"What does he want?"

"Not here, let's go outside where we can talk."

"Smithson wants a smoother operation this winter. The stockyards are divided among too many interests—a union of workers and owners would be better for the sale and distribution. He hopes you are on side." Pat O'Brien was well aware of the talk of reorganizing the stockyards and unionizing the workers. He also understood how the rapid growth had expanded the yard's haphazard network of corrals and slaughter houses into a disjointed puzzle discouraging the smooth exodus of beef and pork products. If the trains reached Chicago as predicted, the amount of exports from the

Chicago stockyards were sure to double and triple. Smithson wanted a large fraction of the profits, naturally. Not all owners were on side, there was dissension—many did not want to give in to Smithson's big plans; they preferred to stay independent.

What O'Brien didn't expect was Smithson's threat. O'Brien would be arrested as a conspirator against amalgamation—charged with inciting riots and violence—his career destroyed, his future left in limbo. He could reconsider, however, if O'Brien openly agreed to comply with the new proposals—come on board with Smithson. But there was also a special favour attached—he would voluntarily release Little Raven—she was to be handed over to Armstrong as part of the deal. "You have one day O'Brien. I will be by to pick her up. She comes with me or you go to jail."

Pat O'Brien stood among the bones and entrails, the swishing carcasses above swinging around passed within inches of his face—he didn't flinch, there was no strength in his legs, his blood ran cold—he felt as dead as the butchered animals stacking up behind him.

The news was not well received no matter how delicately he disclosed it. Mrs. O'Brien wanted to storm down to Smithson's office first thing in the morning with her rolling pin and give him a good crack on the head. Mr. O'Brien of course would not agree to handing over Little Raven and he attempted to restore calmness by guaranteeing that the charges would never stick and if he was arrested he would be released within a day or two. Lil was truly upset as she confessed to being the cause of the horrible threat; it was her fault directly and she immediately offered to give herself over to Smithson. She considered the inevitable—he would get his own way in the end, why prolong the misery? But the O'Brien family would have none of it.

After supper the next day, Sheriff Armstrong appeared at the front door as promised, a deputy at his side—his appearance and credibility questionable at best—Pat O'Brien was escorted to the jailhouse. Shannon and Lil were sure to remain upstairs hidden in the farthest corner of the back bedroom—Mrs. O'Brien however greeted the man herself with a scowling face, scornful eyes and fierce words; she stood a breath away from his arrogant posture and insolent attitude, firing a series of expletives at full volume within a dog's hair of the parameters her Christian tolerances would allow—not that it did any good.

Armstrong responded with an audacious smile and impertinent touch of his hat brim, "Evnin' Ma'am." Feigning cordiality was the only weapon available to him to counter her acerbic diatribe—and it sliced through her Irish pride like a butcher's blade through raw flesh. If she held a pistol in her hand, she would have shot him.

Mr. O'Brien's last words included caution not to worry and a promise to return. She watched her husband leave, his arm tightly squeezed in the fist of the deputy; they disappeared into the shadows of the evening. She closed the door quietly and began to sob without restraint. The November winds picked up that night, so cold; winter was looming—she would see Him tomorrow.

Charles Smithson was not available at his office or at the jailhouse. Armstrong explained that no State Prosecutor was available in Chicago until January, and it would only be from him that evidence concerning Mr. O'Brien's case could be discussed; he would remain behind bars. His unyielding attitude continued to provoke Mrs. O'Brien, his haughty air, his slouching posture in the chair, those slanty eyes, the crooked smile so confident—so exasperating. She stood straight, withholding every urge to commence begging—to beg before this man would mean reducing her pride to a delicate pinch of dust easy enough for him to blow away or stomp upon—she couldn't do it...yet.

"Of course we could come to some sort of agreement until the prosecutor arrived. I could be persuaded to release your husband until the trial; the cost of bail would be the half-breed. Bring her here now and I will hand over your husband to you. He would be confined to the town limits, of course."

"Could I visit my husband?"

"Of course."

Mrs. O'Brien reached through the bars and together they embraced as best as possible. "Lil is not part of our family, why should you stay in here for her?" She spoke quietly and sensibly through her tears. "You can't trust that man. I will bring Lil here, you can come home with me." She whispered her plea close to his ear.

Pat O'Brien took her hands gently and removed them from his arms. "No. I will be fine. He can do nothing to me here. I will be home soon, you'll see. You must protect Lil, don't give into him."

She backed away from the bars, she could feel her Irish temper rising again. "Why are you being so stubborn? This girl means nothing to us. Smithson will have his way. She will go to him, she will be forced, this will all be for nothing. You are making no sense." She whispered close to the bars.

O'Brien would not relent. "You go home now. I'll be fine."

Armstrong appeared at the door. "Ah such a sad scene. Daddy won't come home to Mommy? Better get used to it, he's going to be here for awhile."

Mrs. O'Brien pointed an accusing finger at her husband. "Stubborn!" She pushed past the Sheriff in the doorway. "Get out of my way!" She left abruptly.

His back remaining pressed against the door jamb, slouching, smiling, Armstrong offered a final comment to his prisoner, "She's a tough one." O'Brien sat on the edge of his cot in the cell, holding his face in his hands, he began to weep.

For all his physical strength required for daily routines at the slaughter sheds, for all the brute enforcement used with his work crews and the reputation he had developed as a task master, the even disposition he harboured and maintained concerning survival in Chicago: cruel winters, infectious animals, sick and lazy employees, inconsistent income as prices fluctuated, demand dipped and rose without warning or reason—Pat O'Brien was in fact a very sensitive person. He thought the protection of Little Raven was an honourable endeavour—he had witnessed the cruel removal of the Potawatomi, the unjustified execution of three Indian women, the destruction of their camp, the mistreatment of Mick, and above all the vicious control wielded by Charles Smithson upon Chicago. Mrs. O'Brien had imparted Lil's story and what she had endured: he could not release her to that man—it was tantamount to enslavement, perhaps torture, perhaps repeated violations.

O'Brien did not however consider the false charges brought against him might stick—he assumed they would be dropped, he assumed he would be home within days—he was wrong. He cried because he had failed his wife, his daughter and possibly Lil—the one person he hoped to remove from the clutches of that man: Smithson, my God how he hated the sound of the name.

Siobhan O'Brien, her Irish pride waning daily, did in fact visit the jailhouse again to barter with Armstrong. Smithson remained unavailable, the new Mayor was in Boston, no Circuit Judge or State Prosecutor arrived in town, and even if they had, Charles Smithson would be sure to intercede; the case would remain in limbo, O'Brien would remain locked up. She could not convince her husband to release Lil and no amount of begging would change Armstrong's mind. She became distraught, her home became an empty, quiet, heartless structure. Church members visited frequently; the town sympathized—friends brought food and good wishes on a daily basis, but a spark had been extinguished.

Lil's emotional guilt escalated, her withdrawal to private corners returned; Shannon's efforts became fruitless once again. There seemed to be no worse torture than the futility, the helplessness, the total inability to shift or change the circumstances she now faced, as the power and will of Charles Smithson, finally accepted, was omnipotent—she was wrong.

39

The small room behind the kitchen was sufficient enough, it was drafty, damp, but the cot was comfortable and the window, when opened, allowed the cool air to freshen the place. Francis didn't require much room—he only had one small bag containing a change of clothes and Rising Sun's amputation kit. Father O'Reilly had greeted him with great gusto—a wide sunny smile (brown gums and rotting teeth persistent as always; there had been no improvement in this aspect of his 'sunny smile', and Francis reacted with the inevitable response: astonishment mixed with a bit of disgust (Sister Felicia giggled, Sister Hieronymo immediately scolded her) although that was his way with all visitors, temporary or full time: cheery, smiley.

The Father's expectation for Francis, was a long term stay presumedly picking up where Dancy had left off. Francis was not a cook however and this consideration in particular was of great concern for the priest—who would provide the meals? That would be a conversation saved for the dinner table. The Sisters together, scrounged through the kitchen and prepared a satisfactory meal— Father O'Reilly was happy—this result remaining key among all the results attained and safe-guarded at St. Mary's.

During that first meal at the manor, before the Sisters retired to their shared room upstairs—they had explained that their mission in Rochester would not include servitude or satisfying gastronomical indulgences for the good Father. Father O'Reilly ultimately turned to Francis expecting a positive reinforcement of his requirements and was happily rewarded when Francis answered typically, "I'll do what I can." Francis of course had no intention of cooking or cleaning in the manor, at least not over the long term, he was offering the Father the gratitude he expected—keeping the situation amicable.

Over the next few weeks Francis shared labouring tasks with brick work on the church and the hospital—but was called away often to aid at the Almshouse with the Sisters. A new doctor did arrive from Boston as was promised, his expertise was greatly appreciated as the numbers of penniless patients continued to grow: all forms and styles of fever (typhus, typhoid, cholera, yellow fever, malaria), broken bones, infectious cuts, septic wounds, rotting teeth, famine—it was endless. The Sisters were exhausted most nights and the thought of a quiet, private moment with Sister Felicia—and those thoughts were regular enough—had become rare and often impossible.

Father O'Reilly wanted to hold a Christmas Eve Mass in St. Mary's and, as the final pews were set in place, there was every reason to believe it would happen. The Church was not totally finished; there was much more work to be completed on the interior walls (every wall and pillar painted with biblical scenes), decorative wooden framework around the windows. There were beautiful stained glass murals arriving from New York for the windows and a custom crucifix carved by Louis Rebisso, a wonderful sculptor, arriving by coach from Cincinnati, Ohio—both arrivals promised by Christmas and Father O'Reilly was sure to include a prayer every day for their expedience.

The Sisters washed and cleaned the manor house to a level demanded by Father O'Reilly, however the facial expressions he often made after close inspection of the mantel piece or the cabinets when he assumed Sister Hieronymo was not watching, included raised eyebrows, a curled corner of his upper lip and a very clearly pronounced "Harrumph". The Sister sighed, but refused to add more effort to the situation. As well, the Sisters shared the meal preparation every breakfast and evening—for lunch Father O'Reilly was on his own—Francis did not cook. Father O'Reilly's appetite was rarely satisfied, nor was he seldom in a good mood considering the unfinished state of his church and hospital and obliged now to prepare his own lunches—at times his typical jolly demeanour was indeed forced. Sister Hieronymo was rarely in the mood to appease his demands; she had her own considerations and they generally resided outside St. Mary's at the Almshouse—she instructed Sisters Felicia and Martha to follow her lead—they always complied.

As Christmas approached and work on the church was nearing completion—the stained glass installed, (the crucifix was yet to arrive) Francis had an opportunity to improve his living arrangements; when he relayed the information, the Sisters were pleased, Father O'Reilly thought he had been abandoned. Dr. John Lobbins needed Francis on a daily basis now in town at the Almshouse which was quickly becoming Rochester's new City Hospital. Room and board had been secured for him in a house very close by (the owner was a wealthy businessman who had become the hospital's main contributor) and he was offering regular wages. This opportunity was too great to refuse; he had agreed whole-heartedly. He explained to Father O'Reilly how the church was almost complete and honestly St. Mary's Hospital was far from opening—not for at least another six or seven years— the work was progressing so very slowly. He would not spend his first night in his new home until the week following, but he wanted to be settled before Christmas.

If Sister Martha had been scheming, if she was searching for a wedge to drive between them—she had not yet found it. For her, the small gap already growing between them was secretly celebrated as joyous vindication, perhaps Francis' choice to move to a new location would be success enough. For Sister Felicia the loss of private time between them—more like a chasm than a gap—was falling deeper and deeper into an area where she felt the wonderful close relationship they had begun in Kingston might never be reached again. She rarely worked with him now—Francis cooperated closely with Doctor Lobbins, a middle-aged doctor from Boston who had agreed to offer his aid and expertise after receiving repeated pleas from the Rochester Women's Society. He was the only single doctor on staff at the Massachusetts General Hospital that could spare a few months away; he would stay until spring. He graciously offered Francis his first look through a microscope at bacteria, as well as observing cultures growing in specialized dishes in the lab, (Lobbins introduced Francis to the experiments being carried out by Louis Pasteur). Francis improved his surgical skills and studied human anatomy from texts as well as from cadavers—he was enthralled and entranced—the experience couldn't have been better for him. In particular, Doctor Lobbins mentioned to Francis on more than one occasion how impressed he was with his scalpel technique and his crude but efficient surgical methods. He relayed a casual but significant dose of serious respect, and it was well received.

Sister Felicia decided to scheme on her own, the Almshouse men's residence required a renewal of firewood—the stoves were burning continuously now that December's fierce winds battled relentlessly upon the thin boards and whistled at the highest pitches through cracks and crevices—not a single wall could proudly boast of sufficient protection or structural integrity. The crew for restoring the woodpile was newly delegated daily from within the ranks of the patrons sharing space in the residence—however if they were too weary or too sick they could be excused; Sister Felicia decided she certainly could replace them for one day anyway, with a little help from Francis.

No horse was available, but an old sled with decent runners could be pulled with some effort along the path, through the snow to the tree lot not ten minutes behind the hospital. The cords stacked there were still healthy enough to replace the required supply for at least another two months; they merely had to pick and load, then return. The return trip through the heavy snow of course would be a considerable challenge compared to the trip out.

Together they trod as a team, the rope gripped tightly in their hands behind them, stepping along in the footsteps of their predecessors, the wooden runners sliding smoothly over the trail, winter's cold wind slashing their faces. Sarah asked about his work with Doctor Lobbins; he responded with a stream of stories, his voice often rising with the excited chortles of a young boy discovering the wonders of nature for the first time. She smiled; she was genuinely pleased with his new position. She mentioned how everyone missed him at supper at St. Mary's, but he doubted that Sister Hieronymo or Sister

Martha cared, and Father O'Reilly would be amused with his absence at best—his stomach properly attended to, his furniture polished.

The load was sufficiently stacked in the sled—too much and they would not be able to pull it back—there was a moment for a short break, they were breathing heavily—frost was accumulating on their eyebrows and Francis' moustache (thin yet, but growing steadily). Sarah asked Francis if he ever thought of her. She knew perhaps, the short affection they shared in Kingston might be considered by him as unimportant, forgettable—not worth discussing, she was ready for a cold response. This was the first time in weeks they had been alone together, she had thought of nothing else, she was prepared for the worst answer, she promised herself she would not be heart-broken. She had prayed every night to be forgiven for the deviations from her vows, she had tried to redirect her focus. Every night she fell asleep satisfied that her desires had finally dissipated—yet every morning upon arrival at the breakfast table, Sister Martha's accusatory eyes digging deep into her face—the thought of Francis' kiss came charging back, the thought of him holding her, warming her soul once again—a soft glow returned, a secret satisfaction remained.

"Of course I think of you."

"What do you think?"

Francis looked down at the snow at his feet. "I don't know." He wasn't sure what to say. He was shy, but more to the point, he did not want to offend her. She had vows. He thought of her every night when the challenges of the day were complete, when the candle blew out, when he was alone in the dark. His new room at Mrs. Campbell's boarding house was warm, the wood stove was more than sufficient, the meals were good, he often fell asleep with Sarah on his mind—her blonde hair, her soft blue eyes, her lips—and that kiss…how could he not? But Sarah was a nun and the chances of another kiss were remote, and asking for one would be rude, disrespectful.

"Look at me Francis."

Francis raised his head, their eyes met. She smiled. She gently brushed the snow and frost from his eyebrows and upper lip. Her breath—soft mist swirling and dissolving. She leaned forward and kissed him.

"Is it alright?" He smiled but was definitely caught off-guard.

"I miss you Francis. I don't want to lose this special feeling I have for you. Do you still like me?"

"Yes, of course I do, I just don't know how to feel." Francis was seventeen, Sarah was sixteen, they knew nothing of love, their feelings were fresh, innocent—the impetuous moment was filled with excitement...and fear—they kissed again.

They headed back, their secret tucked away, their thoughts and desires colliding, their composure giddy—plans for a subsequent rendezvous began to dance about in their brains.

Christmas Eve meant special meals for the residents at the Almshouse, the bells freshly installed in the bell tower rang out joyously at St. Mary's and Father O'Reilly presided over Mass—he was truly thankful to God and to all the parishioners who had made the day come to fruition. Francis had been invited for supper at the good Father's request—he enjoyed a wondrous meal with the Sisters, but declined when asked to join them for Mass—he wasn't sure about becoming a Catholic—he didn't feel comfortable sharing their holy space—he preferred to be associated but retain a detachment. There was no judgement made upon him.

The congregation was sure to move swiftly away from the church upon their exodus as the temperature had dropped significantly, the snow falling was heavy with thick fluffy flakes. The bells continued to ring past midnight.

Christmas Day 1847—a day of celebration in Rochester and in so many cities and towns through the Christian world. The moon was high and full, casting a brilliant glow between the clouds, its shining face poking through intermittently, the snow slowly tapering off. When exchanging the good wishes of Christmas Day and offering farewells for the evening, Francis and Sister Felicia met and stood together at the church door—he had waited for her as promised. Sharing a momentary special glance, they embraced with their eyes, with their smiles. He turned and left, following the path to his bed at Mrs. Campbell's, pulling his hat down tight over his ears, waving goodbye in the moonlight.

The bright moonlight cutting through the naked tree branches, created sharp greyish-blue shadows that stretched across the white blanket like the dark claws of a scavenging animal; winter's curving patterns uniquely sculptured by accumulating waves of drifting snow, sparkled and reflected. That same brilliant night light shared by the Catholic congregation in Rochester so early on Christmas morning, flooded the streets in Chicago, six hundred miles away; yet for Siobhan and Shannon O'Brien, for Little Raven and for the Parishioners arriving back on Main Street after their service, the sacred morning would become a shocking disaster, a regretful time better forgotten than embraced.

40

Charles Smithson was drunk, there was no doubt about that. He sat deep in his chair in the dark, his head resting back on the top curve of the fine leather. Each cylinder in the tumbler of his revolver clicked cleanly with each pass, spiralling over and over as he spun it around—he loved the sound; so smooth, mechanically true—dependable. The gun held the promise of life and death. He shared Christmas with nobody—he hadn't since Kate died; he didn't care, it never concerned him—only one thing lay festering on his mind; his daughter…Lil. He wanted her home…now…with him, and he would have her.

He left the dark recesses of his dismal office, the door smashed hard against the jamb behind him, then blew open in the wind; the snow blasted in, drifting, covering the floor with a thin layer—like white dust in a dormant tenement. Fighting the bitter wind, he trudged to the jailhouse and busted in, waking up the deputy on duty.

"Give me the keys!"

Deputy Josh Keller was rudely awoken, but was quick to his feet when he saw the huge figure of his unannounced visitor. The keys to O'Brien's cell were passed over.

"Well O'Brien, Merry Christmas." Pat O'Brien wasn't asleep, but he was absolutely dumbfounded by the sudden appearance of Smithson. The cell door was opened. "Let's go." Smithson pointed the gun at O'Brien and waved the barrel towards the door. O'Brien rose and followed Smithson out. Keller was a new deputy; he was filling in on Christmas Eve, the other deputies out-ranked him. He stood back and watched the entire charade unfold.

Once in the street, the cold wind billowing—cutting like knife blades, slicing his face into frozen pieces—O'Brien wrapped his arms about himself attempting to break the wind's strong bite—he had no coat or hat. People in the street gathering to bid each other farewell for the evening after their church service, stopped suddenly as O'Brien entered their vision—his lone body bent forward fighting to remain vertical against the wind and snow—the huge black silhouette of Smithson looming behind. "Get out there, move!"

Mrs. O'Brien and Shannon pushed through the crowd of church-goers realizing her husband was being freed. They scurried from the boardwalk and ran to him—Smithson's frantic orders from the street bellowed out echoing through the frigid air at the same instant, "Stop, he's escaping!" He fired off two shots—the bullets ripped through O'Brien's back—he fell face down into the snow at his wife's feet.

On their knees at his face, Mrs. O'Brien and Shannon turned him over. Cradling his face in her hands, she softly cried. "No...no." The red blood was quickly saturated through the white snow, it oozed out and disappeared, soaking into the street, the ghastly mixture of bold shades terrifying in its contrast. Mrs. O'Brien could feel her spirit dissolving with her husbands's blood—together they slipped away—tiny red rivers of life ebbing down through the snow lost forever, the devil playing his final hand.

Josh Keller ran out and stood beside Smithson. He was speechless, he was confused and scared. He had witnessed the entire murder.

"Get Armstrong, we're going after the girl." Smithson's order was direct, subtle, almost casual.

Siobhan whispered to Shannon. "Get home, get her out. They are coming for Lil." Shannon didn't move. Her beloved father was lying dead at her feet, her eyes were blind with tears, she couldn't comprehend the moment. "Go. Go!" Shannon raised up, she pushed her way through the people standing in frozen groups, astonished and incredulous; they dare not move for Smithson remained steadfast in his pose, a smoldering gun in his hand, unpredictable.

Keller followed Smithson back to the jailhouse. Siobhan O'Brien remained bent over her dead husband's body, alone in the street, the snow blowing wildly, her bonnet whipping, her face buried in his chest, her hands dark with his blood.

Within minutes Shannon arrived at her home. She raced upstairs and yelled fiercely; Lil woke with a start. "They have killed Father, they are coming for you. Get up, get up!"

"Where are we going?"

"I don't know, get up! Hurry!"

Lil was stalling. "I am not dressed. I am not going."

Shannon pulled back the blankets. Lil was curled in a tight ball, cradling her legs, attempting to achieve a secure anchor; she was digging in. She was cold and frightened. Shannon was distraught, scared and angry. "My father was killed in the street for you...you spineless, useless half-breed. His death will not be for nothing! Get up or I will drag you out!" She had no time for patience or barter. She didn't ask for this impossible night; she wanted her father back, she wanted this woman out of her house. She would not be rebuked! She grabbed Lil's ankle and pulled her out of the bed. Frantic, she pushed her through the bedroom door. Lil had no shoes, no coat, no clothing of any kind for the escape—a thin cotton shift loosely covered her naked body. Shannon gripped her elbow tightly, directed her down the stairs through the salon, then out the kitchen door. Bitter winds instantly smashed them like an explosion of a thousand glass shards; Shannon relentlessly pushing from behind. They forced their way through the drifts to the horse shed. Lil stood shivering inside, her arms bound tight around her. Shannon had no time for a blanket or saddle—she tied a rope around the horse's snout and pulled him out into the storm. She jumped up then reached down to Lil with her hand. Lil did not move.

"Grab my hand. Get up. Get up!"

Lil grabbed Shannon's hand, she was pulled up behind her on the horse's back. "Hold on to me tight!" Shannon steered the horse out of the yard; instantly breaking into a gallop, they charged down the lane. Lil wrapped her arms tight around Shannon's waist, her bare buttocks pumping up and down on the animal's back as the horse deftly whipped around the bends in the lane, her shift flying up to her thighs—every part of her naked body chilled to the bone, her long ebony hair flying with abandon in the wind. Shannon bent her head down deep bracing against the wind; the horse cut clean tight curves around every post, every snow drift, the intermittent moonlight bright enough to illuminate his way—his stride increasing faster and faster, his footholds sure and even, galloping into the night—away from Chicago, away from the blood, away from Smithson.

They followed a well-used path west out of town, across meadows, through heavy thickets—the stark, empty branches of the black poplars lining the route like steadfast soldiers, their backs bending and twisting in the violent winds. They galloped through narrow paths, over fallen tree trunks, across frozen streams—spruce bows disregarding their flight smashed across Shannon's face, the heavy laden branches exploding with snow blinded her vision—her focus never waning, she pushed her horse on and on. The night was a confused logistical challenge of heavy snow clouds and pelting wind spaced periodically with moments of bright moonlight that gave clear negotiation along the narrow paths—combined with overwhelming cold that burned their skin no different than hot whips of steel pulled directly from a fire pit. Shannon knew of a trapper's cabin, far off the western trail; she could find it with luck—but she was well aware of Smithson who would be in fast pursuit.

Suddenly the trail ended—she had made a wrong turn. She pulled her horse to a quick stop—tall bushes and trees closed in their forward movement—a wall of snow-covered evergreens. "What is it?" Lil wanted down. She was willing to hide in a snow bank, dig a hole in a snow drift—she wanted the ride to end.

"This is wrong, we have to go back."

"No I want to get off. You are lost. I am freezing to death. Stop!"

"I can find it. Give me some time." Shannon was not listening to Lil. She pulled the horse around, they returned back down the path through the trees. She found the devious fork, it was snow-covered. She forced the horse through the barrier, they galloped on.

Smithson and Armstrong entered the O'Brien home finding no one. The hoof prints in the backyard were still visible. "They have ridden out!" Mounting their horses, they galloped along the trail following the direction of the tracks, hoping to gain distance before the wind filled in the deep impressions.

The tracks lead them through the woods on narrow trails, they stopped. In the distance through the blowing snow, they could see a small cabin in a tiny clearing. They dismounted, pistols at the ready. Armstrong was ordered to advance, Smithson stayed with the horses.

Shannon had led her horse to the rear of the shed out of sight. Inside they crouched down low—there was no lock or bolt on the door—they would be cornered without an exit if Smithson found them. Shannon pulled an old blanket from the wall, she covered Lil—she was shivering uncontrollably, her hair and face were thick with encrusted snow—her facial muscles were too frozen to allow the movements required for crying or arguing, her bare legs shook violently, their colour: a purplish-blue, she tried desperately to shake quietly. Shannon searched the space for a weapon—there were no guns or knives—nothing to fend off their attackers—she would have to bargain her way out of this ridiculous situation. *Why did I ever start this stupid ride? I'm only going to get us both killed.*

But then…something on the floor in the opposite corner; a dark stick. A hatchet! A rusty hatchet with a very long Danish blade for cutting thick bush. She grabbed it and sat down near the door. She instructed Lil to remain silent. Lil couldn't possibly know or understand anything that was happening, she was barely conscious.

Armstrong stepped slowly along the path, his boots landing in the prints made by the horse when he could—the snow was deep. The clouds had moved across the sky, the moon still full and bright illuminated the scene—the cabin was clearly in sight—the roof was heavy with snow, spruce bows overhanging the sides covered the end where the horse was tied. His instincts were sharp, he knew they were inside. Approaching tentatively—within ten feet—he called out. "I know you're in there. Come out. We won't hurt you. You come on out now."

Armstrong looked back to Smithson who stood thirty feet away at the end of the narrow path where it left the main trail, in the shadows of tall snow-laden trees, holding the horses steady. He gave a wave of his gun to Armstrong beckoning him to continue on. Armstrong blew warm breath on his hands, raised his revolver, and continued through the snow.

Shannon raised a finger to her lips demanding silence. She crouched low in the shadows waiting for Armstrong to enter, the little hatchet clutched tightly in her hand.

The door slowly creaked open. "I know you're in there. Now come on out." He let the door swing freely on its hinges, it blew open; he could see Little Raven huddled in her blanket crunched into a tiny vibrating bundle. His gun hand cautiously entered the dark space, "Well hi there little lady." He was so confident, so impressed with himself. Shannon's hand came down in a flash—the blade of the hatchet sliced his hand off at the wrist, blood splashed across the room, the gun fell to the floor. He grabbed his bleeding wrist with his other hand, fell backwards out the door into the snow, screaming madly. "Bitch, bitch!"

"You got that right!" Shannon ripped the gun out from his severed fist; she stood ready to finish the job. Armstrong reached into his waist belt, drew out another revolver with his left hand. Before he could fire Shannon cocked the pistol and fired a bullet into his head—he dropped back as if he'd been hit by a block of limestone. "Bastard!"

Immediately Smithson started firing. Two bullets hit the door frame above Shannon's head, she dropped down, crawled back into the cabin closing the door. Smithson carried only one revolver, no extra ammunition. He had fired two rounds into O'Brien, two into the cabin, he had two left. He yelled to Shannon. "I'm going to kill you both. You can't get away."

Shannon answered his threat, not knowing about his ammunition. "You'll have to come down here, you stinking coward."

"What are you doing?" Lil finally spoke. She wanted to leave, she was ready to go with him.

"Stay back and be quiet. I want to kill this man."

Smithson slowly started down the path, staying in tight to the trees. He was going to shoot to kill, he wanted to get close, he didn't want to waste a shot. When Shannon could finally make out his form, she fired a shot through the window. It hit the tree trunk close at his shoulder. Smithson instinctively fired back two shots—they hit the door, lodging there. "*Damn!*" He was out of ammunition. He decided he would sneak away, not alarming them, return with a posse and shoot the cabin to pieces.

Shannon was confused by the delay. She carefully raised her head up just in time to see Smithson riding away. "Coward! Come on, let's get out of here before he returns."

"No I'm not going."

Shannon grabbed Lil by the arm and jerked her up off the floor. She'd had enough of this whining Indian. "Yes you are." She pulled her arm back and slapped her hard across the face. "Get!"

They left the cabin—stepping over Armstrong—Shannon reached down and grabbed his gun belt—it was full with extra bullets. They mounted the horse and fled north through the bush.

41

S pring in northern New York State arrives early. Blossoms filling the trees explode with floral displays which include numerous species of fruit, turning the bleak shades of winter into a colour pallet overflowing with pinks, whites, reds, fuchsias, and violets for cherry, apple, peach, pear, plumb and grape. Lush deep reds and yellows of the tulips and roses announce life's renewal in every flower bed and garden throughout every town. Ice on Lake Ontario, cracking and buckling, pressed into high dams of immovable walls against the shoreline, continuing to prohibit the use of boats from the harbours—until the hot rays of summer's sun, eventually reduce them to floating chunks, jostling and bumping. They push along to their inevitable destination: the St. Lawrence River and the Atlantic Ocean.

Canada geese, their majestic 'v' formations covering the vast azure skies with thousands of weary feathered travellers, gallantly following their path back home—north across the lake from winter vacations deep in the south—their wings powerfully propelling, their voices heralding their return with resounding honks, signalling a predictable and welcoming promise of a new season.

The sap begins to flow in the maple trees, syrup cooks in the pots in the woods; green buds sprout on birch, poplar, willow and chestnut trees, and young people begin to stroll about arm in arm down by the lakeshore, dreamy-eyed, hopeful—the inevitability of nature's eternal cycle beckoning.

It may have been the renewal of the season, the sights and sounds of spring, but more than likely it was impatience and the premature misjudgement of her decision to join the Order at fifteen—the rapid circulation of youthful hormones must also be held suspect. Sister Martha knew she was slipping away—much to her dismay—Sister Hieronymo had her suspicions on that first day in Kingston when he took the time to bandage her blisters.

The long sinewy branches of the willow tree dipped low into the water, most of its tiny buds already green, unfolding; the grass beneath was soft—the flood waters from the ice dams had vanished. They sat in the shade watching the ducks dip for food near the shore: heads, then tails…heads then tails. Sarah explained that the Sisters took her in at twelve, there was no family to care for her. The fever had taken both parents that winter—the Order cared for orphans, gave them an education, secular as well as religious, but it was Sarah's decision to become a novice. When she told Sister Hieronymo that Jesus spoke to her, the reaction was incredulous, but the other Sisters gave her such affection—she bathed in the attention. She was younger than most, but her age was not that unusual. She was carefully instructed and warned about such a life-changing decision—but she had remained adamant, virtuous, obedient—there had been no doubts...until now.

Her habit was neatly folded under the tree, she stretched out on the blanket—the freedom of the dress she brought was exhilarating. She rested her hands under her head, her feet were bare, she answered every one of his questions. She didn't know of any nun that had left the order, but she was confident, "There are no chains." Francis laid beside her, the golden strands of her hair shining in the sunlight—her eyes beckoning—they kissed. She took his hand and placed it on her breast. The love making was as much a discovery lesson as a passionate embracement. They held each other tight, fumbling and pawing, their gestures at first so awkward—then finally surrendering to a natural rhythm. Francis offered no apologies, no need, they shared a mutual deep affection—Francis asked her to marry him almost immediately upon completion. He said he loved her and would be devoted to her forever. Sarah smiled and dressed back into her habit, reminding him of the issue of the Order and her circumstances in that regard. "I can't just marry you, there will be some kind of formality I suspect."

"Well when will you know?"

'I don't know, but you must give me time to talk to Sister Hieronymo."

The love Francis now held for Sarah was as true as life itself—it gave him clarity, it was all-consuming. When he kissed her the honesty was deep; doubts about his direction, about Little Raven or Charles Smithson were dismissed, he saw his future now—it was with Sarah and nothing else mattered.

Sarah still had concerns about marriage. She loved Francis and wanted to be with him, but to disregard the Order, the Sisters, all that they had done for her, and the faith that had redirected her when she needed it so badly—she couldn't throw everything away so fast. She would wait. The relationship would have to remain a secret for now and Francis would have to understand.

Francis, although tempted, refused the offer from Dr. Lobbins to return with him to Boston to continue working alongside him at the Massachusetts Medical Centre. The doctor had to return—it was summer, his short contract was up. Moving to Boston would give Francis a tremendous chance to work his way into the medical profession—he couldn't become a certified doctor; he would never be allowed to attend Harvard—however as an assistant his skills would soar. He had become one medical assistant on a team that included many young men like himself who did not possess medical degrees, but were encouraged to participate along side a doctor. The Almshouse received its Charter in 1847 and more doctors began to arrive monthly—of the eventual 142 physicians coming to Rochester in the 1850's only 20% had been to medical school. By 1861 (the start of the Civil War) less than 50% of the physicians working at St. Mary's and Rochester City Hospital were orthodox practitioners with MD degrees. Francis was young, but with his experience, he was quickly accepted. The respect he received was keenly appreciated; he began spending more time with his medical partners discussing terminology, techniques and bacteria.

Separation from Sarah was out of the question. She had not agreed to marry him, her vows still prevented her from capitulating completely, their relationship remained clandestine—however, his sights were set on a future in Rochester: a home, a family. His love for her only soared even as private, sensual moments remained scarce.

The hot, humid days of summer rapidly surrendered to another autumn; Thanksgiving dinner at St. Mary's was meant to be a time of reunion, of rejoicement, of thanks for all the wonderful success at the Almshouse, the steady (but slow) progress of St. Mary's Hospital—Francis was invited; he was excited to donate fresh bread and pumpkin pies—Mrs. Campbell was excited to bake for him.

The repast was particularly sumptuous; Father O'Reilly, in a truly festive mood, congratulated the Sisters and retired early to his chair in the salon before the trouble started—he hadn't begun to light his pipe before he commenced a series of voracious snores. The quartet cleared the table, gathered the dishes, removed the pie plates, brushed the crumbs—an unrehearsed smooth transfer from consuming to collecting and cleaning. Francis gave Sister Felicia what he thought was a secret smile and a familiar wink; he handed her the wine glasses—it had been so long since they stood so close together. Sister Martha missed nothing; seizing her opportunity—she dove in head first.

"I assume you will be announcing your wedding soon?" This announcement was released in a whisper—the good Father would not be privy to her accusations—but it was loud enough to startle Sister Felicia, almost to the point of dropping the Father's precious lead crystal.

Sister Hieronymo was not amused, she simply scolded Sister Martha while continuing to scrub in the sink. "Stop that nonsense."

"Is it nonsense Sister? They have been planning for months."

"Don't be ridiculous, why would you say such a thing?" Sister Felicia was flustered. Her eyes expanded to the fullest proportions—she stared at Francis, searching for support.

"You shouldn't say those things." Francis whispered, somewhat tongue-tied, not knowing how to deal with the shocking accusation.

"They think they are clever. You have been seen. People talk."

"You are a mean person." Sister Felicia began to cry, she rushed out of the room.

"Francis, I think you had better leave now." Sister Hieronymo gave a curt direction. Francis offered a heartfelt thanks for the meal and a sinister stare to Sister Martha.

"Thank Father O'Reilly for me." He left.

Alone together in the kitchen, Sister Hieronymo turned to Sister Martha. "Now what is this all about?" She knew there might be something to the accusations—Sister Felicia was overcome with fear, not with anger—she needed the truth. She wanted to believe the situation was merely a misunderstanding, she wanted to believe Sister Felicia was caught in a silly infatuation, something that could be resolved with punishment and faith.

Francis raised his head to the wind—it was fresh coming in off the lake from Canada—winter was close, yet the days were warm. He brushed the fallen leaves at his feet with his boots, guilty at first, *I should have said more*, but with more kicking and more fresh air, guilt turned to victory, *now she will leave the Order—we can get married.* Francis was naive, familiar with nuns and the Catholic Church, but in no way could he comprehend the influence of Jesus and Sister Hieronymo, nor the vindictive relentlessness of Sister Martha. He stopped in the park; he looked up into the black branches of the tall poplars. He wondered why the few dry leaves, vividly orangey-yellow in their autumn shades, remained so stubborn, sticking tight to their anchors at the edge of the long naked switches. *Why haven't they fallen and flown away like all the others?*

Sister Martha spoke about rumours she had heard (*they were seen together at the lakeshore—Sister Felicia was wearing a dress*). She also described her suspicions of their times together in Kingston. She would say or do anything now to separate them, to force Sarah to deny her foolish infatuation. She wanted her punished, she became exhilarated at the thought of Sarah receiving serious punishment:

hours on her knees on hard stones, perhaps flagellation, cloistered in her room, praying to God daily, nightly, begging for forgiveness. She would be there when Sarah finally relented, finally giving in to her faith, her vows. She would follow direction, she would become her little minion—any misstep quickly relayed to Sister Hieronymo—her constant threat. He would be gone.

"They have been copulating like rabbits for months, I'm surprised she's not pregnant." Sister Martha released her jealousy past the point of control, she began lying without restraint, she was caught in a vortex, she viciously condemned Sister Felicia, she wanted no doubts left in Sister Hieronymo's mind. She lied and lied. Upon completion, she was breathless, the exhilaration had winded her, she swallowed hard. She dropped her head.

"Look at me. If you are lying to me, you will suffer the greatest punishment God can grant." Sister Hieronymo pointed a stern finger in the Sister's face, searching for the truth.

"I would never lie Sister."

Sister Hieronymo was there when the Order took Sarah MacDonald in, an orphan, a child without faith, without a home. She loved her, nurtured her, agreed to accept her application for the Order, she could not abandon her now; now when rescue from the edge of the abyss would be her divine obligation, her duty.

There was indeed a series of long, serious lectures; Sister Felicia did indeed spend many hours on her knees on the cold bare stone floor, alone in the bathroom—she could not tell Sister the truth, she could not reveal her love for Francis, or her desire to leave the Order—she didn't know how; she didn't have the strength. Sister Hieronymo was sure to impose the harshest encumbrance of guilt upon her, the heaviest burden of sin, the powerful wrath of God, her corruption and betrayal of Jesus her Saviour. She was not permitted to see

Francis, and he, subsequently, was restricted from St. Mary's. Francis however was not afraid of Sister Hieronymo, he visited the manor quite often—his entrance, strictly prohibited. Sister Hieronymo did not discuss the accusations, she would not listen to his excuses. Sister Felicia was not allowed to leave the manor; no visitors were permitted at Christmas. Father O'Reilly mentioned in passing at Christmas dinner, "We don't see much of that boy anymore." He had other concerns, and they were well-founded. (In fact his persistence actually resulted in St. Mary's Hospital officially opening before The Rochester City Hospital, as much a surprise and delight to him as anyone else.)

Weeks carried on into months, spring was once again arriving, the time had dragged on—Francis had been tortured long enough. His days were spent searching for her in the hospital, on the streets; his dreams at night: a twisting relentless pursuit—her running, him chasing—union never achieved. He longed for her, his love becoming desperate—the detachment, the estrangement, remained steadfast—Sister Hieronymo had made certain of it.

Watching Sister Martha work at a distance, clumsily feeding patients suffering from fever, his courage and anger boiled over—Francis finally approached as she stood alone in the prep room, close to the end of the day. Sister Hieronymo was not at the hospital.

"How is she?"

"You must not speak of her."

"Please I only want to know how she is. Has she been punished?"

"Sister Felicia has come to her senses, you are no longer of any interest."

"Has she spoken of me?"

"You are a fool. She will never speak of you again."

"You are cold-hearted, you hate her."

"No I care for her, for her spirit, something you know nothing about. You will never see her again."

Nothing Sister Martha said satisfied him, he wanted to scream, to grab her arm—twist her around; he wanted to take a knife out, cut her open, show her a cold heart. He was sweating from his evil, impulsive thoughts. He forced himself to breathe slowly; he composed himself. "Is she well?"

Sister Martha looked at him with the eyes of a pompous, self-righteous master possibly relenting for a sacred moment to a poor soul so desperate for her precious word. "Well if you must know, she's very sick. She may not last the week." She passed on the news as if she was reading a recipe: (*"She might die—include a pinch of salt!"*) Francis couldn't believe her casual words—the feelings of anger and desperation were overwhelming, his hands squeezed tightly into fists, he was shaking. He had no words. The vision of the platform in Chicago, the three swinging bodies, Smithson, Ogden—he had been angry before, there was an uncontrollable force reawakening.

He pushed past her purposely hitting her arm hard. He raced from the hospital up Main to West; he began smashing his fist into the door of the manor. He screamed "Sarah, Sarah!" with each punch. He tried the latch—it was open—he burst inside, up the stairs. Father O'Reilly was in the Church, the house was empty. Sarah was lying in her bed, the curtains pulled tight—her face in shadow. Francis halted abruptly, frozen, shocked, scared. He spoke to her softly, "Sarah." She did not respond.

Francis crossed to the window; he gently drew open the curtains. The sun was setting, yet a glimmer of light spread across the room— soft shades of white caressed the tiny contours of her face. The pink of her face had turned ghostly pale, her eye sockets were dark and sunken; the dim evening light highlighted the drops of perspiration on her forehead and on her upper lip: tiny translucent beads at rest. Her mouth was open, her lips dry and cracked—she struggled to breathe evenly. Francis knelt at her bedside, holding her hand, he whispered her name. "Sarah." She opened her eyes. He moved in close.

She smiled, faintly, she whispered his name. "Francis."

"Sarah." He repeated her name again. "I didn't know, I didn't know." Francis had seen the symptoms before: cholera—or at least a bacteria causing rapid dehydration and very high fever. He took the cloth on the small table, dipping it in the cool water, he placed it carefully on her head. The fever had raged for so long, he knew it would be difficult to break it; he hoped it would offer some relief.

Francis poured water into the glass from the wash stand, he checked the clarity up to the light from the window—it was mirky, there were floating bits, he frowned disappointed—he could not give her a drink from this source. He wiped the cloth from her head across her lips—she tried to lick, the effort was too much. He replaced the cloth, he watched her closely. His heart was breaking, he was crying. Sarah whispered, "Don't cry Francis, everything will be alright now."

Francis could not possibly understand what she meant, he had treated patients for so many months, typhus, typhoid, cholera, malaria—now he faced the nemesis so directly, vicious and cruel—he had no power, no medicines. His skills tested, had failed. If only he could have known sooner, maybe there was something he could have done. Nothing would ever be right again. She was delirious. She was slipping away. He kissed her hand. "Sarah don't go, please don't go. I love you so much. Sarah." She closed her eyes, her breathing faded away, her hand so cold, became limp, like a clutch of weightless feathers from an injured sparrow. He continued to look into her face, watching her eyes, praying for their return—she was gone.

A heavy dark weight pressed hard onto Francis' shoulders—it spread like a fiery virus into his flesh, through his bones, down to his soul—it festered there, septic, seething. Sister Martha had been giving her tainted water. All water from the wells had to be boiled, no water from the canals was to be used at all for anything. He would confront her when she arrived, he would slice her open, he would spread her entrails across the room—Francis was reaching out beyond all sanity, he was wrought with pain and anger...He collected his thoughts for a moment, he pulled the cover over her face—he left the manor.

Nuns don't celebrate death with a funeral service. She had not confessed to Father O'Reilly, there was a chance she would not be permitted to enter Heaven. Francis stood beside the grave in St. Mary's cemetery—it was located at the very fringe of the property—a soul like hers could not be associated with those that had confessed; besides she had broken her vows, she was a lost soul. Dead leaves from the poplars and chestnut trees filtered down, dusting his head floating on a delicate breeze, snowflakes dotted the air—he was lonely, he wanted to go home. He picked up a chestnut and broke the skin back. The nut was smooth, he rubbed it in his hand; then whipped it high as far as he could throw, to the moonlight, to Heaven.

42

*L*il sat quietly by the kitchen window, staring blankly out into the evening sky—the first snowflakes swirling about, leaves collecting on the sill—her favourite place. Emilia Murphy was baking bread, the smells were euphoric, the pastries brimming with jams and cinnamons stretched across her table like obedient soldiers in straight lines—Christmas treats for the church. There would be no celebrating for Lil, she had buried her stillborn baby four months ago, the pain lingered. The pregnancy was horrific—so much discomfort—although Charles Smithson was the father—the thought initially unbearable—she decided to have the child and raise it. Everyone said it's death was a blessing, it was not right, it was deformed—the pain and the horror of the fateful day of its conception would only be recounted with every awkward, pitiful glance of its contorted face and mangled figure—better that it died. For Lil the pain remained anyway.

Shannon had fooled Smithson's posse that night and returned to the little shack after his men had abandoned their search in the snowstorm. They stayed the night, although without a fire—there was no flint. They huddled together under the blanket until morning when Shannon rode back to town. She was an outlaw, she had killed William Armstrong, and there was a warrant out for her arrest. The horse was stabled at the edge of town—she snuck home, down allies and through back streets to retrieve clothes, blankets, flints and food. Mrs. O'Brien was unconsolable—relieved to see her daughter—however the comfort she required to withdraw from the deep well of depression in which she now sank, could not be successfully provided by her daughter, nor from the throngs of church women so often arriving at her door.

Shannon would take Lil to her Aunt's home in Milwaukee, a long difficult journey, but with luck, they would not be found. For twenty days Shannon and Lil suffered the hardships of bitter cold weather, scant food, lost trails, and reluctant efforts from Lil. There were more than a few occasions when Shannon considered putting a bullet into Lil's head, leaving her in a snowbank and heading back to Chicago— the woman had become a useless burden, an annoying boil on her backside. When Lil revealed her pregnancy, she hoped to receive some sympathy—Shannon had none for her—there were a hundred miles to cover, gunmen on their tail, few rabbits, and frostbite threatening every second.

Mrs. Murphy, Siobhan O'Brien's sister, was weary of the two strangers at her door that wintery night—she would not recognize her own niece until well into the evening after the fire had melted the frost, natural colours returned, and familiar stories eventually convinced her. The murder of Pat O'Brien was a shock, they wept together, Little Raven seemed oblivious, detached. It was absolutely a miracle that neither had suffered frostbite let alone lived.

Shannon stayed for a month then headed back to Chicago. Aunt Emilia agreed to hide Lil, but it was Shannon's plan to adopt a disguise and return to her home in Chicago that gave her stress—it seemed an unlikely solution, but Shannon was adamant, her mother needed her.

Mail passed along the Green Bay Road more regularly in the spring and summer, Shannon could communicate with her aunt, news of the baby's death arrived with distress, yet there was a justice—no one wanted to see that baby of Smithson's survive in Chicago's harsh social environment that would question every aspect of Lil and her life—to live a decent life as a deformed person in Milwaukee would be just as impossible. Lil wasn't convinced. So she spent her days staring out the kitchen window; each day Mrs. Murphy's tolerance would be tested, each day Lil would receive a reprieve and a smile.

43

The air on the upper deck was cooler, the smoke and gay sounds from the saloon below so amusing at first, quickly became tiresome—the girls rowdy, the gamblers noisy, the air thick and dirty. Francis could now feel the space around him, he needed to breath, to see the shoreline, he needed to be alone. The Hudson River at least was calm; travel by water still did not agree with him, but the distance to New York was easily covered by the Erie Canal and the Hudson River in two days (one night in Albany). He cut a fine handsome figure on the deck; in the last five years he had grown to a fraction just shy of six feet, his shoulders broad, his hair short and dark, his moustache full and thick, he remained however, impossibly thin, most would say skinny—women aboard gave him nods and smiles, he returned their favours in kind with the tip of his hat. He had saved a serious quantity of money from his employment at the Rochester City Hospital; he carried himself as a gentleman—

he was well-dressed, confident and aloof. He had not contacted his old friend Doctor Lobbins, at the Massachusetts General Hospital as previously planned, because he left abruptly. However he assumed once he was recognized, the amiable times they shared together would come rushing back (he should have considered the few short months they worked together five years ago, could be quickly forgotten by a busy doctor). He would then be offered a position on the spot, and advance warning would have been proven unnecessary. Francis had no accommodation secured in New York, he reckoned a good hotel would be available near the river boat dock—he would stay one night, then continue to Boston in the morning. He carried one bag—a change of clothes, Rising Sun's amputation kit; he wore a full-brimmed hat and carried his coat. The bag never left his side, he patted his inside breast pocket every few minutes (all his money in the world residing there), he carried his coat, he talked to no one, he trusted no one. He considered carrying his buffalo skinner on his back, inside his suit, but decided against it—it just wasn't a gentle-manly thing to do. While his right hand was usually fumbling about in his trouser pocket, Little Raven's leather pouch habitually ma-nipulated by nervous fingers—the locket and ring inside, constant companions—he would practice strutting about on the upper deck.

Two doctors of note now permanent in Rochester, had written letters of introduction; they explained that their presentation should suffice when seeking a position—Francis had become a well-respected staff member, albeit with one minor exception—no bedside manner. There was at least a two year period after Sarah MacDonald's death where even the faintest of smiles or a semblance of cordiality was impossible. His demeanour was volatile, his patience thin, his attitude offensive. These negative attributes, however, with the passing of time, began to wane to a point where any medical staff member would have been more than glad to write such a letter, and in fact his presence would now be sorely missed.

In order for Francis to retain this pleasant professional attitude, however, meant the distance between himself and Sister Martha would necessarily remain excessively wide, as the powerful urge to gut her like a pig continued to well up in his cerebral constitution, and he was sure he might lose all control if forced to stand within ten feet of her miserable penguin persona. The about turn required to pull off this new personality took training—continual practice, and strict discipline—it was achieved by watching the other doctors and copying their idiosyncrasies; in the end it didn't seem too difficult at all.

Francis considered taking a sample of water from the bedroom, examining it under a microscope, then pursuing an investigation into the slow murder of Sarah—but he realized he could not prove that Sister Martha was responsible or even knowledgable. Most importantly if he could prove her guilt, he knew he wouldn't wait for an arrest or trial—he would do the job himself...fast...no hesitation. He was not ready to hang. He has learned to control his impulses, especially when he is strutting about on the top deck of a river boat steamer cruising south to New York on a fine sunny day, full and pompous like an arrogant doctor ready to discuss a new diagnosis or government legislation concerning the amalgamation of railroads.

Francis didn't have to feign confidence in every regard of course. He could still butcher a carcass with extreme deft, be it porcine or bovine, and present perfect cuts in all their various appointed dimensions—the correct and sharpest of tools being available and requisite. There was no doubt about his medical skills be it reducing a fever, setting a bone, amputating a limb, or the extrication of a baby. There were several occasions in Rochester when patients referred to him as 'doctor'; his fellow colleagues with less experience often asked for guidance—although rarely.

The true confidence that Francis desired however, the spiritual serenity that alluded him, remained subject to the unconditional acceptance within the social parameters of his medical colleagues. There was no fraternizing after rounds, after lab work, after staff meetings—Francis was an 'assistant'—it left him somewhat disillusioned, and certainly doubtful. This lack of acceptance often left him defensive—questioning his qualifications was one thing, scrutinizing his skills quite another. Segregation during a staff party would never invoke jealousy or consternation, but cast doubt on the quality of his sutures and Lord help the questioning physician. Ask him his opinion on a diagnosis, and the light from his eyes could light up a room. Ostensibly however, Francis wanted to fit in, to be an accredited doctor, to be considered an equal among the leaders of the medical community.

Something about the time seemed right to him; the hospital was near completion—there were over one hundred full time doctors now, much of the fever was under control, memories there often weighed heavy on his mind—Boston was a new beginning, a plethora of possibilities!

He woke up, packed his few belongings, said good-bye to Mrs. Campbell, caught the first canal boat east, and was gone—no regrets. He had warned the hospital administrators weeks ago, they wrote the letters—they wished him well; it was just a final date that was missing.

The river was windy, the sun hot, the music annoying—his disposition positive. Francis held the rail at the extreme forward edge of the boat; his smile was not jubilant, but more of a smirk—resolute. But fate has a way of wiping away smirks, of stealing a young man's dreams, wrapping them around the horns of a charging bull and throwing them into the burning fires of destiny.

44

The coach ride from New York was a disaster—so many stops, questionable passengers with questionable roving eyes buried deep within large dark floppy hats, (each character resembling some sort of outlaw or criminal), baggage thrown on top carrying the dirt and trail grime of a thousand dusty miles, the hardest of seats—the leather covering and scant stuffing worn down to a bare nip and tuck—protected no part of anyone's delicate posteriors. Francis quickly realized the rail would have been the best choice after all. He had been sadly misinformed: "Yes the trip to Boston by rail was fast, but so expensive—better to travel by coach." The particular coach he chose to ride, displayed a small worn brass plate at the place where a hand grip used to attach to the side of the carriage (to assist leverage upon lifting up onto the step). The leather strap had long disappeared, the ripped remains hung pathetically by a whisker, the leverage required to haul one's body up and in, reduced to whatever amount of strength and unaided agility the passenger could muster. Upon the brass plate was inscribed 'VEAZIE AND BARNARD, TROY NEW YORK'. Veazie had been building stage coaches since 1815, and this unlikely relic was undoubtedly one of the originals.

The coach stopped about every twelve miles to pick up or drop off passengers, allow for a latrine break, switch horse teams, or more importantly to grant the drivers a drink—usually beer of some sort, or perhaps a local beverage with doubtful ingredients, settling loosely within the dubious description of 'premium refreshing libation'—always a wise choice when blindly guiding a six-horse team over rough terrain during the darkest hours of the night at breakneck speed. The two hundred miles to Providence was slowly covered in three days—three days more than Francis could bear—the choice to switch to the New York Providence and Boston Rail Line was an easy and smart decision—the final fifty miles was a wonderful, comfortable trip—albeit smoky. Apparently Louis Susini (cigar and cigarette entrepreneur) introduced a new cigarette to America's eastern metropolises from Germany, and absolutely everyone was smoking them; negotiating a path and locating one's compartment was tantamount to losing one's bearings in a thick Boston morning fog—sitting and choking within the fog for three hours was decidedly worse.

Francis finally, thankfully, soon stood upon the lawn before the newly renovated Massachusetts Hospital across the Charles River on Fruit Street, he couldn't have been more delighted, or relieved—he felt as though he had smoked at least fifty cigarettes without having touched even one.

The Bulfinch Building was huge: a series of six great columns supporting a massive portico styled in the Greek revivalist fashion. The walls encasing over 36,000 square feet were constructed of

Clemsford white granite, and divided the building into two long wings with a central section. Francis climbed the wide stone stairway and entered the building. The reception area was grand by anyone's description—beautiful hardwood accents, tall ceilings, a wide foyer—Francis was impressed immediately. The old man at the desk, who desperately wanted to help Francis, could only suggest he sit and wait as Doctor Lobbins was in surgery and his availability for the next few hours was quite impossible.

Francis patiently waited, his stomach growling, his eyes meandering from window to ceiling to doorways, back and forth—he dosed off almost immediately—a polite nudge on his knee woke him, the time was near seven o'clock, it had been five hours.

"Excuse me sir, this is Doctor Lobbins." Startled, Francis shot up, facing the doctor extending his hand, unbalanced, dreamy visions of Sarah floating about the lakeshore in a partial state of undress rapidly vanishing—he almost fell over his bag.

"So good to see you again, wonderful to finally have arrived." Francis was smiling, his most cordial expression, his hand vigorously shaking and shaking. Doctor Lobbins obviously tired, confused and definitely bewildered, staring, wondering who this travel-weary person with the dusty suitcase and wrinkled suit might be.

"What can I do for you?"

"John, it's Francis Tumblety. Don't you remember me? Rochester. We worked together at the Almshouse in Rochester. You taught me so much."

John Lobbins, exhausted from an eight hour stretch in surgery with Doctor Warren, was attempting to put the face and name together, his back aching, his lids closing, his stomach also grumbling. "Yes, yes, of course. Young Tumblety. What can I do for you?" Although still not entirely sure of the time spent with Francis so long ago—so much had transpired since then (marriage, children, promotions) he did recollect something, however, he tried to remain interested for the sake of good manners.

"Well I am here...finally." Lobbins' face remained blank. "Your invitation, don't you remember? You asked me to follow you to Boston, to work here with you, to continue my education."

"Tumblety that was so long ago. Yes I think I do remember. But I don't know if there's a position here for you, now."

The discussion in the lobby of the Bulfinch Building might have continued until Francis obtained some sort of satisfaction, as Lobbins was willing to listen, as least he was humouring Francis—attempting to give a positive impression—he didn't want to end the impromptu visit burdening Francis with a discouraging and empty prediction. Lobbins was well aware of the journey from Rochester, he had made it, he was sympathetic, but truly he was not involved with hiring medical staff.

The moment was saved; two young doctors, stepping lively into the lobby, asked Lobbins in passing if he was catching supper at The Bell in Hand—they were starving—Warren had kept them overtime. Lobbins graciously declined, however never discouraged—impetuously grabbing the dusty bag from Francis—they quickly marched off together into the evening, into Boston, into the first of many suppers, the first of many shared beers at The Bell and at Clancy's.

Stokie (Ralph Stokins) a young medical student, short—his face fat and continually red as if overwhelmed by fever—suggested Francis stay with him for the night until accommodations could be arranged. He was sure Mrs. Hollis had room at her small boarding house not fifteen minutes from the hospital. Doctor Dave Putnam (a first year doctor, and Warren sycophant) explained that positions for new doctors without credentials were "next to nil my friend," however, he could arrange an interview later this week—perhaps Francis could begin working in the labs in the basement. Putnam was absolutely on route to becoming a high level medical snob, Francis identified the traits immediately: long nose waving high in the air, eyes without depth cutting low at the heart, ordering servers about as if they were his personal scum—suggesting the morgue and ablution rooms, the incinerator, might best suit him. Francis hated him immediately. Ralph was frank and agreed securing a position would be difficult. Francis presented his letters, they seemed to help; Putnam of course tossed them aside as if they might be used to wipe his dirty back end.

Francis, not inclined to drink beers on an empty stomach, although the beef stew and buns helped, staggered into Stokie's loft bedroom and dropped to the floor—exhausted, drunk—if he was at all coherent, he would have admitted to sublime satisfaction as a footnote—but he had passed coherent an hour ago.

Doctor Putnam may have had an alternate reason for approaching Dr. Warren first in the case of Francis Tumblety, however the interview was scheduled, and if Warren received prejudicial comments and opinions from Putnam, he clearly dismissed them—Francis was received graciously, perhaps it was just his style. Doctor John Collins Warren accepted the post as Head of Medicine and Dean of Harvard Medical School following in his father's footsteps. He was the first registered surgeon at Massachusetts General, he was famous, well-regarded, a leader in the field of modern medicine, a supreme surgeon. At a medium height, a clean-shaven face—his jowls drooping in long exaggerated lines down his cheeks—Dr. Warren was a pleasant man, stern and dedicated—but fair in all regards. In the summer of 1853 when Francis was first introduced, Dr. Warren was seventy-five years old, close to retirement, but in no regard could he be considered less than fully astute in every way.

Francis was encouraged almost immediately to sail to England where the sourcing of medical staff was of the highest concern—if it came to war in the Crimea, many doctors would be needed. Upon review of the letters of introduction, Dr. Warren gratefully offered Francis the opportunity to receive a letter from him for the War Office in London. The only position available to Francis was in the basement—cleaning, washing cadavers, possibly some dissections, assisting on some autopsies. *Perhaps Putnam was correct.* Francis turned down the letter for London and accepted the position as assistant.

Mrs. Hollis was a wonderful little lady who had watched many young doctors come and go in her boarding house. She welcomed Francis immediately; she commented on how much she missed Master Stokins, *'what a nice gentleman he was'*. The room was small, it doubled as her sewing room—there were little piles of fabrics about, a machine for stitching, clothing projects in partial completion hanging on door knobs. The bed was soft, the blanket: duck down, the food was glorious. Francis was receiving a decent salary—the cost of the room would take a very small amount of it—he thought it would be difficult to consider better circumstances, unless of course he could somehow be miraculously promoted to doctor.

Stokie would invite Francis for beers at The Bell or Clancy's on Friday nights. He was impressing the pathology doctors with his technique, he was learning so much, Boston had been a good decision after all. The conflict in the Crimea did commence as Dr. Warren predicted, in October 1853, and several young doctors from Massachusetts General enlisted, sailing to England to join a British Regiment as staff doctors. Francis when asked again, was too comfortable in his routine, and the thought of the ocean voyage was a major discouragement—he couldn't possibly consider it. He also assumed the few spaces opening up from the new resignations might open opportunities for him. He remained hopeful.

As the months passed, a regime clearly surfaced. It became almost a regular routine, not every night, but often, and the regularity was increasing—Francis would extend his washing and scrubbing down every floor and hallway on the bottom floor including behind closed doors marked 'ENTRANCE NOT PERMITTED.' His turn to work nights was a responsibility scheduled for one week during a one month rotation—he didn't mind. Eventually there were no corners or closets left unknown to him, his curiosity was boundless, his clandestine investigations thorough. There was a ledge in the custodial room above the basin marked 'keys'; his task seemed obvious. One night he was caught.

45

Walking the dark corridors alone during the deepest hours of the night on the lowest floor of a hospital— the residents occupying the rooms being the grey lifeless remains of humans now in various stages of decomposition and often without many of their internal organs or appendages— would for some be alarming, even impossible. Francis often assumed the task of delivering amputated appendages and discarded organs to the incinerator—the lifeless bodies residing in the basement couldn't possibly give him any grief. He did however struggle with personal demons—their source resided deep within his own personal cerebral corridors, not in a hospital morgue; here he was at home. Here the halls had beginnings and sharp corners, there were exits and stairwells, the demons within the rooms were dead; in his mind at night, visions floated about—their origins undetermined, their route a mystery—there was no way out, nowhere to run. The darkness was often littered with bloody bones, wild dogs stealing and chewing. The flesh and bones he carried now to the hospital incinerator were not much different than the carts of butchered animal remains from the Chicago stockyards—at least they were real—they couldn't hurt him.

Gas lamps lit the hallways at night—enough to allow a custodian the safe maneuverability he required; the hidden corners and narrow alcoves remained covered in shadow—Francis knew his way well enough.

The sign on the door was clearly marked: 'Dr. W. Morton, ENTRANCE PROHIBITED'. It was always locked—Francis gave it a push, it easily swung open. There was no light. *Had Dr. Morton forgot to lock up?* The initial impression of the vast collection of glass tubes, cylinders and beakers was more akin to a glass blower's factory than a medical lab. There were no sticky formaldehyde jars containing discoloured viscous layers of slimy specimens barely identifiable to a layman's curious stares.

There were no white porcelain or shiny steel tables with shallow blood gutters; no trays displaying the usual vast assortment of knives, retractors, saws or probes associated with surgery or dissection. This was, after all, a chemical laboratory not the morgue. Francis slowly followed a curvy pathway past the rows of tables, free-standing iron and glass apparatuses, a myriad of shelves with hundreds of marked bottles; weaved throughout the maze of tiered beakers and bottles, tapered funnels and glass tubes and rods—to the back wall where a faint light cast a dull glow.

"Can I help you?" Doctor Morton did not rise up from his stool or turn, he did not lift his eye from the lens of the microscope—yet he knew someone was standing behind him.

'I'm sorry Doctor, I didn't know anyone was here. Your door was open." Francis was caught off guard, he fumbled for words.

"Please approach." Doctor Morton remained seated and beckoned Francis to stand beside him. Instead of a reprimand, Francis was invited to look into the microscope. "Have you ever seen anything like that young man?" Francis adjusted the focus and watched with fascination as a collection of lines squiggled and flipped about in the solution.

"No Sir."

"Bacillus anthraces—its bacteria, and it kills people. Have you heard of Doctor Ferdinand Cohn?"

"No Sir."

"Doctor Pasteur?"

"Yes doctor."

"Those gentlemen believe these small living organisms, left to multiply in the human body, eventually kill it. It's the basic ingredient of infection. Do you believe it son?"

"Yes Sir.'

"Well, good. I wish the other doctors in this hospital agreed with you."

'Is that what you are doing here Doctor, finding an ingredient that will kill bacteria?"

"Actually, no. This is not my area of research, but I must continue to follow the lead presented to me by my colleagues in Europe. The American medical community is lagging far behind I'm afraid. No, I am developing an anaesthetic that will render a patient unconscious long enough to complete a surgical procedure, and not kill him. Have you heard of ether?"

"No Sir."

Doctor Morton looked at Francis and realized for the first time, that he was not talking to a student, but to a janitor. "Who are you son?"

"I am Francis Tumblety. I am an assistant down here in the morgue. I have been studying medicine with some of the other doctors, assisting with dissections and cataloguing details during autopsies." He hoped his interruption would not result in his dismissal. "I am so sorry I have bothered you."

"Well I can see you are not studying tonight. Not at all, I am not bothered." Doctor Morton regarded Francis, his coat and mop, his keen awareness and reserved attitude. Morton then asked Francis to turn on all the gas lamps in the lab. The equipment was overwhelming, a labyrinth of glass—every shape and size from floor to ceiling. The technique used to develop ether was explained in every minute detail: the vapour-phase hydration to create ethylene (using acid catalysts), the dehydration to ethanol and the mixing of sulphuric acid. The temperatures had to be carefully watched and the balances between ethylene and ethanol carefully controlled as they wanted to naturally change back. There was a distillation process of the ether to prevent it from reverting back to ethanol. All this was fascinating to Francis and he listened carefully, although his chemistry background was severely weak, his knowledge in this area slim to nil. Doctor Morton explained that he had perfected the production of ether, that was not the problem now—it was the application, as too little was not enough to render the patient comfortable and too much was lethal; also the mixture was highly volatile, and explosive.

Francis held the small beaker up to a gas lamp to look at the mixture.

"Not too close son. One touch of a flame and this whole lab will go up."

"Yes Sir." Francis noted the mixture was absolutely clear— it could have been water; it did have an odour, and a close deep inhalation would knock him to the floor—he was careful to hold it away from his nose.

Francis asked many questions. Morton regarded him with a curious affection—his questions were clear, intelligent, astute. Morton was impressed, and when asked, Francis quickly agreed to aid him in the lab whenever he could. They would soon become great partners.

Over time Morton came to share his excitement and all his concerns with Francis; this included his great defeats. His first application of ether on a young patient for the extraction of a tooth left the patient in a coma, and later she died. The technique he needed to perfect now was in the application—how much ether and for how long. Together Francis and Morton collaborated on perfecting the application using animals—dogs in particular. Although Francis had yet to witness the use of ether on a human patient, he was confident in Morton's skills. Dr. William Morton was ready for a public demonstration.

By the summer of 1854, the war in the Crimea had been raging for almost one year, medicine and infection control, antibiotics, amputations, guns, cavalry and ships were the hot topics of conversation at the Massachusetts General. News from Britain included stories of horrific battles and terrible deaths—and for the first time photographs were being relayed from the battlefield. For the most part people were enraged at war—it apparently wasn't all romance and heroics—it was undignified brutal suffering and bloody death. There was a cry to the War Office for relief, sanitation, anything that proposed improved conditions for Britain's sons—although heard, the cry was never really fully addressed. Francis didn't offer his attention or opinions in regard to war—in fact he had no idea where

"The Crimea" was. It didn't concern him—besides if Putnam gave the situation any serious concern—then Francis, typically, would not.

Francis was now a well-known personality at the hospital, not many doctors considered his opinions valid (*tiny bacteria killing whole humans, anaesthetics being necessary during surgical procedures*), however he never backed down from an argument whether at the hospital or at the Bell in Hand on Friday nights.

Stokie and Putnam listened to Francis and this exploits that carried on down in Morton's lab. Stokie was very responsive and thought Francis might become a great pathologist someday. Putnam dismissed the whole discussion as ridiculous and implied that Morton was a fraud and a quack—"You know he killed a patient." In any case, both young doctors were invited to the lecture hall to witness Morton's latest demonstration in anaesthetics—Putnam being absolutely convinced that the man would make a fool of himself, and if the patient died, "A jail cell for the rest of his life would be too good!"

Francis was never discouraged by anything Putnam ever said; most importantly, he was invited to attend the demonstration—and that was the finest outcome he could ever imagine.

In order to fully appreciate the entire ensemble, the mirror would have to be adjusted. Francis reached forward with his left hand and gripped the finely carved wood of the frame that completely bordered the long mirror and tipped it forward on its central swivel axis. Stepping back, he could now receive his new persona in all its splendour from the top of his head to the toe of his boot. He reviewed himself up and down and up again. He pulled on the cuffs of his coat and remarked to himself at the fine precision. He concluded that Mrs. Hollis was indeed a fine seamstress or, perhaps 'tailoress', if that was the correct term to be used in this case, as befitting the alterations of a gentleman's garment.

He was almost convinced that his clandestine integration into the upper echelons of Boston's society tonight would prove undetected, as he now wore the suitable attire and he was, after all, properly invited by Dr. Morton himself.

Francis ran his hand through his hair and lifted his chin in a haughty gesture. The man in the full length mirror looked back and raised an eyebrow; leaning back and a little to one side. He then smoothly tucked his left hand into his coat pocket purposely leaving his thumb cocked and exposed. His other hand gripped his lapel and he spoke as an orator after his opinion was requested from an important journalist, with a pouting lower lip and a raised eyebrow. "I am..." Then he paused.

Spying Mrs. Hollis' sewing mannequin behind him in the reflection, he cautiously turned and retrieved it; then gently rolled it to the mirror. The hourglass curves of course would not be entirely appropriate, as no gentleman tonight would exhibit such dimensions, and the chances of a lady being present at such a lecture would be absolutely out of the question; however, Francis decided it would suffice for his short pantomime.

He turned to the naked, headless, legless figure and continued his address in a professional manner properly suiting a member of the College of Surgeons and Physicians.

"...Tumblety, Doctor Francis Tumblety. I am a surgeon here at Massachusetts General and I have grave doubts about this ridiculous display this evening. I fear the man has no business indulging in chemical experiments that will only mildly amuse and most certainly embarrass the medical community. I only hope Harvard's reputation will not be spoiled, for we cannot afford to discourage the generous endeavours of the Associates." He thought the haughty discourse was a good reflection of Doctor David Putnam, so he had it right—he thought, *what a complete ass he is.*

The attending delegates had no idea if Dr. Morton knew what he was doing or if the demonstration would be a success or a dismal failure, as was the case in his first attempt at applying an anaesthetic during surgery, but they naturally arrived with their biases, deciding it would be acceptable to disagree with anything new in medicine, which seemed to be the rule rather than the exception with most doctors in Boston. Francis retained every confidence in his mentor.

Francis was convinced that he could pull it off, he desperately hoped that his position as a medical assistant would not jeopardize his chance to associate with the upper crust of the Boston medical and business community. It was so unlikely that an employee of his lowly stature would ever be invited to such a lecture. If Putnam could keep his mouth closed, he doubted if anyone really cared about his attendance.

He tweaked his tie and pulled on his coat sleeves. He lifted his chin up above the high stiff collar. He brushed his whiskers at the side of his face with his fingers. *This might be the most important night of my life*, he thought.

When he was satisfied with his presentation, he bid farewell to his unlikely companion with a deep dramatic bow and dashed down the stairs. Mrs. Hollis stood at the door with his hat in her hand.

"Ah you look wonderful dearie," Mrs. Hollis exclaimed with her usual cheery smile.

"Thank you, Mrs. Hollis." Francis tried to look older and 'doctorly', but he just couldn't control the smile that seemed to be glued across his face. Typically his expression should be sour and critical—the very serious demeanour of a Boston doctor.

"Good luck sir." She bid him good evening and Francis tapped his hat on the top to secure its place and he stepped lively down the steps and across the street.

The Dome Theatre at the Massachusetts General Hospital was ornate in its design with seven rows of tiered balconies reaching high into the vault at a very steep angle. A glass skylight at the pinnacle would admit light, albeit a limited amount, to the floor of the room during daylight hours. The viewing was semicircular reminiscent of a true Greek amphitheatre, and although Francis was sequestered at the very top (its lofty geography in perfect reversal to his social status), his line of view was directly over the small stage floor at the centre, thirty feet below, and he reckoned he could see well enough. Below in the second tier sat Stokie and Putnam; he waved but they were focused on the action before them.

Dr. Warren and a handful of gentlemen were standing in the centre when a gurney was wheeled in followed by Dr. Morton. Dr. Warren introduced the lecture and things began to happen very quickly. As Dr. William Morton was (officially) a dentist, Dr. Warren proceeded to begin the amputation of the patient's horrible ulcerated lower leg—the result of a fracture, and the lack of any medical administration up to this point. The leg was infected and gangrenous—it had to be removed in any case, with or without anaesthetic, or the patient's life would certainly hang as precarious as his pathetic leg, swollen, ugly and stinking as it was. The brave businessmen in the audience, not familiar with surgery especially in this cloistered proximity, covered their faces to abate the odour. Francis had seen worse and smelled worse.

The patient was obviously in considerable pain as Francis recognized the pale facial skin, beads of sweat, and the constant writhing of his head to and fro, side to side; yet the poor man, impressively, was successfully suppressing any verbal anguish—as he released not a cry, nor a whimper.

Dr. Morton held a type of cone-shaped metal strainer over the patient's mouth and nose and dripped the clear liquid slowly into a cloth, as Dr. Warren held an amputation knife in his hand in preparation for a swift cut. An assistant was careful to move a gas lamp away from the patient's head—in clear acknowledgement of the volatile nature of ether. With a nod from Dr. Morton, gesturing that his patient was indeed under a controlled anaesthetic sleep, Dr. Warren began.

The lecture theatre was silent: not a sound, as everyone, including Francis leaned forward on their benches anticipating a violent outburst—a primal scream, as steel cut into flesh. The tourniquet tightened, the knife cut around the appendage, the skin flap pulled back. Then a saw cut through the bone, and the lower leg was removed. The arteries were sewn; the blood was wiped and the wound was sealed with a generous length of cat gut sutures. The tourniquet was removed. Dr. Warren, a master surgeon, finished the job swiftly and precisely. Not a sound escaped from the patient's mouth; not a jerk or a movement of any kind. *Was he dead?*

The gallery remained silent as Dr. Morton removed the cone from the patient's face and stood back. The amputation was a clean procedure, but the demonstration would be a failure if the patient remained comatose, or worse—dead.

Everyone doubted Morton's claim, and the cloud of apprehension was thick. The room was heavy with consternation, as skeptical eyes and ears leaned forward to full extent eager to chastise and ridicule.

Francis was astounded by what he witnessed next, as was everyone, collected together as they were to share medical history that day. Dr. Morton tapped the patient's face lightly and asked,

"How do you feel?" The patient responded, "A bit tired sir. Have you begun?" The gallery at first was awestruck and offered no response; then an uproarious din exploded as a great round of applause erupted and shook the great dome from floor to skylight.

"Gentlemen this is no humbug." Dr. Warren's famous exclamation, forever reverberating within the curved walls the "Ether Dome" (as it would now and forever be referred to), called out to the jubilant crowd. His endorsement gave Morton the validity he needed.

Francis had only one thought, *I'll either make it or steal it.*

The grand reception commenced almost immediately, everyone wanted to be the first to shake Morton's hand. Doctors and businessmen from the first two rows were quick to enter the foyer, grasp a glass of brandy, light a cigar (or in many cases, new German cigarettes) and search out Dr. Morton and Dr. Warren. Francis shook Stokie's hand—receiving a "Well done" from his friend and colleague meant the world to Francis—Putnam wasn't about to congratulate Francis even if he had cured small pox, leprosy and cancer—all with the stroke of a scalpel with or without Morton—Francis could have cared less.

Dr. Morton introduced Francis as his assistant to a Mr. James Donahue, a very highly respected businessman and philanthropist— an important associate of the hospital. "And this is Francis Tumblety; he has been a great service to me in this endeavour, a wonderful asset to this hospital." As Francis reached out to shake his hand, a deep voice interrupted from behind the heads of the men standing about. The dark broad shoulders towered over everyone—a huge mountain of a man turned to face them.

"Tumblety did you say? A rather unusual name."

"Yes sir, Irish, no different than Kennedy or Timothy really." Francis stared up, deep into his eyes, It was Charles Smithson, no doubt about it. The beady green eyes, the immense shoulders, the deep resounding voice, his presence overpowering.

"No, I don't think so. Tumblety is very peculiar. Are you from Chicago?"

"No sir, Rochester, I've never been to Chicago." Francis knew Smithson had never met him, he assumed there would be no recognition, no association. He always thought if he saw Smithson again, he would pounce on him fast, slicing him open like a trout fresh out of Lake Michigan—but he was in shock, frozen to the spot, scared—totally confused and unprepared.

Charles Smithson was no fool. He took the time to examine the face of this young assistant, so highly regarded by the 'man of the hour'—he was highly suspect. It had been twenty-four years since he looked into the eyes of Margaret his daughter; that stormy night so long ago. He hadn't totally given up on finding her, he often enquired around when conducting business in Boston—without any results—until now. He could see his daughter in the face of this young man, a man who shared the same name as the boy that met his brutal demise on that Chicago pier the night before her disappearance. He hated that name. This was no coincidence.

Francis could feel the tension, this man was not buying it. He needed to get out fast—this man was unpredictable. "Well, congratulations Dr. Morton, unfortunately I must be off, I will see you again shortly, good evening." Francis grabbed the arm of Stokie; he whispered in his ear about exiting fast—and they were off. Smithson watched, scowling, planning—then also dismissed himself.

Francis gave Stokie a flimsy excuse for their hasty departure, they separated. Francis was cutting through the narrow back streets of Boston, he could feel the hot vile breath of Smithson on his neck— he turned...nothing, he was sweating, he was becoming paranoid, delusional—of course Smithson couldn't follow him home, *how stupid!* He ran past The Bell, past the park, cross to Fulton street, home. Mrs. Hollis' boarding house never looked so beautiful.

Sleeping that night was impossible—there were so many scenarios chasing each other about in his brain—most having to do with his buffalo skinner and Smithson' neck. *How could I do it? How could I find Smithson in Boston? How long was he staying before returning to Chicago? How could I corner him, then slice him?*

The early golden rays of sunlight pierced through his bedroom window, they stabbed his face, he could smell coffee wafting up from the kitchen downstairs—he was still in his suit. After breakfast and the refreshing walk to the hospital Francis began to organize his thoughts; his anxieties began to wane, he would consider Smithson's demise over the next few days. Someone here at the hospital knew him—he was invited to the Ether Dome after all—he would locate his hotel; he would murder Smithson in his sleep. The thought frightened him. It was one thing to ruminate about murder for seven years, quite another to come face to face with the bloody deed. Smithson was strong, he wouldn't be taken down easy; *he was also a drunk—get him when he's passed out.*

By evening Francis had considered many angles although the exact plan had not been finalized, he was sure the killing would play out, just a few more details. His shift concluded, body parts neatly shovelled, floodways cleaned, doors locked, he left the hospital. The evening was cold, Francis held his head low, bracing against the wind—plans battled back and forth in his mind—there were many doubts; leaving the issue without resolution, however, was not a possibility. Francis turned a tight corner...suddenly a hand reached out, a crack to his head left him stunned; he began to fall—his legs lifeless—void of all strength—someone caught him, he was dragged through the streets to a dark alley, then inside the open doors of a large building.

The smell! Horse manure, moldy hay. Vile. He was dizzy. "Get up!" He knew that voice. The shadows were heavy, faces were unrecognizable. Each of his arms were being braced up—one man on either side—they pulled him up balancing him, preventing his collapse. A trace of blood slid down his face. Smithson inched closer. "I know who you are Tumblety. Tell me where my daughter is and I will prevent my two friends here from beating you into a pile of ground beef."

"I don't know what you mean." Francis was being coy, foolish, a tactic that made absolutely no sense, yet he could not trust this man, that much he knew.

"Search him." The little leather pouch was grabbed from his pocket and handed over to Smithson.

"Give that back to me."

"Well it appears we have something Mr. Tumblety wants." With a nod of his head the signal was subtly relayed—Francis received a powerful punch in the guts—he fell to his knees, breathless. Smithson removed the little locket and ring—he recognized them immediately: inside, faces he hadn't seen for years. He lifted his boot, he resisted driving it into Francis' face.

"Give that back to me." Francis could threaten no one with his arms pinned back, his knees scrapping in the horse manure low on the barn floor, blood dripping into the corner of his mouth.

"Our Mr. Tumblety wants to make a deal."

46

*N*o need to rush breakfast, why not finish?—*the best meal of the day really, besides there was time, the hospital wasn't going anywhere, and if all went according to plan, it might be one of the last great breakfasts I'll ever have.* He raised his cup and Mrs. Hollis graciously filled it with another generous helping of coffee. There were no trees that morning, no rushing people about, no carriages or horses making deliveries, no early cool breezes to awaken his spirits, (clean the cobwebs)—his focus was set on the plan; there was an order, a system—he would set everything down, his mind was clear—the streets of Boston disappeared.

Smithson would return the ring and necklace in two days, at the deserted horse barn where his men smacked a club against his head; punched the wind out of his lungs. He convinced him that his mother could be located, he just needed a little time—Smithson agreed to meet at midnight in two days—return the ring and locket for the information. It gave Francis enough time, if all the pieces could be carefully slotted together. First Dr. Warren would give him that letter of introduction for London and the War Office, then book passage on a boat; steal some ether from Dr. Morton, attack Smithson from behind, use the ether, cut his throat and sail out on the morning tide. Francis wasn't sure about his two henchmen. He couldn't attack three men and kill them all—that was the piece that didn't fit. He considered Stokie as a partner, but adding accomplices just made the situation more complicated. He would size up the tactics once he arrived at the horse barn in two nights. For now, Dr. Warren had to be convinced of his earnest and immediate departure for England and the Crimea.

Entering the grand foyer of the Bulfinch Building, Francis checked the front desk—empty—the building was quiet. He then caught sight of a matron he recognized from the medical floor. She remained focussed on her task and did not respond when Francis called out. The space from her chin down to her waist was hidden by a huge stack of sheets weighing heavily on her chest supported by her crossed arms beneath. He called again, his swift gait quickly covering the distance in two strides, stopping her from proceeding on her determined mission. Finally responding, Francis was politely informed that Dr. Warren was on the surgical ward. He turned quickly to the stairway left, then followed down the hall to the pre-surgery room where Warren was discussing the upcoming procedure with a patient on the bed.

Francis remained at the doorway out of range while Dr. Warren examined his patient. To interrupt him at this time would be unacceptable and he was very aware of the importance etiquette would play today in order to secure his request. As Dr. Warren concluded his examination he turned and left the room, raising his head he spied

Francis in the doorway. "Good morning young man. What are you doing up here today?"

"So sorry to bother you Doctor, but what I have to ask is rather urgent." Francis thought the best approach might be a direct one—there were really only a matter of hours until Smithson and that wretched horse barn.

"Well son, follow along will you, we can talk on the way. What a great day yesterday wasn't it? Dr. Morton's little demonstration will go down in history you know—and you with it I presume, young Tumblety. I have a devilish amount of preparation today—three surgeries you know, and none of them straight forward I'm afraid. You could observe you know."

"It's the position in London, Dr. Warren, Sir. I have reconsidered and if at all possible, I would like to leave immediately." Francis hoped Dr. Warren maintained the same heartfelt desire he displayed when he first mentioned London many months ago. They continued to walk along to Dr. Warren's office side by side, Dr. Warren never looking up, Francis remaining vigilant in his hopeful stare down at the doctor.

"Well son we'll be sad to see you go, young lad. Why the sudden change of heart? I hope it's not the Massachusetts General?" Although Francis believed Dr. Warren was probably genuinely concerned about his request, even as it was blurted out without warning, he was forced to relinquish not one inch of stride as the doctor increased his blistering pace down the hallway, not flinching for a moment from the news.

"No sir, not at all, of course not Sir." Francis hadn't really formulated a lie and hoped he wouldn't have to dig in too deep now. "No Sir…it's just that…" Dr. Warren broke in.

"Not a girl is it lad? Hate to think you're running away from a broken love affair. I've never found that they are worth the effort and concern we give them you know." Dr. Warren, true to the Victorian standards of the sexes, couldn't possibly justify a major change in one's life—as in uprooting and travelling across an ocean to procure a shift in one's profession, as Francis was suggesting—strictly for the sake of a woman.

"No Sir."

"Well then I hope you haven't murdered someone," Warren added with a chuckle. Francis swallowed hard, with some difficulty. "And here we are." Warren stopped abruptly at the end of the corridor before a set of marked doors: 'HOSPITALIA'. He rested his hand on the ornate brass handle, turned to Francis completing his sentence before continuing his fastidious industry, "Well if you are certain, then you are in luck. I am dining tonight with Captain John Smith of the American; he is sailing in two days to England, Liverpool, I believe. I shall enquire about passage for you. I shall write you a letter to present to the Purser. You will need a letter for the London Hospital. Dr. Chilton is my connection there. If anyone can secure a commission for the Crimea, it will be him. Well, sorry to see you go, good luck."

Dr. Warren removed his hand which had been resting on the door lever throughout his conversation, and offered it to Francis. There was a brief but sturdy shake, the third time Francis had received one—but this time he couldn't help but consider the lack of good faith inherent within—so contrary relative to the two previous times. He was asking Dr. Warren to become an accomplice to his escape after the bloody rendezvous planned two nights hence—regretful… but necessary. Dr. Warren reminded him to drop by tomorrow and his secretary would have the letters ready.

"Thank you sir." The short answer was all Francis had the time to say in response to the doctor's quick and generous offer; the door closed, followed by the quick clipping of Warren's footsteps, they echoed on the wooden floor on the other side, accentuating his hurried pace across the room, slowly fading, then stopping. Francis completed an about turn; he left.

Dr. John Bernard Sweet Jackson continued to compile information from his endless work on the cadavers Francis wheeled into the pathology lab, week after week. The important data would eventually be compiled in a text book co-authored with Dr. Warren (Gross Pathology) —there was no one more precise when executing the fine applications of dissection, no one more fastidious when laying out the organs, flesh and bones. Francis watched the style, absorbed the skills, copied the techniques; but with two days remaining, he had lost focus, he had asked Dr. Jackson to repeat himself more than once—that was unacceptable. "Where's your mind boy? I said visceral cartilage...write it down!"

"Yes Sir."

The specimen had contracted a cancer of the throat—the respiratory tract was coated with a heavy, black tar-like substance. Dr. Jackson was tall, the sleeves of his lab coat were short, barely reaching half way down his forearms—but settled precisely at the position he required. He remained bent over, his face inches away from his work—his glasses pressed tight to his face, were secured with a string which tied in a knot at the back of his head; he used no gloves—he continually wiped his hands with a cloth from his side pocket after each exchange of his implements. Francis was recording every word while calculating the number of scalpels, and tongs used—he was shopping. Jackson picked up the cutting and stared at it closely before the flicker of the lamp. "Neoplasm. Never seen one so black."

"Yes Doctor."

"Slice a series of cuttings for me and place them on slides for this afternoon. I have a meeting."

"Yes Doctor."

"And get your head out of your ass."

"Yes Doctor."

"And stop saying 'yes Doctor' like you're some kind of idiot parrot."

"Yes, Doc...." he caught himself, shut his mouth, stopped talking.

Once Dr. Jackson left, Francis made a mental note of the implements he would include in his bag tomorrow before leaving the hospital for the last time. The idea was to abscond with a precious few, yet leave no visible evidence that any were missing. The rest of the day dragged—a laborious, endless routine that included washing down the tables and sinks in the pathology labs, sewing up cadavers, covering them and storing their ridiculous remains, stuffing specimens in jars, sweeping and cleaning floors—it all seemed so wasteful now; the deed weighed heavy on his mind, the burrowing eyes of his grandfather, the deep slice, the end of it all.

Seven o'clock did not bring sunset—the evenings were still long, Francis walked along the path south of the Bulfinch Building to Clancy's; Stokie would be there, they had made a date. He raised his head at every corner, spied around the rows of buildings lining each street—up and down—he could see no one following him, yet he knew they were there. He purposely selected the longest narrowest alleys, still a pair of curious, dark scum-dwellers refused to emerge. Francis stepped into Clancy's.

But Smithson's men *were* on his trail. They had received strict orders to follow him and report back. Smithson wanted to know the location of his daughter. They were also told to reel him in close with the locket and ring, get the information then kill him, tomorrow night.

Stokie was in fine form; he wanted to joke and sing with the crowd. Some western boys were singing 'Snow-clad Hills'

"I've left the snow-clad hills

Where my father's hut doth stand

My own dear Dalkarlia

For a stranger land."

He couldn't possibly know the lyrics and they went on and on forever. Francis attempted to tell Stokie that he might be leaving Boston, but the opportunity just didn't seem to arise—there was too much noise and singing and beer; he gave up, ordered another beer and together they left very late—Stokie requiring a gentle shoulder to balance upon, Francis was glad to respond—he assumed it would be the last time they would ever be together. Smithson's men followed behind dodging in and out of shadows, then returned to Smithson's hotel. There would be no sleep for Francis that night.

47

He left his travel case on the bed, it was packed and ready—he would return after it was done (if he survived)—pick it up, then head to the harbour. He couldn't possibly go over the plan again—he was determined to stay focused throughout the day, leave very late, arriving at midnight to the selected spot. He carried his medical bag today; he considered slinging his buffalo skinner on his back, tucked away out of sight, but after rehearsing his moves in the little sewing room (Mrs. Hollis' mannequin doubling for his victims) he decided a quick slice with an amputation knife would work better. *A time to kill, a time to heal, a time to kill a time to heal.* He had gone through the moves over and over. He must attack quickly from behind—if they had pistols, he must slice before they had time to aim. It was all so desperate, so impossible—but his nemesis was before him—he would not be deterred.

The letters addressed to The Purser on the American, and to
Dr. Chilton were available later in the day—he slipped them into his
breast pocket. Dr. Warren and Dr. Morton were not in the hospital,
there were no farewells; *just as well.* Francis remained somewhat
recluse deep down within the dark, secluded grotto of the labs and
storerooms until well after eight o'clock. He collected two bottles of
ether from Dr. Morton's lab; he filled his bag with scalpels, forceps,
tweezers, scissors, a sewing kit and cat gut sutures, syringes and probes
from the pathology lab. He debated over the leather tourniquet with
the brass-handled screw, *too snobby*, but ultimately shoved it is as well.
He added some good amputation knives and a saw. His medical bag
was complete. He wore a dark coat that dropped down to his knees,
a high collar, a dark hat. The sun set behind Boston, he stepped into
the shadows; steps of murder, steps of retribution.

The time was nearing midnight, the early hours of Boston's
warehouse district were dark, damp, gloomy—a miserable place fit
for the likes of rats and drunken sailors. A slip of a quarter moon
slinked in and out between thick, heavy clouds—there was a hint
of rain in the air. A few gas lamps rested high on iron posts at the
wide intersections where draft horses and long carts navigated tight
corners during the busy day, when barrels of whiskey and bags of oats
arrived for storage and distribution. But the lamps were cold—the
posts stood silently, stiff; vigilant iron sentinels. The watchman had
not arrived tonight to light them, or the gas was not moving through
the pipes. He smelled no gas. *Did they snuff them out?* He passed
close to the wall of a large brick edifice—by the smell of it, maybe
an iron works. He strained his eyes through the darkness across the
wide intersection—there was no watchman; without the dull glow
from the lamps, he easily slid into the inky shadows undetected. He
considered immediately that Smithson and his men were doing the

exact same thing—lurking, watching, waiting. *Where were they?* He waited...a dog sniffed the lamp post nearby; he lifted his leg.

Francis crossed the cobblestone street; cautiously arriving at the abandoned livery stable. He waited again for a sign, an image, a presence...something. There: a shadow moved. Inside the barn door, an obscure figure slipped across the narrow opening. The barn was designed with two large openings opposite each other located across the vast expanse of the entire width of the building. These openings were covered by huge double doors that travelled upon a rail above— when open an entire rig could manoeuvre easily through, pulled by a team of horses. The door was open—a narrow width, space enough for a slender man. The barn was abandoned—the operation had moved, or perhaps had gone bankrupt; in any case it was recent as the residual odours from years of accumulating manure and rotting hay drifted up into the faces of any person passing by.

Francis watched. The man left the space and walked deeper into the barn, he spoke to someone—Francis silently slipped in, darting to a pillar to the left near a corral. Hiding there, he waited in the dark. The two men spoke, their words were muffled; the other man lit a cigar, then left to stand outside at the far door. Faint moonlight inter-mittently cutting in, cast a pie-shaped dart on the dirt. His friend turned, he walked back to the street-side door close to where Francis hid. Francis had two victims, where was Smithson? If he waited much longer, they might leave. They were separated now, this was a good chance to catch one off-guard. He bent down and removed the ether from his bag. He poured a large amount onto his cloth, *better make sure*. He reached into his pocket, he checked for the long amputation knife—ten inches, long, slim point—razor sharp—he was ready.

The man stood at the door peeking out into the street through the opening. Francis rushed up behind. He whipped his left arm around the man's neck, squeezing his throat—bringing his right hand up, he pressed the cloth tight to his nose and mouth. There was a muffled choking gasp, a short moment of twisting; Francis held the cloth firm, forcing in with his body and knees, pulling backward hard. The man went limp. Francis dragged him inside to the corral behind the post. He quickly checked his pockets for the ring and necklace—nothing. *The other man must have it.* The man's breathing changed, he began to cough, he began to shift in the dirt. Francis reached into his pocket and pulled out the knife. He slashed across the man's throat, the gash was deep, down to the spine. He slashed the man's groin—first the left, then the right, cutting the femoral arteries, the blood squirted and flowed. Francis rose up from the dirt; the blood was rapidly beginning to pool. He turned to face the other set of doors—a cold white slice of moonlight directing his path. His fist, sodden with blood, dripping with black ooze in the shadows, held the knife handle tight, the long blade seeking its fleshy scabbard.

Francis stood inside the barn just at the edge of the opening; the man approached—he had a limp—he stuck his head in, "Mick... Mickey." He whispered for his friend. Francis gripped the man's head from behind and pulled him in. The cloth freshly anointed with a generous amount of ether was pushed into his face. This man was smaller—he went down faster; he went out in a second. Francis dug through his pants. Success! He held Little Raven's leather pouch in his fingers. He checked for the locket and ring, again, success! He carefully stuffed it in his pocket. He turned the man over and without a moment to consider his actions, he sliced his throat deep and clean; he sliced through the groin—two slashes. Standing up, Francis moved to the corner away from the moonlight; he waited for Smithson. No one came. He left.

48

To Francis the morning was like any other: dark, lonely, cold, and foggy—it seemed to be forever foggy, each and every morning in Boston. Mrs. Hollis would not rise to prepare breakfast—it was too early: 4 am. He knew the fantastic ineptitude of the Boston Constabulary would delay the discovery of his work for hours, perhaps days, and he remained secure in his assumption that he would be well on his way to England by the time those two pirates would finally find a cold table in the mortuary on which to stretch out. Only a few hours had passed since he left them bleeding in that stable. By now he doubted that even a drop of their cursed blood remained in their bloating corpses as the steady, sticky dark flow mixed with the filth of the street and drained without hesitation down to the vile gutters below. The rats, he suspected, would already be scurrying around their lucky find, fighting over which bit to nibble first.

He had been packed for hours—since before his meeting with Smithson's men. The walk to the pier was considerable, but he was not concerned; he was confident that there would be enough time. He quietly left his small room, careful not to alarm Mrs. Hollis, and departed the little boarding house, then turned east towards the harbour. The thought of leaving Boston behind and embarking on a new life was invigorating; it gave him a new sense of purpose. He did not linger on the bodies—he now considered their murder no more than a temporary inconvenience (consciously considering that his swelling confidence might cloud his judgement)—nor did he dwell on Smithson, although a small corner of his brain would always be reserved for that man. If he wanted, Francis could bury the loathsome image of that dreadful man deep within the folds of his subconscious and not visit his virulent features for days or even weeks at a time. Then, without warning, something would trigger it's revival—a curious smell, a drifting shadow, a familiar voice perhaps—something nebulous and indistinguishable, yet to Francis, unmistakable—and his grandfather's formidable figure and piercing eyes would arise, confusing his thoughts, intercepting his logic and redirecting his focus—but not this morning. He continued on to the harbour, clearheaded and resolute. He considered the position at the London Hospital a diversion only; a respite. He would return, and he would find Smithson when the time came. He didn't really plan past London—the Crimea remained well beyond his interests. His final thoughts on that man this morning, but for only a moment, stirred dark, warm emotions: he would not hesitate to draw a knife blade across that man's throat. It would suit him; it would be a sweet killing. Then he tucked the thoughts away.

The narrow cobblestone streets were wet and his footfalls echoed a moist but clean rhythm of regular taps off the sooty damp walls of the old brick buildings along the way, as each heel came down hard and crisp with the contact of the sodden clay brick underfoot. He was alone all the way, save for two sailors laying facedown outside of Clancy's. They weren't dead, just drunk and their attempt to find lodgings or their ship after their gin-soaked evening ashore had obviously failed miserably. They were lying oblivious to the cold in a large puddle of water that had accumulated during the night's short rain shower. Their vulnerable presence had already obliged some scavengers as their clothes were torn open, their pockets pulled out and empty, their shoes—missing. Their day would begin, no doubt, with regret and frustration, thought Francis, but he stepped lively over their limp bodies giving them no extra mind and faced the task at hand—locating the American.

Down to the end of Main and left onto Purchase and the harbour should come into view. A thick shroud of cloud and fog filtered the early sun on the eastern shoreline as it had not yet breached the horizon, and even with the most strenuous concentration, Francis could see nothing. The sounds of the busy docks however were clear enough: screeching gulls overhead, diving in to steal fresh catch as every type of fish and sea creature poured onto the streets from arriving fishing vessels; dock workers yelling commands as they swung ropes and baskets overhead filling the ships' hulls with goods for export as others unloaded supplies from vessels newly landed.

Francis continued to strain his eyes through the dense grey curtain that surrounded everything, transfixed in his spot at the perimeter of the activity, salty air blowing his hair over his eyes; the strong stench of dead fish filling his nostrils, and everywhere, dancing and diving invisibly all around him somewhere in the fog, seagulls and more seagulls—screeching and screaming as if commanding the entire scenario with their irritating orders, requesting a rapid pace and demanding more fish!

In a short time, more light began to brighten the misty air from grey to white and Francis thought he could see trees in the distance—a forest of black tree trunks rising up into the sky, their edges unclear; their tops disappearing far above fading out of sight. The sun's warmth began to penetrate the thick canopy and the tenacious fog began to lift, yet ever so slowly. Remaining steadfast in his position as if on guard, and gripping the handle of his case tightly with the fingers of his right hand, Francis watched the transformation with youthful amazement. A metamorphosis unfolded in the sky as the unlikely apparition he had foolishly mistaken for a forest of trees, slowly transformed into giant black masts as the smoky mist rolled away—a forest of ships' masts—thousands of them of every size and in every direction, rigid and towering, as the harbour was filled with hundreds of ships moored to the docks and anchored in every corner of the bay. The sight was overpowering, and Francis thought that every ship in the world must be here today floating in Boston Bay.

The American was the largest ship in the harbour and Dr. Warren had pledged that its identification would be without difficulty as it had no rival in terms of length, breadth or sheer beauty, and he had convinced Francis that he would be able to spot it immediately upon first glance at his arrival onto Front Street.

Francis dipped his left hand into his front trouser pocket and with a soft touch he gently fondled the little leather pouch to confirm its safety.

Through the wall of crates, around the limitless lines of slimy fish tables, past the pyramids of stacked barrels and bulging grain sacks, Francis finally arrived before the great black hull of the American— his home for the next three weeks. He approached and became one of hundreds of persons weaving through the congested port, stepping lively so as not to be knocked about by rising booms or flying sacks. The docks were waking up: ships were arriving and others were preparing to depart. High tide was peaking.

A rumble, low and uneasy erupted from Francis' stomach; he wished he'd grabbed a cake from Mrs. Hollis' kitchen. The pungent fish smells were awakening his repressed hunger, although he wouldn't normally consider seafood for breakfast—any source of food at this time would be welcomed.

Francis now stood at the bottom of the long narrow wooden gang that spread out from his boots on the dock, high up to the deck of the American before him. He stretched his neck up. The tall masts and yardarms dominated the skyline. The view included a confused network of ropes and buckles crisscrossing the space like a jumbled spider web tangled after a storm—drooping and swinging but still, desperately, hanging on. There seemed to be no order to their display—truly only a seasoned sailor could ascertain the function of the apparatuses necessary to secure the safe manoeuvre of such a huge vessel as it negotiated a path through the unforgiving seas of the north Atlantic.

Francis knew nothing of ships or the sea. Except for the short trip on Lake Ontario from Port Dalhousie to Toronto (a disastrous trip he'd sooner forget), the torturous fourteen hours stoking a steam engine from Toronto to Kingston, and then to Rochester with the Sisters, on the little canal boat. His knowledge of sailing ships and ocean voyages however, was limited to sailor stories at Clancy's or his readings from the new Boston Herald. It was impossible to consider the boat trips on Lake Ontario without the beautiful vision of Sarah flashing by—he quickly dismissed it. An author, Herman Melville, had recently published excerpts from a new novel, and described the sea as a ferocious enemy that contained all the power of the world within a single wave. His story included the heroic adventure of a whaler searching for a monstrous white whale. Francis hoped his trip across the ocean might conclude with few dangerous exploits such as these.

In fact his time aboard The American would include tutelage in more than nautical jargon and tales of white whales or analyzing the adept skills and peculiar habits of sailors at sea and their crude superstitions. Social life in cramped quarters aboard ship such as this one for extended trips often become a test of one's mettle; that mental courage one develops in order to answer the sea's scrutiny, close as it is to hell's fury and trial, was no different than the physical contest of the body bracing toward a fierce wind as it lashes across the foresail threatening to rip legs out from under feeble contortions, thwarting all balance on the slippery deck, and tossing the useless remains into the briny as easy as tissue paper in the jaws of a lion. For all the tests and tribulations tendered by the sea and ships, the saddest student was the passenger, the one so poorly versed in the ways of the ocean that every movement, every gesture and every maneuver would face a challenge, and it seemed that Francis would fail every time.

Before stepping onto the gang Francis observed the length of the ship—over 420 feet of iron plating; a hull so deep the upper deck was not visible from the dock even as she sat deep and full in the harbour. Among the masts and yards and yards of rope, two tall, black steel stacks spouting smoke, rose like stumpy afterthoughts near the stern above the deck. The American was a new screw ship that combined steam power and propeller as well as sail to push her through the toss and turn of the ocean's relentless provocations. The furnaces were stoking and the boilers were hot—the black smoke encircling the masts billowed and danced, giving warning of an imminent departure.

A fresh wind blasting his upturned face from the south east rattled the turnbuckles and rustled the curled sheets over the yardarms; Francis leaned forward to brace his balance.

The American was massive—the largest ship yet to be built in New England. She could carry more cargo and cross faster and safer than any ship afloat. With three masts and heavy rigging, two large coal furnaces and triple boilers, the American boasted a direct drive piston engine and a massive screw propeller. With a full cargo hold she could make 12 knots—the surface being smooth and the winds hard and consistent. She would be operated by a larger crew and included upgraded quarters for all aboard. The romantic days of the square rigger and tall ship were fast closing.

Francis gripped the handle of his case tight and stepped up onto the gang. He reached for the rope looped through the standards evenly spaced up the length of the narrow planking and cautiously climbed up to the top deck, carefully regarding his footfalls as he went.

A table was positioned close to the top of the gang and there, sitting in a dining chair quite out of place among the boxes, trunks, cartons and kitchen stores coming aboard, a very skinny man in a black suit bent over his ledger, quill in hand looking stern with eyebrows squeezed tight and lips pursed. This was the man, Francis presumed, that would be interested in his arrival, and he was correct.

Mr. Carter was the Purser—a short balding man with many more whiskers on his face than on his head: moustache and mutton chops all around with a pimple of a nose upon which balanced wire rim glasses with angular lenses, through which Francis could see a busy pair of tiny eyes frantically scrutinizing as they feverishly dashed back and forth and up and down between the long rows of minutiae scratched on the pages before him in long straight columns. Dropping his bag to the deck, Francis reached in his breast pocket and pulled out his letter.

"I am Francis Tumblety, sir. I am to sail on this vessel I believe." Francis wanted desperately to appear confident and capable, yet his approach remained humble and so very unsure—his words folded over his lips like lumpy gravy dropping onto cold potatoes—arriving more as a muffle than a salutation, and the gruff retort signalled an indignant response from the little man sitting there.

"Eh, what's that? Speak up! And don't call me Sir. I'm not anyone's Sir!"

Francis remained calm, and repeated, "Tumblety. Here is my letter of introduction for Captain Smith," and he held it out under those tiny spectacles so Carter would be sure to notice.

"Eh?" Mr. Carter ripped the letter from Francis' hand, unfolded it and drew it to within an inch of his eyes, not once looking up to consider the man standing before him. Dipping his quill, he then completed the necessary information in his ledger and returned the letter. "The captain's not on board. He will direct you to your quarters when he arrives. Move along." Francis was dismissed with the quick brush of the quill through the space above the ledger as if waving a wand and perhaps magically with that simple gesture, this irritating passenger would be gone. The results proved fruitful; Francis quickly stepped away.

Past the crates of tea and barrels of flour, Francis managed to find a vacant space near the rail forward and starboard side. Some members of the crew were on deck, however it seemed to Francis that no one was particularly busy or assuming any task in any diligent manner as they were milling about in groups of two or three and appeared to be preoccupied with observing him more than their duties. Their stares were indignant, their attitude wary. This ship was a service vessel, merchant marine, and passengers were an uncommon sight. Their stare made Francis uncomfortable, he turned away.

Holding the rail with both hands Francis peered down to the dock and over the roofs of the warehouse buildings. Boston was a bustling port and he wondered when he would see it again.

To the right and left, a thousand masts and shrouds of every sort tangled together weaving a tapestry of timber, canvas and hemp pressed together so tightly that even the smallest flying creature searching for a scrap of discarded catch would discover that darting between the open spaces would become almost an impossible task. Francis considered the unlikelihood of a unified exodus—all the ships leaving port simultaneously—how they would crash and bump their way into an impossible tangle of timber and steel bound tightly together with rope and sail—a puzzle so tightly congealed that a year of disassembly would avail no headway.

As Francis was casually considering the humorous result of such a ridiculous occurrence, he heard his name called out from behind, and startled out of his daydream, he turned.

"Mr. Tumblety, I presume?" Mr. Blessing approached from the wheelhouse, his hand out, a broad smile about his cherry face.

"Yes Sir!" They greeted with a firm handshake (he would soon begin to lose count). William Blessing was an old sailor from the British Admiralty who now served as the America's First Mate on route to full retirement, not so far along in the near future, as Francis would soon discover. He was short and pudgy, his once form-fitting uniform now stretched to capacity about his chest and rotund girth. His full set of whiskers were bright white save for the area around his droll little mouth where yellow stains from years of pipe tobacco smoke had painted amusing patterns across the moustache and just below his lower lip. Between the whiskers a full ingratiating smile expanded and Francis regarded the half-moon curve on his top teeth, that when closed tight, the mouthpiece of his pipe would slide in and sit comfortably—a snug secure fit like two pieces of a puzzle. On the end of his bulbous nose balanced wire rims securing a set of small lenses, positioned well below his eyes, dangling by what seemed to be two tiny lucky hairs, naturally selected for their job as brakes.

"Pleasure to meet you, your accommodation is all in order. Have you seen Mr. Carter?"

"If Mr. Carter is the man with the ledger and quill at the top of the gangway, then yes."

"He is indeed. The Purser, the most powerful man on the ship, I should say...next to the Captain, of course. Keeps close records of everything pertaining to this vessel: goods and personnel alike. If his ledger is lost, we are doomed. At least he likes to think so, hey Tumblety?" And with a laugh and a bite on his pipe, Mr. Blessing reduced tensions instantly and Francis began to feel the slow relief of comfort and compliance.

Francis pulled out his letter and presented it. "My letter of introduction from Dr. Warren, Sir."

Mr. Blessing received the letter with enthusiasm, glanced at it briefly, looked over his spectacles and replied, "Splendid, lad splendid! Follow me to your birth and we'll get you all settled." Francis picked up his case and followed Mr. Blessing down the deck. A positive elation rose in Francis' heart; taking a deep breath of salty fresh air, he directed his attention upward to the towering masts and swinging rigging crisscrossing the clear blue sky far above. His thoughts of those two unfortunates were melting, any anxieties with regard to them were vanishing, quiet satisfaction of surrendering to a new home—albeit a temporary one—were beginning to settle.

Mr. Blessing rounded the corner of the wheelhouse and just as Francis was about to follow the turn, a voice—deep and raspy, almost inaudible—caught Francis off guard and he jerked his head in response. "Landlubber, if I ever saw one."

"Excuse me sir?" Francis directed his enquiry to the only person within speaking distance, one who was not rushing about lifting crates, pulling lines or climbing masts—a sailor, slim and somewhat dishevelled in appearance, leaning up against the central deck house. James Snodgren's hands remained lightly tucked into the front pockets of his breeches; he slowly raised his head, two dark eyes narrowed, they stared directly into Francis' face.

"Landlubber, I'll give you a week." He turned and walked away—a sullen gait, a careless, confident stroll.

Francis was left dumbfounded. An unpleasant character to be sure, he thought, confused about the threat and wondering in part if he should be concerned in any way. He watched the sailor—he seemed to slither away, slow, almost shuffling; a carefree attitude, then, all his compatriots about him on deck and high above in the canvas were now suddenly and purposely engaged, attending to their chores, hauling, lifting, pulling, so deeply engrossed in preparation for departure. This man's behaviour was so contrary to the obligations of a crew member during such a critical time in the ship's schedule, that Francis was obliged to consider his actions as even more disconcerting than his verbal threat. *Why was he so special?*

Two twin buildings were positioned port and starboard on either side of the wheelhouse, midships, and Mr. Blessing stopped at one, opened the door and indicated to Francis that they had arrived. Francis moved past Mr. Blessing to stand in the doorway. Saliva wedged in the stiff folds of cartilage lining his gullet and released a bitter taste; immediately attempting to swallow—he could not. His upper lip coiled and trembled. A rank odour of damp coiled hemp saturated in salt brine fused with tar and oil smacked hard and square in his face, no different than if a swinging boom in a swirling gale had released its total fury crashing with full force to rip his head clean off—he steadied his feet and held his breath. Their dual figures standing at the threshold cast a deep shadow into the opening but as Mr. Blessing stood back to welcome Francis to his new accommodations, the gruesome sight was revealed. Yards and yards of heavy folded rope blackened with tar were stacked to the ceiling and cascaded down to the floor; they laid limp and clumped in all manner of disarray in every corner and space. Stacks of shackles, pulleys, sheaves and blocks originally ordered and paired, now collected in haphazard piles and disorganized conglomerations. Francis detected no place for him: no bed, no basin, no shelf and he was mystified and disappointed. *Was this stinking, filthy disaster to be his accommodation for the next three weeks?*

"This is the Bosan's locker and there is a birth there, you'll find it alright, just move a few things along." Mr. Blessing waved his hand in a dismissive way indicating that he was not responsible for the disgusting assemblage, sight or smell, and Francis was expected to 'get along' one way or the other.

"I'm sorry Mr. Tumblety, this is all that is available for a passenger who signed on at the last minute." Mr. Blessing turned sharply and reminded Francis of dinner at six—he was invited. Francis wanted to be grateful, he wanted to thank Mr. Blessing but the words caught in his throat, buried deep within the tart saliva—they continued to stubbornly remain immobile. His quiet reply, a faint "I see." He didn't choke on the words but a more confident response was not possible.

He dropped his case and searched low for the feet of a bunk, and he found them lost alone under the weight of a hundred pounds or more of block and tackle. A shift under his feet and a jolt to the left—the American was moving!

Impulsively he darted away from the shed and moved quickly to the rail, port side—the hunt for the rest of his bunk would follow soon enough—Boston was quickly disappearing. The harbour was fading away and the city was becoming a dark smoky series of rectangular white blotches hidden behind the contorted puzzle of a hundred moored ships on the horizon, as the sun continued to rise and bounce a shiny reflection on their wooden faces. The American deliberated a gradual entrance into the open waters of the Atlantic following a north-east bearing.

The outstretched wings of a gliding seagull tilted and curved above the wake. Without effort he rose and dipped in the air currents swirling above the churning waters; the propeller cut a clean swath of white brine through the green water behind. There were no pickings for him—the cook had yet to throw scraps over. Francis watched as he rose up higher and higher, then abruptly turned about sailing west, following a course back to Boston where competition for scraps would be fierce but plentiful. Lifting his beak—was he mocking Francis, he who could turn and float away effortlessly on the airwaves, not bound by iron or sea, orders or attitude? His flight, his gliding: true freedom—sailor of the wind.

Francis strolled to the stern rail, squinted through the greasy black smoke billowing out from the stacks marking the newly selected course east; it drew a somber line in the sky back to Boston, to the horse barn where he left the two victims of his knife work back in the dirt, in their own blood. He gave them a moment's thought then turned his face forward to England.

49

The two men relegated to the lower levels of Massachusetts Hospital, to view a pair of corpses—the remains in question having rotted away for at least a night and a day, and were decidedly stinking and wholly disgusting—were Constable Michael Langley and Detective Patrick Crookshank. Prepared with a hand over each prospective mouth, the other on the hip, regarding with professional aplomb and cool expectations, the sheet was quickly withdrawn. Crookshank stood displeased as Langley did not keel over as was his great hope, therefore immediately removing the adolescent opportunity to ridicule and chastise back at headquarters; Langley being the rookie, Crookshank being the veteran, this was his deepest desire today: not the ripped throats of the scum on the table, but the tilting angle of Langley's posture and the vacant open space below on the floor where he might soon lie. Crookshank disappointingly switched his attention to the business on the stone slab, however continuing to glance at Langley periodically throughout the investigation, ever the optimist.

The throats of the bodies before them were gaping open with such a wide gash that all muscle and tendon could no longer support the heads; they fell back exposing all the internal anatomy of the neck and throat. The colour of their faces was so white and pasty that all recognizable human features had been erased and only ghostly bloated carcasses remained. Langley had difficulty believing they were ever alive; Crookshank had to admit the nasty scene was at least unique.

Dr. Thomas Frederick worked exclusively with cadavers and began explaining his examination without hesitation, delicately disregarding any human sensitivities, particularly to those shared by the visiting policemen. Originally Dr. Jackson had examined the bodies—but considering the deaths rudimentary, had given the case over to Frederick—he couldn't have been more delighted. To him the bodies boldly exposed in their cold grievous state were no more than a welcomed source for his enthusiastic studies in biology and anatomy.

"Normally a victim with a sliced throat wouldn't be of concern to me gentlemen, and certainly not to Dr. Jackson, as we are well aware of the results of such a wound." Dr. Frederick was a very slight man whose slim body was truly hidden deep within the empty spaces of his huge lab coat. His hands were continually held before him, but up high just under his chin; his fingers wiggly—he appeared like a giant rodent appreciating his catch before diving in for the gastronomic rewards of his sneaky efforts. His beard and moustache were dark and thick. His front teeth were buck and protruded forward only heightening the weird image. "But here we see something very unusual," he continued with his lecture, eyes widening, arms now coiling tight to his body as if relishing the odorous, grim specimens before him, their violent injuries cruelly disclosed. He then quickly released his arms and wiggled his fingers aggressively gesticulating his find with excitement. "Look here gentlemen!"

Crookshank had seen it all before, although not to the extent exhibited here; he was not particularly impressed by naked corpses or blood, but he was still hoping Langley would succumb to the scene, perhaps even knock himself out when he hit the floor. He tried to focus once again on Dr. Frederick and the autopsy. Dr. Frederick reached forward with both hands to the crotch of the body closest to him. *What is he up to*, thought Crookshank, *grab the poor man's penis?* But the doctor pushed the limp member aside and revealed two slices deep within the crotch area on either side of the inner thighs.

"Our victim here required no fatal throat-cutting in order to guarantee his death."

"What are you saying, Doctor?" asked Crookshank appearing at last to be interested, but truly puzzled by this new injury and information.

"Exsanguination was quickly accomplished by these two expertly placed incisions," explained Frederick as he carefully lowered his head closer and closer to the area in question, holding one of the wounds wide open with the careful spread of his fingers on his left hand.

"Ex...what?" replied Langley desperately trying not to look anywhere near that general area, squeezing both hands ever tighter around his nose and mouth in every attempt to repel the repulsive stench.

"Exsanguination" clarified Frederick. "He bled to death, and very quickly. I don't believe he has an once of blood left in his body. This one either, actually," as he flipped his flapping phalanges towards the other body adjacent, to offer clarity and direction, although neither was required. Dr. Frederick continued with the explanation of his examination, never once looking up from the bodies, maintaining a hungry rodent posture: fangs out, eyes wide, claws extended. "Both femoral arteries were severed, which allowed for rapid elimination of enough blood to stop the heart in a matter of seconds. He might have been dead before he hit the ground. I think the neck wound was an afterthought, and totally unnecessary, or perhaps visa-versa. In any case, this is a question of an over-zealous attack…very odd indeed."

Crookshank viewed the evidence, yet remained sceptical. "I've never heard of anyone intentionally stabbing someone there, unless of course a jealous girlfriend who missed her mark, if you get my meaning Doctor?" Crookshank placed one hand on his hip and traced the fingers of his other hand through his hair in a posture that reflected confusion. Langley stood quiet and looked for an expert conclusion from either man, received nothing, and was ready to exit the cold room, when Frederick continued. "This was no accident Detective. The stabs are perfect, on the mark, and obviously successful. Your suspect knew exactly what he was doing."

"No sign of a struggle or fight, Doctor?" Langley asked.

"None—no protection wounds on either arms or hands. This procedure was accomplished very fast, with the killer facing his victims straight on. Don't know how anyone would allow this to happen to them." Doctor Frederick was beginning to react with a sense of bewilderment himself.

Crookshank stroked his chin and pondered. "Could they have been drunk doctor and therefore not able to defend themselves?"

"I suppose that's a possibility, but they'd have to be dead drunk not to know a ten inch blade was bearing down directly at their groin," responded Frederick, looking less hungry and more satiated.

"A ten inch blade!" exclaimed Langley, with a fair amount of astonishment. "The blade cut directly down and through a length of ten inches. He wanted to be certain that the incision would be accurate and successful on the first cut—he used the correct knife, there are no slashes or missed cuts; its precise—its textbook."

"Are you saying our suspect is a doctor…Doctor?" asked Langley directly.

Doctor Frederick finally looked up and scanned the eyes of his two detectives. Placing his hands in the large pockets of his lab coat and allowing his fastidious fingers to receive a short respite, he released a sigh, "No, but if I was performing a dissection, I couldn't have done it better."

50

The American was a floating community; a diverse collection of people and activities separated by their social stations and connected by their collective needs: survival being premier. Desperate to maintain order and balance even as the cruel Atlantic smashed and tossed, dipped and swayed, the sailors adhered to a strict understanding of the unwritten laws that guided their voyage and their destiny.

The undisputed leader aboard was captain Jonas Smith (John to his friends); he was stern, serious, anti-social—he was aloof... preoccupied. His task above all else was directing his ship through a safe voyage and arriving timely with the ship and all cargo in tact, everything else was the concern of Mr. Blessing, Mr. Carter, and Mr. Simmons. His officers included men who understood routine and order; their attitudes and behaviours were predictable. If the ship maintained course, if the crew remained diligent, if the cargo arrived safe—they were satisfied. But not unlike the crowded urban centres of the time, the American had a dark underbelly where often a blind eye was turned to secure a momentum—a texture, a smooth pulse—one that rocked in synchronicity with the waves; an order and, for some, it offered relief from hard labour and tedium; for others—the chance for game, to steal money and abuse weaker sailors and inexperienced passengers.

James Snodgren was a criminal; his nefarious activities aboard ship were tolerated as he carefully maintained the balance weaving and conniving under the slack, retiring eyes of Mr. Blessing and the naive demeanour of Mr. Simmons. He did not work alone: Billings and Wraiff were bullies—mean, despicable and easily coercible—perfect companions: they did their jobs well, above and below deck; they followed Snodgren's lead gaining meagre but acceptable profit. These men no longer shared a bunk in the crew quarters forward in the fo'c's'le; they were not welcome nor did they care. They preferred a private space deep in the hold aft: a dark, ensconcing hole; a dismal cavity where their prohibited gin could be buried; where illegal gambling games could be carried out; where evil plans could be calculated, and where dire conventions devoid of decency could be shared with the slimy cockroaches and stinking rats. The crew gave them a yard or more of distance when passing, watched carefully for derisive signals and were keenly aware of their own predicament, as even the slightest falter in this regard would mean a quiet farewell—a final wet rendezvous. Impetuous disregard was rewarded swiftly: swallowed lustfully—lost to the sea without a sound in the night… and forgotten.

Francis would meet Snodgren soon enough. He often passed silently—a dark whiff of cool salty breeze—carefully brushing Francis' shoulder as the poor sick patron spewed his guts over the rail, night after night. He measured Francis' stamina at each brush, and watched his legs shake and buckle with each sour heave. The time was near.

Francis was sick. His stomach had not stopped churning and complaining throughout the first three days and nights aboard the American, and he was exhausted. There was nothing more to purge. His stature was in a constant curl: shoulders bent, hands sweating—resting on his midriff or his forehead; his station: at the rail, always at the rail. Passing sailors tipped their caps and shook their heads—their mouths curled at the corners with ridicule. That first meal on his first night in the Captain's Wardroom was mutton and roast potatoes, gravy, corn and pudding, and he ate it with brave enthusiasm; every piece, every mouthful, talking rarely, gulping rapidly. The talk was England and The Crimea and new steel cables ready to refit the American; all the hemp rope would be left on the dock in Boston—"then the American would truly be the ship of envy." Captain Smith was completely consumed by the thought of new steel cables, he spoke rarely of anything else. Francis sat quietly among the four officers: Smith, Carter, Blessing and Simmons; he was out of place—crumpled baggage among dark navel attire and shiny silverware.

The first bout of vomit emerged within minutes of leaving the Wardroom, as Francis headed to his little storeroom, with no respite insight.

On that first morning Captain Smith arrived on board one hour before sailing, completed a quick inspection of the ship then confirmed with Mr. Carter and reviewed the ledger. Smith's daily routine for the past three days was supervising the cargo: huge bales of cotton, barrels of molasses and crates of food and stores. A signature inscribed on the lines within a ship's ledger was a sacred thing—it stood for integrity, and Smith did not sign until confirmation about each entry was assured.

Smith was tall and robust. His hands were huge and calloused, powerful. He took pride in knowing that he could still haul canvas aloft faster and better than any sailor aboard. His face was weather-worn with deep creases, and his full beard extended proudly forth from his square jaw: full, thick and white. Upon his wide shoulders he carried his black uniform impeccably; not a roll, not a crease— and he expected his officers and crew to follow in kind. When he spoke his voice sounded gruff, but he was not angry. The salt air after so many years had tempered his vocal cords resulting in intonations that retained a growl; but throughout: a clear resonance, soliciting an awareness and demanding respect. Stretching his neck skyward, he carefully regarded the wind and the clouds; his lips pouted in keen affirmation. Smith called to Mr. Blessing, "Where is Mr. Tumblety, Mr. Blessing?" Mr. Carter's inclusion of that name had not bypassed his scrutiny of the ledger.

"Mr. Tumblety was shown to his cabin on deck, Sir. I have made arrangements in the Boatswain's locker, he will not bunk with the crew in the fo'c's'le, as you requested." Mr. Blessing received the ledger from Mr. Carter and prepared to present it to the Captain for his viewing, but Smith turned and with his hands fisted and firmly secured on his waist spoke directly to Blessing.

"Mr. Tumblety comes to us highly regarded as a medical officer, and he will no doubt see action in The Crimea, if it comes to that. Mr. Blessing, he is your ward and you will ensure his safety while aboard. I will not tolerate any nonsense from the crew in regard to his position as passenger. Do you understand Mr. Blessing?" His words were stern but fair, they resounded in Mr. Blessing's ears. Direct eye contact was retained until Blessing responded.

"Aye, sir."

But unfortunately Smith nor Blessing were overly concerned about Francis' welfare as the ship took precedence over all other issues and replacing outdated hemp with steel, shifting cargo, unpredictable wind, capricious boilers, diminishing coal reserves, heavy seas, and tight schedules occupied Captain Smith's mind day and night throughout the voyage. Mr. Blessing's interests lay far away in Cardiff where his wife prepared his favourite meals, where his mind often drifted to an old warm chair by the fireplace; Mr. Blessing wanted to go home—this last voyage was a tedious endurance, a necessary final chapter in a long miserable career. Standing on the foredeck, soulfully searching the eastern horizon for Wales, Mr. Blessing in every way but in body was already home.

Still perched over the rail that first evening spilling his guts into the sea, Francis felt the light touch of a kind hand on his shoulder. Breaking his diligence concerning aim and care for his clothes (as only minimal change in wardrobe came aboard with him), he looked up and the man spoke.

"I am Kevin Simmons, Boatswain, or Bosun if you like, and I can assure you Mr. Tumblety it will get better. Your first voyage?" Simmons was young, tall, slender and clean shaven. His face was fresh and reassuring. Using both hands he helped to steady Francis along the rail.

"Yes. I remember you from supper. I'm afraid whatever I ate tonight is long gone."

"I watched you gulp down your supper Mr. Tumblety. You ate too much and too fast, I knew this is where I would find you. However its a lesson, now I suppose you'll be more careful. I am on duty tonight so I shall leave you now. Will you be alright Mr. Tumblety?"

"Yes, thank you Mr. Simmons." Francis lied, for his stomach was turning and his jowls were sour, not a bit of food left, but more heaves were ready to erupt.

"I shall look you up again later Mr. Tumblety." Mr. Simmons carried on down the deck. Francis turned again to the sea releasing a spew of slime and gravy in long sticky strands; the gooey contours carelessly flipping in the wind. Mr. Simmons did not look in on Francis again, and the feeling of loneliness only exacerbated his emptiness and melancholy.

When Snodgren passed close to Francis on that third night after his watch, he saw a pathetic man that had no food for three days, that could barely stand, that was lonely, homesick, lost and scared. Perfect. He would return tonight.

51

The breasts were big, but they were no longer round or firm; they fell stretched and wrinkled as did her waist and her hips. The grass skirt no longer flared and if there was ever colour it had faded and blended into blots of black and dirty indigo hiding beneath a forest of dark hair. But Crookshank could describe it well enough and the anchor tattoo on the other forearm, especially the M.G. below, which was tiny but clear, would be excellent evidence for identification. This man had two easily identifiable tattoos and a gaping mouth—no front teeth—evidence he would use to find a connection during his investigation. The other victim had anchor tattoos as well but not particularly unique, however that one single silver tooth and that old scar running down his cheek from his left ear to his lip would be very useful, and Langley agreed.

Two woeful eyes peering up over his fingers still clutching tightly around his nose and mouth—finally surrendering and silently pleading for conclusion and retreat—were answered with a regretful nod from Crookshank. Without hesitation Langley completed a hasty about-face and cut a quick circuitous path through oozing floor drains and steel tables harbouring questionable implements giving him no cause for curious contemplation in any way, past glass cabinets of chemicals and sticky specimens, a row of stone slabs upon which lay the remnants of unlucky clients whose better days were long past, all of which relentlessly emitted vapours so positively revolting that hell's kitchen could not have competed or exceeded without envy, and raced to the iron skeleton ensconced in the farthest corner of the grisly pit: a staircase and exit—ascension and liberation.

Each volatile step released a resounding squelch as the loose risers connected to the bolts protruding from the stone foundation walls slid in and out; the whole staircase rose and sank in tandem with each press of his boot bouncing Langley about, but failed to deter his defiant escape; he graciously sucked in volumes of fresh air from the street above—even as it was thickly laced with the daily aromas of fish guts and horse manure—immediately upon his arrival in the street above.

Detective Crookshank bade farewell to Dr. Frederick leaving him pondering feverishly over his customer, needle and thread carefully poised in hand, then followed Langley out and decided to continue the day's investigation alone but not until congratulating his partner on his tenacity; its true Langley's eyes were red and watery, his face pale and sorrowful, but not a morsel of food had left his stomach nor had his legs given way allowing for a clumsy fall, and Crookshank, although somewhat disappointed, assured his partner that he was mindful of this.

Redirecting his police pursuits elsewhere and dropping this whole case had entered Pat Crookshank's mind, but there was something here that grabbed his curiosity and wouldn't let go. This was no knife fight over a game of cards or a woman; the men were not found together and there was no evidence of a struggle or fight; there were no weapons of any kind found anywhere. Frederick had convinced him that someone with extraordinary surgical skills and a ten inch knife might be slinking through Boston streets at night with no logical reason but to cut victims not once but three times and in doing so very closely removing their heads. He had never seen such a thing and he couldn't let it go. Of course there could very well be a good explanation for these murders; either way he was determined to see the case through, or at least make an attempt. Someone in this town knew them and Crookshank knew where to begin. Clancy's.

52

Far below in the lowest level of the ship, down among the coal bins next to the huge steam engine that drove the heavy screw in monotonous prediction; down with the wretched rats that scurried about searching for stale pickings—anything left behind, anything rotting and no longer fit for human consumption; down where the air was damp and stinking, where breathing easily was as impossible as gripping a cold slippery handrail in a gale—you think you've got enough to answer the need, then in an instant...its gone, you will choke or you will slide away, either way you are struggling for your life: it being squeezed out of your throat and thrown into the sea—there among the vile vermin lay Snodgren, swinging in his hammock, stinking of gin, his dissolute mind floating and scheming.

"What say we gives Mr. Tumblety a visit, eh? Sees what he's got for us, eh lads?" Clasping his fingers together behind his head,

Snodgren released a belch, followed by a slow smooth exhale of thick sour effluvium. The question was offered as casually as if asking to pass the bread—not that mannerly discourse was ever exchanged between these crusty sailors at suppertime, or at any time for that matter.

Wraiff and Billings were half asleep in a gin stupor when they reluctantly received the invitation and reacted apathetically with total disinterest until Snodgren took a few minutes to compose an extension to his initial proposition. "Eeze got money in that case to be sure and who knows what else. I plans to snatch it and if he refuses I'll throw him over. He walks the deck every night, who's to say he didn't drop over, him puken' his guts up at the rail every five minutes, eh lads?" Snodgren's eyes continued to stare directly up to the iron ribbing on the ceiling of their tight quarters. His voice was shallow but loud enough. A team of cockroaches sat in a quiet cluster on the lip of the flange of the iron support above his face; he regarded them with queer fascination. The ship rocked and they began to stir and shift their position. One was pushed over the lip by a sudden swoon of the ship's hull and as it fell threatening to land in Snodgren's face—it was clipped in midair and subsequently captured within the closed fist of a rapid-fire hand shooting out from behind his head.

Opening his hand, he viewed the helpless insect with odd curiosity. Holding his fingers a short distance before his eyes, he pressed his forefinger and thumb together, squeezing, crushing, releasing the thick internal juices. He gently rotated the gooey fluid of the insect's guts about—first circular, then back and forward. Like a clumsy entomologist studying the viscosity of its loose anatomy, he pulled his fingers apart just slightly watching the sticky band as it continued to remain attached to the skin on the pads of his fingers. Snodgren's thoughts were not so scientific. He raised an eyebrow and considered a different victim he might like to squeeze there; someone who would squirm, someone who, even with the least amount of pressure he could rip apart, expose all his hidden treasures. It would be so easy he thought.

Francis lifted his face to the evening sun, a short breeze brushed through his hair. Little Raven sat next to him swinging to-and-fro on the porch swing. She faced the western sky radiating with saffron and crimson in the late hours, the fields in every direction washed with a golden glow. Standing to her side, Sarah—her golden hair long and flowing, her smile wide, her bright eyes enticing. The house: a white clapboard, and a white picket fence all-round bordering a vegetable garden—the herbs and spices grew tall and rich in their abundance. Rising Sun bent forward selecting the best from her crop, gently turning her face to smile at them—upon her face: not a wrinkle, not a mark. Francis reached out to retrieve a bouquet of wild roses from her hand that she offered, but his wrist was suddenly grabbed by an iron clamp and the searing pain jerked him vertical. His brow wrinkled in confusion as he fruitlessly attempted to pull away.

"Well Laddie, how's Mr. Tumblety tonight, eh?" Snodgren's ugly, evil face smiled down, discharging his rancid breath into Francis' face.

Billings grabbed his other wrist and Wraiff quickly stuffed an oily rag into his mouth. Francis was startled; he could only twist and pull his arms forward and back as if running on the spot yet his legs were not moving. The locker room was black and the images of his dream had nearly faded when the three faceless shadows were upon him holding tight, pressing down, pinning him to his bunk.

"Close the door," Snodgren whispered in a dry throaty order to Wraiff. "Let sees' what Mr. Tumblety 'as for us tonight."

Sea sickness had drained him; not an ounce of energy remained in his body, the will to fight was strong but the ability was gone. If he could get to his knife, he could cut these pirates up, he could toss them into the sea, they would suffer the same consequences others had faced before, he was not about to go down at the dirty hands of these filthy sailors, he would…but the sway of the sea and the churn of his guts left Francis reeling; instantly they were on him.

Wraiff and Billings forced Francis down tight to his bunk. With every jerk and twist, Francis could feel his attempts at breaking free were wasted. Snodgren reached for the oil lamp on a crate next to the cot and pulled out a flint from his pocket. He turned and checked for any activity on deck through the door—no one. The door closed with an easy swing and Snodgren dropped the latch.

Total blackness inside the small space elevated his uneasiness; Francis assumed the worst: the quick smooth sting of a knife blade carving across his throat—clumsy and uneven, or perhaps the powerful thump and searing pressure of a stab in the back or chest, a chance of missing vital organs, resulting in a slower painful death. These impetuous idiots had no knowledge of procedure and he would rather be bound and tossed overboard to face the final plight with the cold predictable ocean than be carved up by these clumsy butchers. Yet with this notion Francis began to relax his struggle, he would face the inevitable with a measure of courage, giving them no pleasure in witnessing his fear. It was a hollow gesture, he was shaking with terror and shock; how could he have let this happen? He was captive, vulnerable; his surrender disgusted him. For his own safety he attempted to lie still and complacent.

Snodgren struck a flint and lit the end of a string. Sweat dripped into Francis' eyes, stinging—he blinked staring at the fiery red glow; the only thing visible in a box of black. The two men holding Francis tightened their grip, breathing heavily from between clenched teeth, their stinking body odour wafting generously into his face. The faint glowing string floated in the dark nebulous space then suddenly flashed into a bright yellow flame as Snodgren lit the lamp. He held it high searching the corners: the ropes and blocks, the crates and hooks, "So where is it Laddie? Hiding it on me are ya?" Snodgren grunted out the rhetorical question not taking his eyes away from the deep, black recesses, continuing to search concentrating on the areas illuminated by the faint glow of the lantern. The rag was foul and the oil burned his tongue and the inside of his mouth. Francis' muffled verbalizations were ignored; he was pressed harder into the ropes of his cot. Snodgren lowered the lamp and spied the corner of the small leather case under the cot. "Here we are Laddie, something for the poor crew of the American." With one hand holding the lamp steady, Snodgren reached under and pulled the case out, his expression lifting, his eyes widening. "Here, take this," and Wraiff grabbed the lantern as the ship pushed him back into the door. "Watch it you clumsy fool, we'll all burn up!"

Snodgren rifled through the case rapidly. Within seconds he lifted his head, he held the medical bag aloft. "A fine cache of knives for me Laddie." Immediately he ordered Francis to be rolled over onto his stomach; Billings complied and flipped him over pushing Francis' face down into the folded blanket. He then reached down with both hands and ripped the trousers from Francis' hips exposing his naked buttocks; a cruel gleam flashed across his face and he smacked him hard. "How's that Laddie?" The shocking sting made Francis tense up and clench, releasing a small squeal. Then...

Footsteps on the deck outside the locker door and Wraiff whispered, "Simmons!"

Snodgren threatened with a fist in Francis' face, "Not a sound Laddie, or it's over the side." Wraiff blew the flame out, total blackness engulfed the locker room...they cautiously waited, frozen still, balancing on the shifting toss, fighting the need to slip or trip, holding their breath in the cold blackness: an invisible iron weight fusing their iniquitous enterprise. Waiting. The footsteps passed. Snodgren searched the pockets of the trousers and found Little Raven's tiny leather pouch. "Well this is something, isn't it Laddie?" Francis squirmed and jerked, he grunted a muffled protest, twisting his neck knowing his precious property was now in the hands of a vile creature, someone who should never touch it; never look at it! Billings thrust his knee into Francis' back and punched him alongside his head, the squirming stopped. The sudden blow stung and his head pounded!

Snodgren grabbed the little black medical bag and opened the door, peered out cautiously and summoned his two compatriots who quickly followed. Snodgren cautioned, "Not a word now Laddie or Tumblety will survive alone as a single inky scratch on Mr. Carter's list, just another lost soul at sea." They slithered away on the salty air.

The American held tight to a lofty position peaking high on a swell, then plummeted rapidly deep into a cavernous greeny-black trough; the lantern, its flame quickly extinguished by Wraiff before leaving, now rolled across the floor leaving a slimy streak of coal oil; Francis watched it tumble and crash into the rope piled in the corner, then slide clumsily back as the ship rose up again mounting the crest of a fresh wave. His eye was throbbing and his mouth and lips stung, but neither pain compared to the aching torment that filled his heart. He whipped the rag from his mouth and threw it to the floor. Emotionally drained, he held back tears; resisting the urge to cry, he held both hands to his head and cradled it there with soulful compassion, disbelieving the terrible events that had passed only moments ago. From his sitting position now at the edge of his cot he rotated his face slowly upward and stared through the open door to the rail on the deck and the night sky; stared through his open fingers placing them loosely over his teary eyes. He jerked up his trousers and stepped out to the deck. He could feel his pounding heart beginning to relax and his breathing became more regular. The deck was slippery; he quickly grabbed the rail. Seawater beaded there and sparkled like tiny pearls on the shiny wooden surface, rolling forward and back as the ship rocked in the silent swells. There was a full moon but the glow was dull and intermittent, shrouded in thick grey clouds; wind, wet and salty, slapped Francis in the face as he bent over hopelessly searching through the ocean's cruel, paradoxical industry: allure and torment, for resolution. He faced a solitary vigil, no one could know; he could confide in no one. He respected Snodgren's threat, he could do no other. But he was not yet destitute, another two weeks or more remained on this torturous journey and he decided there would be time to plan; he would deal with Snodgren in his own way, in his own time. His property was everything. He had lost all his knives, Rising Sun's amputation kit, his buffalo skinner—everything. His wallet and money, however, were tucked away under a heavy load of rope, a wise choice. His mother's ring and locket—lost to grimy hands of scum once again.

Well below the unforgiving wind, below the sea-washed decks, Snodgren reviewed the contents of the case and was not satisfied. The unusual collection of old Indian knives was interesting, some of the medical tools were interesting, the buffalo skinner was a rare find for sure. The bottles of ether smelled bad, the small vials of laudanum, camphor and carbolic acid were foreign to him, and the other few items were useless and nondescript. There was no change purse, no money. The silver chain of the delicate necklace twisted in his fingers; he swung the heart pendant in a tiny arch back and forth: a pondering pendulum for a conspiring mind. The Claddagh ring had been clumsily squeezed tightly on the first joint of his pinky finger—the blatant contrast between the beautiful simple artistry of the jewelry and his grungy bony fingers was remarkable...and disgusting. His eyes remained in deep concentration, observing and calculating. The round white naked cheeks of Francis' buttocks came to mind and a sinister smile slowly expanded across his face.

53

Some say Isaac Beasley sailed 'round the Horn and lost his fingers on a frozen rail—ripped off when he attempted to pull them free in a winter storm that lasted ninety days; some say he lost them in a bet when the loser was forced to cut off his own fingers if he was caught in a lie—Beasley lied all the time. Perhaps his shrivelled right leg was the result of a whale bite; others claim it was tangled in a line and hoisted fifty feet aloft—most of the skin and muscle torn off to the bone; a six inch line cutting deep into what's left just below the knee. Either way a lifetime at sea had rendered his body useless, no ship would have him—it was all slinking and slipping now among the harbour thieves: a missing crate here, loading contraband there, and exchange for coin: information. He knew when ships were arriving and what they were carrying, he knew crews and criminals, cut-throats, thugs, dirty officers and barrels short of their fill, forged ledgers and missing documents. He proudly wore his marlin spike on his hip—a crudely carved piece of narwhal tusk displaying notches each chronicling a story, fiction or fact, but worth a drink or two at Clancy's and he limped and cackled like a parrot in the dark corners collecting a coin here or a shot of rum there.

Beasley spied Crookshank sitting alone at a table near the door and he knew it was him he was looking for. Limping up to the table, Beasley watched Crookshank turning a coin over and over attempting to procure a balance on its edge, a delightful attraction and one that would not be missed or considered insignificant by the likes of someone like Beasley. "Takn' time for a wee dram are ya Detective?"

"I've just been to see two of your friends." Crookshank stopped the coin, sat back carefully scrutinizing Beasley's face for a reaction from his coy comment, tapping a steady beat on the table with the coin's edge.

"Not my friends, I don't have any friends." Beasley wasn't about to give up anything easily and Crookshank knew a hard strike to the heart of the issue would loosen up the game; he was not in the mood.

"Sit down and tell me why you carved up those two miscreants and I'll buy you a drink before I haul you off to jail."

"Not my doing Detective, I don't know nothing about it." Beasley sat down. Crookshank waved a finger and caught the attention of a barman and ordered Beasley a rum, his favourite; the gesture was much appreciated and Beasley started to talk. "I heard there was a murder, but to be truthful Detective, I don't know who you've got down there, I don't, I don't."

"One man has an island girl tattoo on his right arm, and an old anchor on his left, the letters M. G. below; he has no teeth. The other is a slimmer fellow, one silver tooth and an old scar on his face, left side, might have had a limp. Crookshank gestured the direction of the scare with a slice of his thumb down his face in duplication for effect. Do you know them Beasley? Tell me what you know now, or you'll be takn' a walk with me."

"I don't think I know them, they sound fairly familiar, but I can't say for sure." Beasley was gambling for another rum as the first had slipped down his gullet fast enough. Crookshank ordered another and the tension in his face tightened stiff enough so Beasley could see that perhaps the meeting was heading for a quick conclusion and this would be his final hand. "I did know a fella with a tattoo similar with a name Mickey Gilhooley, and he and Charlie Stanzy did a job for this big businessman that came into town last week. It could be them; I'm not saying that it is."

"What businessman?"

"Smithson, Charles Smithson, a huge big man from Chicago, I've seen him before, comes about every six or eight months. He had Mickey and Charlie runin' errands all over the city." Beasley looked down at the coin turning over in Crookshank's fingers, assuming maybe he was finished.

"What business?"

"Guns mostly. Guns and pistols, ammunition, shipping them to Chicago."

"Where's Smithson now?"

"Left Boston three days ago, just about the time, them two found themselves cut up, he caught the first train to New York; on his way to Albany, I think...pretty sure, I don't know who did it that's the truth." Crookshank peered long and hard into Beasley's face; he passed the coin, it was snapped up in an instant. He pulled out another—the tapping continued.

"An' you can offer me a whole bag of those an' I wish you would, but it won't do you no good, cause I don't know who cut them up, or why, and that's a fact."

"Have you seen the new jail on Charles Street?"

"Yes I have."

"It's a big one isn't it?" The Suffolk County Jail at 215 Charles Street was brand new, a huge granite fortress, ominous and frightening. Crookshank's question was sly; a provocation no doubt; Beasley maintained eye contact.

"T'is."

The fastest way to Albany from New York was on a riverboat and they sailed the Hudson regularly; Crookshank considered the trip, but he doubted City Marshal Tukey—the new Chief Commissioner—would agree. A three-day head start; it was becoming more difficult and Crookshank wondered if they were worth it. He tossed the coin to Beasley, rose and left Clancy's.

Who the hell was Charles Smithson?

54

There was only one choice for Erastus Corning: The Delavan House. It was the biggest, most luxurious, most prestigious hotel in Albany, perhaps in all of New York State. His guests would relax in the elegant comfort of the most gracious, most opulent furnished rooms, and dine on the most exquisite cuisine sure to satisfy the most demanding gastronomic pallet in all of America—he would see to it. A five-story masterpiece of nineteenth century classic architecture, covering an entire city block on Broadway in the heart of Albany, the Delavan would welcome delegates from all corners of eastern and north central America, and he would win them over. Congress had passed legislation in April, only 3 months earlier, and his vision of uniting ten railways to form the New York Central Railway was only hours away; he could taste it.

Corning was a very wealthy man, a shrewd man, there was no denying that; most metal goods and steel products manufactured in New York, Connecticut and Massachusetts ended up in his huge hardware warehouse on the Hudson River in Albany, a depot for distribution to all corners of the country, but in particular to the west. Charles Smithson was a stakeholder and this is where he was headed when he stepped onto the Daniel Drew, docked on Pier 45 on the Hudson River that fateful morning. His gun purchases concluded—small arms and rifles from Smith and Wesson, Springfield and Remington, all loaded on railcars to Chicago—he would meet Corning and other major stockholders in Albany for the final vote.

The Henry Clay was charging her boiler and the game was ready. Smithson bit down hard on his cheroot and smiled at Captain St. John from the deck of the Drew—a thousand dollars riding on the victory. A seven hour race straight north on the snaking, twisting Hudson and all aboard were screaming and waving at the challenger: the mighty Henry Clay, until then the fastest steam paddle wheeler on the Hudson. Smithson was there to make history and watch the Clay fall miserably behind in her wake, as the new side wheel steamer began to prepare her fires and charge her boilers.

Racing paddle wheelers on the Hudson had been outlawed as it had become so dangerous, but Smithson had been putting his deal together for three days now and finally John Tallman, part owner of the Clay and her Captain, had ultimately succumbed. Many wagers had been finalized and if the Drew arrived first, Smithson was guaranteed to receive a handsome sum.

People in their finest and most fashionable sailing costumes crowded together at the rails yelling, whistling and waving to each other across the narrow distance between the two boats; the Henry Clay and the Daniel Drew jostled for position ready to churn forward at the sound of the gun. The bands played and the banners flew in colossal colourful pageantry of red, white and blue. Charles Smithson stood with Captain Alanson P. St. John carefully observing Captain John Tallman across on the forward deck of the Clay; Tallman reciprocating his scrutiny of St. John on the top deck of the Drew. Finally a six pounder exploded on shore with a blast, and they were off. Wild cheers rang out; boisterous cries competed with the roar of the steam engines and the crashing, spinning wheels on the swirling water below!

Each vessel bombarded their fires with coal; teams of sweating stokers began shovelling and screaming orders, the huge paddle wheels began to turn and the water bubbled and splashed as the huge blades smashed at the river. Black smoke rose and billowed in voluminous thick clouds above the great stacks, the boilers hummed, their sides forced to stretch to maximum restraint, and the powerful blast of the steam whistles blared their message for all aboard and to everyone on shore—the race had begun!

The great challenge for the pilots was to keep that delicate distance between the boats while carefully regarding sand spits, capable of grounding the boat, and floating logs, which could get caught in the great paddle blades and destroy them in seconds. Once a boat gained a lead it could navigate from the centre of the river and the challenger would have to find the spot to pass—a most difficult manoeuvre considering the curves and spits in the river. But until that time when a boat might overtake the other, it was head-to-head and the chance of side-swiping each other was a very real prospect, the result of which could be catastrophic and signal the end of the race and possibly the sinking of a boat!

The Drew was long and sleek, 244 feet, with two decks: one above and open to the views and the throngs of passengers screaming their excitement to the crowds on shore and to the passengers across the water to the Clay; and one deck below—a covered deck that included plush salons and bars, luxurious card rooms and magnificent dining rooms. Two smoke stacks above expelled the residue from the huge coal furnace; the massive boiler produced tons of pressurized steam, pushing and pulling the 12 foot pendulum on the crank shaft which turned the double wheels at maximum speed, capable of pushing the boat up to twenty two miles per hour—the fastest of any paddle wheeler on the river—or so Smithson gambled. She was called 'The Jewel of the Hudson,' and she proudly presented her title in every way. The Henry Clay was a bit older but had proven time and time again to be a very fast and reliable boat. She was shorter, 198 feet long, but just as beautiful; the wrap-around promenade deck above was considered a tasteful addition and below she was outfitted with the finest fashions available. She could match the Drew's speed, and John Tallman had bet on it…heavily.

The Hudson was not so wide and straight as a boat pilot would like, there were definitely difficult turns to navigate, and Charles Smithson, being a regular returning customer, knew them well. It was within minutes when, as the Drew gained speed and he quickly became dissatisfied, he barged into the wheelhouse. The Clay remained even and close alongside the Drew, and although the crowd on the deck was visually and verbally excited, and Captain St. John appeared stoic and pleased, Smithson was very near exploding with rage. "What are you doing you idiot? Pull ahead of that boat or I'll be taking over that wheel!" Not a patient man, Smithson wanted results immediately, and the pilot called down to the stokers in nervous response.

"Head up steam there!" Willie Burns looked to Smithson, then to Captain St. John with apprehensive reflection wondering who was in charge, and what to do. Smithson's towering figure stood head and shoulders above the little pilot and his gruff manner and evil grimace was enough to scare anyone on deck, employee or other.

Captain St. John had followed Smithson into the pilot house and attempted to calm him down. "No need to worry Charles, Burns knows this river well."

"Not well enough for me. How much money does he have riding on this trip?" He didn't wait for an answer. Smithson whipped his cigar on the floor of the wheelhouse with a powerful fling of his arm; he turned back to Burns, "Now give her full steam, I want her clear ahead by Harlem and Yonkers." By Dobb's Ferry the river starts to open up wider so that by Tarrrytown she was twice as wide—almost 2 1/2 miles wide. It was there that the Clay might try to catch up, if she could, but Smithson did not want her beside him at Crotonville; there the river started to change. There the boats would have to follow a channel quickly reduced to half the width—but still allowing room for them to navigate together side by side if necessary; but for the pilots their skills would begin to enter a new level of concentration— with no room for error.

Smithson and St. John moved to the port side window of the wheelhouse and watched the Clay with anxious anticipation; she was moving fast and true, the Drew was making no gain, and they were passing Yonkers. The boats sailed side by side each gaining a small advantage then losing it again over the next eight miles. Just as Croton Point came into view on the port side, Smithson could see the great spit reaching out from the east bank over on starboard, and he knew shallow water and a hidden muddy bottom was looming perilously close and ordered the wheel pulled hard left. Burns quickly complied and the Drew swung left cutting off the Clay. She inched ahead through the channel pulling forward slightly and beat the Clay through the narrows continuing to gain speed for the next challenge. The river was open now and Smithson knew Tallman would use this opportunity to catch up and cut the Drew off at Tomkin's Cove, knowing that the channel would then shrink to a distance so narrow, passing would become impossible.

"Watch that boat you idiot!" Smithson yelled at Burns as the Clay began to reach her port side, just aft, challenging for the lead. "Give me that horn,"—Smithson grabbed the horn and screamed down to the stokers, "Give me speed, give me speed, now, you useless idiots, she's gaining!" But the Clay maximized her momentum slowly and steadily, gaining on the Drew, continually pushing forward, until she was directly bedside her and Tallman leaned over the rail, smiled and waved at St. John in cruel mockery. Smithson nearly ripped the lip of the window frame from its position on the pilot house squeezing his massive hands in powerful frustration, "By God, move this boat!" he screamed, but the Clay took the lead at Tomkin's Cove and entered the narrow channel ahead of the Drew and all she could do was follow in distress.

The boats carved a smooth round curve to the right then cut their speed to control the sharp dog leg left at Iona Island where only 500 feet of river passed between the banks on either side. Smithson knew it was a tight passage now all the way to West Point, but there was a sand point half way at Con Hook on the east bank and if the Drew could lay upside the Clay at this point maybe she could force her over. Smithson demanded more speed and although the fire was producing at its maximum, he had to admit the Drew, being a heavier and longer boat meant acceleration and speed might be jeopardized after all, and this was the test.

The Clay reached Con Hook first and followed the river around the spit at West Point as she slowed somewhat to navigate the hard left turn. The Drew was in tight pursuit on her tail and Smithson's new plan was already clearing in his head. If she could maintain this speed there was a space wide enough after West Point between Cornwall-on-Hudson and Newburgh for overtaking the Clay. She had to be successful there as the channel became too narrow after that all the way to Kingston, there would be no other chance for regaining the lead.

St. John at this point had reluctantly given total charge over to Smithson; there was no controlling him—he was vile, barbarous, contemptuous, adamant. He was dangerous. Smithson's face remained contorted, his speech: loud and venomous. He paced from the window to the helm and back again; he stared at the boiler and raised his head to the stacks, searching fruitlessly for more speed. He could not be contained; he would not be denied! He absolutely hated viewing the Clay from its ass-end, *this was intolerable!*

The two boats followed each other around the bend at West Point and now Smithson demanded absolute obedience—she would catch up at all costs before the river narrowed again at Newburgh. He jumped down the short companionway from the pilot house to the furnace level and shook his fist at the stokers and told them to double their load or he would shove them in! The pace did quicken and back on deck Smithson pressed his face to the window encouraging the Drew forward, leaning into the small cabin, crushing his body on the window ledge; leaning in as if he alone, using his powerful body, desperately remained the last force the Drew could use for the necessary acceleration required to propel the Drew into the lead.

Tallman on the Clay gave his helmsman a smile; he knew the Drew was in trouble, after Newburgh it would be clear running all the way to Kingston and then to Albany and the sweet smell of victory; cash in his hand from a man such as Charles Smithson, would feel so good. He gave orders to maintain maximum speed as he watched the Drew carefully following so close now on his tail.

The open water was a gift to the Drew and she began to gain after Cornwall-on-Hudson; Smithson began to smile, something he hadn't done since they tossed the lines ashore at pier 45. He yelled down to the furnace, "Give her hell, give me speed!" The Drew began to pull up beside the Clay and Tallman raced to the deck rail starboard side, glaring at St. John who stood there to receive his shaking head; Smithson's teeth clenched tight in his face and he grabbed a new cheroot from his breast pocket in reward.

The boats sailed side by side within a few feet from each other as they raced around the narrow spit at New Hamburg on the east bank. Crowds on deck rallied and cheered raising their hands and waving hats; Smithson grabbed the horn and blasted the stokers, "Now you idiots, now!" But the Drew fell behind at Poughkeepsie and the channel narrowed; Burns dare not attempt to pass now as shallow water and a very narrow passageway would only allow the Drew to continue to Kingston in second place.

Through the next series of smooth, slender curves, the Drew cautiously trailed the Clay, there was no alternative, but Smithson was not yet defeated. It was approximately 15 miles to Rondout Lighthouse, just before Kingston, maybe forty-five minutes, and there Smithson would make his move.

The day had been beautiful and sunny—a clear blue sky, with little or no wind, but now as Captain Tallman reviewed the clouds collecting and billowing overhead, he reckoned the wind was picking up and its direction from the north teasing his bow, would affect his forward speed without doubt. This slight change in the weather had not escaped the keen senses of Captain St. John and he passed the information quickly on to Smithson, who smiled and allowed the Drew to slide in tightly within the slipstream behind the Clay; a perfect position—here he would wait patiently.

Almost within forty-five minutes exactly, Rondout Lighthouse appeared off the port bow and the channel opened. "Gain speed Burns!" Smithson ordered. "Now, now!"

St. John couldn't have guessed Smithson's next move, but as the boats passed the lighthouse on the right, the Drew came up next to the Clay and Smithson pushed Burns aside and grabbed the wheel, "Move out!" he yelled, and cranked the wheel hard left and the Drew began to sail directly towards the Clay. As the long narrow spit just south of Kingston appeared to Clay's port side, she hit! The Drew rammed the starboard side of the Clay and the people on-board screamed in panic. They jostled and fell on the deck, they grabbed the rail and cried, they slipped and crashed into each other, desperate to stay on board. Tallman gave orders to pull hard to port, but Smithson drove his boat into her again! The Clay and the Drew, side by side, went careening full speed into the point at Kingston smashing onto the beach. Chaos ensued on board as the catastrophe was sudden, extreme and terrifying. Captain St. John yelled out at Smithson, "What are you doing?" and attempted to remove Smithson's hands from the helm.

"Get away from me!" Smithson pushed at St. John and the man crashed to the deck and sprawled down beside Burns who was holding his head; blood oozing from a cut on his forehead. Smithson quickly ordered reverse and full power; the boat began to jerk and the paddles chopped and spun—the Drew began to lift from the beach. "Move this boat out, move it, give speed there!" he ordered down to the furnace. Two passengers standing over the rail at the farthest forward point on the bow, flipped over at the sudden jerk as the gears slammed into reverse, and toppled to the beach below.

The Drew pulled out and Smithson cranked the helm over, "Forward, forward." The great cam reversed once again and the Drew moved into the channel past Kingston leaving the Clay on the beach. St. John was dumbfounded and rose to his feet glaring at Smithson in bewilderment, in total disbelief and without resources of any kind to rectify this impossible situation. Smithson was smiling, chomping his cheroot, steering the Drew and climbed to the position of victor: his chin high, his ego firm and supreme.

Tallman on the Clay quickly engaged in a damage check and cautioned passengers to move away from the rails. His officers attempted to compose the crowds of screaming woman and crying children, but they could see Tallman was not beaten. He ordered the Clay to reverse her gears and pull out from the beach, as no major damage was reported. He examined the hull of his boat closely over the rail as she gently slipped off the beach and within minutes she was racing after the Drew, in spite of the riotous defiance from her crew and passengers.

But the Clay was damaged; her boiler was cracked and the pressure building now as Tallman demanded more speed, jeopardized the integrity of her iron casing—she was perilously close to exploding. Tallman continued to press on hoping desperately to catch the Drew and teach that scoundrel Smithson a lesson. He vowed that the Drew would never sail again and Smithson would be clasped in irons!

Tallman never heard the explosion; he was ripped apart in an instant and his flesh was flung in bloody clumps in every direction throughout the pilot house as it shot thirty feet into the air and smashed to the river into a thousand pieces. The Clay burst into flames, the hull collapsed at the centre, the stacks rocketed into the sky, the great wheels buckled and spun into the air twisting and devouring people left and right like a slicing guillotine. Passengers were flung overboard like burning cannonballs, unidentified body parts whipped and flew up and over the deck, the engine crew at midships were jammed deep into the crushing hull below water, gasping for air, frantically reaching for escape. The Clay burned and sunk in a matter of minutes.

The shocking great din of the explosion and the massive mushroom of black smoke rising high into the sky behind them was terrifying and caused panic on board the Drew, but Smithson with both hands gripping firmly on the helm, now concentrated on Albany; he couldn't collect on even one wager, and...he was late for his meeting.

55

Detective Patrick Crookshank stood rigidly stoic on the wharf at Pier 45, his face anchored to the north—observing and studying the Hudson River; an inquisitive manner embracing his posture—his hands pressed square on his hips, feet wide apart, chin firmly rising up to meet the cool chill in the breeze. Passengers about took notice and perhaps they could sense the official nature of his stature; they dispensed with pleasantries, in fact they ignored him entirely; that was absolutely acceptable to him. The sky was overcast and a stiff wind attempted to remove his cap from his head; he lifted his hand quickly to save it—he scowled. He hadn't arrived to investigate the catastrophe aboard the Henry Clay, but he might as well have—as there was no other news worth discussing here it seemed. Everyone was chattering and discussing, chortling and mussing, arguing and scolding. Why did they allow these races when they know they are so dangerous? When are they going to outlaw the use of these infernal steam machines? Who is responsible for the deaths of all those people? Where can I get a ticket for the Armenia scheduled to leave shortly for Albany? In fact if Crookshank had arrived yesterday he would have been a passenger on the Drew or the fateful Clay and that bit of astuteness should have been raised to the top most section of his inquisitive mind, but it wasn't; he wanted to catch up with Smithson, and the Armenia was the next boat ready to depart.

At Kingston everyone rushed to the port side and attempted to get a glimpse of the wreckage. There was a bent smoke stack and a twisted frame left from a paddle wheel, some boards floating—black and burned, nothing however really resembling a boat. The Armenia sailed past, her speed maintained, her direction solid and true; men removed their caps, women cried, then everyone returned to the lower salon, disengaging from the biting wind; it was nasty after all—ladies hat fashions were just not designed for such intrusive climes.

Anthony Davis stood beside Crookshank on the foredeck when the Armenia passed the returning Daniel Drew about a mile or so north of Kingston, where the river widened, and boats could pass easily without concern for their safety; he was the Captain and he was in a foul mood, understandably. A somber salutation was exchanged between the boats: no cheers, a few waves, mostly quiet, not morose but a chilling reception. "It's barbarism. It's tantamount to murder, and this river may have seen its last race."

"Then you suspect foul play Captain?"

"I do indeed," responded Davis, and there will be an inquiry, mark my words." A stern index finger directed at Crookshank's nose punctuated his threat and the Captain sauntered away, head down shaking side to side, hands embraced behind, fingers knotted, leaving Crookshank deep in his own thoughts: not racing river boats, but rather carved up sailors and wandering butchers in the night, and most importantly, catching up to Smithson.

The Armenia did not arrive in Albany in record time, however Crookshank realized he was in a race himself and escalated his pursuit. The distance from the wharf to the Hotel Delavan was farther than he realized and Crookshank appreciated the sofa in the lobby when he finally arrived. He considered ordering a beer, but when the server arrived, he quickly changed his mind realizing time was imperative; instead he asked that Charles Smithson might be announced.

Charles Smithson had already checked out.

Crookshank received directions to the train station upon hearing of Smithson's recent departure from the hotel; a trot turned into a gallop and a gallop into blind panic—the train was due to leave for Chicago in minutes! He hadn't travelled all this way at the behest of his Superintendent to watch the rear end of a train casually disappear into the western horizon, leaving him stranded and embarrassed on a vacant, windy platform a mile from a cold beer, and 170 miles from Boston (directly along that new Line—thank you Mr. Corning.)

There was a small crowd on the platform, the train was steaming, conductors were waving, people were leaning from coach windows. Where was his man? The situation looked hopeless and Crookshank was becoming desperate...then...a big man, a huge man, with impossibly wide shoulders, wearing a long black coat and carrying a custom black bag, a fresh black cheroot extending almost vertically up and out from between his teeth, stood alone ready to board.

"Mr. Smithson! Mr. Smithson!" Crookshank ran up beside the man, puffing and panting, calling his name, assuming the identity was correct, following descriptions given to him from Beasley and Captain Davis of the Armenia, calculating the size of this man, how could he be mistaken; yet when Smithson turned, he said nothing, only stared down, his whiskers pouting, his cheroot twisting.

"I am Detective Patrick Crookshank and I'd like to take a moment of your time." Smithson squeezed the handle on his bag tight and lifted his hand to his face. He pulled out the cigar, his eyes burning into Crookshank's face, responding at first with not a word, only an incredulous glare.

"I have a train to catch and I had nothing to do with it." Smithson incorrectly assumed Crookshank wanted to interrogate him for the mishap on the Hudson. "Talk to that stupid Captain, if you want answers. St. John. He has no idea how to pilot a boat. Leave me out of it." Smithson turned to enter the train, when Crookshank pleaded once again.

"I am from the Boston Constabulary Mr. Smithson. I am asking about two men in your employ there, Gilhooley and Stanzy."

Smithson's eyes opened up and his demeanour changed somewhat. "What about them?"

"They were found dead Mr. Smithson, murdered most definitely. Would you have any idea who would want to do it?"

Smithson stepped up to the train and dropped his bag on the floor inside. The train whistle blasted and the slow chug of the engine wheels began their steady slippery rotation. Crookshank began to run along side as the train moved away; Smithson's car inched ahead. "Mr. Smithson! Mr. Smithson!" pleaded Crookshank. "If you know anything, please tell me! Mr. Smithson!"

Charles Smithson squeezed his head out a small window in his coach and yelled, "Tumblety, Francis Tumblety! That's your murderer. Ask Dr. Warren at the hospital. He's a killer. He stole my property; he killed them. Tumblety."

The train to Chicago picked up speed and headed west. The New York Central Railway's first trip under that name. Corning's deal had been a success, and as a reward he had been elected the first President of the new railroad in the bargain.

Pat Crookshank had a train to catch back to Boston, (thankfully he would not have to consider a return trip on the Hudson) but first maybe a beer at the Delavan would be in order.

Who the hell was Francis Tumblety?

56

The cutting clang of the ship's brass bell ripped a hole in the serene moments of early morning—Mr. Simmon's duty was up; eight am. The pathetic, hunched figure drooped over the rail, not unlike a load of discarded soiled sheets, was too familiar; he had witnessed it every day for a week. "Mr. Tumblety you don't look well. My guess is you haven't slept or eaten all night." Mr. Simmons approached and was shocked at the face now turning to him. The cheeks were gaunt and hollow, eyes were dark and vacant; no evidence of life reflected from any corner—the chance that he was regarding the same Mr. Tumblety was questionable, and he quickly reached in with aid, holding Francis' shoulders, offering balance and comfort.

"I have not been well Mr. Simmons; I fear I may not survive this journey."

"Nonsense Mr. Tumblety; you'll come with me now." Mr. Simmons held Francis up as they worked their way to the companionway forward and down to the galley. A tasty chicken broth was served with soda bread and a small glass of brandy from Mr. Simmons cabinet. "Not too much at first, eh?" A warm blanket was carefully wrapped about, followed by soft comforting talk. The engagement was short but sincere, Francis was grateful.

The constant westerly wind was finally settling and the deep swells were shrinking to less than half of the volume from the very first day. Francis was invited to sleep on the bench in the galley and he complied without hesitation. Later in the day, pacing the deck, he could feel the steadiness begin to grow in his legs and the soup stayed in his stomach—an overwhelming victory without doubt.

Francis did not consider disclosing the situation concerning his three nemeses, their fate he felt would be in his hands alone, and because now his stamina was possibly improving, that course might be more rigorously planned. He supposed Snodgren had taken everything, and therefore further chastisement and brutality would be not forthcoming, unless bullying alone would satisfy his callous needs. The bolt on the inside of the locker would be secured and Francis would remain inside throughout the night; hopefully if seasickness returned he could use a bucket; he borrowed one from the galley.

Francis was beginning to appreciate a more optimistic outlook; his legs were responding to the welcomed gentle rolls of the sea, his stomach had settled, the sun was reaching mid-point above the horizon and the warmth on his face was well appreciated…

Snodgren appeared at the rail, his schedule nearing noon victuals. "How are we today, Laddie?"

"You have my property, I want it back." Francis was direct, his attention was focussed squarely into Snodgren's eyes, there was no hint of fear or trepidation, (he was feigning). He waited for a response.

"Well now, I likes me knives and new jewelry, and I suppose I'll be keepn' it. You, I think Mr. Tumblety, will be careful now won't ya?" Snodgren walked off, flirting with a wink and a smile. Francis seemed less concerned; a poor dissolution.

Francis didn't know Snodgren in any way.

Francis had a mild supper, he didn't want to overdo it: soup, bread and dumplings, sponge cake and coffee. He ate alone in the galley—his appearance in the officer's mess or the Captain's Wardroom was not permitted unless invited, and no such invitation had arrived. He strolled along the deck towards the stern. The evening breeze caught in his hair and tousled it about his ears and eyes—he would have to consider a cut when he arrived in England. A vast red, cloudless sky spread across the entire western horizon; shades of crimson fused with fuchsia creating a pallet rich and divine; the grandeur displayed could only heighten one's level of spirituality, something Francis knew little about, but perhaps now as his health and optimism was improving and the vision so wondrous and beautiful before him seemed to heighten his delicate demeanour, perhaps the sour taste of previous events might begin to dissolve and he could begin to relax, maybe even enjoy the remainder of the trip. He emitted a cautious smile.

Arriving back at his locker shed, Francis entered and pulled the door closed. Whatever divine spirit attempting to enter his soul on the deck—pretentious comfort—it was instantly sucked out like rancid bilge water through a hose pump. The bolt was gone, ripped out! He swallowed hard.

There was no way now for securing the door; Francis would be easy pray inside without a barricade—he immediately left. While heading for the galley various scenarios crossed his mind; one that included stealing a knife from the galley, followed by slicing Snodgren up into pieces and offering him to the variety of scaly species swimming about in the sea—an easy toss away. His disappearance may not be a major concern for many on board but somehow the blood and the knife and the questions from Wraiff and Billings would only complicate the matter, and Francis was not prepared to face an inquiry, and there was very little time to plan all the necessary refinements of such a murder. Another solution would involve soliciting the ship's carpenter to repair the bolt; however that might involve some sort of work order and Mr. Blessing would undoubtedly enquire about its current destroyed condition. He reviewed the tangle of ropes and buckles—they were too big, too bulky, they could never be arranged to secure the door—there was nothing.

The galley was closed; no knife and no hiding place. Would he run about the ship all night attempting to allude his adversaries; dodge about between pipes and bulwarks, crates and barrels, jump overboard? By four am there was no need to concern himself anymore about his destiny aboard the American; Billings and Wraiff suddenly appeared forcing Francis into the Bosun's locker; they threw him on the bed—Snodgren lurked in a dark shadow deep inside. Face down, Francis' hands were tightly bound and wrapped around the cot at the head, his trousers were whipped down and his legs were violently spread apart; a rag stuffed in his mouth. Billings kept a tight hold on the door and a keen eye and ear to the deck. Snodgren stood behind Francis prepared and erect. Francis left the little shack, rose softly on a cloud and drifted to the prairies—golden grasses and flowing wild roses of red and violet reached up to the bright glowing sunlight, its radiating warm rays washing the land, purifying and cleansing. Sarah's long golden tresses tickled his nose as she bent down over him whispering softly into his ear, caressing, comforting; he felt secure and loved.

And then they were gone...

Every section of his body was resonating; a pulsating vibration, rapid and consistent. His hands were shaking. His heart continued to thump hard and fast in his chest. The locker remained dark and hollow, and although the ship was reeling, he didn't feel it as the motion lingering in his head and stomach was due to the repetitive jamming and crashing of that filthy body, invading again, and again. They were gone but the vulgar enduring pulse remained, and it would remain...forever.

Far below the decks the dull hum of the engines continued to send their pounding signal to the screw blade, the ceaseless reverberations oscillated through the legs of the bunk up to his chest; above, empty silence enshrouded the decks. The canvas high aloft remained full and firm—night watch had secured them tight; block and tackle were stretched and pulled to their limits. Wraiff had thankfully untied his wrists from the bunk before he left.

Lifting his body over from his face-down position angered every bone and muscle, and he hesitated. Pain emanated from every fibre, from every corner and every joint and sinew. Finally, lying on his back he carefully turned his neck to the door. The dark sky over the waves was a painted black canvas and dotted between the hasty silver clouds were critical twinkling eyes that had silently witnessed his horrific vigil; how dare they remain so steadfast and true. He tried to rise up away from his bunk. On one elbow, he lifted a tortured hand to his mouth and gently pulled away the rag, softly caressing his lips and cheeks; the skin there raw and bruised—blood had crusted around the corners. *They hadn't even asked about his money. They didn't want his money.*

This was a time of sorrowful contemplation and desperate revelation, as he knew now they would not stop. The ship climbed and sank; the stars shifted above the doorway and then down again. Francis painfully pulled up his trousers and sat at the edge of the bunk holding his head in his hands and he wept. He had come to the end, there was no place for him here. His deliverance: a mere two steps away.

He stared at the deck rail through the door opening and listened to the relentless waves hitting the ship's great hull far below. Each one desperately encouraging his approach, calling to him, offering solace and peace. There would be no more pain; no vengeance. The black burdensome weight of guilt, defeatism and unwavering disgust and rancour would be over. Francis stood; balancing on the door frame, he was spent, fragile; he peeked down the deck...no one was about. He shuffled cautiously to the deck rail and hung on, peering down into the inky black churning abyss. The cold Atlantic wind jostled his hair and smacked hard against his sweating brow. The salt spray from the wake stung his mouth on the open cuts and he winced. It would be over, no one would know or care. As the ship reached up to the top of the crest he raised his head to the stars and stepped up on the bottom rail.

The clouds above shifted and curled, the wind scowled and surged, the ship twisted; Francis slipped and was pushed forward. In an instant he would be tossed overboard. Frantically he instinctively grabbed on and then, only for a brief fraction of a moment, a frothy vision appeared in the spiralling wake far below. Little Raven held out her hand to him beckoning his rescue; her eyes glassy and wanting. The ghostly image was overwhelming, her message clear. In a flash he realized Charles Smithson would never face restitution for his actions; that Little Raven would be left on her own without help and be subjugated to Smithson's wrath; that Snodgren would continue to rape and murder without forfeit. To surrender was selfish; he had to live, he had to return to Chicago somehow, to save Little Raven; and those damnable sailors would be made to pay!

Francis stepped down and returned to his little shack in the cold, in the dark, alone, less confused but unsure of how to deal with tomorrow night's unwelcome rendezvous with his three adversaries... if they returned.

Will this sea ever settle, will this restless stomach ever find peace, will this damn ship ever reach land...will this nightmare ever end, will I ever be granted a reprieve—a small relief of any kind? Francis whispered and begged for enlightenment, for salvation. It didn't come.

The abuse, indignity and perversion continued unabated throughout the next week by Snodgren, Wraiff and Billings, over and over again; Francis felt helpless in combating them in anyway. Emotionally drained, physically injured and exhausted, spiritually purged, he maintained a disconnection from the horror, a detachment from reality—a coldness; he established an invisible construct—a bitter, tenacious wall—he felt nothing, he was numb. His survival response was intense, desperate...but also something else: he began to develop focus, direction, and perhaps...purpose. Anger twisted and bent into dark resilience; it exposed a faint willingness of hope— hope for a solution; the vision of Little Raven returned to him often, but his plans did not involve dreams or aberrations; there would be no mystery or ambiguity surrounding his actions. *A time to kill, a time to kill.*

Finally a day passed—Snodgren did not come on deck. The waves began to flatten—three days until the American made port in England; a promise of smooth sailing passed about the ship from the pilot and Mr. Blessing. Continuous card games were played out below, each sailor hoping to gain his money back before their duties concluded; gin and rum was sold and greedily consumed in generous quantities keeping Snodgren and his mates busy. Francis appreciated the relief and accepted the Captain's surprise invitation to supper in the Wardroom.

"Well Mr. Tumblety, it's been a fine voyage; glad to see you are well. Have you enjoyed your time then?" Captain Smith did not look up from his potatoes. It was the second time Francis had seen the Captain in three weeks. Francis answered politely.

"Yes sir. Thank you sir."

"Fine lad, fine."

In fact no one looked up from their meal; the atmosphere was quiet, unsettling, almost tense; the cold distance Francis felt between himself and the officers was palpable; it seemed odd—a severance; a disassociation. His face was pale to be sure, and there were bruises about the sides of his face, but his long hair covered most of it. When asked about them by Mr. Simmons many days previous, he explained that an unexpected wave had pushed him into the rail, and this excuse seemed to be reasonable. He had not taken any time to socialize with the officers, he had been sick, true…but there was something else here…

They knew! Somehow they knew! What else? They were guilty. Guilty of irresponsibility, guilty of abandonment, guilty of gross negligence, guilty of poor seamanship. Guilty. Guilty. Guilty and guilty. How long had Snodgren and his cohorts been playing their foul games aboard this ship? How long had the officers known about the illegal contraband and gambling? How long had Captain Smith and Mr. Blessing been irresponsibly tolerant of theft, rape and probably murder? Francis' body stiffened and his fists curled around his cutlery, the urge to remove himself from the table was overwhelming, but he reluctantly remained seated; he asked Mr. Simmons to pass the salt, hopefully without revealing any clue about his assumption and possible revelation. He was learning how to control his anguish, hide his thoughts—they festered, evenly, secretly.

Throughout the course of the meal—roast chicken, corn, potatoes and dumplings—new information was disclosed that sealed a plan for Francis. Mr. Blessing was not sailing to Liverpool and disembarking with the rest the officers and crew; he would be leaving the American off the coast of Wales near the port of Cardiff where a small cutter would be sent out to pick him up in two days. This imposition would save him travelling all the way south from Liverpool, a disheartening prospect as he was old and tired, and the trip would be more than discomforting; that was the core argument for his request. The change in course was at least two hundred miles out of the way from the channel at Ireland and Captain Smith would lose at least 20 hours or more, but an exception was made due to fact that Mr. Blessing was going home for the last time, and the American had made good headway in the past three days; to this everyone raised a glass and bid him farewell, and the best of luck.

Francis acquired permission to disembark with Mr. Blessing, as he explained he was on his way to London with a special letter of introduction and Liverpool was certainly out of the way for him as well. Without much clarification Captain Smith seemed to be more than happy to oblige. In two days Francis would leave this damnable ship; the jubilation in his heart was overwhelming—reserved but overwhelming. To guarantee his personal safety he asked to sleep in the galley—although that was certainly his reason, the explanation he offered was more to deal with the disagreeable cooler air above on deck, and the need of a good night's sleep before he left the ship. Mr. Blessing agreed whole-heartedly. Although his intuition about Snodgren keeping busy through the night deep below was correct, he was taking no chances at this juncture.

He must be patient, just a little patience…

57

Patience. Had he not been patient long enough? Yet the time was drawing close; he could hold on—he had no choice. There was no clock on the wall—no pocket watch for exactness—but he felt it was too early. The night watch had ended— he had heard the bell's harsh clang ring out at midnight, followed by a parade of scratching clomping boots, as the gamblers scuffled along the deck, past the galley door, then scramble to the companionway leading to their den, deep below, that greasy pit, that stink hole. As wretched as that place was, they raced to arrive, they fought to arrive—the promise of gin and game seducing them. A few hours had passed since then, or maybe more—not nearly enough time. He could wait. For this particular severance he would wait a thousand nights, and a thousand more, knowing they would be risking more tonight than a few shillings, more than a few bottles of their crude gin. Tonight they would risk everything and Francis would play the final hand.

Mr. Blessing expected his cutter to arrive at four or five am, just before sunrise, and Francis assumed the time would coincide precisely with the conclusion of the game and well past the limit of their gin tolerance.

He completed his preparation for debarkation: wash up, remove vomit stains from shirt, smooth hair behind ears, place hat and coat neatly on the bench. He now required only one more thing: to retrieve his possessions from Snodgren and then to put their mutual disagreements behind them...forever.

Francis left the galley and closed the door behind him, then followed a direct path forward, then port side up to the wheelhouse. The ship rocked slightly—Francis held the rail all the way. Not a star in the sky for there was no sky to see. He knew Wales was just off the port side and he strained his eyes peering deep into the fog but could see nothing. The breeze was brisk and Francis pulled his arms about his shoulders attempting to gain some warmth.

"Good evening Mr. Tumblety. All set then are ye? Mr. Blessing's not on deck yet Sir." Mr. Polson greeted Francis as he kept a sharp eye out, maintaining tight hold on the great wheel, but had flicked his face around just enough to identify the person arriving in his wheelhouse so unexpectedly.

"I've just come to check the time Mr. Polson. I'm a bit anxious I suppose," remarked Francis, rubbing his hands together feeling the chill, blowing some warm air into his cupped fingers.

"Four on the hour, Sir. Mr. Blessing'll be on deck soon Sir, then off you'll be. Terrible fog though. I can't pull in too close for fear I'll ground 'er. But don't you worry lad, we'll be alright 'soon's I spy the light at Lavernock, then I'll know." Mr. Polson nodded with affirmation and smiled. Francis couldn't possibly consider how he knew where he was. There was nothing but dense fog on every side.

"Thank you, Mr. Polson. I'll wait below. Good night." Where could he go? To that stinking Bosun's shack? Never again! Back to the galley—it was his only choice, there was no salon or ante room. It was too cold on deck. He would wait on the bench among the sacks of flour, bags of potatoes and chicken cages. His case on the floor, his money retrieved…patience.

"Night Sir" was Polson's reply, never once removing his cold stare from the square glass before him, squeezing his hard knuckles tightly around the thick wooden spokes of the great wheel—the left hand over, the right hand under—miraculously manoeuvring the great ship with a keen sense shared by only those who understood the sea; the fog being no stranger to him in these waters.

Francis turned and headed for the companionway aft, that lead to the deck below. Four am, not much time now. If they were still playing, would he wait? If the cutter arrived, he would have to leave— he would have to square things up with Snodgren on shore. Francis desperately wanted to finish it now; he may never find him again once they went their separate ways.

Francis stepped down the long staircase gripping tight to the rails on each side—he arrived on the next lower level, below the top deck. The gas lights were flickering in their brass holders—three mounted on each wall, staggered to eliminate shadows; he could follow along without trouble. No one was about. He continued with careful purpose; without hesitation. He arrived at the companionway midship, then stepped down, then down again and once more, finally to the lowest deck.

As the ship slipped back and then slowly forward again, faint creaking whispered in the dark corners. The ship was asleep, enjoying an early morning slumber in the calm shallow shores, as if, perhaps, grateful for the respite from the Atlantic's ferocious tribulations and proud of her success—arriving unscathed and punctual as she was. Francis followed along aft, listening for human sounds from the card room near the stern; possibly a pair of drunken sailors lingering over a final hand. There was nothing, it was empty, and Francis stepped along to the storeroom adjacent, at the very end, just before the engine room.

Only one lamp was flickering and it was behind him, halfway down the long corridor. There were six large storage rooms along this section on this deck, each one filled with crates and barrels, sails and rigging. Another three hours before the bell clanged. (*"Watch out for Snodgren. He runs a crooked game down below, deep down by the engines. Stay clear of that one."*) Simmon's words were not forgotten, although the choice of staying clear was unfortunately never up to Francis. He was thankful for a dark space outside the room, if indeed this was the room he so desperately required this morning. But now the dark space was closing in; the unbearable realities of this deepest and most hideous sector of the ship was embracing him and his trepidations. Here, in such close proximity to the engine rooms, the machinery groaned incessantly; their monotone moaning playing a repetitive dull dirge with such intensity—the iron sheathing, binding the ship together, vibrated like a great shivering skin covering the giant's bones as she rocked ever onward through the cold, black sea. A pulsating rhythm of pistons and gears, engulfing the chamber like a smooth oily blanket; a weight pulling everything down, smothering walls, pipes and fixtures—everything continuously vibrating and moaning in unison. The heat was intense, the furnaces raging, the great boilers bubbling, the steam hissing. The sour odour of coal smoke seeped surreptitiously from under the door and a sticky residue covered the walls in a fine black slime. There was no ventilation and the air, so palpable, choked and stuck in Francis' throat. The storeroom door was slightly ajar. He pressed his hand to his mouth holding back a cough, and cautiously, slowly, pushed the door open.

Black. There was nothing but a black void—nothing to use for orientation; no corners, no walls. *Was this the right storeroom?* He began to doubt his calculations. He pressed the door open to its full extent and the dim light from the corridor offered just enough illumination to grant Francis a dull view of the interior. Directly before him: three swinging hammocks; their sagging bottoms full with the weight of three stinking sailors. Their smell smacked into Francis' nostrils and he was almost overcome: a vile concoction of sweat, dirt, grease, oil and gin; compounded by the fact, no doubt, that not one of these putrid men had bathed since the commencement of the voyage.

The hammocks swung from thick hemp ropes above, securely fastened to sets of huge steel hooks that were bolted to the iron frame of the ship. They swayed in rhythm, all three together: a ballet of black, sweaty bags following the direction of an invisible conductor as the waves commanded the cadence; the crunching ropes squeaking tight when they reached the height of each swing against the bolts to add intonation to this ridiculous symphony of sleeping scum. To the left, a particularly disgusting smell: the ablution pail—it obviously had not been dumped for a few shifts. Then to the right— an unmistakable sound: the scurry of little claws: rats. The place was absolutely the most impossible of spaces to imagine; however Francis stood firm and began the task he came to complete.

His eyes now accustomed to the darkness, spied a bag in the corner directly before him, and he moved toward it. A glance at the face in the first bunk to his left and Francis identified Billings. His mouth was wide open and from within, a series of cranking bellows emerged at every inhalation. The leather valise on the floor was his medical bag, and it now received all of Francis' immediate attention. He turned sideways and slid inching along between the swaying hammock before him and the steel bulkhead wall at his back. If Billings awoke he would, without hesitation, beat Francis down, kill him and toss his body into the sea without a speck of guilt or remorse—as was his threat for the entire three weeks, and Francis had no doubt that he'd follow through, even now on the last night. Francis was betting that the deep sleep and loud snore was induced by a healthy amount of gin and Billings wasn't about to wake up too soon. Still, he had to be cautious.

Squatting over the bag, Francis opened it and immediately found Rising Sun's amputation kit. The soft, leather buck skin roll contained all the knives and tools Francis had been missing since that first day. A calculated blind survey in the dark was accomplished by delicately stroking each instrument between his fingers and thumbs, careful not to glide across the sharp edges. He felt the bottles of ether in his hand; considering them, then rejecting them—not necessary. He knew in a matter of seconds that all the contents were present and undisturbed—all his new surgical tools from Boston. He counted each one in their order. Snodgren had not discarded them or lost them foolishly in a game of cards.

He then selected a slender knife, used specifically for long thin, deep cuts: a good dissecting blade if no bone was to be included in the incision—it was quickly becoming his favourite for this type of operation. Francis rose up to full height in the dark corner, knife in hand, and focussed on Billings. The ship rocked and the hammock swayed slightly—this was a variable Francis needed to incorporate into the procedure, although his speed, he assumed, would eliminate any error provoked by the movement of the ship. It was easy now to visualize the difficult conditions a ship's surgeon might encounter during a sea battle, he thought. *Focus on the job!*

Francis stood beside the swaying body of Billings. He was in a deep sleep; his head at Francis' right, his body stretched out to his left. Francis reached over ready to begin when he realized everything was wrong. This side would be awkward as he would be cutting under his left arm as it rested on Billings' face—pressure he would require to secure head movement which, undoubtedly, would follow the incision.

Francis bent down and scooted under the hammock, then rose up between Wraiff and Billings. He swivelled around to come up beside Billings with his face and neck now on his left side. Deciding this position more satisfactory, Francis began to calculate his point of entry and angle of attack. With a quick twist of his neck he checked the other bunks. Wraiff and Snodgren were asleep—mouths gapping, air sucking.

In order to prevent soaking his clothes in Billings' miserable blood, and to control the splatter, Francis turned the knife in his right hand over leaving the pointed edge out and away, then used his three free fingers to grab the edge of the blanket at Billings' feet and pull it up to his face just below his mouth. He then turned the blade back over again in cutting position ready to begin. He rolled up his sleeves, securing them high just below his elbows and placed his left hand over Billings' face in a hovering position ready to press down the moment the blade struck. He would complete the incision entirely under the blanket to contain the blood there.

He reached under the blanket poised and ready. He raised his shoulders twice and flexed the fingers of his left hand in preparation for the press and hold on Billings' face. Looking down, Francis checked the follow-through area by his right thigh. He practised two strokes: a cutting move, fast and sure above the throat, out of the blanket and over his right thigh. He shifted just a touch to the left as there was a chance the follow-through might cut Wraiff's hammock. He wanted no blood on the floor as he was wary of footprints he might leave behind. He had no way of cleaning up after the aftermath. Following these two attempts, he decided his position was satisfactory for the job.

He was ready. He did a final head check: Wraiff and Snodgren were still deep in their gin sleep. He turned his head and focussed on the face of Billings. He reached under the blanket and pressed his left hand down tight over Billings' nose and mouth. Then...a pause, a slight pause—the ship rolled slightly; an empty bottle rolled across the floor and hit the bulkhead, the shit bucket slid a few inches into the corner. Francis checked his balance; he loosened the pressure on Billings' face. A drip of sweat from his forehead landed on the back of his left hand as it remained frozen in an idle position over Billings' face. Francis crunched his teeth together in anxious tension. His heart was pounding so loudly through his shirt, he was convinced it might arouse Billings from his sleep. The sweat was trickling down his back in rivers.

The small room was so confining and unbearably hot, he could hardly breathe. The putrid stench caught in his nostrils, choked the thin strip of air wedged there so tight he feared he might pass out. The sulphur from the coal fumes from the corridor were burning his eyes—dripping tears blurred his vision. The constant pounding of the engine thumped hard in his head no different than if he was receiving continuous blows from a wooden club. He raised his eyes to the ceiling. He waited. He waited a moment more. By God if this ship didn't settle he would have to give it all up! A second more, and... finally the ship steadied. The time was now! Francis dropped his face down to the work before him and pressed his hand down tight over Billings' face, while simultaneously drawing the knife blade across his throat, pushing down and following through with one rapid stroke. The cut was accomplished in an instant. It was smooth, deep, and clean.

Billings predictably arched and shook. The air entering the gash chortled as it mixed with the blood blasting from the wound. Francis continued to press down hard on his face and over the edge of the blanket. Billings began flailing with his arms; he was strong and wiry—he could roll himself right onto the storeroom floor with his gyrations, waking up the other two and ending all chances of finishing off all three. He wrestled for air; he fought for his life. Yet in less than a few seconds, Billings' shakes subsided—he lay motionless, the blood continuing to ooze—soaking the blanket. Francis removed his hand: no blood, and no blood on the floor...yet.

Careful not to touch any blood, Francis delicately reached under the blanket, he searched for the opening in Billings' trouser pocket— no leather pouch. He knew the likely pocket where he would find it, but he would have to check them all in case its ownership had switched throughout the week, from game to game, from loser to winner.

His job was not finished, not yet. He turned to the two bunks swinging at his side, sagging low...stinking. The corners of his mouth lowered and remained level—*to work.*

He slid under the bunk and came up face to face with Wraiff's ugly countenance. The sounds rolling forth from his face were as nauseating as the stench accompanying it. With the knife still clutched in his hands, he reached forward and pulled the blanket up over Wraiff's face. His right hand slid under the blanket and with his left hand, he crushed Wraiff's face, confidant now in his technique, he ignored the rolling of the ship—there was no time! He sliced through Wraiff's neck: deep and true, fast and clean. The follow-through was generous—lots of room and the blood remained under the blanket. The jerky gyrations quelled within seconds and Francis withdrew his hand, turned and quickly reached under for his pockets—no necklace, no ring. Snodgren must still have it—if not, then it's lost forever, there was no time to search elsewhere, the cutter would arrive soon from Cardiff. He must finish.

His method now was so precise, so clever—so fast. Francis didn't hesitate; he decided to finish off Snodgren in the same manner. There was no time to consider motives or consequences. These men were evil rapists and thieves. They had violated him without hesitation—they would die without hesitation. Snodgren would go down with the others, and his death would be the most precious. He must work fast!

Moving around under Snodgren's hammock, Francis raised his knife and lifted his left hand to the vile face of his nemesis. A grip of steel grabbed his wrist, "What are ye after Laddie, my money?" Another hand whipped up—his right hand holding the knife was stopped before Francis could even think about slicing down. They wrestled and twisted; together they crashed to the floor—Snodgren on his back on the deck, Francis above, the knife blade hovering over Snodgren's throat. An equal struggle of strength followed that allowed for no advantage to either—the knife continued to waver above Snodgren's face; the twisting back and forth finally resulted in Snodgren gaining advantage on top, and the knife shot out and hit the bulkhead near the open door. Snodgren wrapped his hands around Francis' neck and began to squeeze; Francis grabbed Snodgren's wrists attempting to pull his hands away without success—he was so strong. "Thought you'd come down for a quick see, did ya Laddie? You'll never take my money." Snodgren goaded Francis feeling his strong grip beginning to weaken his adversary. Francis couldn't breathe, he felt dizzy, he was losing consciousness. Frantically he brought his knee up and jammed it into Snodgren's groin—a hard metallic jingle rang out; Snodgren released his hold just enough— Francis grabbed his throat with his left hand and reached for the marlin spike hanging at Snodgren's left side. In an instant the spike was in his hand, "I don't want your money you stinking pig...I want your liver," Francis declared viciously through tense lips, his sweat pouring into Snodgren's eyes. He drove the marlin spike up under Snodgren's ribs and twisted, then removed it and jammed it in again, and again...and again! Snodgren laid still on the floor, Francis' shirt was bloody; blood dripped down his wrist to his elbow, then to the grimy deck at his side.

What was that? Still bending over Snodgren, Francis jerked his head up quickly. Silence. The engines had stopped, the American was slowing. *Cardiff!*

Francis crawled over to the door and grabbed the knife; he wiped it on Billings' blanket and dropped it into the bag. Standing to leave he could see the blood dripping from the hammocks and pooling on the deck underneath; the area around Snodgren's body was a grotesque collage of blood scrapings and oozing guts—not his style. With bag in hand he stood at the door, stopped and remembered. Searching through Snodgren's trouser pockets he located Little Raven's leather pouch, and within...the locket, and ring. He held it to his eyes, smiling briefly. The large lump that jingled at Snodgren's groin gave Francis a thought and he reached in and pulled out a huge leather bag thick and heavy with coins...would he be a thief as well as a murderer? *Yes!* Into his case it went, and out the door he ran—up five decks to the galley forward. Quickly...washing his hands in the sink, wrapping his coat tightly around his body—hiding the bloody evidence of his work—

grabbing his hat, and case, scrambling onto the top deck where sailors were hustling about—lowering Mr. Blessing's chests and boxes to the cutter below—he arrived!

"Well there you are Mr. Tumblety, I thought we might miss you."

"Yes sir, Mr. Blessing." Francis handed his case down and waited his turn to descend down the ladder.

To the east, a faint glow of diffused yellow light eagerly struggled to bully its way through the thick grey shroud that enveloped the morning in every direction. Francis watched the dull light hopelessly strangled by the mist; he wondered about the city of London which lay somewhere hidden in that distant direction—his new home waiting for him—as he sat pensively behind Mr. Blessing in the little cutter. He listened to the oars softly raising and lowering in the water, quietly dipping through the black, placid liquid that expressed no volatility now, no anger, no threat—strangely the sea now offered serenity, a smooth path to tranquility—to liberty. Their bodies jerked forward together in tandem at every stroke. Francis watched the American slowly recede in the distance; the tiny golden flicker from the lanterns on deck gradually waning with each stroke; the crew on board shrinking into small grey dots, slowly dissolving into the fog...until they disappeared.

Those three dead pirates—not even a moment's thought.

End of Volume One

Be sure to follow Francis in Volume Two
Fruition, as he continues his perilous journey
through the 19th century on route to epic
infamy.

https://RMorton.ca

https://pagemasterpublishing.ca/by/robert-b-w-morton/

To order more copies of this book, find books by other
Canadian authors, or make inquiries about publishing
your own book, contact PageMaster at:

PageMaster Publication Services Inc.
11340-120 Street, Edmonton, AB T5G 0W5
books@pagemaster.ca
780-425-9303

catalogue and e-commerce store
PageMasterPublishing.ca/Shop

R obert B.W. Morton BA, B.Ed. is the author of two published books based on different time periods of his life: *Jointman, Survival Guide for Rheumatoid Arthritis* , and *Rhythm of the Guard* . *Seeds of Retribution Volume One GERMINATION* is his first novel and the first in a series of three books chronicling the legend of Francis Tumblety. Mr. Morton is a retired teacher and history buff who enjoys weaving an exciting story through the wild and cruel 19th century. He lives in Alberta, Canada with his wife Sandy.